W. A. SCHWARTZ

THE WEIGHT OF WATER

Black Rose Writing | Texas

ISBN: 978-1-68513-343-6
PUBLISHED BY BLACK ROSE WRITING
www.blackrosewriting.com

Printed in the United States of America
Suggested Retail Price (SRP) $23.95

The Weight of Water is printed in Minion Pro

*As a planet-friendly publisher, Black Rose Writing does its best to eliminate unnecessary waste to reduce paper usage and energy costs, while never compromising the reading experience. As a result, the final word count vs. page count may not meet common expectations.

"Well, all last night, I sat on the levee and moan.
Well, all last night, I sat on the levee and moan.
Thinkin' 'bout my baby and my happy home."
–Kansas Joe McCoy, *When The Levee Breaks*

"All this land is a country of reeds and brambles and very tall grass."
–Pierre Le Moyne, sieur d'Iberville, Explorer, March 1699

CHARACTER LIST

Rachel Thibodaux: Sister of Talia Fontenot married Daniel Thibodaux, a wealthy socialite living in Uptown, New Orleans.

Talia Fontenot: Younger, sister of Rachel Thibodaux, the two have not seen each other in many years.

Nina Fontenot: Mother of Rachel and Talia.

Janie Lucille Paradise: an inmate on death row at Marietta State Penitentiary in Louisiana, convicted of murdering an off-duty police officer during Katrina's aftermath.

Daniel Thibodaux: Husband to Rachel, CEO of AmHealth Corporation, and member of the old and powerful New Orleans family.

Alex Thibodaux: the 19-year-old daughter of Rachel and Daniel Thibodaux, artist and student at Tulane University.

Jeb Thibodaux: Son of Rachel and Daniel Thibodaux, Straight-A student, Star athlete, working in high finance after college.

Virgil Barrons, MD: Forensic (Legal) psychiatrist at Central Lockup in New Orleans assigned to evaluate Janie Lucille Paradise for her competency to be executed.

Camilla James, RN: Nurse, working with Virgil Barrons at Central Lockup and previous nurse administrator at AmHealth corporation in 2005

Francine James: A nurse's aide on duty at Good hope during Katrina and daughter of

Catherine (Cat) Landry: A wealthy socialite living in Uptown, New Orleans, a good friend to Rachel Thibodaux, and wife of Rick Landry. Cat is closely connected to operations at AmHealth Corp.

Rick Landry: V.P. at AmHealth Corp and husband of Cat Landry.

Errol Gentry: boyfriend of Nina Fontenot

Ray Larson: Partner with Nina Fontenot during high school and shortly afterward.

Pink: Live-in girlfriend to Ray Larson during the 1970s and 1980s.

Matt and Nadine: Pink's children who lived part time with Rachel and Talia during the 1970s and 1980s.

Antoine and Oscar: Talia's adult male friends in New Orleans.

"Jimmy": Boss and pimp at the strip club in the French Quarter, where Talia works in 1992.

Nona (Magdalena) Fontenot: Mother of Nina and Grandmother of Talia and Rachel

Tommy Lee: High School boyfriend of Rachel.

Ellie and Bernard Cohen: Residents at Good Hope

Miss Gloria: Talia's neighbor in the Lower Ninth Ward

Charmaine: Talia's neighbor in the Lower Ninth Ward (Niece of Miss Gloria)

Beaumont: Guard at the front gate at Marietta State Penitentiary

Luanne and Carly: Two inmates on death row who Janie Paradise befriends at Marietta.

PROLOGUE

There's a road runs along a waterway out east of the city. It's low and long and even, like a ribbon that's been pulled tight. The white cypress leans thick on the waterside, blocking the view for miles at a stretch, branches blinking open here and there to allow a peek of the bayou, fat with moss, heavy black against the white-hot sky.

At the end of that road, there's a house. Or there used to be. Not large, not a wealthy man's house, just three rooms, and a tiny yard, but it had a heartbeat. It breathed; it lived for a century. Now it's just bones. A ruined box, broken windows stare onto the road like unlidded eyes— skull mouth open, hungry. Curls of sweet jasmine wind through the trellis around the porch, dropping pale petals onto the dry patch below. The old steps, half gone now, a layer of mushrooms sprouting in the mud beneath the remaining boards. The roof sways deep, the ceiling inside too low for a full-grown man to stand.

The grass has come back, lush and thick with weeds: sweet spire and tickseed and cat-o'-nine-tails punching skyward. The magnolia trees that used to flank the house are gone; vanished, as if they'd never existed at all. No markers but the bluegrass growing over their graves, only a few remaining slabs of concrete slow the encroachment.

A broken pathway splits the weeds and juts forth, going nowhere. A kid's bike, missing a wheel and grown through with dandelions, lies in the yard, one of the chrome handlebars at an odd angle, like a fractured limb.

A modest porch, the portico is gone, washed away years ago. The narrow columns battered and forlorn like stranded soldiers. They no longer have a job to do.

No one lives there now—no one human. Still, there's life. The nutria and the snakes came first. Later, the cicada and tree frogs and, with them, the herons and egrets.

It's the water coming back. Up the long road from the West, into the little street and across the sidewalk, up the steps, inside the house. Soon there won't be a house at all. Only the memory of one.

THE
WEIGHT
OF
WATER

PART ONE: HEAT

2005. They'd come up in a borrowed bass boat, wearing rain slickers and boots they'd been lucky to salvage. Two of them. Not young. Middle-aged, at least. The water mean, stinking and ink-black where it bellied up against the side of the boat, pallbearer to a dead city. Flotsam. Baby bottles, hubcaps, street signs, kitchen appliances-a refrigerator that's lost its door half-full of rotting food. Every once in a while, a body. The heat was nearly unbearable. Way beyond that. But the whole situation was hell, anyway.

The front door and all the windows of the little brick house on Charbonnet Street are blown out. If not for the water, a man standing on the rickety porch could clearly see through the tumble of overturned furniture and soggy debris to the remains of the concrete back stoop.

Inside, the air goes quickly rancid; the smaller man covers his mouth, stemming the urge to vomit. Thigh-deep in wreckage and standing water, the thick heat induces a claustrophobic panic. Like being trapped beneath a hundred feet of water. "I got it," shouts the bigger of the two; he's already taken his flashlight and made his way to the attic. Light bounces back and forth across the hatch. Yellow circles dance off the walls of the ruined kitchen. The small man steadies himself against a rusty appliance, no longer identifiable. The closeness of the kitchen, rotting food, death. The sick in his gut is getting worse. "Hey, Chief," he calls out.

If it comes at all, the reply is smashed to silence by the sound of gunfire overhead.

CHAPTER 1

New Orleans, Uptown

July 21, 2020

The tablecloth is too long. It puddles on the floor beneath Rachel Thibodaux's feet, catching and twisting around the heel of her pump every time she moves. The Uptown Debutante Prep Committee ladies sit at a T-shaped set of banquet tables in a room with fourteen-foot ceilings, elaborate crown moldings, and an eighteenth-century French chandelier the size of a small automobile. Creamy linens and heavy silver. Peony blooms clustered in bowls of baccarat crystal down the center like little sailboats. A few have lost petals, and the pale pink shreds lie in little heaps beside the bowls. Her feet ache, and she considers kicking her shoes off, hiding them inside the folds of fabric. She looks around and thinks better of it. None of the other forty-three women in the room appear to be removing articles of clothing. She jerks her heel free of the cloth and straightens in her chair. Margaret Bocage, the chairwoman, is speaking, and Rachel forces herself to focus.

"Ladies, please turn to the third page of the handout; you will see a list of specific tasks." Margaret is a large woman in her mid-fifties. Not shy and with a penchant for bright colors, she appears a bit stuffed into a fuchsia-colored suit and cantaloupe blouse buttoned to the neck today. Margaret, who put her own four daughters-sturdy girls, each with the slightly sanctimonious countenance and space-occupying physique of their mother through the debutante process, became self-appointed committee chair last year following the untimely death of the previous chairwoman, Elizabeth Cornay. Untimely, meaning poor Elizabeth swallowed fifty anti-depressant pills and drove her Range Rover into Bayou St. John.

Rachel feels suddenly sad, thinking about Elizabeth and her three motherless children. All grown now, for sure. What were their names? Something alliterative. Maybe "C" names. Callie, maybe. No, Calliope. And the other two were boys, too young to have been friends with Jedediah. Perhaps she never knew their names. Rachel flips open her handout-Margaret is exceptionally fond of handouts. She turns to page three. Collin? Was that the boy? No, Carter. That was it. Carter.

"Rachel?" She looks up. Sunlight passes through Margaret's corona of blonde hair. "Rachel," Margaret repeats. "Did you hear me, hon?" (Except for people she really likes-who she calls by name-Margaret calls everybody, hon.)

"Oh," says Rachel because she can't think of another response.

"We were wondering if you've talked with the Comeaux brothers. Are they available to help with the move?"

A broken vent on the wall behind Rachel sends thick spirals of frozen air down over her right shoulder while her underarms are sticky with sweat. "Yeah, yes. Sorry. It's fine. They'll be there." Margaret smiles and makes a note in her folder. A bright pink artificial feather is scotch-taped to the pen in Margaret's hand. It dances around enthusiastically as she writes. Rachel is a bit mesmerized. She makes a mental note: Two Xanax is too many. The pills she took before the meeting are now paradoxically increasing her anxiety. The ladies understand she's spacey and distracted. She picks up her water glass, takes a long sip, and sets it down, carefully inside the wet ring on the table.

She wouldn't have needed the Xanax if it hadn't been for Camilla's phone call. Jesus. Camilla James, a nurse she hadn't spoken to in nearly fifteen years. *There are some things you need to know.*

The call had come before daylight, waking Daniel first. His breath was warm against her neck. Rachel had been dreaming. A blue-green waterway. Cypress is big around as truck tires. Thick, black swamp mud caking her shins like frosting.

Your phone, Rach, I think that's your phone.

She opened her eyes. The room was warm despite the air conditioning. A sheen of sweat bathed her body despite the fan blades turning lazy circles, creaking softly overhead. Outside, a half-moon the color of beeswax. The cicada trilling.

Hello? Rachel said, sleep still croaking her voice. Clouding her thoughts. At first, nothing. The indistinct murmur of television in the background.

Mrs. Thibodaux? A woman's voice, hesitant. Rachel leaned over and switched on the bedside lamp. Her reading glasses were next to the table, and she slipped them on. The little crystal clock read 4:45 am.

Yes, this is her. Who is this?

Suddenly, a rush of blood made her dizzy, and her heart was thudding in her ears as the memory of another early morning phone call flooded back. Mrs. Thibodaux? A male voice had come out of the darkness that night so long ago. Hello Mrs. Thibodaux. Do you have a son by the name of Jedediah Thibodaux, middle name Mason?

She shook herself out of the memory. Focused on this call. Now. Right now. She said, "My daughter. Alex. Is she ok?" The words tumbled from her mouth so quickly she wasn't sure they were intelligible.

Oh god, I'm sorry, said the voice. No, this is not about your children- But Rachel was already out of bed, down the wide hallway, past the guest rooms. Pushing open her daughter's bedroom door. She let go of her breath and dropped the phone to her side. Her twenty-year-old daughter slept peacefully. Most of the bedcovers kicked to the carpet—her legs like ivory marble in the moonlight. Nearly colorless blonde hair splayed out across the sheets like water. Gently, Rachel pulled closed Alex's door. Lifted the phone back to her ear. Irritated. Who is this?

The surge of adrenaline that had accompanied Rachel's absolute certainty Alex had been killed, or maimed or, at a minimum, jailed, drained from her body with an acuity that turned her legs to jelly. She sat or, more accurately, fell into the nearest chair. An S-shaped contemporary-vintage monstrosity Daniel purchased on one of his many trips abroad and then insisted on displaying in the hallway. Her tailbone slammed into its hard-plastic surface, and she clenched her teeth to keep from cursing.

"This is Camilla James, Rachel."

Pause. Breathe.

"This is who?" Perhaps she'd misheard.

"Camilla, Camilla James. It's been a long time, and I'm so sorry for calling so early, but something's happened." One beat of silence. Another. *"I need to speak to you urgently. It's about Good Hope. There are some things you need to know."*

After the phone call, Rachel could not go back to sleep. She lay in bed for a long time, remembering.

It was 1981, the year she met Camilla for the first time. She'd met Daniel and Camilla both on the same day. Broke, alone, terrified, and so incredibly young Rachel hadn't even been 18. A terrible summer storm engulfed the city that morning and, by the time Rachel reached the streetcar stop and climbed aboard, she'd been wet to her soul. It appeared the city might wash away. Dissolve in the hot, fat raindrops that hadn't stopped falling for days. Late June, and already, the sticky heat had her undone. Unable to sit still, she pulled at the plastic buttons of her blouse and repeatedly released and smoothed and refastened the clip that held her now drenched hair in place.

The car was crowded. People jumped on faster than off as it rolled down Saint Charles Ave toward the Central Business District. Halfway to the Lee Circle, just past the Loyola campus, and already, it was standing room only. Anyone near a window was leaning halfway out to get some air. Up at the front, at least a half-dozen young men were balanced precariously on the steps leading down to the track, clinging one-handed to the silver pole, a foot waving dangerously off the edge, raindrops bouncing from their shirtsleeves and baseball caps.

Outside, steam rose from the asphalt and Spanish moss hung heavy from the branches of live oaks lining the avenue. Smells of sweet dogwood and chicory and hot tar. Despite the heat and the crowd, Rachel usually enjoyed this part of the ride. Particularly the iron-gated Victorian mansions near the university. With their formal porticos, decorated by urns overflowing with maidenhair and feathery lady fern. Elegant facades, draperies pulled back to allow only a wink of view beyond the double-hung windows. Lush gardens. Flowering dogwoods and brick walkways bordered by rows of pansies and marigolds. Most days, she'd enjoy daydreaming about living in a mansion on St Charles. She and Talia. In the morning, they'd throw open the front doors and step barefoot onto the porch and then sit quietly together and watch the streetcars trundling by. They'd be safe—someday.

Today, however, her nerves were jangled, and she was thinking of nothing but AmHealth Corporation and the looming interview she'd rashly accepted. She was, she realized, pathetically underqualified for the position—for any position. At seventeen, she had no skills, no meaningful work experience, and lacked even a high school diploma. This interview, she thought, was insanity. She'd promised to be there, and be there she would.

Rachel hopped off the streetcar at Carondelet and walked two blocks to the building. AmHealth headquarters occupied several offices in a twenty-story building named Trinity South. The name was a mystery to Rachel. As far as she knew, there was no *Trinity North* or *Trinity in any other direction*. She thought the name made the building sound like a church.

Inside, she found a bank of glossy-looking elevators, each with dozens of buttons. Sighing, she rummaged in her purse for the paper scrap upon which she'd scrawled the office address.

"Where are you headed?" A man's voice came from behind her.

She turned to find a tall, thin young man, dark-haired and dark-eyed, dressed in an expensive-looking suit. He was grinning at her. Rachel felt suddenly annoyed.

"Uh, AmHealth," she said. "But I'm ok," she added, pulling the crinkled bit of paper from her purse. She pressed the button for the ninth floor.

"Ah, AmHealth. That's my destination, too," he said, tipping his head at the button panel. "You're new, right?"

"Not new, just interviewing." Rachel kept her eyes fixed on the numbers over the elevator doors. She didn't want to encourage conversation. He was increasing her anxiety.

"Ah, ok." The doors opened, and he stepped back to let her in first. A second later, they were alone in the elevator. She stood stiffly, bag pressed to her side, eyes on the lights above the door. It was a slow elevator.

"Who are you seeing?" he asked. "Maybe I can give you some tips."

"Uh," she hesitated. "Director of Staff Resources, I guess."

He nodded. "The Director is a good lady," he said. "You'll be fine."

Rachel mumbled something like thank you, and a thousand years later, the elevator came to a smooth, silent stop, and the doors slipped open. She stepped out.

"Well, good luck to you," he said. "I'm Daniel, by the way. Daniel Thibodaux." As he switched his briefcase to his left hand and held out his right to shake hers, Rachel couldn't help but notice the lovely watch peeking out beneath his shirt cuff and, on his ring finger, a thick band of pale gold.

"I'm Rachel," she said. "Rachel Fontenot." His grip was firm, his skin warm and dry.

"Nice to meet you, Rachel Fontenot. I'll see you around." He smiled again and walked off down the broad, carpeted hallway. His lanky frame and shock of black hair were briefly reflected in the elevators' polished brass doors. She'd known, even then, that she'd see Daniel Thibodaux again.

And Camilla, Rachel thinks. Nearly forty years later, she still remembers the office's details as she sat waiting for her interview with Camilla James, B.S., R.N. Director of Staff Resources at AmHealth Corporation. An unsmiling, efficient young woman had escorted her in. "Have a seat here; she'll be with you momentarily." Left alone, Rachel perched on the edge of her chair. She felt like a trapped bird. Her heart fluttered; her breath came too fast. She leaned forward and lifted a creamy business card from the silver rack on the desk. She imagined a tall, blonde woman with sharp features, long silky legs, and a cool smile. She'd lean back in her desk chair and ask Rachel impossible questions. Rachel felt panic coming on. She inhaled, slowly, counting to three, exhaled even more slowly, reminding herself the worst that could happen was she could leave without a job. No worse than the situation she was in now. Except that wasn't exactly true. Humiliation plus unemployment were much worse than unemployment alone. Stop it. Stop it.

There was no clock in the little office, and she had no watch. It seemed she'd been left waiting a long time. She tapped her foot repeatedly and resisted the urge to get up and stick her head into the hallway. She tried to recall the comforting words of her friend Ruth Myers who'd gotten her the interview. Just go on over there and talk to 'em, Rachel. They don't except you ever done nothin' work-wise. They won't be expectin' much. All they need is somebody to clean up around the office a little and bring 'em coffee and whatnot. Quit worryin'. Thinking about Ruth only exacerbated Rachel's stress. Her thoughts quickly ping-ponged to the future scene where she'd tell Ruth that she'd messed it up. Rachel's brain did that a lot. Bouncing forward to the worst-case scenario.

Ruth was an older woman, a waitress at the Napoleon Grill, where Rachel had been briefly employed. When they let her go after discovering she was underage (the grill employed only those eighteen and up), Ruth, feeling bad for her, had her husband-a night janitor at AmHealth- put in a word for Rachel.

A few days later, a call came in. AmHealth is considering hiring another assistant to clean up after meetings, run messages and errands, type, and file a little. Would she be interested? Rachel, who did not know what an assistant did, had never filed a thing in her life and had no typing skills beyond the two-finger method, accepted the interview and felt immediately terrified.

Instead of abating (as Ruth had assured her would happen as soon as she arrived at the interview), Rachel's nervousness escalated into sick, heart-thudding dizziness. She picked at a loose thread in the hem of her polyester blouse until it unraveled completely, leaving three inches of hem hanging free. She stuffed the raw fabric under and shoved it into the ample waistband of her skirt. The white blouse and navy skirt, both borrowed from Ruth, were at least three sizes too big. She'd had to fold the elastic band over a few times to keep the skirt from falling.

She looked down at herself, dismayed. Thought briefly of leaving. Imagining the cool relief as those glass doors swung shut behind her, and she hit the street. Squeezing her eyes shut, she reminded herself why she was here. You need this job. You need the money. Tee, think about Tee.

Rachel yanked again at the hem of her blouse, then set the business card back in its tray and looked around the room. A bookshelf crammed with titles like Organizational Development in Health Care. A few potted plants. An unidentifiable yarn object that looked as if a child had made it. A wall of framed certificates. Degrees. Awards.

This is crazy, she thought again. I'm a seventeen-year-old high school dropout with zero skills. She took a breath, blew it out, cheeks puffed, and pushed herself out of her chair. She'd leave. Before anyone noticed, she'd just disappear and save everyone the embarrassment of this interview.

Rachel was at the door, hand reaching for the knob, when it opened inward, almost knocking her back.

"Whoa there, girl!" said a large, grinning black woman. "Where are you going? We haven't even met yet, right?" She was shoving her hand toward Rachel. "I'm Camilla James," she said, still smiling. "And you are, Rachel Fontenot. Am I right?" The woman dipped her chin and almost crouched to force Rachel to look into her eyes. Rachel felt the flush in her skin as she looked up at the striking woman.

"Hi," said Rachel. "And yeah, that's me."

In a voice so amiable and warm, Rachel would have sworn it caused her body to physically relax. Camilla James said, "Well, come on then, sit down; we have some talking to do."

That had been it. Camilla James saved her life. Got her the job. Changed everything. After that, they'd been friends for what? Over twenty years before losing track of one another. Or maybe it had been Rachel who'd lost track of Camilla. Either way, they'd had no contact in over a decade, and now, now this.

In the morning, Rachel had second thoughts. She had agreed to meet. More, she'd kept it from Daniel. But that was ridiculous. She'd had no contact with Camilla in almost fifteen years. Not since it all happened. The woman might have experienced a psychotic break in all that time. Or dementia-how old was she? Or maybe she'd had an accident. Brain trauma, Rachel had read brain trauma could make people delusional.

She decided over her first cup of coffee; she would not meet this woman, certainly not alone. She'd talk to Daniel first. She sat in her robe at the table, reading the news on her phone. Scrolling through headlines without paying much attention as her coffee grew cool. And then she saw it, the Good Hope article. But it wasn't the headline that stopped her. Her gaze caught on the name printed further down in the text. She stared for a long time at the letters that formed the words, the digital dots that made up those letters. Studying the screen until she heard the clipped sound of Daniel's English shoes coming down the wooden steps. Then she set the phone face down on the table and got up to kiss him good morning.

And so she hadn't talked to Daniel. Not while they ate their breakfast of scrambled egg whites and toast, not while they chatted about their schedules for the day, and again, not when he kissed her goodbye before leaving the house. Instead, she'd taken two Xanax and called Uber for a ride to the meeting. Vowing to sort it out later. Later, being a time almost always preferable to now.

CHAPTER 2

Devereaux, Louisiana

1975

Buffa's Restaurant in Devereaux, Louisiana was a long, low building, pushed up against the highway's edge, so close to traffic, it was possible to feel the weight of the air displaced by the cars as they whooshed past. The brick façade, painted white decades ago, was littered with greasy fingerprints and layers of dirt. Someone had jammed a bunch of miniature American flags into the weedy earth beside the walkway— leftovers from Memorial Day, but that was weeks ago.

Rachel watched as her sister Talia bent to snatch bits of the purple love grass that poked up through cracks in the cement. Pinching a stem carefully between her small thumb and forefinger, she stood, clutching the straggly weed in her palm. Tee was not quite five, too young for what was happening. She just stared up at Mama. After a moment, she stuck the stem in her mouth.

Nina Fontenot crouched in front of the double glass doors and stuffed a crumpled bill into the pocket of ten-year-old Rachel's shorts. "Y'all go inside. Take that money and ask the lady to bring you somethin." She was looking at Rachel. "Anything you want, baby. A couple of those chocolate ice creams you like." Her voice sounded strange. Far away, like she was saying the words and thinking something different.

"I don't want to, Mama," Rachel said. "I don't know them, people."

"It's just for a little while. I'll be right back."

"When?"

"Well, let's see." She glanced over her shoulder and then back at Rachel. "About an hour. I think that'll do it. Can you be my big girl for me?" It wasn't really a question.

"Where are you goin'?"

"Wanna go with you, Mama?" Talia whined. Dropping her flower, she held out her arms to be picked up.

"Where are you goin', Mama?" Rachel repeated, but Nina didn't answer. She wiped her eyes with the back of her hand, then she pulled both girls close and held on for a long time.

A teenage girl came up the walk. Silky straight hair, bell-bottom jeans, and a T-shirt covered in tiny rainbows. Over her shoulder was a long suede purse, the fringe brushing her thigh as she walked. She was the sort of girl Rachel wished to be. Rachel straightened.

"We'll be alright, Mama," she said. Not at all sure that was true.

Behind Nina, Errol sat in the driver's seat of his rust-eaten pickup truck. Parked up against the curb, motor running, he wore cheap mirrored sunglasses, and his hair, short in front, ran to a skinny tail in the back. Errol had tattoos up both arms, knitted close together, showing hardly any skin. The truck radio blasted country music, and he tapped his fingers on the steering wheel along with the beat. He glanced over and caught Rachel's eye and looked away.

Beyond the truck, between blackened utility poles, the sky extended flat and white to the horizon.

They'd been living at Errol's place in Devereaux all year. Ever since Nina left Pichette. Pichette ain't got no use for me, and I ain't got no use for it, Nina said. Devereaux and Pichette were less than an hour's drive from one another, and yet, they hadn't been back. Not even for a visit.

Living with Errol hadn't been so bad at first. Rachel and Talia didn't have a room in the trailer, so they got to sleep together on a tiny couch curled like spoons. The Sunnyside Trailer Park ran along the back of Christmas Bayou-so named because of the Christmas green algae that grew thick across its surface and the bright blooms of star hibiscus that popped up among the palmettos like mammoth red lollipops. Folks called it a wasteland, too soft to build, too soggy to plant. A wide swath of swamp grass ran along the water, and the girls spent hours there, fishing with poles they rigged from cypress branches and wire, hunting frogs and crawdads. Sometimes they only sat, watching the egrets as they swooped overhead and landed like dancers in the hollow formed by the gum trees across the way. Rachel even liked the school; her teachers were friendly, encouraging, and all the kids were the same. They were flawed, their families were poor, and it wasn't like Pichette. Devereaux was a metropolis compared to her tiny hometown. It lacked Pichette's incestuousness, and Rachel welcomed the relative anonymity.

Most of all, Mama was happy. For a long time, she smiled and laughed, and they had fun, and Errol was kind to her. He was kind and patient. He looked at her sweetly and touched her face gently when they spoke. Mama helped with Rachel's homework. She was never too tired. They even started a small garden. Errol mostly ignored the girls, but occasionally he brought little gifts, candy or bubble gum. Once a set of miniature stuffed animals. Once packs of candy cigarettes, which Mama threw away.

If things hadn't changed, Rachel supposed they could have lived that way forever.

But Nina and Errol's fights got louder and meaner. Errol started hitting. After a while, he did it all the time.

One Sunday, Nina fixed boiled crawfish and corncobs and set the picnic table outside with a white paper cloth and a mason jar full of wildflowers in the center. But Errol never came home. Nina said nothing. Just carried the Tupperware back up to the trailer and then went out and stacked up the unused paper plates and brought them back, too. Then she pulled the whiskey down from the cupboard over the sink and sat down on the sofa, still wearing her good sundress, and drank it straight out of the bottle.

If Errol had stayed gone, things might have been alright. But he stumbled in before dawn. Rachel lay on the sofa, pretending to be asleep. One eye opened to a narrow slit. He stank of stale alcohol and cigarettes and something else she couldn't identify. He pulled open the fridge, took out a beer, peeled back the metal tab, and tossed it into the sink. Then he sat down in a chair beside the sofa, blue light from a bulb outside streaming over his arms and hands. Rachel could see the half-moons of dirt under his fingernails. The knuckles of his right hand were scraped raw and bleeding. After a while, he got up and pulled open the door to the tiny bedroom and disappeared behind it.

The girls awoke later to the sounds of crashing. Nina and Errol cursing at each other.

"I work hard, Nina," he said. "I work my fuckin' ass off all fuckin week to take care of you and those two brats and what? Your gonna bust my balls over one fuckin night?"

Nina's response was unintelligible, but it must have made Errol mad because, after that, she wore oversized sunglasses around for two weeks, trying to hide the bruise.

Once, enraged that Rachel had tried to intervene in a fight (throwing her small body in front of Nina's to block a punch), a shirtless, drunken Errol dragged Rachel out back of the trailer and smacked her hard across the face. "You ever git in my way again, I'll kill you," he said, his face so close she could smell his breath. Errol straightened up and hiked his jeans up over his sunken belly. "And if you tell your mama about this here," he said, pointing at the ground between them. "I'll fuckin kill that baby sister a yours too."

With a cupped hand, Rachel held her bleeding mouth. Tears welled in her eyes as Errol walked away, tiny clouds of dust kicking up under the heels of his boots.

As Mama stood, preparing to leave them at Buffa's, Rachel noticed a crack in the cement. It ran from Mama's boot-heel across the sidewalk, ending at the truck's front right tire. Mama said a quick goodbye, kissing each girl on the head, then she turned and stepped toward the waiting truck. As she climbed up and disappeared, Rachel imagined the crack sucking her down inside. Swallowing her whole, the way an alligator does a marshmallow when you toss it off the side of a skiff. Chomp.

· · ·

Three hours later, they sat close together in a booth. Solemn and waiting. Four small feet dangling under the table, not quite reaching the floor.

"She ain't comin' back," Rachel whispered, running the tip of her spoon around the bowl and scooping out the last dregs of ice cream. "She ain't comin' back," she said again, this time looking at Talia, who had picked up her dish and was holding it to her face, shamelessly licking the bottom. Rachel grabbed the smaller girl's elbow and jerked at it. "You hear me? Tee? She ain't comin' back. We got to do somethin'. We can't just sit here like babies."

Talia let go of her dish, which clattered to the table but did not break. She stared up at Rachel, a tiny furrow between her eyes. Her mouth twisted into an angry pout. "Mama." was all she said. At nearly five, Talia spoke less than other children, but she wasn't stupid. And everyone loved her. Talia, with her wide eyes and soft dark-blonde curls and the way she had climbed up into anyone's lap for a hug. Anyone. Rachel worried about that.

"No!" said Rachel. "No, that's what I mean. She ain't comin'. It's gettin' dark, Tee." Rachel pointed at the window. Beyond a row of palmettos and over the highway, a clump of oak trees was deeply shadowed against the paling sky.

Talia shook her head and curled her fingers into tiny fists. She closed her eyes tight—something she always did when confronted with bad news, which was often. "No," she whispered. "Mamas comin'. No. No." Rachel slid across the vinyl booth and wrapped an arm around her sister's small back. She could feel Talia's ribs under the threadbare sweater. She felt her resolve weaken.

"Open your eyes, Tee," whispered Rachel. "It's ok. We can wait longer." It felt like a lie. Rachel used her free hand to pull the change from her pocket. They had three dollars and eighty-seven cents left from the money Mama had given them. Everything they had in the world. Rachel leaned close to the silky whorl of Talia's ear. "Hey, you wanna have another ice cream?"

• • •

Through the dirt-spattered window, Rachel watched as gray clouds gathered across the highway. The rumble of a storm in the distance. Heavy and foreboding. The customers at Buffas were almost all gone. A skinny boy, not too many years older than Rachel, was mopping the floor. He had a plastic bucket on fat wheels like roller skates, and he kept pushing it around near their table, squeezing the mop's brownish water out on the floor so it puddled under Rachel's feet. She glared at him, but he only grinned. He was missing one of his two front teeth.

It was the cook who finally came over and asked after them. "You two been here a while. You waitin' on someone or what?" He was wiping his hands down the front of his apron as he spoke. He was a big man. Bigger than Errol, around the middle anyway. But he was smiling. His blue work shirt sleeves were rolled back, and a band of white skin encircled his suntanned wrist, marking where he wore a watch.

"Yeah, we're waitin' on our Mama." She looked down at Talia, who'd fallen asleep and lay stretched across the vinyl booth, her head cradled in Rachel's lap. One of her plastic sandals had fallen off and gotten lost under the table. Her foot was bare, and Rachel could see the red polish remnants where Nina had painted her toenails the night before. The sight made Rachel's heartache.

"Yeah? What's your Mama's name?" the man asked. "I think maybe we ought to call her to come fetch you two. We're fixin' to close up."

"Her name's Nina," said Rachel. "Nina Fontenot, but she ain't home. And she don't have no phone anyway, even if she was home."

"I see. Well, is there anybody else we can call?"

"No, sir," said Rachel. "She said to wait here."

The cook narrowed his eyes. "How old are you two, anyway?"

"Thirteen," Rachel lied. "And this here's my sister. She's five." Not such a big lie.

"You ain't thirteen," said the cook.

For a moment, Rachel was afraid. She knew about kids who got left places. Some were forced to live with a dozen other kids in dirty, crowded foster homes, like the one run by Mr. and Mrs. Limon. Rachel's third-grade friend Colleen had lived with the Limons, and half the time, Colleen hadn't even made it to school.

But the cook was smiling. He didn't look like the sort of man to send a kid to a foster home just for sitting alone at a diner a little too late.

"Hey," he said. "I ain't gonna make you tell me the truth. Tell you what, you give me your names, and we'll see what we can find out for you, ok? Meantime, how 'bout somethin' to eat. Besides ice cream, I mean."

Rachel's stomach rumbled at the mention of food.

By the time Granny Nona arrived, Talia was awake, and the restaurant was closed. Rachel watched through the window as Nona climbed out of her truck and scurried across the blacktop. She held a magazine over her head, trying to keep dry from the rain. But the drops were fat and dense, splashing up from the pavement and drenching her jeans to the knees. Just outside the entrance, she stood for a moment and dropped the soggy magazine in a trash can and shook out her hair and stomped her feet a few times. Then she pushed on the door. It was secured. Rachel could see an angry expression on Nona's face as she yanked on the door twice and then pressed her face right up against the glass. One waitress made her way over, pulling a ring of keys from her pocket.

Nona was a small, hard woman, with hair she kept bleached, like straw. When it was wet, it lay in pale strips across her scalp, dribbling water into her ears and down her neck. Catching sight of the girls, she came flying across the empty restaurant, cursing even before she reached them—the rubber soles of her tennis shoes squelching as she came.

"What in hell am I supposed to do about this? Huh? Where in hell's your Mama? Just leavin' y'all here to what? Take care of your own selves till god knows when."

Talia was sliding down into the booth, burying her face in Rachel's side as if she were terrified. Rachel pushed at her.

"Tee cut it out." Everyone knew Nona had more bark than bite. No bite at all, really. And she especially loved Tee. Tee wasn't afraid of Nona. She just didn't like loud. Not in any form.

"Oh, for pity's sake, look at this baby." Granny Nona's voice softened, and she let loose a deep, tobacco-wracked sigh. "Well, come on then, let's get. It's an hour back to Pichette, and the weather's already on us."

Rachel and Talia said nothing as they climbed out of the booth. Nona looked around, bent to see under the table. "Nothin? She didn't give you no clothes or nothin'?"

"She said she was coming back," Rachel whispered. "She promised." Nona only scoffed and rolled her eyes.

"Yeah, well, come on now." Nona whirled around and started for the door. Rachel had to push Talia from her side and force her to walk. She'd closed her eyes again.

"Tee, come on. You gotta look where you goin'." But she refused to open them. Rachel guided Talia out the doors of the restaurant and toward Granny Nona's old Ford. As they climbed in, she whispered into Talia's soft baby hair, "It's ok, Tee. Mama will come tomorrow. Everything will be ok now. You'll see."

Nona said nothing on the hot, bumpy ride back to Pichette. It was late by the time they pulled off the main highway. Rachel squinted out the window, trying to see if anything had changed during their year up in Devereaux. The one road through town was still covered in white rock and seashells, and the gas station was already closed. The main street was dark except for the fireflies that buzzed Nona's headlights on the dark road.

A cacophony of bullfrogs and cicadas greeted them as they got out of the truck. The familiar tiny clapboard house was stuffy and hot, but it smelled of back fat and red beans and just a little of the swamp.

The girls slept together in Mama's old room. Side by side in a bed barely big enough for the two of them, their heads touching on the pillow. Rachel tried to explain things. She rubbed Talia's tummy and whispered; her lips pressed close against the top of her sister's head. She could feel Tee's baby breath, dry and warm against her neck, smell the sweet, earthy tang of her. Like peaches.

Long after Talia fell asleep, Rachel lay awake in the dark. Finally, she closed her eyes, imagining Mama was there kissing their cheeks and calling them my baby girls, her strong arms and long, soft hair falling across their bodies in the night.

CHAPTER 3

New Orleans, Central Lockup

July 21, 2020

The lobby vestibule is stuffy and crowded with visitors. Waves of hot air waft inside every time the door opens. Bodies pressed together, creating a stench: sweat and fear. Virgil Barrons takes a position at the back of the line just inside the entrance to the jail.

An elderly black woman in bubble gum-colored support hose and orthopedic shoes waits in line in front of Virgil. A teenage boy, maybe her grandson, stands slope-shouldered beside her. They visit a father, brother, or uncle—someone who mattered to them once. The boy is all angles and teeth. His face is sullen. He wears a button-down shirt that was likely ironed when he put it on but is now badly wrinkled and sweat-soaked under the arms. Sockless ankles. Feet stuffed into a pair of dirty tennis shoes. It's a long haul down here for most of these people, especially without a car.

The woman reaches up to place a hand on the boy's shoulder, and the boy jerks away. "Quit," he says irritably, and she withdraws. Otherwise, they don't speak.

DiMarco, the correctional officer (C.O.) manning the metal detector, spends a long time with the old woman's bag. He pushes his hand around inside aggressively like he might encounter something he'll need to fight. He produces a plastic comb, a rolled tube of mints, and a compact mirror, which he confiscates on account of the glass. When he hands the purse back, the boy makes a disgusted face, shakes his head, and blows out his breath. DiMarco glares at him, holding the stare until the boy looks away. Finally, the cop waves them through. The vestibule is nearly empty now. It's Virgil's turn.

"You see that, doc?" asks DiMarco. His voice was low.

"Yeah."

"Little sonofabitch giving me attitude. I swear, some of these kids. Might as well arrest right now. Am I right, doc?" DiMarco smiles. Tobacco-stained teeth.

"Uh," says Virgil. "Yeah." Agreeing with a bigot like DiMarco feels like shit, but it's been an awful morning. Virgil slept poorly. Thoughts of the warden's late-night phone call (meet me in my office at nine) plagued him throughout the night-then, driving in the car producing a strange high-pitched "thweeeep" every time he braked. Finally, the reminder call from the warden's secretary came in on his cell phone while still in the parking lot. All Virgil wants is to get to his office, shut the door, and be left alone for a few minutes. Getting into a debate about social inequality and race relations with this numbskull would certainly put another curve in his day. Besides, you don't argue with the guys who have your back while you're on the inside. Right? That's right. It would be stupid to do otherwise.

"Hell yeah, I'm right," Di Marco continues, encouraged by Virgil's silence. "Ever one of 'em is slingin' dope. Ever goddamn one. If it was up to me, doc, I'd just..." says DiMarco, handing back Virgil's briefcase after a cursory check. Virgil, half a foot shorter than DiMarco, has stopped listening and is studying the guard's chest. There's a dime-sized stain on DiMarco's white uniform shirt near his badge. Ketchup maybe. Virgil retrieves his briefcase and passes through the metal detector and down the hall as quickly as possible.

Because of its location, squeezed into the middle of the city, Central Lockup (Orleans Parish Jail) is built vertically. A multi-storied complex of gray concrete and steel. Row after row of narrow slits for windows lend the structure an intimidating aura from the outside and render it dark, dank, and echoing with the unsettling sounds of an old prison movie soundtrack on the inside—steel on steel, clanking chains, human cries. Virgil has grown used to it. Mostly he doesn't notice. During the day anyway.

Strangely, jail comes to him in dreams. Nightmares. He's alone in the building, first rushing, then sprinting through the corridors, although he's not sure why. Sweat pours into his eyes, and he's unable to catch his breath. In his mouth, a putrid substance he's unable to spit out. He grows panicked, hunting for an exit: nothing but dark foyers, closed doors, and hallways built into complicated, insoluble mazes.

Virgil passes into a narrow airlock, less than half the size of a jail cell. A small pane of glass set into the steel door is his only view out of the tiny space. Through it, he sees nothing but an endless pale green hallway. He shifts uncomfortably, one foot to the other, as he waits for the buzzer showing the inner door is unlocked. He wills himself not to touch the door. Several seconds elapse without a sound. He looks up at the camera. A white eye set high in the corner. There's another one on the opposite wall. They can see him and most of the guys on duty, like Virgil. They like him because he's a shrink and having a shrink around makes the job easier. Nothing like ten milligrams of haloperidol to knock the danger out of a 300-pound psychopath. But there are a few, one or two, who enjoy screwing with him. Maybe taking an extra few seconds to open the steel door at the opposite end of the airlock, for example. Virgil waves an arm at the camera. Five more seconds, and there's a loud buzz followed by a click. Unlocked. He lets go of his breath and steps out.

He crosses the hall and gets into the open elevator. Another box. Smooth steel walls with cameras in all four corners. No buttons. Once inside, he holds up a hand, thumb and forefinger together, showing he wants to head downstairs to floor zero. The doors shut, and the elevator lurches and moves. The smell of cold metal and bleach and vague man sweat.

The office Virgil occupies is in the basement, or what would be the basement if New Orleans had floors existing below ground? A windowless corner on the lowermost floor of a sinking building. But

Virgil doesn't mind. It is an office with a door that shuts, which is more than most employees can boast. He fought five years to get the space, arguing he needed a place to make confidential phone calls, draft reports, and, mostly, store the stacks of files he was required to audit and review every day. The one communal space, which had to be shared between the medical nurses, psych students, the one physician's assistant, and rotating specialists, was, he explained, inadequate. He discovered that logic carried no weight—the unspoken consensus among the non-physician administrators seemed to be that doctors, as a lot, believed themselves, superior genetically, and therefore entitled to never share space with the great unwashed. The result was that Virgil spent those years pushing a cart similar to a shopping cart piled high with records back and forth to the secure file room every day.

What mattered was the chummy relationship he developed with the director of nursing. Camilla James, a fifteen-year veteran of the state bureaucracy, a New Orleans native, and a formidable physical presence at nearly six feet and two hundred plus pounds, took up Virgil's fight, eventually wrangling this office from the rotating psych residents. The latter now had to scramble for desk space wherever they could find it.

Virgil checks his watch. Forty minutes until the warden expects him. He stares at the stack of charts on his desk. Well into the twenty-first century and the New Orleans jail is still paper record dependent. The administration has made a terrific mess of the attempted transition to electronic record-keeping over the past few years. The result: every patient record is now maintained in both paper and digital format. Nearly doubling the workload for everyone on staff.

He leans forward and slides the first chart off the top. Flips it open and begins reading. As the only full-time staff psychiatrist for the jail, one of his duties–among many- is the dubious task euphemistically named chart evaluation. What it really amounts to is maximizing denial of care. They replenish the chart stack on his desk at random intervals, often several times daily. He will never make it all the way to the bottom. His job is to read each record and decide diagnosis, disposition, referral and medications then enter those decisions into the computer system to be shared with the rest of the staff.

He's never laid eyes upon most of these patients/prisoners and never will. Besides being medically unethical, the charting process probably qualifies for malpractice in five different ways. But there's no money. At least there's no money available to hire docs: three hundred prisoners, one mental health doc. This is triage regressed to somewhere around the level of a surgeon's tent in the Civil War. Anyone too sick or too well probably wasn't gonna get a lot of help.

In his early years at the jail, marking nearly every chart as urgently needing full evaluation made Virgil incredibly unpopular with the higher-ups. After receiving a third CEO reprimand for his apparent inability to recognize the limitations under which we are operating at this institution, he got more creative with his processes. Suicidal and potentially violent patients get seen. Everyone else waits. Maybe forever.

He reads that this inmate was a forty-one-year-old alcoholic arrested for bank robbery, now threatening to kill himself. A sticky note left by one of the social workers marks it URGENT. Social workers label every chart as urgent. They are the good guys. Virgil is reading the arresting officer's report when there's a knock on his door. "Yeah," he says. "Come on in."

He looks up, and Camilla pokes her head in. "Hey, Virgil."

He smiles at her and sets the chart down. "Hey Camilla, morning. Come sit."

"You busy?"

"Nah, never busy," he grins. "You know this guy?" He reads the name. "Macalory J? Came in over the weekend. You think he's really suicidal?"

She pushes open the door and steps inside, closing it carefully behind her. "Yeah," she says, lowering her heavy frame into the one spindly guest chair. "I saw him. Sad situation. Weighs about a hundred pounds. Rotten teeth. Meth. Xanax. Alcohol. The whole deal."

Virgil shakes his head. "Yeah, the guy stumbled into the First Bank of Metairie. Got the brilliant idea they had money, and he needed money. No weapon. Nothing. Handed the teller a note. Bank robbery by goddamn note. GIVE ME ALL THE MONEY, scribbled on a deposit slip, only he ran out of the room. There's a picture of the thing right here." Virgil turns the chart so Camilla can see the photo. Both sides of the deposit slip. GIVE ME scrawled messily on one side and ALL THE MONEY on the back.

"Idiot. And Old Metairie, for god's sake. Home of the rich, white xenophobes. He might as well have waved his note around at the Bank of Beverly Hills."

"I think maybe he lived there at one time. He used to be some kind of engineer," she says.

"Poor dumb bastard, looking at a life sentence for one desperate, drunken mistake." Virgil makes a note, signs the chart, and moves it into the pile of NEEDS TO BE SEEN ASAP.

He looks up at Camilla, noting for the first time, her face is puffy and strained. He worries about her. Well into her sixties, overtired and overworked. She doesn't say much about her personal life, but Virgil can see it in her sometimes. No family. A daughter who died long ago. Virgil has heard that loss resulted in Camillas stepping down from a remarkably prominent position she'd held in corporate healthcare. The company was AmHealth, Virgil thinks. Camilla never speaks of it, and he never asks.

"Hey, are you ok?"

"Yeah, thanks. I'm ok but listen, I need to talk to you before you see the warden." She glances over her shoulder, then turns back toward Virgil. "I think you may have a problem."

CHAPTER 4

New Orleans

July 21, 2020

Rachel checks her watch and decides the Uptown Ladies meeting must wind down, for god's sake. Waiters circle the tables, carefully lifting cutlery and china plates out of the ladies' way. They have left most of the lunch tragically untouched. Eating in public is not really done. Food is served and then sent back. Rachel hopes someone on the catering staff takes it home. At least her plates are cleaned. She shoves a heaping forkful of chocolate bread pudding into her mouth. She takes two more bites, sets the fork down, carefully balancing the tines against the edge of the Wedgwood dessert plate, and waits politely for the approaching, white-aproned young man to ask her, "Are you finished with that?"

She picks up the handout. Tells herself to focus. She'll also need to stay awake. These meetings are mind-numbingly dull and interminably long.

She squints, trying to read the shrunken font. Hopeless. She cannot make out more than a handful of words. No matter. Most tasks will be fluffy, make-work projects like counting the required corsages or addressing thank-you notes by hand. These affairs have become like an academy awards night and the Audubon Ladies Club hires professionals to do the real work like the other debutante societies in the city.

A high-pitched squeal explodes from the unnecessary speakers, followed by the crackle of static. Rachel snaps to attention; a surprising hitch in her stomach catches on the bit of cake, still making its way down to her gut. Jesus. Margaret has let her lips drift too close to the microphone again (she appears to be giving it some tongue). Now she's set off an ear-splitting feedback loop. She has a lot of trouble with technology, Charwoman Bocage. One reason she's attached to paper handouts. She taps a chubby finger on the mic several times, sending mini-explosions across the room.

Rachel suppresses a yawn. The insomnia is back, and Ambien isn't cutting it anymore, even at a double dose. She makes a mental note to add Talk to Dr. Mifflin about the pills to her list of things to do. Thinking of the To-Do list makes her feel instantly more impatient and fidgety.

The tablecloth has produced a sort of Gordian knot around her foot, and she's unable to get free. Frustrated, she finally gives it a good yank. There's an ominous ripping sound as the heel of her pump catches the material. Heads turn. Leaning down, Rachel gently lifts the edge of the cloth and checks for damage. A gash runs at least eight inches down the middle of the drape. She winces and sits up slowly. Then, when she's sure nobody is watching, she tries kicking surreptitiously at the cloth to push the evidence further out of sight. Without warning, the entire table setting shifts. Her crystal water glass rocks once, then twice. Horrified, Rachel lunges. She misses and is left, gaping, arms outstretched, as the glass tips in what seems like slow motion, rolls on its side, and dumps its contents into the lap of the woman sitting beside her, eighty-five-year-old Dominique Henry.

Dominique lets out a sort of bellow—much deeper and more frightening than Rachel would have imagined the tiny woman capable. The meeting grinds to an ugly halt—silence in the rapidly cooling air.

"Oh shit," Rachel blurts. Mrs. Henry has a napkin in her bony fingers and is dabbing uselessly at the wet sections of her dress. This revered woman is the oldest and the richest in the room, and a half-dozen supplicants shoot out of their seats and rush towards her like combat medics. Rachel secretly tries to invoke her unique invisibility powers while babbling apology through the gaggle of middle-aged women surrounding Dominique.

It's fifteen minutes before Mrs. Henry is sufficiently dried for the meeting to resume.

Eugenie Atherton is staring at Rachel. Lips pursed, she raises her eyebrows in the self-righteous expression of a teacher's pet. Turning away, her blonde hair shifts on its own, in one solid piece, like a helmet. She and Carolyn Bichum exchange a few whispered words, and one of Eugenie's almond-sized diamond earrings catches the sunlight as she shakes her head. Rays of white light bounce off the walls and ceiling. Despite its exclusivity, this club has many members whose family wealth was largely squandered over the years. Irresponsible relatives. Poor business management. So many women like Eugenie and Carolyn cling to their social class. Their birthright. It's all they have. Rachel wishes she knew what they were saying.

She suddenly thinks of James P. Lawless Grammar School, back in Pichette, before they lost Mama. Before Earl. Before everything. Despite the essential poverty afflicting nearly every child who attended the school, a hierarchy existed—Rachel's family at the absolute bottom. Like crème de la crème, only upside down. Trash de la trash.

She'd tripped, stumbling in the cafeteria. Nearly dumping her lunch tray on a table full of older boys from a part of town known collectively as The Trailers. Life in a trailer park, nasty as it may have been, was still considered a step up from the swamp shanty Rachel Fontenot and her family occupied. "Hey, spastic, watch out!" screamed a skinny boy named Loomis. Then in a lower voice, so the lunch duty lady wouldn't hear, "What's a matter with you. You high?" They all laughed, and he kept on. "Hey, guess what I heard? I heard your Mama was so fuckin high last weekend she fuckin blew ever guy over at the Moonlight. Just lined em up and fuckin sucked em off like they was on an assembly line." The boys found that hilariously funny, laughing and high-fiving each other like fools. Loomis was an enthusiastic user of offensive language. The F-Word is often a bridge to fill in for his lack of vocabulary. "Yeah," said a fat boy with a baby face and a mouthful of cafeteria mystery meat. "Fuckin' blow job assembly line." This prompted another round of hilarity.

It wasn't true. Rachel knew it wasn't. Rumors swirled around Pichette like mosquitos in summer. Especially for Nina Fontenot. Granny Nona said it was all on account of her being too young and too pretty for her own good. Barely sixteen, when Rachel was born, she cared for both girls, mostly alone except for Granny Nona's help. It was hard working all the time. So, what if sometimes she went out? Besides, Mama said it didn't matter what folks said. They were just a bunch of rednecks anyway and didn't get what was, so Rachel and Tee should ignore them until they had the money to get out of town. Sticks and stones, Mama said. Sticks and stones.

Rachel, who had just passed the table by the time the fat boy added his comment, turned around. Setting the tray on the boys' table, she picked up her milk carton and peeled it open. Then, never taking her eyes off Loomis, she dumped out the entire contents over all their lunches.

The punishment hadn't been too bad. A visit with Dottie Larson, the school counselor, who expressed her "concern about Rachel's angry feelings" and wanted her to share what had prompted "such a malicious act." No way would Rachel tattle, no matter how much she hated Loomis and his friends. Tattling was a sure way to turn a person into social dog chow. Rachel took the one-day suspension rather than explain her actions. She didn't care. The suspension/ was not the problem and would have been well worth it had the retaliation she'd taken done anything to ease her rage and humiliation. Mama had been wrong about something. People could hurt you with words. And the hurt was just as big as sticks and stones. What people thought and what they said about you mattered.

Rachel arranges her face in an engaged-with-the-process expression, picks up her pen, and gets busy scribbling nonsensical notes on her legal pad.

It's been five years since Alexandra, now an art student at Tulane who shuns all things frilly and feminine-wears only paint-splattered overalls and doc martins and is student leader of the campus LGBTQIA organization-was forced to don the white gloves and gown and endure the deb presentation. Alex spent most of the months leading up to the ball, pretending to be sick to get out of dance lessons-going so far as to stick two fingers down her throat in an attempt at vomit induction, interrupted only by her older brother's urgent need to use the bathroom. It was Daniel who'd insisted Alex take part, but it was Rachel who carried the burden of forcing their daughter to do the work.

She sets down her pen and looks around at the creamy, well-tended faces. For so many years, Rachel has worked to fit into this world. Almost twice as long as she lived in that other place. A place where women ten and twenty years younger than these women were already bent-backed and gray-skinned, bare shadows of their girl selves. She's fought to lose the feeling of being an unwelcome outsider. She'd like not to care. She pretends to not care. She hopes she's successfully taught her daughter not to care. But Rachel? It still matters to her. Goddammit. It matters, and it's her own fault. These women, most of these, are not cruel or haughty. They don't judge her. She no longer feels the heavyweight of their eyes on her as she passes. Most are not old enough to care about her background. They know her only as a Thibodaux, Daniel's wife. Eugenie and Carolyn do not dislike Rachel because she comes from the swamp. They dislike her (if they dislike her because who really knows) for her money. And possibly for the beauty she once possessed. It makes Rachel smile now. That beauty lingers a bit, but the power it once wielded is gone.

Still, she owes this committee a debt. After Jeb died, when Rachel couldn't get out of bed, her brain a post-apocalyptic wasteland, and her heart a broken thing, they'd all come. Singly or in groups, they'd brought casseroles and cliché words of support. Little by little, she'd allowed herself to be pulled edge-wise back to her life. For her daughter. For Alex.

Not without scars, of course. Beyond the cavity in Rachel's chest, where half a heart lies petrified and splintered, there are other marks. She doesn't drive outside of town anymore on the highways or bridges. And the worries are nearly constant: campus shootings, hurricanes, contagions that kill college students like meningococcal disease, and car accidents.

Her internist had a solution. "Take one of these at the first onset of the symptoms, Rachel," he'd said, smiling, passing her a paper prescription. "And then, just take another one if you're still feeling poorly a half-hour later." That was three years ago. The pills aren't working so well anymore.

Margaret is wrapping up. She's finally given up on the microphone. "I think we've done it for today, ladies." She flips her leather binder closed with a flourish, tapping bright pink nails across the cover and eyes her audience. Despite the over-cooled air in the room, Margaret is flushed and perspiring. She picks up her napkin and waves it furiously at her face. "So," she continues. "If there are no more items on the agenda-"

Fantastic, thinks Rachel, with a surge of euphoria that feels a bit over the top. She remembers reading that chronic sleep deprivation could make a person manic.

When the meeting is adjourned, Rachel folds her napkin, lays it across the table, and gathers her purse. She glances down at her notepad before sliding it into her bag. Half the page is covered in random inky circles and rudimentary drawings of daisies—the other half in her own handwriting. Line after line, closely spaced, letters perfectly formed, she's written JANIE LUCILLE PARADISE.

CHAPTER 5

Devereaux, Louisiana

1975

Rachel guessed the air conditioner at the Shop-n-Save must be on the blink. It was hot as blazes in the checkout line. Plus, they'd been waiting for about a hundred years. Granny Nona said the girls who worked the registers were a bunch of ninnies, which was the problem, but Rachel thought it had more to do with heat. Rachel leaned her sweaty forehead on the shopping cart, forearms against the handle. She pressed her face through the baby seat and watched her little sister. Talia had climbed atop a twelve-pack of Pabst Blue Ribbon and was perched precariously, one chubby hand outstretched toward a row of orange-haired troll dolls that lined the shelves nearest the registers. Rachel glanced at Granny Nona, waiting for her to notice. Granny Nona always noticed because she had eyes in the back of her head.

"Quit it," said Granny Nona, swatting at Tee's fingers without looking up from her magazine. "And quit makin me tell y'all to keep them hands down. Only what we came for. What I say about money?" she said without turning around. She was licking her thumb and flipping pages of a gossip magazine. Nona didn't believe in gossip magazines because they were Trash, sold for Idiot Trashy People with too much time and too little brains.

Tee screwed up her face. "It don't fall on trees?"

"No, silly. It don't fall outta trees, Tee," said Rachel. Talia looked confused.

"Well, it doesn't matter," said Nona. "We just ain't buying anything we don't need." She pressed the magazine back into the rack, smoothing the cover down neatly, then yanked at her nylon headscarf. Two pink curlers popped out from underneath, emerging at the nape like off-board motors. Rachel giggled. Nona ignored her. "Holy crow, I don't get why you two gotta be so grabby all the time,"

Nona made the drive up to the Shop-n-Save in Devereaux once a week, and now that the girls were staying with her, just until your Mama comes to her senses and comes around to get you, they had to make the trip with her on account of there wasn't anybody to look after them. Pichette was virtually an island at the southernmost portion of Acadiana, bordered by Lake Salvador to the south, multiple bayous to the West, and the vast waters of Shelter Swamp to the north and east. Except for the dock, which sold fishing bait, tackle, ice cream bars, and the Tesco, which sold gas and snacks that tasted like cardboard, Pichette had no stores. Growing up on the island, Rachel had become accustomed to trips up into Devereaux for almost all the essentials. Mama came up to buy groceries, just like Nona. But Mama always used the Piggly Wiggly. She said they were a lot more flexible about food stamps. Nona said food stamps were just a damn shame. Rachel would rather be with Mama at the Piggly Wiggly, but the Shop-N-Save was good on account of the toy dispensers.

Granny Nona usually gave each girl a dime to use in the dispensers by the door while she transported the shopping bags to the truck. Talia always used hers for a ride on the rusty mechanical horse out front. Climbing up, she stuffed her dime into the slot and waited, short legs dangling against the peeling purple paint. The machine was so old; Rachel was always worried it might not start up, but it always did. Talia had absolute faith. That was one difference between them.

Rachel agonized over her choice. Pacing the row of coin-operated vending machines, she bent to peer through the glass. Plastic bulbs stuffed with toy rings or multi-colored bouncy balls or superhero stickers. The best machine had packs of tiny colored pencils, four each in a little clear case, each with an eraser no larger than Rachel's pinky fingernail. But the pencils cost two dimes, and she'd never had the willpower to save her money from one trip to the next.

Talia had finished her ride and was sitting on the frozen mechanical horse, petting its steel mane and crooning into its unresponsive ear. Nona had finished putting the bags away and was standing by the truck, hands-on-hips, calling them, impatience threading her words. "Come on, girls. Let's get it. Right now!" Nona liked to remind them how they dawdled. Do I look like a waiter to you? Then why do y'all keep me waitin?

Rachel jammed her dime into the machine with the rings and waited for her treasure to drop. Nothing happened. She banged the machine. Nothing. She kicked the steel pole upon which it sat, then kicked again and then bent and peered up into the shoot, sticking her hand inside the machine as far as it would go. She had four fingers in there when a voice came from behind, so startling her, she yanked her arm back, scraping the skin along her knuckles. She was too scared to pay any attention to the pain.

"Need some help with that girl?" the man asked.

Rachel turned slowly, an egg-sized lump in her throat. The man loomed. So tall, he blocked the sun. His face shadowed and unrecognizable—store manager, for sure. They would arrest Rachel for... for something. She wasn't sure what. But it was probably illegal to beat up one of these contraptions. Private property and all. And It was definitely illegal to steal, which she wasn't doing on account of already giving her dime to the stupid thing, but would this man believe her? She studied his face. Nope, he would not. Jail. Straight to jail. She swallowed hard, took a breath, and stammered, "Sorry. I'm sorry, I just uh..."

"Lemme see that," the man said and crouched down, one big hand splayed across the top of the glass dispenser. He tilted his head, closed one eye, and peered up into the metal shoot with the other. He smelled of cigarette smoke and winter green. Rachel recognized the smell from the little Christmas Trees Mama hung from the rearview mirror in her car. Rachel stepped away. Talia slid down off the horse and approached slowly.

"Yeah," he said, smiling. "This ain't no problem." He had his long fingers up inside the machine and made a funny face. Talia approached, her eyes wide and unafraid. She was always so unafraid. The man stuck his tongue out further, exaggerating his effort. When he saw Rachel looking, he made his eyes go crossed. Both girls laughed. Using his free hand, he gave the whole mechanism a couple of big jerks and then pulled out two plastic capsules and handed them to the girls, one for each.

Inside, the transparent capsules were rings. Turquoise for Rachel and bright pink for Talia These were the sort Tee liked to call princess rings because the cheap shanks were decorated with bits of brightly colored plastic like jewels. In Talia's world, only royalty owned jewels.

Rachel studied this queer man. He had a broad smile and thick brown hair with a funny hank that flopped over his forehead. He wasn't old, no older than Mama, but there were crinkles in the tan skin around his eyes, blue-green like the ring jewel. Like Rachel's.

All of this happened in a matter of seconds, although in later years, Rachel would remember every detail and it would seem stretched, the way taffy can pull so much longer than one might expect before it develops holes and falls apart.

Suddenly, there was Nona, marching back toward them from the car. She crossed the parking lot and the cement walkway, and Rachel could see her lips making the sounds of curse words under her breath. Nona didn't curse-it was the devil's language- except silently, when nobody could hear, or when she was extra mad. As she grew near the little group by the vending machines, her mouth dropped open, and, for the first time, Rachel could remember, Nona was struck silent.

"Well, hey Magda," the blue-eyed man said, smiling. "How y'all been?" Rachel cringed. Not because this strange man knew their Granny Nona, but because he'd used that name. Magda. Magdalena. Nona hated her given name. Rachel didn't understand it, but Mama said Nona forbade anyone to use it. Mama always used it in secret.

"Take your sister to the car," Nona said. When they didn't move, she added, "You go now." She didn't take her eyes off the man.

"But," Talia started.

"Right now," said Nona without raising her voice. "I need to speak to this man for a minute." The uncharacteristic formality and quiet tension in her voice sounded dangerous, like the low, high whine of a tornado coming at you from a distance.

"Magda, come on now. I came all this way just to spend time with 'em. I think I deserve a little..." He sounded wheedling and a little mean, and his face twisted like a face reflected in a funhouse mirror, like a face made of wax, and suddenly Rachel didn't care about his pleasant eyes. She didn't like him.

"Nothin, Ray. You deserve to nothin'." Nona had her fixin' finger (*Get over here, and I'll fix you right up),* sticking straight in Ray's face, and her kerchief had come loose, floating half off her head like a flag, and she looked about as scary as Rachel could remember her looking. "Don't you say another word, or I swear you'll get nothin'. Never again," Nona continued. "Not one word."

Despite her overwhelming curiosity, Rachel was glad to take Talia's hand and head back to the truck. Tee resisted, craning her neck to watch what was happening behind them. Rachel ignored her protests, concentrating instead on the steady thwap-thwap sound their rubber flip-flops made on the hot parking lot macadam.

"Who is he?" asked Talia. She stood, pressing her face up against the window. Her tiny nose was so close, Rachel could see her breath condensing against the glass.

"Don't know," answered Rachel. "Don't care," she added. Did she, though? Did some part of her know?

"Maybe he's a prince?"

"He ain't no prince Tee. That's just dumb."

"I think he looks like a prince," says Talia. "Like in my book. The girl who don't know she's a princess and then the prince comes across the ocean and tells her she is, only she never knew on account of she got stolen when she was born." Talia stared out the window.

"That's stupid," Rachel repeated.

"It's not."

"We don't have princes here, anyway."

"He's not from here," Talia said decisively. "I just told you."

"Ok, then. Where's he from? Exactly?"

Talia turned toward Rachel, her face grave. A tiny wrinkle between her eyes as she forced a serious expression. "The future. I think he's a prince from our future."

Rachel thought for a moment. "Ok then, maybe that's right."

They watched their grandmother and the man for a bit. Nona's hands flying like she might bash him in the face, the man smiling with just his lips and leaning out of the way.

From a distance, the man grew younger. He stood in profile, and his thinness was more apparent. His jeans hung around his hips, held up by the leather belt he wore, and his arms were much thinner than Earl's or most of the others she knew from Pichette. He didn't have tattoos either. He wore bracelets around his wrists—different colors, made of thread and beads.

It was a long time before Nona came back, and when she did, she was in a mood. She drove with both hands tight like iron on the steering wheel. Leaning forward, she stared straight into the road. A thick vein pulsed in her neck, and Rachel knew better than to ask questions.

Something had shifted. A force as inevitable and unstoppable as weather or time or death had laid claim. Rachel felt it, the same as she had the day Mama left them at the restaurant a year ago. Life had a way of putting up signs, and if you were smart and kept your eyes open, you could spot them. Rachel had known Mama wasn't coming back that day at Bubba's, only she'd pretended it wasn't so. On account of being afraid. No more being afraid. That was for babies. This time, she saw the sign, and she was ready—nothing to do now but wait.

Rachel noticed her sister wearing the plastic ring she'd pulled from the capsule. She pulled Talia close, and, all the way home, they both watched the pink plastic stone as it danced and flashed in the sunlight.

CHAPTER 6

New Orleans, French Quarter

July 21, 2020

The French Quarter is sticky hot. The sky is overcast. It rained earlier, and the narrow streets glisten sharply in the early afternoon sun. A breeze picks up along the walkway as Rachel approaches the back patio at Galleys. It seems like forever since she's been here. Fifteen years at least. Rebuilt since the storm, it's a little bigger and cleaner but still has the same low white walls, broad-bladed, slow ceiling fans, and colorful local art on the walls. The waiters are different. Nobody she recognizes. That's true all over the city, of course. So many people left and never returned.

She nods at the hostess-a girl with bright eyes, long limbs, and impossibly smooth skin. "Just meeting someone," says Rachel, and the girl dips her head and smiles. As she passes through the restaurant, she notices the waiters, the busboys, everyone, who appears to be about fourteen. Since when has the working world been populated by people younger than her daughter? She shakes off the discomfiting sense she's missed something.

Out back, off the kitchen, the brick patio is open to the pale blue sky—the air moist and copious smells of shrimp creole and cooking gumbo. Along the black-slat fence, prehistoric lime-green fern and bromeliad overflow pots of every description. A small bird is caught beneath the mosquito netting that drapes half the courtyard. It bumps itself against the material in an increasingly frantic attempt to escape. One of the staff, a dark-haired boy slightly older than the hostess, is up on a ladder yanking, somewhat hopelessly, at a corner of the netting.

As he reaches for the material, his white shirt rides up. His black jeans gape away from the lower curve of his back. Jeb, Rachel thinks suddenly, and her heart lurches. Jeb on the ladder, Daniel below, and they are stringing Christmas lights. That must have been six or seven years ago? She should have taken more pictures. She is staring at the boy when he glances over his shoulder and makes eye contact. She takes too long to look away.

The patio, like the rest of the place, is crowded. Although Rachel has only a vague idea of what Camilla James might look like now, Rachel scans the tables. Suddenly, from behind, a gentle voice.

"Rachel?"

She knows who it is before she turns around. The two women embrace awkwardly, then Rachel steps back.

"I can't believe it, Camilla. How are you?"

She's trying to sort out what she feels. Confusion? Anger? Distrust? Elation at seeing this woman she'd felt close to so long ago. Camilla is different, of course. Older, as expected, but so much older. Her face was worn and tired, and her beautiful caramel-colored skin was heavily blotched and shadowed. Her black hair was nearly all white and cropped close to her head. She's a tall woman, but her once-powerful frame looks puffy and weak, her shoulders rounded, and it surprised Rachel to see she's breathing heavily as if the walk to the restaurant has exhausted her.

A few minutes later, they sit at a tiny corner table near a clump of palmetto fronds. Overhead, strings of miniature light bulbs flicker even though it's daylight. The boy has finally set the bird free, and it's quiet.

"We don't have long," says Camilla, reaching a hand to cover Rachel's. The nurse's fingers are bony, the back of her hand-knotted with veins under the dark skin, but her touch is warm and dry. "I'm sorry, but I had to see you. You need to understand some things." Her forehead is shiny with sweat, and she looks around, shifts uncomfortably in her chair. She's almost whispering.

"Camilla," says Rachel. "Are you ok? What is it?"

Camilla takes a sip from her water glass and sets it down. Beads of moisture drip from the rim, making messy streaks down the sides. She runs a finger up and down the glass, then looks at Rachel.

"Nothing is what you think, Rachel. They've lied to you."

"Who?" Rachel feels her body tense. "Who's lied?" She knew this woman once, but that was decades ago. She does not know what's happened to her since. What she's been through. She tries to see something in Camilla's dark eyes. The truth?

Camilla sucks in her breath. "Everyone," she says. "The company, the people who reported what happened at Good Hope. Maybe even Daniel. Honestly, I'm not sure."

"Good, Hope?" Rachel feels the harbinger of a headache-a pinpoint pulsing- beginning behind her left eye. Absently, she rubs at her forehead. "Daniel? Lied about what? I don't understand."

"I'm sorry, I'm not making sense." She pauses as the waiter sets down two white China cups and saucers, followed by a French carafe, a pitcher of cream, and a silver sugar dispense. The aroma of pressed coffee settles across the table. After he pours the drinks, nods politely, and goes, Camilla continues. "Look, something happened at Good Hope. I won't claim to know the details because I don't, but something was happening before the Water. And afterward? They cleaned it up, you know. They're still cleaning it up. They did something."

Before the Water, thinks Rachel. That's how people think of the disaster now. Anyone who suffered through it. Anyone who lost someone. Not the storm, not the hurricane, and certainly not by name. It's the Water. Hearing it out loud makes Rachel shudder.

"Something? What does that even mean? And how do you know? You weren't working there, right? You were still at headquarters," says Rachel.

"I know. But Francine," she says. "My daughter, Francine. She was working there. I got her the job." She dips her head, then adds, "She died there that day."

Rachel sighs and softens her voice. Oh my God. How had she forgotten about Camilla's daughter? She'd met Francine only once years ago when she was still a child, nine or ten. She'd been tall for her age, powerfully built, the way Camilla once was, with an enormously beautiful smile and wise eyes. Rachel slides her hand across the table and lays it atop Camilla's. Beneath the pad of her forefinger, she can feel the throb of a vein that runs over Camilla's bare-knuckle. For several seconds, Rachel has no words. Finally, she says, "I know Camilla, and I'm so sorry."

"Thank you." The older woman pauses and drops her gaze. Then pulls her hand away and picks up her water glass. For a moment, Rachel thinks she won't continue, but then she looks up and says, "She knew something. Two days before, Francie told me she was concerned about how things were being handled. We argued. I told her the budget was tight as it was at most nursing homes, but AmHealth did a good job caring for patients and, well, you know, blah blah." Camilla made a quick intake of breath, as if trying to steady herself. She closed her eyes briefly, and when she opened them, Rachel saw a new resolve. "I cannot believe I was so naïve. So stupid. Francie knew what was happening. She was right there, working as a nursing assistant. And Landry, I know you're close to them, the Landrys." It made Rachel uncomfortable how Camilla said *you're close to them*, but she said nothing. "Anyway, he was hardly ever there. He was covering the whole southeastern region. But that weekend, because of the storm, he was there. Francine called me and told me. It was strange because they did not inform me of that beforehand. I assumed someone higher up the ladder than me had sent him over to monitor things in case the storm got bad. That alone should have made me think."

"I remember that, of course." Rachel was certainly aware of Landry's position. In spite of working for the same company, Landry was practically Daniel's nemesis, although she and Landry's wife, Cat, had been friends for so many years. In the disaster's aftermath, she suspected it had been Daniel to send Rick Landry over there to "handle" Good Hope since it was one of the AmHealth facilities in the worst potential place concerning the storm. Of course, Daniel had no way of knowing how catastrophic a storm Katrina would be.

Camilla continued. "So, Francine seemed worried. Like she knew things weren't right. She gave me no specific information; only said she'd talk to me about it later." She pauses, shaking her head. "I was a director at AmHealth, Rachel. I should have known if anything wasn't right. But I knew nothing. Then my Francie died, and they said it was an accident and...." Her voice trails off.

"It was an accident, Camilla. An accident and a tragedy," says Rachel.

"No," says Camilla, straightening her back and narrowing her eyes. She is no longer the grieving mother, but a warrior. She is assessing Rachel, taking her measure before she speaks again. "Look, Rachel, you must believe me. This isn't for me. It's for you." She pauses, breathing without moving her eyes. "They killed her. Maybe intentionally, possibly through negligence. But they killed her, and then they covered it up to avoid taking responsibility."

"Jesus, Camilla. Do you hear yourself? What you're saying?"

"She was strong. She could have made it up to that roof. When they found her, she was... with the residents. But near the exit. She could have made it. The explanations I got never made sense. They prevented her from getting out somehow." She takes a breath and then says, "And they killed all those other people as well."

Rachel has heard enough. It's the reference to an un-named 'they' that does it. "That's crazy," she says and immediately regrets it. "I'm sorry, Camilla. But there's no way." She remembers the terrible stress of those years after the flood. The questions. The investigations. It hadn't seemed right. City officials, state political leaders, and everyone ultimately exonerated Good Hope's administrators and the parent company (AmHealth). There'd been no vehicles available, and they'd done a heroic job of getting as many out as possible. The water had simply risen too quickly, just like the rest of The Lower Ninth Ward. There was nothing to be done. Tragic? Yes. But criminal? "No, Camilla," she says more gently. "There's just nothing to that. Everyone tried. It was no one's fault."

Despite her words, Rachel felt a new kernel of worry. She thinks everyone had exonerated AmHealth, except for some of the family members. They'd continued their accusations, and what had Daniel said about them? He'd called them greedy or delusional. His lack of empathy had bothered Rachel. The unkindness with which he spoke about grief-stricken people. Daniel, who had never known adversity or pain. Might he have been lying? No, not lying. More likely, he'd gotten involved in something he'd rather Rachel not know about. But intentionally lying? That sounded... sinister. No, she didn't believe that. Daniel had been a hard man then. Tough in business, but not evil.

"You're wrong," says Camilla, pushing a stray hair from her face.

She looks unwell. And so tired. Rachel is also feeling increasingly ill. Her headache escalating. "Can we," begins Rachel, but she's interrupted.

"Good Hope wasn't like they said. Look, just take this, ok?" She's pulling something from her purse. A folded piece of notepaper. Pushing it across the table. "Don't open it here. Read it later."

The pain in Rachel's head explodes across the left side of her face and temple. She can't get a full breath, and her chest feels heavy. She's fumbling in her purse. She needs a pill. Something.

"Are you ok?" asks Camilla.

"Yeah, I'll be fine. Just a headache." She's still rooting around for the bottle of Xanax. Not there. Suddenly she remembers she left it in the car. "I'll be fine," she repeats, placing her bag under the table. She takes a drink of water and grits her teeth against the pain. Looks at Camilla. The nurse's face is serious, strained, but her eyes are clear. She looks sane. "Ok, so suppose you are right. Something happened. Why now, Camilla? It's been almost fifteen years. Why call me now?"

Camilla sighs and looks down for a moment. "You want to know the truth? I should have done this a long time ago. I should have done it right after everything happened. But I was a coward. I tell myself it's because I didn't really know anything, but that's an excuse. I'm ashamed to admit how afraid I've been. For myself. For the rest of my family. For anyone involved. Fear kept me quiet." She pauses, inhales, and says, "But now, I can't wait anymore. They're about to do it again."

"Do what?"

"Take another life."

"I don't get it."

"There's a woman, an innocent woman, up at Marietta. At the prison. Her name is Janie Paradise."

Rachel starts. *The name again.* She tries to push the thought away. *It can't be. How many millions of people must have loved that name? Used that name. Called themselves by that name? Few,* the obvious answer. Almost no one. It would take a particular sort of woman to choose a name like that. It would take someone like Talia and Rachel knows it. Still... there's no way. Absolutely no way. It makes no sense. She shudders. "No," she says. "No, no."

"Hey," says Camilla, looking confused and concerned. "Are you ok?"

"Sorry. Yeah, I'm fine. I just."

Just what? Just have no idea what to think. Just feel like I'm losing my mind. Just don't want to tell you or anyone else the truth?

"I read about her," says Rachel. "She killed a cop. She's no innocent." Her voice sounds tight and shrill, but the words comfort her. She feels more confident.

"She was an employee of AmHealth," says Camilla, "and she worked at Good Hope."

"So, did lots of other people, and AmHealth employed a thousand. The company was all over New Orleans. All over the South."

"I knew her. Janie is a good person, a terrific nurse's aide. She was on duty that weekend and that Monday. She escaped the water Rachel—one of the very few. I don't know what happened after that, but I know for sure Janie is no killer."

"Ok," says Rachel. "And?"

"And now her execution is scheduled to go ahead. It's less than thirty days away."

"Right, I read that as well."

"So, I started poking around, asking questions, upsetting things, I guess. And the next thing I knew, Rick disappeared."

"What? Are you talking about Rick Landry? He's not disappeared. I just saw Cat yesterday." Rachel stops. Cat, yes, but Rick. She hadn't actually seen Rick, but then she doesn't normally see him. "Wait, what do you mean disappeared, exactly?"

"Well, I'm not at AmHealth, so I don't know any details, but I have friends there, and I hear he's not been at work. Vague excuses from his staff. He's left messages. He's at out-of-office meetings, that sort of thing. Nobody seems to know much. Honestly, I don't know. I'm hoping you can find out." Camilla unfolds a piece of notepaper she's holding and pushes it across the table toward Rachel.

This is crazy, Rachel thinks. Camilla is grieving, perhaps more than grieving. Depressed maybe. She's come up with some nutty conspiracy theory to distract from the pain.

Rachel picks up the notepaper, runs a finger across its edge, and then looks at Camilla's face. "I'm so sorry about your daughter," says Rachel. "I lost my son." She pauses and looks away. "Three years ago. He was twenty-two." She tells no one about Jeb and does not know why she shared this. Quickly, she adds, "A car accident. Just a stupid accident. Not even speeding, as far as the police could tell, could have been the dark." Rachel swipes at her eyes. The half-lie comes so smoothly now Rachel almost believes it herself. *But it wasn't just an accident, was it? It wasn't even exhaustion from working sixty hours a week in his first year at a crazy job.*

"Oh, God, Rachel. I'm sorry. I'm so sorry. I didn't know."

Rachel changes the subject. "So, what is this?" Rachel picks up the paper Camilla slid towards her.

"An address. Go there, see for yourself."

"What address?"

"It's where they found her afterward. A week later. It's Janie's address. Well, her former address. Also, there's the name of someone I think you should speak to."

Rachel looks at the name and phone number on the slip of paper. A doctor, Camilla, has given her the name of a doctor. "Who is this, Camilla?"

"Barrons, Dr. Virgil Barrons. Just call him. Please. I know him, and I know you can trust him."

Rachel sighs. "Camilla, why me? Why do you want me involved in all this?"

"You're Daniel's wife. You can get the information that I can't. You can find out what's happened to Rick Landry. Also, I think someone is following me. I could cause more problems by trying to help. And..." She hesitates.

"And what?"

"Janie's life depends on this."

Rachel hesitates before asking, "Camilla, what are you not telling me?"

"Look, trust me. This is for your family. Look into it, Rachel. Please. Go to this place. Just see what they did to her. To Janie."

"This Janie Paradise? I know the name, don't I?"

Camilla smiles slightly and shakes her head. "I have to go. Like I said, I think I'm being followed. Probably best if you stay a while, so we are not seen together." She pushes back her chair to stand. "Thank you, Rachel, for seeing me." And then she is gone.

Rachel sits in the chill, green shade of the patio. Late morning light shimmers against the stones. Someone has propped open the back gate, and she peers out onto the street. The Quarter is coming to life. Drivers on Bienville honk impatiently at clumps of pedestrians. Still drunk on last night's alcohol, tourists shout at hotel guests who hang dangerously off centuries-old balconies. Strains of jazz and zydeco drift over from the musicians at Cafe du Monde. The smell of beignets and coffee, someone nearby practicing the saxophone.

The waiter approaches to take her order, looking mildly perplexed at the absent seat.

"She had to go," Rachel says apologetically.

"Sure," says the waiter, collecting up the silverware and half-empty drink glass. He tells her about the lunch special, but she's not listening.

Rachel looks at the note re-reading the lines written in Camilla's elegant hand: 1161 Charbonnet St. The Ninth Ward, she thinks. The house will be a ruin if it is still standing at all.

CHAPTER 7

Pichette, Louisiana

1975

They were down at the swamp, crouching low between the horizontal branches of a dead tree, slapping at mosquitos and watching the water for frogs.

"Ain't no frogs down here, Tee," said Rachel. "I'm telling ya. They only come out at night."

"Shh," said Talia. "Are too. Just hush." She was holding onto a moss-covered cypress branch and leaning out over the dim silvery water.

They'd been living with Granny Nona for two months now, and she'd quit taking Rachel and Talia with her into Devereaux. She never said why, but Rachel knew. It had badly shaken Nona the last time they'd gone up to the Shop-n-Save. She'd spent the rest of the afternoon having a lie-down, and both girls knew that when Nona had a lie-down, it meant something serious had happened.

Talia had worn the plastic ring all the time, refusing to give it up until it snapped into three pieces one night as Nona removed it for a bath. Talia went to bed with the bits clutched inside her small fist, her body folded around it like an oyster with a pearl. After that, her memory of the man at the Shop-n-Save seemed to fade. Anyway, she stopped begging to go along on the shopping trips, and, for the rest of the summer, once a week, the sisters had an entire morning to themselves.

"You might get tadpoles if you get lucky." Rachel watched Talia for a few seconds, then added. "Or gators, maybe a hungry gator."

Talia snapped her head around. "Gators? Really?"

"I'm kidding. Nah. Come on. Let's look somewhere else." They took a few steps up the bank, warm mud sucking up between their bare toes. After a minute, they came to a spot where the palmettos cleared, and the steep bank gave way to an expanse of blue-green bulrush. Pond lilies like elephantine rafts floated lazily on the still water below. "Look there, Tee," said Rachel, kneeling carefully between the branches. "But hang onto me. It's steep."

Talia clung to the back of Rachel's T-shirt and peered over her shoulder. "That's Japanese Lilly," said Rachel, pointing at the enormous spiky-petaled flowers perched atop pads of emerald green on the water.

"I'm gonna get one," said Talia, moving down the bank. "For Nona. Purple is her favorite."

"No, you ain't," said Rachel, grabbing hold of Talia's arm. "You ain't got no idea how deep it is right there, Tee. Look over there," she pointed east toward the estuary. "You got currents merging over there, Tee. It'll get strong underneath. Plus, y'all are smarter than to go swim in water you don't know nothin' about."

"Lemme go," said Talia, wrenching her arm free. Immediately, she slid down the bank and landed on her bottom with a splash. Startled at first, she didn't move, only sat half-submerged, eyes wide. Rachel thought she'd scream, probably cry, but Talia only giggled and pushed to her feet.

"It's only to here," she said, standing in the muddy water to her thighs, grinning wide.

"Ah dammit, Talia, get up outta there. Come on." Rachel scanned the surface for snakes as Talia turned away from the bank and continued to wade forward, stretching a skinny arm out, reaching for one bloom.

"Wait, I got it!" called Talia over her shoulder. She was now waist-deep and still three feet from the nearest lily pad.

"Come on back here now, Tee. This ain't no swimmin' hole. If I gotta come in there. I swear-"

That's when she saw it.

Just below the water's surface, which had suddenly gone motionless except for the ominous shadow turning towards them. Noiseless. Surfacing. Discernible from the swamp's brownish-gray only by its independent movement and the wake it left as it rushed at Talia, torpedo-like beneath the water.

CHAPTER 8

New Orleans, Lower Ninth Ward

July 21, 2020

The twenty-minute drive from the Quarter, over the canal into The Lower Ninth Ward, isn't like Rachel remembers. She takes Bourbon Street down to Bienville and makes a left onto North Rampart, then follows the Saint Bernard Highway along the river to the bridge. There's been some progress since the storm. She can see it in the new construction, new streets, restaurants and shops in the Garden District, especially. But the brightness dims as she heads east. Peeling paint. Worn-out porch fronts barely support collections of random aluminum furniture. Graffiti. Weeds. Damaged cars. Boarded windows.

Further on, nearer the bridge, nature is making progress too. Everywhere there is evidence of its rush toward repossession of the land. Fat vines overtake rooftops, spidering down walls, in and out of shattered windows; shoulder-high weeds curve over walkways, obscure sidewalks; a few structures are so overgrown they look as if god's world (if you believe in god) has completely consumed the man-made structures beneath, leaving a tangle of root and vegetation and living creature behind. Dangerous house shaped topiaries.

The man-made structures that remain appear well-guarded. Locks, bolts, grates, fences and security bars of every kind. On windows, doors, shopfronts. Was it always this unsafe? This depressing? She can't remember.

Rachel looks more closely at the people as she passes. They sit outside on their battered furniture, in their partially annihilated neighborhoods, in twos and threes. Occasionally alone. Mostly older, a few young women with children. Some bodies are withered with age, some sagging with fatigue, but often, Rachel sees pride in their eyes. Or maybe just an assurance. Or something. They study Rachel. Some nod. Some wave. Some ignore her completely. Rachel tries to think. This isn't her poverty—this ruined city.

Hers was rural poverty. Wicked in its own way. Insidious in the way it spread itself out: everyone had nothing, and everyone you ever knew had nothing. So familiar, you forgot you had nothing and stopped expecting different. Rural poverty was a liar. It hid behind the pale sunlight and warm mud of the swamp- being shoeless hardly mattered. It crouched behind family-those were your people, where you belonged, and the only place you'd ever be safe. Leaving meant betrayal. It slipped into your dreams and brought down the curtain on your performance. You hoped to graduate high school, not college. You fantasized about managing the little restaurant where you worked; maybe you'd get to Florida on a beach vacation one day. Worst of all, poor slithered inside your soul from the moment of birth. Perhaps it was in your genes. Yes, it was in your genes. Even if, by some miracle or tragedy or goddamn random strike of the universe, you got out; you were still as poor as your eyes were blue, and you'd spend the rest of your life trying to hide it. That's it, Rachel thinks. None of these people are trying to conceal a thing.

When she arrives at the ramp onto the bridge, she slows the car. Drivers behind her bang their horns impatiently. It's been nearly three years since Rachel has driven beyond the quarter. Even longer since she's pushed herself to go over a bridge.

You can do this, she tells herself, forcing deep breaths to quell the panic already tightening her chest. You must do this. Somehow, Camilla's request seems even more urgent now. Don't think, just drive. She inhales deeply, grips the steering wheel with both hands, and steps on the accelerator, sending the car up the ramp and out into traffic.

The Lower Ninth Ward. It's closer and dirtier than she recalls; So many of the houses and buildings abandoned. Vacant lots-some with a brick mailbox still standing are littered with trash or the detritus of abandoned construction. Some ruins, heavily overgrown with trumpet vine, weirdly juxtaposed by garish new structures thrown up cheaply and quickly in the months after the storm. Nearly all the streets, cracked and pot-holed so deeply in spots they could swallow a small car whole. She maneuvers around them as if they were landmines. And there is so much sky.

It takes a minute to sort out what's missing besides people. What aberration makes the sky seem so vast it gives the land the appearance of a barren moonscape. Trees. There are virtually no trees. Fifteen years after the hurricane, the trees have yet to return. Rachel remembers reading the storm wiped out something like 320 million trees across Louisiana and Mississippi, most never to be replanted. But in Uptown and the Garden District, things were not as bad. Like nearly all New Orleans antebellum mansions, a plantation owner had built Rachel's house nearer the river on higher ground. Because of being slightly less below sea level than neighborhoods like the Lower Nine, they'd experienced virtually none of the flooding that occurred in the rest of the city. The three-hundred-year-old oaks flanking Rachel's entranceway still stand, unblemished by the disaster. Suddenly, the discrepancy feels intentional and sinister. Her lack of awareness, her complacency feels conspiratorial.

With the trees went the creatures who depended on them for life. There are no birds here. There's a threatening stillness in this neighborhood. In absolute silence. In the utter blueness of the dome of sky. She pulls over and rolls down the window. The cars on Pontchartrain Expressway hum faintly in the distance, and a few streets over, she hears a woman calling out. The words are muffled, but she sounds stressed. Her voice is high-pitched and strained. There are no family sounds. No shouts of children. No games. No water slides or sprinklers. Nothing to show everyday life.

"Shit," she says aloud. "Shit, shit, shit." This isn't her fault. She didn't bring on a fucking hurricane, and she didn't create a system that failed to help. She checks her phone. Two bars. Service is sketchy out here, and she's unsure where she's going. She inhales. She can turn around. Go home. This is stupid.

But what if Camilla is right? Rachel squeezes her eyes shut, gripping the steering wheel so hard her hands hurt. Go home, she thinks. Just go home and mind your own business. You don't need to deal with any of this. It was a long time ago. Nothing you do will bring any of those people back. But Camilla, she thinks. Camilla believes something happened, and she practically begged you. There's a burn in Rachel's chest, a poison dart. A sting. A goddamn bayonet. You owe Camilla. You owe her, and you know it.

• • •

When Rachel opens her eyes, she sees a girl coming out of the clapboard shotgun across the street. Although it leans precariously to one side, the house is well kept, with pots of marigolds on the porch and a small patch of lawn someone has tended and coaxed to a green sheen. The child is maybe eight or nine, skinny with blue-black skin and knobby knees. She wears cutoff shorts and plastic flip-flops, and her belly protrudes a little beneath her purple tube top. Her hair is in braids. About fifty of them. She isn't smiling, but her head is tilted slightly, and her eyes are bright; she looks curious and unafraid. She holds something in her right hand and, as she crosses the street and approaches the car, Rachel sees it's a green plastic tumbler. The girl balances it carefully, watching it as she walks, tongue between her teeth, concentrating.

"Hey, lady," she says in a voice slightly shrill and young. She's not even eight. "Whatcha want out here? My mama says y'all could die in the heat." Finally, she smiles. She's missing her two front teeth. "Here, you need to drink this." She pushes the cup through Rachel's window.

"Oh," says Rachel, shoving sweaty hair out of her eyes with the heel of her hand. "Thank you. That's really kind of you." She takes the cup and sips at the water, which is achingly cold and delicious. The girl watches. Her eyes are enormous and up-close. Rachel sees they are specked with gold and quite beautiful. "Do you live there?" Rachel asks.

"Ah, huh."

"I'm Rachel."

At first, the child doesn't respond, appearing to consider. Then she says flatly, "I'm Monique."

"That's a beautiful name." The girl nods, says nothing. "Have you always lived here?" The girl nods again. It occurs to Rachel that Monique is too young to remember anything before this post-apocalyptic landscape. This atrocious stillness and silence. And the child's mother? How old could she be? Rachel glances at the flowers in their yard. Down at the cup of water she still holds.

Even amidst fierce flames, the golden lotus can be planted.

The words float across her mind from nowhere. Where had she read that?

Monique chews on her upper lip for a moment, then says, "Lady, you ain't s'posed to be out here. You should go." Her eyes move up and down the street like she's looking for something. Taking a measure.

"Yes," says Rachel, although she only vaguely understands. "And thank you again for the water, Monique. And thank your mama, too." She hands the empty cup back through the window, and the child takes it.

"I gotta go now," says Monique, but stands there another few seconds, the cup dangling from one hand. She's going to say something, thinks Rachel. Ask something. But then she turns and skips off, disappearing behind the screen door of the little house across the street.

Rachel turns the ignition and rechecks the address, then pulls slowly away from the curb. She makes a left at the end of the block and then a quick right onto Conti, which runs along the canal. She pulls past a rusted chicken wire fence in less than a minute and arrives at her destination.

There are no gates. It's hard to tell if they've been stolen or washed away. The parking lot macadam is badly cracked and buckling and the white paint that once marked out individual automobile spaces is now almost undetectable. Not that it matters. Nobody parks here anymore. It is so desolate and intimidating that Rachel doubts it is visited much, even as an amphitheater, for youthful mischief.

The long, low building remains standing only as a shell. Every window is devoid of glass. There are no doors, and the iron railings leading up to the front entrance are bent at a violent angle. Still, the concrete steps are mostly intact, as are the outer brick walls. Much of the low roof sags inward, and, in several spots, enormous holes expose the inside to the elements. Nature is reclaiming the structure—long tendrils of ivy crawl up and over the building's top across its left side. A grove of dead oak trees along the right is thick with Spanish Moss that has merged itself to the roof's overhang, like webbing. The greenery gives the entire structure the appearance of having been sloppily decorated for the holiday season. Graffiti covers much of the building's facade. A giant penis in black with the words FUCK THIS PLACE beneath it. In red, someone has written the word JAYDOG in an odd blocky script. The rest is illegible.

Rachel gets out of the car, slams the door, and treads slowly toward the building. She feels something crunch under the toe of her right shoe. Looks down—broken glass. Tiny shards cover the parking lot, stretching as far as she can see. How had she not noticed it? The asphalt glitters like diamonds. "Jesus," she says out loud and looks around as if expecting to see the person responsible for shattering the glass. She continues forward, approaching the gaping doorway. Beer caps, broken bottles. Cigarette butts. So much for this place intimidating the mischief-makers. Up the cracked concrete steps. A steel sign, badly rusted now but still bolted to the brick over the entrance, its lettering flaked but still legible:

GOOD HOPE SENIOR CARE

"We Care the Way You Do."

The lobby smells heavily of mold and decay. Prehistoric-looking vines grow over the entrance and up the walls. Rachel pulls her collar over her mouth to block the odor, but it's useless. The stench is powerful enough to permeate concrete, let alone the flimsy silk of her blouse. The walls are covered in black mold and filth patches—the hallway littered with rusted wheelchairs and broken gurneys, and other unrecognizable debris. The scene is so dramatic, so bizarre it looks artificial. Except for the stink, the place could be a movie set.

Everything is dry now, of course, but marks on the walls reveal the level to which the water rose that day. Mostly, the yellowed lines run parallel to the floor about a foot from below ceiling height. Well above the drowning level. Rachel shudders, thinking of the floodwaters rising in minutes. Ten or fifteen minutes, she's been told. Good Hope sits mere feet from the canal. It was a wall of water that came across the parking lot and slammed into the glass doors at the building's front. There was no time to get the patients out of harm's way. They died where they'd been before the levees broke. In their rooms, lying in their beds. Sitting up in chairs in the hallway. Some are in the dining room waiting for breakfast.

A handful of the staff made it up to the roof. Everyone else perished.

In the weeks following the storm, stories emerged that nobody could explain. What happened to the young woman, Francine, Camilla's daughter, was one of those stories? They found her body with several others pushed up against the inside of a set of heavy doors. Her fingernails scraped raw. Hundreds of marks and scratches in the paint down the inside of the door. She'd apparently beat on the door with the back of a broom handle, and then, when she'd lost the broom-a fragment was left jammed into the door frame-she scratched at it with her fingers while the waters rose over her head. And there were others. Very elderly patients, bound to their beds, or imprisoned in their rooms, long after an impending disaster was clear.

Family members who'd lost loved ones filed complaints, and a state task force investigated every report. Ultimately, the investigations were closed, and authorities explained away the tragic outcomes as a series of unfortunate events. "Acts of God," they said. "A confluence of negative factors," they said. But nobody's fault. The head of the task force announced on national television six months later that the tragedy "simply could not be blamed on wrongdoing by any one individual or corporate entity."

Rachel and the children had evacuated to Baton Rouge, missing the storm and most of its aftermath. When the company was cleared, she'd been relieved. Although not directly involved in Good Hope, Daniel handled the overall functioning of twenty-five nursing homes owned by AmHealth nationwide. That included Good Hope. His reputation and the reputation and viability of the entire company were on the line. And so, their reputation and their wealth intact, Rachel had let it go. Like it had never happened.

Daniel, Rachel thinks. Is this possible? Her Daniel? The man she's loved for nearly thirty years.

But it had happened.

Rachel advances cautiously beyond the nurse's station and toward a set of double doors behind. They must lead to the administration wing, she thinks. Or storage. They are heavy steel security doors meant to separate patients from this part of the building. Despite the filth and muck coating their surface, it appears they've survived the flood. There is a deadbolt that has been sawed off to open the doors. Probably a rescue worker trying to get past the lock. The lock? She runs the pad of her forefinger over the smoothly sliced end of the bolt, then glances back down the hallway behind her. At the peeling linoleum and rotting walls. The high-water marks on one side of the formerly impassable door. The very high-water marks. She glances back at the deadbolt, then up at the marks. She stands there, still, in the silent, reeking ruins.

Slowly, a monstrous idea takes shape in her mind.

CHAPTER 9

Pichette LA

1975

"Alligator!" Rachel was down the bank and into the water before she had the sense to stop herself. Yanking her sister up and out, she dragged Talia by the arm so that her bare heels left deep gouges in the mud.

"Ouch, stop, stop! I can do it myself!"

"No, you ain't. We're goin'. Come on!"

She pulled Talia by one arm and took off through the scrub back towards the house, stopping halfway when Talia screamed and jerked her arm away. They stood panting and looking at one another.

"I hate you," said Talia, but there wasn't much energy behind it. She rubbed at her arm.

"Goddamn, Tee," said Rachel. "You gotta listen when I tell you somethin'. There's a gator down there, big as a truck." Talia's eyes widened with fear and surprise. Her mouth was half-open, but she said nothing. Rachel's anger dissipated. "Oh, it's ok, Tee. Those things look scarier than they are. Still," Rachel put an arm around her sister. "I didn't want you in the water with it."

They heard the rumble of Nona's old Ford. The high-pitched squeal of her brakes as she rolled to a stop at the house. Talia looked down at herself, soaking wet and sticky with a layer of brownish-green muck to her chest. Feet and ankles were black as tar. Tears filled her eyes.

"Don't worry," said Rachel. "We'll just say you fell in on accident or somethin'. It'll be ok."

"She's gonna be mad at you, Rachel," said Talia, wetness rivering the filth on her cheeks. "It's my fault, and Nona will be so mad." She was clenching and unclenching her fists.

"No, she ain't. Now come on. You stink."

"Yes, she is Rachel. You know it."

Talia was right. Nona would be angry. She'd blame Rachel for not taking better care of her sister, but Nona's anger was the gusty, short-lived kind. Like a sharp wind out of nowhere that blows a mess of twigs and sticky fruit off of the pecan trees. All you had to do was hold on to something sturdy until it passed. Rachel patted Talia's shoulder, then wiped her thumb on the clean part of her T-shirt and rubbed some of the mud from her sister's cheeks.

"Don't worry, Tee. It's all gonna be fine. Don't you worry?"

Together, they climbed the bank and headed toward Nona. She was already out of the truck and yelling for them to quit shilly-shallying and come help with the groceries.

•   •   •

In the fall, Nona enrolled both girls in school, Talia in kindergarten, and Rachel in the sixth grade for the second time. She had to repeat her final year of grammar school on account of all the days she'd missed during the time up in Devereaux with Earl. Rachel didn't mind. It would keep her close to Talia for a while, and that was good. Increasingly, Rachel found the idea of being separated from Tee more than a little disturbing.

Something was wrong with Talia. Not wrong exactly. Different? Ever since the Alligator incident, Rachel hadn't stopped noticing it. A sort of wantonness. Wildness. Not the carefree, joyful capriciousness of a young child. She'd never been that, anyway. Tee had always fluctuated from shy to overly familiar. Never lighthearted. Now, she could be fitful, euphoric, or effervescent, and sometimes, lots of times (Rachel wouldn't have known the words), Tee's behavior seemed almost self-destructive. If danger was about, Talia headed straight for it. Sticking her hands near the stove, she'd laugh at the heat; twice Nona caught her on the roof at night, star-gazing, she said; daily, she had to be reminded not to wade into the river without shoes or not to hide from the grownups, so they couldn't find her. Talia was less disobedient than unwary. Less defiant than dauntless. Less provocative than exasperating. She charmed the adults, who secretly laughed at her antics while Nona meted out only token punishments. But Rachel saw it, in Talia's gray eyes, in the way her baby sister held herself, and in the way she was unfurling like a sleeping cat. The thing inside her was strong-scented and smacking and growing bolder each day. Talia was beautiful and lost and a little crazy. Worst of all, she was helpless. Rachel saw it so clearly: Talia was just like Mama.

And, so, in the fall, they started school. Things went better than Rachel had expected. School seemed to settle for Tee. She loved it. She was a smart child, and the stimulation took her mind off some of her other less desirable activities. She quickly picked up numbers and loved learning her letters, practicing on everything she could get her hands on. Crayons on Nona's coupon notebook and markers on the dishtowels included.

Rachel didn't have the same enthusiasm, but it was ok. The teachers were friendly, and Rachel knew almost all the other kids. She'd known them since birth, so even the lousy ones couldn't intimidate her. Something was happening to her body, at least to her face. Her body was having trouble catching up. Her jaw and cheeks, roundish and freckled in her early childhood, were slimming and her features becoming refined. Her large green eyes and thick lashes stood out now, and other kids noticed. Mostly girls, who, in fifth grade, were still kind about another girl's looks. Being beautiful seemed to make her instantly popular, which softened the blow of her sordid family history. Besides, everyone in Pichette had a checker boarded past. Some better, some worse, but all varying degrees of atrocious.

The days unfolded without incident. A slow and predictable routine of school and chores and homework and, when the weather was good, afternoons at the swamp. Talia spoke of Mama less and less, and Granny Nona wouldn't talk about her at all. In late November, the truth would come for them with the ferocity of a train wreck.

CHAPTER 10

New Orleans Central Lockup

July 21, 2020

Twilight as Virgil leaves lockup. The sky behind the jail's concrete complex is going shades of pale pink and indigo. He'd stayed late to see two new guys, both allegedly suicidal. One, a thirty-year-old father of three, hauled in for making threatening phone calls to his estranged wife. A probation violation and a viable threat given his status as an ex-con recently paroled for aggravated assault. The second, an older guy Virgil had seen before. Homeless drug addict nearer fifty, he went by the street name "Sketch." He'd been caught trying to steal a television from Best Buy. Apparently unaware of the security cameras posted everywhere in the store, he'd grabbed a small display TV and stuffed it into an oven-sized TJ Max shopping bag.

"They got me at the exit Doc," he'd told Virgil, looking weirdly sheepish as if he were about fourteen. "Can you fuckin believe that? I was almost there." He held up his thumb and forefinger, pressing them together to show the nearness.

"Yeah, Sketch. Except I think that's what they do, right?"

"Whaddaya mean what they do?"

"I mean, I think they wait to see if you're really gonna steal something. Then, if you are, that's when they grab you. Right?" Virgil was struggling to make it sound like a serious conversation. He did sincerely feel for the guy. He wasn't stupid. Just desperate.

"Ah shit," said Sketch, curling his mouth into a smile. "Nah. They know'd I was gonna take somethin'. I mean, look at me, Doc." He turned his hands over, palms up to show his appearance. Painfully thin, his collarbones protruded beneath the pale skin like knives. Partially bald, a few strands of graying hair slicked down at the nape of his neck and tied with a rubber band. He grinned wider. For lack of several front teeth, his smile was both disturbing and oddly sweet.

"Yeah, you have a point."

"Besides," he went on. "I had all that other shit on me." He leans back in his chair. "That's how come I got to kill myself, doc."

Virgil studied the prisoner. "I'm not following Sketch." This, of course, was the alleged reason for the visit. Never mind that Virgil knew Sketch, despite his circumstances, was no more suicidal than Virgil. The fact was, he was probably in a better mood.

"On account of the amount."

"Uh, huh."

"Yup. Had a laptop up under my parka. Some kinda shit for phones, too. Planned on sellin' it, ya know? Need the money. Came to nearly eleven hundred dollars. That's over the limit." An unmistakable brush of pride colored this little speech, and Sketch sat up taller. Well, thought Virgil, everyone needs something to be proud of. For Sketch, it's stealing electronics from the Best Buy. What is it for you, Virgil? Surely, it's not this.

"You were wearing a parka?

"Yeah."

"In the middle of July?"

"Yeah."

"Did you think maybe that would look suspicious?"

Sketch was nodding his head. Contemplating. "Now you say it, I guess so." He paused. Then shrugged and said, "Didn't have nothin' else, though."

"How many felonies have you had, Sketch?

"You mean countin' this?"

"Yeah."

"Makes three."

"And you think you have to kill yourself because?"

"Uh, well, prison, doc; I can't go back there, and this time, you know I ain't gettin' out." He says this with a bright, upbeat tone that makes it sound like he's going to a boring summer camp, and it annoys him he won't be leaving. Truth is, though, he's right. He's going to prison, where he will not fare well. Old druggies with addled brains and skinny bodies don't do well in prison. Sketch squeezes the end of his nose between his thumb and forefinger, then wipes his hand on his pants. Grimy black half-moons show under all ten fingernails: Virgil grimaces, but only a little.

"Do you have a plan, Sketch?"

"A plan for what?"

"To kill yourself. How you might do it."

"Do I need one?"

"Do you need one for what?"

"To qualify."

"To qualify for what, Sketch?"

"For the program, or what have you?"

Virgil shook his head. "Sketch, just answer the question."

"What was the question?"

"Do you have a plan?

"For what?"

"Do you have a plan for how you might kill yourself?"

"Nah, I ain't got that far yet. I figured I'd talk to you first." He leaned back in his chair and took a long breath. "Hey, you got any cigs? I'm all out, and you know what they cost in there? Crazy."

"Sorry, I don't, and you can't smoke in here, anyway." Virgil wished for a moment he had a cigarette. It would be a small pleasure for the guy. "What was it you thought you'd talk to me about?"

"Well, ain't there some kinda hospital you could put me in? Stead a prison, I mean."

"Not really, Sketch. Not long-term. You'd have to do your sentence, eventually."

"Ah shit," he said. "You know I thought so, but some guys in here they talk a lotta crap. Worth a try."

"Yeah, Sketch is worth a try."

"Hey." His face brightening.

"Yeah?"

"What about double rations? You think you could order me double rations?"

Guys like Sketch make Virgil think about Marvin. Sketch has nothing in common with his brother other than the addiction. But addiction, Virgil has learned, is viciously greedy. When it takes a person, it takes everything. Obliterating love, hope, memories, friendship, kindness, creativity and intelligence leaves a heap of semi-living organic substance that can do little more than burrow, blindly along thoughtlessly seeking, seeking, and seeking, and never finding. In that way, Sketch and Marvin are precisely alike.

Marvin's been dead now five years; Virgil should be over it. Or at least be making progress through the five stages of grief: anger, denial, bargaining, depression, acceptance. Instead, he is just angry. Marvin was forty-four when he died. In his bed, alone, suffering through his second bout of acute pancreatitis. He'd been a drinker for thirty years, and it caught up with him. That's what Virgil tells himself. But he knows it's more complicated.

For years, Marvin had been what people call a functional alcoholic. A term Virgil had always believed people used to excuse themselves from confronting the alcoholic in their lives. Marvin had been married (his wife, a family physician with a thriving practice), kids, lovely house in an upscale suburb of Nashville. He even had his own accounting firm for a while back in the nineties. But he was also a selfish bastard. Prone to violent outbursts, his wife called the police more than once when he lashed out physically in a blaze of drunkenness. Marvin bloodied his hands, punching locked doors, smashed furniture and dishes, and kicked holes the size of basketballs into the walls. Although never directly violent to his family, the children were terrified of him, and the oldest, a boy, was growing increasingly unruly in his own way. It never failed that once Marvin sobered up, he was full of regret and remorse.

Incomprehensible demoralization, he called it. He'd grovel, sob, make promises. Even stop drinking for a while. Once, he lasted almost six months. But, inevitably, it happened again. Worse than the time before. Finally, when the oldest child was thirteen, his wife took the kids and left. She filed for divorce three weeks later.

Within eighteen months, Marvin had been arrested for DUI at least twice (he lied most of the time, so there was no way, to be sure), was addicted to a slew of drugs, and was no longer working. Still living in the family house, he could not pay the mortgage. It was only a matter of time before foreclosure. He spent his days swallowing painkillers and drinking at home or at a nearby bar called Patty's.

After the first hospitalization for inflammation of the pancreas, Virgil and his ex-wife staged an intervention. The kids were there. The moment Marvin recognized what they were up to, he flushed bright red and then purple, kicked at the furniture, sucked in his breath, and fled, cursing their betrayal and general "fucked-upness" on his way out the door.

In the end, having driven away every person who'd loved him, Marvin was left with Virgil as his lone ally. Put another way, Virgil was the last one standing and, consumed by guilt and, he would later learn, bewildered by his unrecognized codependence, Virgil was incapable of walking away

In those days, Virgil tried to make it up to Nashville every few weeks. He relied on a neighbor to check in on Marvin when he could not and told himself that was enough. Virgil was plagued by anxiety, inability to sleep, and problems with appetite, and chest pain. His physical health deteriorated as he struggled with his schedule and stretched his capacity to the limit. But Marvin refused to sell the house at a loss and refused to move down to New Orleans. So, Virgil persisted with the crazy schedule. For months, he kept this going. There'd been no choice; there'd never been a choice with Marvin.

Caring for and later rescuing Marvin had been Virgil's job for as long as he could remember. At least as far back as their mother's death. He and Marvin were both less than ten and their father, who'd caused the alcohol-fueled accident that killed her, never got over it. He had never emerged from the spiral of self-pity and guilt into which it threw him, and he spent the rest of his life wallowing, drinking, and occasionally raging. Virgil's life was marked by his failure to rescue his mother; everything he did was an attempt to make up for that failure. He knew it, and he didn't care.

It was on one of those routine visits, Virgil found him. Marvin hadn't answered the phone for a couple of days, but that wasn't unusual. When Virgil pulled into the circular drive and saw what must have been a week's worth of newspapers piled on the front porch, a wave of nausea came over him before he got out of the car. It was January twenty-ninth, at four o'clock in the afternoon. Five and a half years ago.

The scene inside the house was like something from a grim reality TV show. Pizza boxes, unopened mail and garbage piled everywhere. Food-encrusted dishes dating back weeks, if not months, in the sink, on the counters, some toppled to the kitchen floor—empty beer cans scattered on tables and furniture in the family room and kitchen and bedroom. The smell was intense, the air utterly rancid. Virgil knew immediately what had happened.

Marvin was in his bed, in a pool of dried blood and urine and feces. Face up, eyes open in an expression of surprise, almost disbelief. So thin, he looked emaciated. His skin was the mottled gray of those dead for an extended time, but Virgil could also see the blotches of bruising on his arms and hands where intravenous lines had been inserted. He was still wearing the hospital band around his wrist. Checked himself out despite warnings that he'd likely die if he didn't continue treatment and certainly die if he continued to drink. Prescription pill containers littered the side tables, a few of them open but not empty, and a square plastic baggie held the remains of what looked like cocaine. A hundred beer cans were scattered around the room like dead soldiers. An empty bottle of scotch next to the bed. No glass. He'd been drinking straight from the bottle.

The coroner ruled the death of natural causes—multiple organ failure because of chronic alcoholism. Not a suicide, they said. Virgil disagreed. Marvin killed himself. It just took him thirty years to do it. The coroner did the family a favor since the life insurance wouldn't have paid out for suicide.

What happened was not Virgil's fault. Marvin had a terrible disease, and that disease ultimately killed him. Virgil needs to forgive himself. Let this tragedy go. Move on.

He's heard it all before. And besides, he's a doctor. He knows these things. But that doesn't change the fact that he feels responsible. Like he should have done more. Stayed with him. Maybe forced Marvin into treatment. Marvin was his little brother. The boy with whom he'd walked to elementary school shared a bedroom and buried a mother. A person has a duty to protect a little brother, and Virgil, no matter the comforting words of any therapist or twelve-step sponsor, failed.

Virgil pulls out of the parking garage and makes a left onto Gravier, then another left onto Tulane. Downtown is still busy, cars crawling Claiborne Avenue in both directions. Flooded in the pink light of sunset, the abandoned Charity Hospital looms over the avenue like some colossal city-eating alien out of a sci-fi movie. Virgil lives in a small shotgun house on Bayou St. John, less than two miles west of downtown. In traffic, it will take thirty minutes to get there. He flips the radio to WWOZ and settles back. Wynton Marsalis and the soft opening chords of Sunsettin' on the Bayou. Virgil taps along, fingers against the steering wheel.

CHAPTER 11

Pichette, Louisiana

1976

Rain pebbled hard against the windows. The afternoon had been a blustering, bitter cold, and Nona was late returning from her shopping trip. The storm had marooned the sisters inside the small house for hours. Rachel was sitting cross-legged on the bare wood floor, watching television and messily spooning chocolate puff cereal into her mouth. Meanwhile, Talia wandered the living room, sing-songing a whiny atonal version of Santa Claus is Coming to Town.

"Hmmmmm-ahhhh-hmmm Sanna Class is comin'nn ta town, so ya better not cryeeeeeee-lalalalalala-hhmmmmmm-ahahhh-lalalala!"

"Come watch Paradise Power Girls, Tee. Please!" Rachel begged, holding her hands over her ears and raising her voice over her sister's high pitch and volume.

"Don't wanna. Lalalalalalalalala-hmmmmahahahah-Sanna Clawsss is comin' comin' toooooo town-lalalalalalallalala!"

Rachel tried to concentrate on the cartoon. It was the one where Janie Lucille turns invisible and sneaks into Evil's cave and steals his Master Blaster and hands it over to Sadie Baby, who dismantles the whole thing just before it explodes the entire planet. Talia usually adored watching Power Girls, but today she was in one of her moods. That's what Nona had called them. Moods. Intermittently, she'd go completely silent, frozen, and just gaze out the window at nothing. Right now, however, she was ear-blasting loud.

"Lalalalalalalalala-hmmmmahahahah-lalala."

Rachel lost her temper. "Shut up!" she shouted.

"Will not," said Talia. Putting her hands on her narrow hips, she sang even louder. "You better not pout! Or cryeeeeee!"

"I'm trying to watch this."

"Don't care; I'm bored. Play with me."

"No," said Rachel, who then got up and turned the television volume up, which prompted Talia to run both hands through the Venetian blinds using them as an instrument. Rachel picked up her cereal bowl and scooted forward so that her face was within six inches of the screen.

"Nona says you'll go blind."

"I don't care."

"I'll tell on you."

"Brat."

"I'll tell on you! You said I'm a brat."

"Don't care."

"Lalalalala-" Suddenly Talia went silent and perfectly still, staring out the window, her attention engaged. She stood that way for a long time. Long enough for Rachel to relax. Sometimes Tee did this. She'd crash after an hour or two of activity. She might even fall asleep. Rachel was following the plot of the television show and even enjoying it a little. Then, without warning, her sister shrieked at the top of her voice. "Hey!"

The shock caused Rachel to jerk her hand and send a heaping spoonful of cereal into her lap, cold milk soaking through her jeans in a wet mess. "Shit!" the curse exploded from her, and she looked around, reflexively to see if she was in trouble.

Tee went darting toward the door. Rachel stood up, stamped a few times, and brushed at her clothes to wipe away the milk and puffs. Before she could reach her sister, the child had rushed to the door and yanked it wide open. There stood a man-a rain-soaked stranger-and Tee, bouncing on tiptoes, babbling excitedly, and waving her arms around, laughing as if she'd just found Santa standing right there on her front porch.

The stranger wore blue jeans, scuffed work boots, and a black T-shirt under his rubber jacket. He stood with his legs apart, his thumbs hooked into his belt loops. Rainwater soaked his hair; it hung in heavy slashes, nearly ink-black across the pale skin of his forehead. Rachel saw it was dripping into his eyes, but he didn't seem to care. Even through the water and dank smell of the storm, Rachel caught the heavy odor of cigarettes. She didn't like how he looked as if he might come, going, or staying right where he was, and he didn't mind whichever. Rachel was familiar with that look. In later years, she knew it was arrogance.

"It's you! It's you!" Talia was jumping up and down with more amperage now, clutching at the man's sleeve, trying to drag him forward.

And then, suddenly, he was inside, peeling away his wet jacket and moving down the hall. A stream of words. *Do y'all remember me?'* And *'I sure remember you.'* And *'Ain't you two the prettiest little girls?'* And *'Where's your Nona at, anyway?'*

Rachel backed away from him, tugging gently at Talia's arm.

"You can't be here," Rachel said, irritated at the anemic sound of her voice. She cleared her throat. Tried again. "We don't know you, and our Nona ain't here, so you gotta go."

"No!" said Talia, rushing at the man and throwing her arms around his waist. She buried her face in his belt buckle. Rachel reached for her sister, but Talia kicked a foot out and caught Rachel hard in the shin. It stung, but Rachel bit back the pain.

"Whoa," the man said, looking down at Tee, both hands held away as if she might be contagious. "Hey, hang on now." He was awkward and seemed unsure of how to extricate himself from this child.

"Let her go!" said Rachel, although the words made no sense. He wasn't holding onto Talia. It was Talia was holding him. Rachel narrowed her eyes, clenched her fists, ready to fight this intruder. "Let her go!" she repeated.

Finally, he dropped one hand and patted Talia's head, and pushed her away gently. Most people automatically kneeled and lowered their voices when speaking to Talia. She was small and fragile-looking, and grownups were forever approaching her like she might be made of glass. But this man didn't do those things. His voice was rough and loud, and he spoke the way men spoke to other men.

"Don't worry," he said. "I ain't no stranger. We met over in Devereaux at the Shop-N-Save, remember? I got you those pretty rings, so that means we're not strangers. I'm Ray." He stuck out a hand, but Rachel did not take it.

"I know who you are," said Rachel. When had she known? Was it as soon as Talia opened the door? It didn't matter. She knew all about him now.

"Well, ok, then. That's good. And me, your Nona, we've known each other for," he stopped, rubbed his chin like he was considering. Rachel noticed he had thick stubble over the lower half of his face. "For a long time. I'll put it that way," he said and moved into the living room. "Tell you what? How about we just sit here and wait for your Nona to come back? Meanwhile, you can get me a sweet tea," he said this, looking directly at Rachel.

Talia bounced on her toes and tugged at his arm, yapping about her crayons, her room, her TV shows, and who knew what at all. Rachel wasn't listening. Instead, she was staring at Ray with eyes hard as flint.

After an hour, Nona pulled up. Rachel watched through the window as she got out of the truck and stood for a moment, studying the rusty Chevrolet parked out front. Then, seized by a sudden and enormous swell of energy, Nona whirled around and marched straight for the house. Rachel never did figure out where she got the thing, but Nona busted through the door and came at Ray with a metal spatula—waving it in the air like a sword.

"Get the hell out of here, Ray Larson, before I call the cops. You get out of here right the hell now! I know what you want, and you got no goddamn rights!"

Rachel pressed her back up against the wall, surprised by Nona's fury. Her sharp face reddened and glistening from the rain, the veins in her neck thick as cords. Nona was afraid, and Rachel couldn't remember ever seeing Nona afraid of anything.

Ray untangled himself from Talia and slowly stood up. His voice was calm but tight.

"Magda, put that thing down. You don't want to hurt nobody. Ok?"

"Get outta here, Ray, like I said." She didn't drop the spatula, but neither did she move closer. She just stood there, frozen, inches from him, the kitchen implement raised. Nona was probably a foot shorter than Ray Larson, but if she'd wanted, she might have spit on him from that distance.

"Look, I checked with a lawyer, and I have rights. You know that as well as I do. This is gonna happen, Magda. In the end, there ain't nothin' you can do to stop me."

He said other things as well. Then Nona said things, and then, they argued, but after Rachel lost track. Her gaze stayed fixed on the spatula in Nona's fist. Rachel only repeated the words in her head: This is gonna happen, Magda. In the end, there ain't nothin' you can do to stop me... This is gonna happen... This is gonna happen.

It was Nona's sudden squeal, "You dirty sonofabitch!" that broke Rachel's daze. Nona continued, "You think you can fool me like you fooled my girl? You get outta here right now!" With that, she began whacking Ray Larson in the head with the kitchen implement.

Ray held his arms up and was backing away when one of Nona's swings caught him in the face. A bright blossom appeared on his forehead, producing a dribble of crimson that rapidly gave way to an ugly river of blood. He swiped at it uselessly with the back of one hand.

"Jesus! You cut me. Stop it!" He yelled at her. He sounded much less confident now. No swagger.

She continued to swing at him, although he avoided additional blows. He kept wiping at his face, succeeding only in smearing blood onto his hands and up into his hair. Rachel didn't think she'd ever seen so much blood come out of one person.

Talia, who had been silent, suddenly let out a scream and rushed towards Ray. Throwing herself at his body, she wrapped both arms around his thigh, sat her bottom on his boot, and shut both eyes tight.

Nona dropped the spatula to her side and stood silently, lips pressed together. Waiting. Ray glanced down at Talia. She was crying and clinging to his leg, her weight dragging his jeans down on the left side, exposing a thin strip of hairy abdominal skin the color of candle wax. He shook his head as if to say this pitiful scene was not his doing. He looked at Nona, then pulled a manila envelope from his jacket and laid it on a small table in the hallway. A bloody half handprint now decorated the paper.

"Read that. I'd meant to tell you in person, but..." He shrugged. "Fuck it, right?" He jabbed the heel of his hand into his eye, now covered in blood. "Motherfucker," he said.

He moved to the door, dragging Talia along, and placed one hand on the knob. His unbloodied eye was dark and unreadable.

"I'm comin' back, Magda." He glanced at Rachel, smiled slightly in a way that made her feel simultaneously hopeful and afraid. Then he looked at Nona and shook his head. "You know what? You don't know everything you think you know. That's always been the problem with you. I loved Nina. I loved her more than anything. And you don't know why I want my girls. It ain't all about the money. You're a stubborn, angry old woman, Magda. And that's all I have to say." Then he peeled a screaming Talia off his leg, yanked open the door, stepped out, and took off toward his car.

Talia lay where he'd left her, curled on the floor, her filthy T-shirt now smearing blood and snot and tears into the already stained linoleum tiles. She was screaming and kicking her feet. They gave her a few seconds, but she wasn't calming down. The cries were escalating, her body movements bizarre. She was alternating between writhing, twisting, and beating her hands and feet on the floor. Repeatedly, she howled, "Ray!" Talia howled, only it came out in one long vowel heavy moan. Raaaaaaay.

Finally, Nona moved in to comfort her, and suddenly Tee charged. Teeth bared, she flung herself forward, clearly intending to bite Nona's arm. She looked feral. Worse, she looked almost inhuman. Rachel heard but did not see the smack. Suddenly Talia was falling backward, down and down and down. And then, like a tiny baby, she was wailing.

Rachel's stomach lurched at the sight of her baby sister in a crumpled, bloody heap, cherry red handprint welling up on her cheek. She thought she might vomit. Instead, she bent to comfort Talia, one arm outstretched to keep Nona away. They sat together on the floor, rocking slowly as they both cried.

Nona only looked at them both, saying nothing, then snatched up the envelope and turned on her heel, and walked down the hall.

It took a long time for Talia's sobs to become gentle tears and then soft hiccups. Finally, she allowed Rachel to move her to the sofa where they sat together, wrapped in one of Nona's old afghans, listening to thunder in the distance and rain splatting against the roof.

• • •

It was three days after that when Ray Larson came to take them up to Devereaux for good. Rachel guessed she'd known all along he'd be coming. Even before Nona told them the truth.

It had taken Nona a whole day to get around to it, so they barely had any time to pack. She'd brought the envelope-the one with the bloody handprint left by Ray-and she sat them both down in the kitchen and pushed the envelope across the table like they were supposed to open it. Only nobody touched it. Then she just said the whole thing right out. No stopping or anything.

"Your mama is dead." Nona tapped her finger on the vinyl tablecloth, and Rachel concentrated on the soft pah... pah... pah sound she was making. "Your mama is dead, and these papers say you got to live with your Daddy Ray. He's your daddy, which I guess you might've figured out."

All the words came as a rush and jammed themselves together into Rachel's ears so that they weren't making sense. The kitchen's air was warm and stale, with the smell of last night's grits and gravy. She felt sick. Tried to focus on the finger going up and down. Pah... pah... pah.

Talia screamed. Flinging her body to the floor, covering her ears with her palms, she kept screaming, drowning out the rest of Nona's words. Finally, Nona picked her up off the floor, got her to stand, and walked her towards the bedroom. Rachel caught sight of Nona's face as she left the kitchen. Her heart was broken. And Rachel didn't know it yet, but, in two days, when Ray came to collect the girls, Nona would be broke in a whole new way.

Nina had been dead for a long time. Since that day, she'd left them at Bubba's. She'd fallen, hit her head. An accident, they said, but Rachel didn't believe it. Neither did Granny Nona, who said that "good-for-nothing bastard boyfriend of hers wasn't the sorta man to just let a woman leave him," and Rachel was old enough to know what that meant.

Rachel's grief felt blunted. Like she'd known all along, Mama wasn't coming back. Nina could be unpredictable and volatile sometimes, but she'd never just leave her girls like that. Rachel decided it was best to always expect the worst. It saved a person from a lot of surprise pain.

Talia had never stopped believing Mama was coming back. That faith. That optimism was part of what drew people to Talia. But the price she paid was high.

Talia stopped talking that day, and Rachel worried maybe she'd never say another word. But then she did.

Is Mama really dead?

Yeah, Rachel told her. She is dead.

I don't want her to be dead, said Talia.

I know, agreed Rachel. Neither do I.

And they lay curled around each other on their bed, silent, tearless, considering what it meant. Motherlessness. Each girl clinging, with newly sprung desperation, to the other.

He came two days later. Rachel sat in the backseat and stared out the window as they drove the long flat highway that connected Pichette to the rest of the world. Ray drove with the windows half-down, and Rachel held her face to the warm breeze, watching as decrepit telephone poles and small-town gas stations and amateur road signs came into view and then disappeared behind them. Now and then, the highway neared the water. The cypress and live oak paired perfectly with their reflections on the still surface of the bayou.

PART TWO: WIND

CHAPTER 12

New Orleans Uptown

July 22, 2020

Magnolia Grill is busy for a weekday. A handful of bedraggled-looking tourists sit along the benches outside, waiting for tables, fanning themselves with paper menus. They lean back in unison each time vehicles pass in futile attempts to avoid an bespattering of mucky gutter water. The storm was short-lived but drenching; it left Uptown and Carrolton Avenue specifically rain-slick and dangerously black-pooled. Impossible to tell how deep the flooding went in certain spots; plenty of people attempted to drive through potholes and got stuck—their cars were up to the door handles in floodwater.

The air is sauna heavy, gray clouds low and marbling the sky. Outside the restaurant, the smells of rubber and jasmine and deep-fried cooking.

It was reflex, calling Catherine Landry. Too much happening in too short a time. Rachel felt suddenly desperate for advice. Now she's wondering if she's made a mistake. No, this is good. Meeting with Cat. What the hell is she supposed to do? Camilla James, after all these years? Good Hope? Cat has a way of offering stability in choppy water. Cat knows AmHealth. She's been part of the company even longer than Daniel, not officially but through her husband, Rick and everyone knows that the motivation, the drive behind Rick (maybe the brains too), belong to Cat. Besides, Rachel and Cat have been best friends for more years than Rachel can count. Rachel knows acutely that her friend is emotionally limited and psychologically damaged, but probably no more or less than Rachel herself. Just in different ways. Regardless, Cat possesses the absolute confidence that Rachel lacks. She doesn't question herself, and Rachel needs that right now.

Rachel peeks inside the restaurant. Sunlight spills into the tall, narrow space and across the old brick floor, and customers fill the bistro-style tables arranged along each wall. She scans the tables but does not see Cat. Checks on her phone for messages. Nothing. She's irritated but not surprised. With Cat, late is the rule, not the exception. It was Rachel who made the mistake of being on time. She drops the phone into her bag and steps outside, where not a single space is available to sit. She considers waiting in her car, but that seems odd somehow. Instead, she finds a spot halfway under the eave and leans a bit against the wall. It's terribly awkward. It's growing warmer, and she can feel the sweat accumulating around the back of her neck and under her arms. Why is she wearing linen slacks and heeled sandals? She hates linen. It gets all crinkly and sweaty, and it's bullshit about the fabric breathing. Linen doesn't breathe, she thinks. You know what breaths? Skin. Skin breathes. She wishes she'd worn her ugly, comfy gardening shorts and flip-flops. Rachel blows out her breath and settles in for the wait.

Cat Landry grew up outside of Lake Charles along the Acadian Coast, in a Cajun family big enough to make a baseball team. Seven kids, two parents, and a grandmother squeezed together in a house smaller than Cat's current garage. Aunties, cousins and second cousins stuffed the tiny town of Myrtle Grove; everyone related to everyone. The women spent their days and their night's cooking and canning and washing. Tending to the sick and running after the little kids until there was a girl sibling big enough to help. Compared to Rachel's life in Pichette, it was a decidedly different sort of poor. Cat's mother and aunts grew vegetables, and everyone helped fish the bayou for shrimp and crawdads. The men hunted deer, raccoon and rabbit, and sometimes alligator. Rotten chicken slung from a hooked wire, they'd leave baits out overnight and before dawn ride out in skiffs to check the lines. Pulling an alligator out of the water was dangerous work. Men lost hands, arms. Men died. But the food was plentiful, as was love. What was lacking was hope. Most everyone born in Myrtle Grove died there. But Cat was different: strong-willed, acquisitive, intelligent, and aggressively ambitious from the start. At seventeen, with nothing but a paper-wrapped pile of corn cakes, thirty-seven dollars stuffed into her pocket, an eleventh-grade education, and a voice gorgeously accented with the French of her ancestors, she left Myrtle Grove for good. That was decades ago, and she'd never been back.

At nearly six feet tall with pale skin, icy blue eyes and cheekbones sculpted from marble, Cat Landry had made an immediate impression in New Orleans. Ricky Landry picked her out the minute she walked into the bar at The Columns on Saint Charles Avenue. A year later, they were married. She was barely eighteen: he, just twenty-two.

Rachel met Cat during one of AmHealth's first holiday parties. Rachel, a newlywed, had known no one and spent most of the evening standing beside Daniel, thinking about how much her feet hurt and wishing mightily her husband would stop introducing her to people. Glancing around the room as Daniel chatted with a couple who looked to be in their early one-hundreds, Rachel's eye fell on a woman of striking composure. Her movements so smooth, they seemed almost choreographed, but so well-executed it was impossible to tell. With her waterfall of hair and red sequined gown, she floated around the room, chit-chatting and laughing as if she'd been born to the life. Here was a person-a woman-genetically pre-dispositioned for wealth, class, position, power. Rachel was thinking just that (wondering if it was possible to purchase lessons, or a gene donation, from such a person) when, shockingly, there came the woman straight at her, in her outstretched hand, she held a crystal flute of champagne.

"Hey there. You're Rachel," she said. "I'm Cat. Ricky's wife. I've been looking forward to meeting you."

"Oh shit," said Rachel. "I'm sorry." She felt a blush rise from her neck. She never blushed. Never. Fuck.

"For what? Staring at me like a stalker?" Cat blinked. Straight-faced for a few seconds, then she grinned. "Kidding."

Rachel shook her head, took the champagne, and smiled back. "Yeah, God, you must think I'm so strange. How long was I doing that?" Cat Landry had been sewn into her dress, which fit her so well the pear-shaped diamond pendant she wore fell precisely between her perfect breasts, stressing the decolletage. The entire ensemble might have been some designer's princess dream costume. But here she was, pulling it off in real life.

"Oh, I don't know. Like ten minutes." Then, seeing the horrified look on Rachel's face, she added, "I'm kidding! I don't know. I just saw you look over and thought I'd give you a hard time. Anyway, I really have been looking forward to meeting you."

The bond was almost immediate, and the two quickly became friends. Cat was smart, her sense of humor wry and quick, and she wasn't afraid. Rachel loved everything about her. It would be a long time before Rachel understood what lay beneath the glossy, tranquil surface.

Rachel is pacing outside, avoiding eye contact with other customers. Sweat drips down her back, washes away the makeup she applied earlier.

"Rachel!"

It's Cat stepping from her creamy late model Jaguar, parked illegally directly in front of the restaurant. Rachel waves and watches her friend step over an enormous buckle in the cement and proceed toward the entrance. Cat is the only woman Rachel knows who can effortlessly navigate a New Orleans sidewalk wearing four-inch Prada heels.

"Oh my, you look terrible, girl. What's going on?" Cat approaches, laying a hand on Rachel's arm. With the shoes, she's nearly a foot taller than Rachel, who must peer up to look her in the face. It makes Rachel feel childish, but strangely safe at the same time. "Come on, let's get a table."

The hostess greets Cat by name, calling her Madame Landry. She offers a wide smile and leads them to a private table in the back of the crowded restaurant. Cat has always been more adept at using her status and money to make things happen. She knows everyone. Everyone knows her.

Cat leans back and lets out her breath. She sets her bag on the chair beside her, shakes out her lengthy hair, and looks up at the slowly rotating fans overhead. At sixty-something (Cat has always been vague about her age), she looks fantastic. Rachel knows it's partially down to an excellent surgeon (Cat does not hide it), and there's all the usual stuff: millions of hours of yoga, self-flagellation at the gym, spa time, pro-biotics, fifteen different vitamin supplements, but there's something else. Rachel can't quite sort it out, but there's an iron strength in Cat that makes her seem invincible. It can't be true, of course. She has weaknesses and vulnerability, just like everyone else, but she almost seems stronger as she gets older.

"You know, I'd think this place would have better air conditioning by now. It's a shame what we have to put up with." Cat smiles warmly at Rachel, who sits, clutching her purse to her lap.

Cat furrows her brow. "Hey." She puts a hand on Rachel's. "Talk to me. What is it?"

They both glance up as the waiter puts thick crystal glasses on the table, along with a pitcher of water and sliced lemon.

"I'm not sure," says Rachel. "Could be nothing. But I don't feel like it's nothing." She waits for the waiter to finish pouring, and when she refuses food, Cat orders them both chicory coffee and blackened shrimp salad.

"You gotta eat, hon," says Cat. "You know that you have to take care of yourself. You know those looks of yours ain't gonna last if you don't eat and get your beauty sleep." Cat smiles. Rachel smiles back. Cat has long made a point of teasing Rachel about her looks. Cat, because of her enormous confidence, has never had a problem with beauty. Another woman's beauty. She doesn't compete. When they were young, she pointed out, played up, played down, played to, and used Rachel's beauty for her own benefit, but never once did she act as if it didn't matter. It mattered. At twenty, it was as unmissable as deformity. Cat was striking, sexual. She was a creation. Like a diamond-encrusted Christmas ornament. Bigger than that. More like the whole tree at Rockefeller Center. But Rachel had been something else altogether. The strong features against ivory skin, which, in childhood, had appeared too large, almost masculine on a girl's face, now blended gracefully. Her huge up-tilted emerald eyes and wide cheekbones, and perfectly shaped mouth. Her thick auburn hair changed colors in the light and her long shapely body was both strong and delicate at the same time. All of it made Rachel something like a natural phenomenon. A curiosity. A freak. Lauren Bacall, maybe. People felt entitled to stare, comment, question, invade, and, perhaps worst of all, to assume. To assume everything she'd ever achieved was because of the way she looked. Which, Rachel sometimes thought, was probably right. And so, Cat had poked fun, brought it all down to earth. And it felt good. Now, in middle age, things were different. Quieter. She could go about life anonymously. Her looks might be noticed or might not, but the body she inhabited no longer took the front seat in defining who she was.

"Besides," continues Cat, shoving a piece of baguette into her mouth. "There's no problem so terrible it can't be at least partially mitigated by a big bowl of butter and cream."

When the waiter's gone, Rachel tells Cat about the meeting with Camilla James. The expression on Cat's face is sympathetic, maybe? No less than that. More like tolerant, as if she's listening to a child spin an impossible tale. And the more Rachel talks, the crazier it sounds. Rachel stops talking, takes a sip from her water glass, and digs around inside her bag.

"Camilla wants me involved. She thinks I can help. It needs to be me."

"Why?"

Rachel shrugs. "She says, I'm Daniel's wife. She thinks that gives me access."

"Access to what?"

"I don't know. Records maybe? Information about Good Hope or AmHealth? She wouldn't say. But I think there were other things she wasn't telling me."

"Other things? Like what?"

Rachel hesitates, then blurts out, "Where's Rick?"

"What?" Cat looks completely confused.

"Rick, your husband, where is he?"

"Now, what in the hell is that supposed to mean? I don't know where he is. When do I ever know where he is, Rachel? And when do I ever care? Why are you asking me?"

Rachel stares at her friend for a long time. That's exactly the answer she would have expected from Cat if she were completely innocent. Of course, she's innocent. "Could be I'm going crazy," she says.

"Why did you ask me that?"

"I don't know."

"You know."

"Camilla,"

"Oh my God, what is that crazy woman telling you, Rachel? That I went and did something to my husband? Please." Cat rolls her eyes and laughs in a way that sounds mocking, almost angry.

Rachel stiffens, suddenly unsure how much she wants to share. "No, I mean. I don't know."

"Well, I'll tell you I don't know where he is this minute, but he's been back and forth to Baton Rouge all week, if that helps."

"I don't know, honestly. Like I said, I'm losing it."

"Rach, sweetie, have you thought maybe you're just exhausted?" Cat asks, her voice soft. Too soft, thinks Rachel. "I mean, you haven't really stopped since, since it happened, Rachel. And those pills." She gestures at the bottle Rachel is now pulling from her bag. "And I have to ask you. How many of those pills are you taking?"

Anger flares. Rachel glares at Cat as she snaps open the medicine bottle, dumps one alprazolam-her last- into her palm, pops it into her mouth, and follows with a long drink of the water.

"Since it happened? Do you mean since Jeb died? Just say it, Cat. Jesus. And sure, I take a Xanax occasionally. So what? Should we talk about what kind of happy pills you take?" Her words come out louder and sharper than she intended. Her heart is pounding. A few patrons turn to look. She swipes at her eyes with the back of one hand. She will not cry. "Fuck." She sits back, takes a deep breath, blows it out, and then looks at her friend. More gently, she says, "Oh God, Cat, I'm sorry. I'm really sorry. I know you're trying to help. But I swear this has nothing to do with my being exhausted or anything else."

"Hey," Cat says softly, leaning closer to Rachel. "You know I'm not talking about the pills. Not really, sweetie. This is about you. You've been running like crazy since the accident. Getting the foundation going, taking care of Alex, hitting the gym like a maniac. It just seems like you might need a rest, is all." She pauses, watching. "Look, I know those kinds of calls are upsetting. We used to get a lot of them. Remember? Crazies threatening all kinds of awful. Blaming Ricky for what happened. Blaming me even. But, Rachel, you know what happened at Good Hope. You know the story. You've seen the depositions. There was no question of anyone being responsible. Act of God, it was called. Just a horrible, unfair accident."

"Yeah, I know, you're right. But," she takes a deep breath, "You didn't see Camilla. She's not angry or vindictive. Not like the others. And Cat, you knew her too. Back then. You knew what she was like. A rock. Not prone to hysteria. She wasn't crazy. She's different now. And it's not just grief."

Cat blinks and nods. "Ok, so she thinks there's some kind of conspiracy going on that involves the entire staff from Good Hope or at AmHealth or, for god's sake, the entire state of Louisiana?" She makes air quotes around the word conspiracy. "Please, Rach. I mean, if she believes all that, then she's certainly different." She raises her eyebrows. "You know what I mean? Not in a good way, right?" She waits, and when Rachel doesn't respond, Cat adds, "Ok, so how? How is Camilla different, Rachel?"

Rachel closes her eyes for a few seconds. She can feel the Xanax taking effect. The conversations around them sound pleasantly muffled, and a cozy warmth is spreading through her body. Cat's right, she thinks. This is ridiculous. She's making problems where there aren't any. This is what she does. Create a crisis out of nothing. Her grief counselor said this was a distraction. But then again... She opens her eyes and picks up her coffee. Shakes her head slowly.

"Terrified Cat. Camilla is terrified."

CHAPTER 13

Devereaux, Louisiana

1976

The house in Devereaux was small and low-slung. Constructed as part of a mid-century tract, it was one of the several dozen depressingly identical houses, individually discernible only by their dilapidation. Ray's place, although not the worst, was badly in need of attention. It had a dingy appearance, the tiny lawn-mostly weeds-and almost all the siding in need of paint. A truck tire lay on its side between two red plastic lawn chairs, a kid's bike, badly rusted, was, mysteriously, chained to a broken pipe near the porch, and Rachel could see multi-colored Christmas lights strung from the gutters running clear around the roof.

Ray's live-in girlfriend was waiting at the open door as they arrived. She said nothing, only leaned against the doorjamb, sucking blue Icee through a red straw. She stared at the girls like they had a disease. Ray was ahead, carrying their small suitcases into the house. As Rachel came up, the girlfriend didn't move out of the way, forcing Rachel to squeeze past. Her bare shoulder brushed painfully against the splintery wood of the door frame, but she made no sound.

"This here's Pink," said Ray as they stepped inside. The woman gave a perfunctory nod. She had long gold earrings and the words PINK SPANKY tattooed in delicately scrolled lettering across her shoulder.

Her real name, they'd learn later, was Linda, but she went by Pink on account of the roller derby, which was her primary job, or that's what she said. They'd also learn that Pink had two kids. Matt, a scrawny, pale, anxious little boy with small hands that moved around like hummingbirds when he got excited, and Nadine, thirteen. Nadine was slim and tall for her age. Almost pretty. But she wore a sour, pinched expression all the time and had lank, mousy-colored hair she was forever pulling and twisting around her fingers. Mostly the kids lived with their dad, who Matt would claim invented the Instamatic camera and owned three race cars, but Rachel would think he was probably lying.

For now, though, Pink said nothing. Just stuck the straw back in her mouth, slurped her drink, and eyed Rachel suspiciously. Her stare, Rachel thought, had weight.

"This here is your room," said Ray, standing at the entrance to a small cubby just a few feet inside the front door. He held back the floor-length strands of plastic beads that acted as a partition. Talia stuck her face in between the beads, giggling.

The appearance of Ray Larson had dramatically soothed Talia's grief. Daddy Ray Tee called him. He wanted them both to use the name, but Rachel refused. Tee was in love with the man. Had been, of course, since the day at Shop-n-Save and was delirious with the idea he was her father. For all her hysterics over learning about Mama's death, she was still so young. It seemed to Rachel that, for Tee, life was lived in the moment. Everything either was or wasn't. Memories meant little, drifting into the ether like smoke. The future meant nothing. She could let go as quickly as she could connect. Like a chameleon, she just changed with her environment, seemingly internally unaffected by it. But no, that wasn't true. Talia was changing on the inside, too.

Ray was looking at Rachel like he wanted a response. She said nothing, only looked around. The space was cool and dim. It smelled of tobacco smoke and stale beer and fast food, same as the front entry, but there was something else in here. Tropical fruit, maybe? Pineapple? Glade. That's what it was. Nona hated air fresheners; she called them fluffers for reasons Rachel never understood. Nona said if you were spraying fluffers around your house, then you were for sure doin' somethin' you ought not to be doin'. The thought made Rachel smile. Somebody had tried in this little space. Spraying deodorizer around to cover up the stench. There was a twin bed, and a tiny veneer topped table beside it. The table held a yellow porcelain lamp, its base badly cracked. The only other furnishings were a circular rag rug-definitely homemade-and a slightly lopsided child-sized dresser. Weirdly, a scratched and empty fish tank sat on top of the dresser. There was no room for their suitcases.

"We'll find a place for these later," he said, setting them down. "You can have a fish." Ray pointed at the empty tank.

Rachel scrutinized it. Inside the glass, a greenish scum looked as if it had been there a while. She glanced back at Ray, who was smiling at Talia. Could it be he actually wanted to please them?

"Yay!" said Talia, jumping up and down. "I want a girl fish, and I'll name her Goldie! Goldie, the girl fish!" She clapped her hands together and smiled up at Ray in the desperately solicitous sort of way that let Rachel know it was an act.

"Well, ok then," said Ray, grinning. "A girl fish it is."

Pink appeared, sidling between the purple beads, hip first. She was a muscular woman about Ray's age, with brassy blonde hair and coffee-colored eyebrows. She wore no makeup other than a band of dark eyeliner that rimmed her blue eyes. She was pretty in a harsh sort of way—a second tattoo-a narrow peacock's feather-wrapped her right thigh from the knee to the hem of her shorts.

Rachel stared until Pink said, "What are you lookin' at?" then she pushed her eyes away and let her glance bounce aimlessly around the space.

"I'm hungry," blurted Talia.

"Well, ok," said Ray and then looked at Rachel. "How about you?"

Rachel was not hungry. Instead, she was feeling sick, but she nodded anyway.

"Great," he said and then repeated, "Great." His smile faded a bit, but he clapped his hands together as if he had a plan.

It took less than a week for Rachel to understand that Ray's good cheer and enthusiasm were fleeting, inconsistent things. Diurnal creatures skittering from the darkness of his alcohol-fueled moods. Irritable and sharp-tempered, he sometimes shuffled silently about the house, rubbing his eyes and pushing hanks of his unwashed hair from his face. Other times, he mumbled incoherently or spat invectives directed at various bosses, both present and past. He'd fallen off a ladder in the spring and hurt his back. Had to quit construction. Now he stacked boxes in the backroom at the Shakey's Pizza. He hated the job, but he and Pink fought whenever he said he was going to leave. Ray said it was a shit job for shit people. Pink said he was goddamn lucky to have that job the way he always screwed everything up. It surprised Rachel when that didn't make Ray angry. He just looked smaller. Rachel didn't like him much, but sometimes she felt sorry for him.

The thing was, Ray was never cruel to the girls, and, often, he was funny and sometimes generous. He'd bring sodas or small gifts from the mall where he worked. Plastic toys, playing cards. Things he could fit in his pockets. Rachel figured he shoplifted them, but she said nothing to Tee. Ray seemed to want to be a father to both of them. For Talia, that was enough. But, within Ray's bouts of alcohol seeped from moodiness, Rachel saw what was coming.

Then, there was Pink; she was an entirely different matter. She was a small-minded, reedy-hearted, prickly-skinned sort of person. All bound up inside and set to spring at any moment. Rachel quickly discovered it was best to stay extremely far out of her reach, interacting as little as possible. Pink's son Matt had some kind of "problem." He wouldn't take baths or brush his teeth. He threw bizarre tantrums, raging and screaming obscenities. Rachel heard him call his mother a fuckin cunt. Banging his head or smashing his own possessions against his bedroom wall. The rest of the time, he barely interacted at all. He couldn't or wouldn't look Rachel in the eye, and he ran around the house murmuring single words and phrases repeatedly. Often sentences he'd picked up from movies and TV commercials. Once, he spent a full day singing Libby's Libby's Libby's on the label label label. You will like it like it, like it on your table table table. He didn't stop until Pink locked him in his room and told him to shut the fuck up, or he'd stay fuckin in there for fuckin ever.

When Matt and Nadine visited, Ray and Pink took off to Pink's sister's house, leaving Nadine to babysit. Matt usually cried the whole time, or else he smashed stuff in his room. Nadine spent all her time smoking weed and telling Matt to get the hell out of my room. Once, Matt grabbed a steak knife from the kitchen counter and, brandishing it, threatened to kill them all if they didn't let him watch Porky's on the VCR player. Rachel raced for the phone, ran one finger down the list of numbers scotch-taped to the wall, and called over to Pink's sister's house. When Pink finally came to the phone, she snapped at Rachel for bugging the fuck out of me and then hung up, leaving Rachel clutching the receiver listening to a dial tone, Nadine watching with a bitter *I told you, so* expression on her face and Matt still screaming murderously in the background.

•　•　•

It was a Friday night six months after they'd left Nona's house, and Pink was out with Ray. Rachel and Talia were in their room, trying to ignore Matt's screams. Nadine had just given him his pills, and everyone was waiting for him to pass out.

"No way. I ain't gonna listen to you. You ain't the boss of me... lalalalalalala..." For now, Matt's obstinance was childish and annoying. Rachel wondered what would happen once he grew bigger than Nadine.

Talia sat in her nightgown on the floor with her back up against their bed. Her skinny legs sticking out straight in front of her, hands slapped over her ears. She hated the noise. Few things would disrupt Talia's perpetually sunny disposition, like demonstrations of anger. It seemed like as time went on, she grew more, not less sensitive.

It was late by the time Matt finally calmed down and fell asleep. At least he'd stopped hollering, so Rachel assumed the drugs were working. She checked the clock after midnight. Matt's fits sometimes did this to her. Sent her brain spinning. She'd be up all night. She groaned, squeezed her eyes shut, and tried to force herself into sleep.

She lay wide awake in the narrow bed, curled around her dreaming sister when Ray and Pink arrived home after two am. She heard them come in, giggling and dropping things by the front door. After a while, when they were finally quiet, Rachel unfolded herself from Talia, careful not to wake her, got out of bed, and padded toward the kitchen. Maybe a glass of water would quiet her busy mind.

As she approached the kitchen swing door, she heard a soft moaning. Gently, she pushed it open the door and peeked through.

The overhead bulb was switched off. The room was bathed in an eerie blue-white light coming from a streetlamp outside. Pink, naked from the waist down, sat hoisted up on the counter, both legs up around Ray's waist. Her eyes were closed, and her head hung back so that her long hair brushed the blue Formica of the countertop. Ray, jeans around his ankles, pushed himself against her, his butt muscles clenching and unclenching with each thrust.

Rachel stood frozen, one palm still on the door. Pink's eyes shot open. Rachel held her breath. Shrouded in the hallway's dark, it occurred to her she might not be seen. But then Pink, arms around Ray's neck, squinted and cocked her head, peering in Rachel's direction. Her eyes, in the strange light, black holes in her pale face. Rachel's heart thudded. Pink opened her mouth, smiling slightly, then ran her tongue along her top lip. She saw. She wanted to be seen. Rachel felt sick. She turned and ran through the dark house, back all the way back to her bed.

Rachel knew about sex. Ever since the second grade when Randy Galey, a broad-faced fourth-grader, drew her a picture and explained that's what he was going to do to her. She'd told her mother about it, and Mama had gone ballistic and called the principal. The following week Tommy cornered Rachel at the bathrooms, stuck a thick finger into her ribs, and told her next time she told on him he'd get her little sister. Rachel wasn't afraid of Randy Galey-he was spoiled and stupid and slow, and she'd grown up outsmarting him and his stupid, slow friends- but she couldn't risk he'd put his fat fingers on Talia, so she never told. Instead, she lifted his Magic School Bus lunchbox from the shelf outside his classroom, took it around the back of the school, filled it with swamp mud, and returned it.

So, no, it wasn't the sex that frightened her, although it was decidedly disgusting. It was Pink. Her monstrous muscled thighs glowing in the white of a streetlight. Her empty eyes. Her expression. The hate. It made Rachel feel like she was on the edge of a cliff, leaning much too far out over the edge.

Rachel got back into bed and curled around her little sister. One finger gently circling the tiny scar on Talia's chin. She'd fallen at an ice cream shop in Gulf Shores when she was three, and Mama had made everything perfect with cherry-berry ice cream. Rachel thought about that day-about Mama, Talia and the Cherry-Berry ice cream as she closed her eyes and buried her nose into the back of Talia's neck, feeling the rise and fall of her breath. Then she fell asleep, inhaling the sweet vanilla scent of her baby sister's skin.

CHAPTER 14

New Orleans, Bayou St John

July 22, 2020

Virgil is up early, sleep having become a flighty, problematic thing in his middle years. He leashes Louis, his ten-year-old English lab mutt (Virgil suspects he's got some giant dog mixed in, Mastiff maybe), and they head out for a walk around the Bayou. The thing about Lou is that he makes all the decisions when it comes to his walks. Also, his meals and his naps. Virgil realizes this is not an ideal owner/dog relationship, but it's worked for nearly a decade, and he figures it is too late to change it now. Also, Louis pretty much speaks English, so when he's ready to go back to the house, he says something like, "Ok, I'm ready to go back now, Virgil," and off they go. They've reached a compromise on leashes. Louis wears one (a very loose one), but only because Virgil explained that without one, other humans might become terrified of him, thinking he will attack or go wild. He wouldn't, of course. He's much too civilized.

Back at the house, Virgil spends an hour at his kitchen table, drinking chicory coffee and trolling the internet for information about the latest case. He reads a few of the older articles. The original trial was fast; They convicted Janie Paradise of capital murder in less than two months. The appeals process and subsequent proceedings had been stuttering and excruciatingly slow. In the end, (and this is the part Virgil is struggling to understand), they had dropped the entire convoluted appeals process. Why? Was the woman tired of the stress, the emotional torture, the endless court time? Had she given up?

None of it made sense. Faced with death, living beings desperately want to live. No matter the ugliness, the lack of nobility, the cost, we fight for survival. Life is not Hollywood. In the end, we humans have more in common with rats than Spartans.

He shuts the computer, stands, and walks to the window. Leans against it, holding his coffee. Still dark, but just barely; a thin film of darkness, dissolving, diffusing into the gathering daylight. The last sounds of cicada and night frogs float in through the warm mist. Virgil loves this about Louisiana. Nowhere he's ever been has he experienced such a love in the night, in the dark.

Thirty minutes later, Virgil is pulling onto Interstate 10, heading west through Kenner. He crosses Walker Canal and drives up through the marsh toward Laplace. The road is long and flat, the sky pale blue, cloudless, and still. He lowers a window on the Lake Pontchartrain side and inhales the moist air. The odor was simultaneously fresh and slightly decayed, like old flowers and new grass. At Laplace, he takes the 55 north, and the roadway morphs into two elevated strips of asphalt above thick marsh on both sides. Bright green algae and the golden-yellow fronds of sargassum weed swirl the surface like watercolor. The bright yellow forehead feathers of a pelican. The bird dives across the sky, disappearing for seconds into the blue-brown water of the lake, before re-emerging, beak clamped around a flopping silverfish.

He crosses the bridge at Pass Manchac to Akers, a tiny, waterlogged town where fishermen's clapboard houses perch precariously on stilts above the waterways running like fingers between the cypress. A garage built of corrugated aluminum stands at the boundary of the town. Two young men in waterproof chest waders-the skin of their arms and faces deeply tanned-lean against the wall, smoking. Over their head, a hand-painted sign reads mysteriously: LIVE and BOILED. It makes Virgil smile.

Beyond Goat Island Canal, Virgil turns left, heading for Chafalaya Parish and past that to Marietta, where the water finally gives way to the vast, empty fields of Marietta Plantation. As he drives the last monotonous stretch, he replays the conversation with Camilla two mornings ago, scanning for details he might have missed.

The meeting had not been unusual. Camilla often stops by his office at the jail to chat. Nearly every day, in fact. But this time, she'd been stressed. She'd pushed a copy of the New Orleans paper across his desk. "Look," she'd said, tapping two fingers on the front page. "Look!"

He'd picked it up. Read the headline. "Shit."

"Yeah, I think that's why they want you, Virgil. It's a political disaster. And the guy she killed? A cop. A friend of the mayor. Fishing buddies or whatever."

"Marietta has its own forensic people. They've got, you know, Todd Marshall and the girl, the woman. What's her name?" Virgil knew he should know the woman's name. She was a resident. At least he thought she was still a resident. Who the hell knew? Time moved like a fucking bullet train these days. The woman was probably forty by now.

Camilla rolled her eyes, smiled a little. "Dr. Samson. Virgil, you're thinking about Samson, and no, she's no longer a resident, but she is still inexperienced. Also, Marshall is out on paternity leave." Camilla pursed her lips. "Anyway, I think they want you."

"They? Who are they?"

"I heard the warden and the medical director talking about it, Virgil. They plan to loan you out for this case."

"Ah, shit." Virgil reread the headline: KATRINA COP MURDERER EXECUTION SCHEDULED. He squinted at the blurry photo. A small woman in handcuffs and jail reds flanked by two beefy uniformed cops is headed into the Terrebonne Parish courthouse. Her long hair pulled back into a ponytail. Face turned from the camera, only partially visible. "Is that a scar?" He held the paper up under the desk lamp, peering closely. "Jesus, what the fuck?"

"Yeah," said Camilla. "So, she has the sympathy of many people."

"That's a hell of a wound. Disfiguring. How'd it happen?"

"I don't know exactly. It's a gunshot wound, but otherwise... they found her like that. Up in the attic. Seems like maybe the gun went off.

She dropped a paint can on the guy's head. Skull smashed. Quite a mess."

Virgil had winced. "He had a gun? Service weapon?"

Camilla shook her head. "Unregistered. They found it at the bottom of the attic stairs. No way to prove it was his. The story is it was her gun. Cop found it there. Picked it up, and it went off."

"Wait, I don't get it. She has a gunshot wound; at minimum, that bullet grazed badly her." He peered more closely at the picture. "And it's not self-defense?" He looks at Camilla. "That's crazy."

"It is. But she never countered the story. And, you know, in this town," she shrugged. "A dead cop, a dead New Orleans cop. They need a perpetrator."

"Right." He dropped the paper. "So, the state's case is what? That she murdered this guy in cold blood and then got herself accidentally shot? Jesus Christ."

"Pretty much," said Camilla. "And it's not just the state's case. She confessed on the tape and in writing. And, until now, they've done a good job keeping her away from the media."

Virgil yanked open a desk drawer in search of Tums or Pepcid. Rummaged a bit and found nothing, slammed the drawer, and looked up at the nurse. "Ok, it's awful, but it was years ago. Why's it coming up now?"

"Execution dates coming up. Someone in the outside press finally got hold of the story. Now she's got advocates. They're pushing for an investigation. You know, a closer look. It's a political nightmare. Or it could be."

"It seems straightforward. She's trapped alone in a hundred-degree attic for what? A week? No food. Who knows how much water? She had to be practically psychotic by the end. Some cop comes up those attic stairs, maybe points a gun at her, and she reacts. No way is it murder one."

"That's my point, Virgil. I know how smart you are. You'll figure it out."

"Figure what out, Camilla. You're not making sense."

"Self-defense Virgil. It was self-defense. They weren't there to rescue her. I'm sure of it."

"Ok, so she'll tell me that, right?"

"Yeah, right. Except she's still not talking about it. Except to say she did it. She says she planned it, meant to do it, was in her right mind. You know all that. She's smart. Knows what she's doing. She wants the sentence carried out. But that's the thing. I don't think she's guilty. I think she's afraid. Protecting someone, maybe. But it doesn't matter. I know you'll figure it out anyway, and that's the problem. You can't do that. It's not safe."

Virgil leaned back in his chair. Removed his glasses and squeezed the bridge of his nose between thumb and forefinger. "Hang on, so I'm supposed to go up there and confirm she's the murdering psychopath they want her to be?"

"Pretty much."

"You're telling me she's not that?"

"Right."

"It's no win. Amnesty International. The ACLU. They'll fry me if I let them execute a victim of Katrina. And if I don't," he stopped.

"You'll lose your job," she finished for him. "At the very least."

"Yeah," he drawled. Then he smiled. "The hell with it. Likely it's time for private practice, anyway. Nice cushy office uptown, right? Long lunches at Commanders."

She wasn't smiling. "The thing is Virgil." She stood up and leaned over the desk. Lowered her voice. "Do what they say, ok?"

He looked at her. Her eyes were blazing, her lips colorless. "Camilla?" He said and reached a hand across his desk to touch her fingers. "Hey, it's ok. I'll be fine. I'm just complaining, is all."

She shook her head vigorously. "No, you don't understand. They'll want you to rubber stamp the decision Virgil, so do it. Rubber stamp the execution. I know you always want to do what's right. But this time, you need to do whatever they tell you, the DA, the prison officials, the goddamn governor, whoever. No matter what." She leveled her gaze at him. Eyes hard. "Tell me you understand. Please tell me you'll do it."

They? Who was she talking about? Was she paranoid? Confused? She'd been prone to high blood pressure. She might be having mini-strokes. Or depression? Psychotic depression? He'd wanted to reassure her. Tell her there was no conspiracy. The Louisiana *powers-that-be* might be inept, corrupt even, but dangerous? No. But he'd looked at her and, instead, said nothing. Just nodded his head in agreement, and then she was gone.

Virgil pulls off the main highway and makes a right onto a long nameless road up to the prison. After a while, the wide fields give way to weedy earth patches bordered by a chicken wire fence. The vegetation thins and the long low buildings of the prison come into view. Marietta was once a working plantation, and fields of cotton spread out on either side of the gates. Virgil can see some women in bright orange uniforms working in the fields. Correctional officers on horseback trot up and down the rows monitoring the prisoners. The view is disturbing for about a dozen reasons.

He slows as he approaches the outermost gate. A concrete watchtower to the right and just behind another set of gates, these topped with razor wire. Two guards peer out of the half-open transom windows. Encircled by a ring of weedy dirt and dead lawn, a foreboding steel sign stands beside the road; a few sagging marigolds planted along its base. The white lettering looks crisp, newly painted, or re-painted: MARIETTA STATE PENITENTIARY FOR WOMEN.

A moderately overweight, balding man with slow eyes and a narrow forehead suggesting an undersized brain leans against the doorframe of a kiosk, smoking a cigarette. Virgil pulls up and rolls to a stop. The man is blowing smoke rings over his own head and appears, more or less, like he found the uniform in the back of a secondhand shop and thought he'd put it on just to see how it would look. He's younger than Virgil first thought, maybe less than twenty-five.

He smashes his cigarette into the dirt, then steps back into the kiosk, busying himself with paperwork. Virgil waits. It feels like a long time before the guard looks up and acknowledges his newest arrival. Virgil pushes a folder with his credentials out the car window toward the uniformed man, who looks at it disdainfully before taking it from Virgil's outstretched hand. The man's jaw is rimmed with not-so-old acne scars.

"Yeah," he drawls, slowly flipping a page of the credential packet. "And y'all are coming from where?"

"I'm Dr. Virgil Barrons from Orleans Central. I'm here about one of your prisoners, Janie Lucille Paradise. It's all in there. My clearance. Should be everything you need."

"Yeah," says the guard, only he pronounces it, "Yeeee-aaah." and still doesn't look up at Virgil while he's sifting through the papers.

Virgil watches a thin plume of smoke rise, first inches, then feet, from the half-smashed cigarette butt near the kiosk door. Virgil glances up and sees for the first time he wears a tag that reads Beaumont.

It feels like a long time before Beaumont finally steps back and says he's "gonna need to make a call." Virgil has to restrain himself to keep from making a snide comment. Snide does not work down here. It will only make things worse. "Yes sir," he says instead, ignoring the heat inside the car and the fact that his one good shirt is now sweat stuck to his back and underarms.

The little car fills with the smell of cheap tobacco, sweat and fertilizer as Beaumont snatches up the phone and mumbles something unintelligible while simultaneously picking at his nose.

A sign on the glass window reads: THIS IS A NO HOSTAGE FACILITY. ENTER AT YOUR OWN RISK. Virgil thinks perhaps it's an omen, this sign. Sort of like black cats or broken mirrors. But then he thinks, no. Real omens are never so obvious. Beaumont, however, with his strange slow eyes and scars and poorly concealed hostility, Beaumont is an omen for sure or at least a warning. Virgil should put the old Volvo in reverse and get the hell out of here before it's too late, as they say.

There seems to be a pause of inordinate length before Beaumont replaces the phone receiver, stamps the credential packet, and hands the paperwork back to Virgil.

"Okey dokey partner, yer good to go."

Virgil gives Beaumont a brief salute and drives on.

Virgil parks and hauls his briefcase and testing materials out of the trunk and makes his way toward the prison. The formal prison is a long, low concrete building. It is flanked on both sides by sniper towers and surrounded by electric fences topped by razor wire. Clearly, Beaumont is the prison equivalent of a Walmart greeter, meant to do little more than wave hello. These electric shocks, bullets and knives are actual security, meant to keep the animals in, or maybe to keep the enemy out. It gets confusing, Virgil knows, depending upon your perspective.

Lined up and paying only vague attention to the yellow markings on the asphalt, dozens of family members are waiting. The sun is already bar-b-cue hot, and many of them use their prison paperwork to shade their eyes from the glare. Others fan themselves with the pamphlets while pushing strollers one-handed or jiggling crying babies on their hips. They are all women. No men. No older boys. By the time the boys get to be teenagers, they stop coming to visit. Some were already picked up by the juvenile authorities, too busy learning the street, hustling, or dealing drugs. They didn't have a chance.

Virgil eyes the listless toddlers sleeping sweaty in portable strollers. Some of the older ones dance restlessly around the adults who accompany them or stand solemnly still, resignation on their faces. The young ones drag dirty blankets or stuffed animals. The older ones hold popsicle stick photo frames and glossy clay blobs shaped into ashtrays or little pots. They will confiscate all of it before the families get to the visiting area. It can smuggle contraband. Virgil remembers one eighteen-year-old. Caught selling cocaine to the other inmates- and some of the guards-the dope smuggled in by her seventeen-year-old sister, who'd stuffed it into the rattle of her three-month-old baby.

Virgil sets his briefcase down on the cement, pulls off his jacket, and folds it over his arm, hoping to save it from the worst of the moisture. Sweat is rolling heavily down the center of his back. The air smells of tar and cigarette smoke, and body odor.

Marietta is the oldest prison for women in the state. Built in 1941, its structures, especially its death chamber, were state-of-the-art. Now, the place is a mishmash of mid-twentieth century brick buildings (jalousie windows and flat roofs), pushed up against the newer multi-story prison barracks. Split into four blocks, A through D, most of Marietta's thousand-plus inmates are housed in A, B, or C. Within those, most live in dormitories where overcrowded rows of double or triple bunk beds create submarine-like living quarters.

D-Block is different. It's where they keep the most violent, or potentially violent, criminals. The "Double Reds" they are called. A reference to the specialized color of the prison uniform worn by D-Block inmates. There are twelve individual cells in the solitary section on D-Block. They call this area Administrative Segregation, known affectionately as AD-SEG. Two floors, six cells per floor. This is where they keep the most difficult inmates, the most at risk, and those sentenced to death. Security here is so tight that, outside of hearings, court and the infirmary when necessary, the inmates never leave. Even their "yard time" is restricted to a small courtyard that opens off the back of the building. They get one hour a day, and, except for the accompanying C.O. (corrections officer), they spend that hour alone.

Virgil is required to enter AD-SEG to interview Janie Paradise. Passing through the brilliant fluorescent lighting reinforced electronically controlled steel doors, gargantuan central guard station, rows of television monitors, and the oppressive atmosphere is vaguely nauseating and intensely disconcerting. Virgil reminds himself he has the luxury of leaving. Living here? Virgil cannot imagine.

A C.O. leads him to a small interview room and tells him to wait. The door is sealed from the outside, and although a guard stands duty and would, Virgil hopes, open it should he knock on the window, the setup makes him acutely uncomfortable. They've taken his cellphone and watch (both have cameras and internet capability). There is no clock, no window to the outside, no way to gauge time other than the beat of his heart. Virgil settles back, takes a deep breath, and prepares to meet Janie Lucille Paradise.

CHAPTER 15

Marietta State Penitentiary

July 22, 2020

Janie Lucille Paradise lies on her back, staring up at the ceiling. She is studying three brownish stains, each about the size of a half-dollar. She's fairly sure they are bloodstains, and she's trying to sort out how the blood got to the ceiling. Even in prison, that would be a trick. The bleeder must have been in one sorry state.

"Hey, Jay-Jay." A raspy female voice through the air vent. "You awake?"

It's Carly. She and Luanne Marston are the only other women at Marietta on death row. Their cells mashed up one against the other, allowing for conversation, desired or not.

"Hey, Carly, I'm awake," answers Janie.

"I was thinkin'."

"Thinkin' what?"

"I dunno."

"How can you be thinkin' and not know what you're thinkin?"

"I dunno."

Having sustained many head injuries at the hands of abusive stepfathers, boyfriends, and two of her four husbands, Carly is not a witty conversationalist. Twelve years ago, convicted of jamming a hunting knife so deep into her husband's neck, it nearly decapitated both him and the woman curled in sleep behind him, Carly is unrepentant. The deaths were accidental, she says. She'd meant only to scare them, and besides, they deserved it. The state argued that dousing the bodies with gasoline and lighting them on fire showed both malice of forethought (she'd brought the gasoline along) and explicit knowledge of right and wrong. They sentenced her to death.

"Ok, Carly," says Janie.

"You know what?"

"What, Carly?"

"I'm thinkin' about that date they got on you. I'm real, sorry."

"Yeah, thank you." That's the thing about women like Carly that Janie can't figure out. They can hack to death a couple of people, then turn around and genuinely cry for the crappy situation another person is facing. Carly is sweet. Down deep.

"I mean... well, you know what I mean."

"I do. I know what you mean."

"You doin' ok?" asks Carly, her voice breaking a little.

"Yeah, I'm doin' ok."

"You readin' your bible?"

"Yeah, Carly, I'm readin' my bible," Janie lies.

"You know they say all the answers is in there, right?"

"Yeah, I know."

"You think that's true?"

"Do I think what's true?"

"You think God is true?"

"I don't know, Carly. I've never known that." It's another lie. No way does Janie think all the answers are in some book a bunch of old guys wrote three gazillion years ago. She's not sure there are answers. She's pretty sure there aren't, in fact. But people like Carly need to believe in something. So why not the bible?

"Well, you were s'posed to know; as you got closer to the end you know what I mean?"

"Yeah, I heard that too, but it's not true. Least not for me."

"Oh."

"Sorry about that."

"Well, ok, then. Long as you readin' the Bible, y'all be ok."

"Thanks, Carly."

"Yeah."

"Jay-Jay?"

"Yeah?"

"I didn't know either."

"Didn't know what?"

"If God was true. I said I did. But I didn't."

"That's ok, Carly. That's ok."

Carly has been close. Twice she's been served her last meal and been accompanied to the death room by the priest. Janie imagines what it must have been like. Senses on overdrive. The taste of bile. The smell of your own sweat and fear. Electronic locks clanging open and shut, the sound reverberating up the corridor. And your heart, the sickening thud of your own heart.

Then, twice, a stay at the last minute. But Carly's case is unique. She has advocates, or she used to. Most have moved on now, to more interesting cases, those with more publicity, more hope. Like Janie, Carly is running out of time. But she seems strangely unaware of all that.

Janie gives up, staring at the stains and turns her head to examine a slim shaft of light hitting the opposite wall. Dust motes dance along its length. Twenty-four days, four hours, and approximately thirty-eight minutes. Dead, she says the word inside her head, trying to make it make sense. Not present. Never having existed. Only that's not right. Dead is different. It's what is no longer rather than what never was.

Footsteps outside. Heavy keys clanking. They don't use keys in this wing anymore (all the doors are opened and closed electronically), although, on Janie's few trips to other parts of the prison (the infirmary, the priest's office, and twice for hearings), she's noted the giant steel key rings carried by some guards, hooked onto their belts like weapons.

The door opens. It's Officer Wilmers, and he's got something to say. Janie can tell when Brad Wilmers is about to give her bad news. He has the proverbial cat that ate the canary smirk, and his narrow, sloping shoulders shake a little with internal giggles. He leans against the doorjamb, mean and scrawny, and smacks his lips.

"There's a guy coming to see you today," he says.

She sits up slowly and looks at him. He's going to make her talk to him, and the sooner she does so, the sooner he'll go away.

"A guy?" she asks.

"Yeah," he says. "A guy. He's coming up here to see how crazy you are. Some special kinda shrink. Knows all about freaks like you, Janie." He pauses, giving her a sneer she thinks is probably his regular out in the world face. "And you know how come?"

"How come what?" Of course, she knows. Her lawyer told her.

"How come they're sending some big shot doctor up here?"

"Nope, Officer Wilmers. I got no clue."

He bends his mouth into the shape of a smile. "So, they can kill you, Paradise. That's how come. So they can prove you ain't too fucked up to kill." He pronounces kill like the verb that means capsize: "keel." Wilmers is an idiot.

That last message was the reason for his visit, of course. He didn't need to come. He'd probably spent the morning salivating over another opportunity to remind Janie about her impending execution. Seems like recently, he'd come by her cell daily for that very purpose. Wilmers wants her to hate him, but she doesn't. She's too tired to hate anyone anymore. Especially an inconsequential fuck like Wilmers. Watching him step out of the cell, she thinks, she almost pities him. Almost.

After he's gone, Janie sits up and leans forward, resting her elbows on her knees. She pushes the heels of her hands into the sides of her head as if she can squeeze control back into her brain. How much time now? Twenty-four days, four hours, and approximately thirty-four minutes. The shaft of light has paled and is quickly disappearing, dissolving into the wall. Taking with it the dust motes, leaving not even displaced air behind.

CHAPTER 16

Devereaux, Louisiana

1978

By early 1978, life in Devereaux had settled into a rhythm. Rachel had become accustomed to Daddy Ray's erratic moods. Strings of grumpy mornings interrupted by inexplicable bouts of generosity and good humor. He took the time to teach Rachel how to shoot. Rather, he took the time to *almost* teach her. Ray was like that. He started and stopped projects, left a lot of things unfinished. Pink complained he had the "attention span of a goddamn retarded gnat." They'd gotten as far as taking apart the gun, a hunting rifle, and putting it back together. Ray had even driven Rachel out to the woods, where they took aim at a few beer cans, but he ran out of bullets after a handful of shots, and they had to come home. He wasn't supposed to own a gun on account of "some kinda legal whatnot," so he'd had to borrow one from Pink's younger brother, LooLoo. After a while, LooLoo, who had been pretty much living on the sofa, decided to "move on along" and took his gun with him. Ray never got around to borrowing another. Rachel didn't care on account of despising LooLoo and being so happy he was gone.

Occasionally, they went to the movie or out for a happy meal. They went bowling sometimes, just Rachel and Talia and Daddy Ray. He'd sit back, grinning and drinking beers while the girls took turns heaving the heavy balls down the alley, Talia squealing when her ball bing-banged dramatically off the gutter guards. Those were good days.

Rachel thought Nona was probably wrong about him. Rachel knew Daddy Ray got the checks every month. She'd seen Pink tear open the official-looking envelopes. Nona was positive that's all Daddy Ray wanted—the money. But Rachel didn't think so. Daddy Ray was one of those people all mixed up on the inside. He was trying to do right by her and Talia; he just didn't know how. In her short life, Rachel had known a lot of mixed up people like that. Still, Ray had a certain pathetic appeal about him. She didn't exactly like him, but it made her hate him less.

Besides the drinking, the biggest problem with Daddy Ray was leaving all the parenting up to Pink. Even at fourteen, Rachel knew that the tattooed roller derby queen had the mothering instincts of a lizard. Nevertheless, the girls were sorting the situation out. The main thing to know about Pink was that she hated kids. Even her own kids, pretty much. So Rachel worked hard to stay out of her way and ensure Talia also stayed under the radar. It wasn't difficult unless Matt was around. He liked to stir up trouble unnecessarily.

Matt was a liar. His lies becoming increasingly elaborate and devious as time went on. He'd learned that by breaking one of his own possessions (a hairline crack in a prized ceramic pencil cup, for example) and then attempting to hide the break (superglue in the gap), he could blame the entire break/repair/hide conspiracy on Rachel and Pink would believe it. After a while, Rachel gave up professing innocence. A quick admission of guilt resulted in far less punishment than persistent denial. Pink only shook her head and gave Rachel a stupid, fake "I'm disappointed in you" look, then told her she'd have to do Matt's "chores" for a week. This made no sense since Rachel always did all Matt's chores, anyway.

Granny Nona visited regularly. To check up on things and take the girls out. Shopping for school supplies. Up to the river or over to the shopping mall to wander around in the air conditioning. At Rachel's request, they sometimes went to the library to check out books. Reading for Rachel provided a respite from the chaos of home. Learning, she discovered, was something she loved and at which she excelled.

During those years, Talia seemed to settle. She slept less restlessly. Stopped sucking her thumb and crying at night. She laughed more. By the fall of her sophomore year, Rachel felt herself relaxing into life as a teenager. They were a stitched-together patchwork version of a proper family. Sort of Adams Family meets The Brady Bunch with much less money and more beer and fighting. But it was ok. It was what they had.

After LooLoo got his gun and took off, he didn't come back for the rest of the year. That was good. When they'd first arrived at Daddy Ray's, LooLoo was always around, sprawled on the sofa with his eyes closed and a half-drunk beer balanced on his small, rounded belly. He stank of stale alcohol and sweat and grease, and he enjoyed harassing Rachel with rude, often embarrassing remarks. LooLoo was skinny, with stick-like arms and a concave chest above that protruding stomach, but he was scary. His real name was Edgar. Daddy Ray said everyone called him LooLoo on account of him being crazy. Pink said that wasn't true, but offered no alternative explanation. Ray said it was so true, and what about that time LooLoo got drunk down at Hazel's Bar and had an argument with another guy he was convinced called him fag or something like that. LooLoo reached over the bar, said Daddy Ray, and snatched up a steak knife and jammed it into the other man's head. Pink said that never happened, and anyway, he was only sixteen and he shouldn't have been allowed at Hazel's in the first place, and besides, the guy didn't even die.

Rachel was glad LooLoo stopped coming around, and, mostly, things were good. By the end of that year, Talia had five more goldfish, all in separate bowls, and she'd developed an interest in drawing. She spent hours sketching fish and wild birds, and Rachel helped her plaster the pictures all over their tiny room. Talia slowly began speaking more in public. She made one or two friends, and Rachel thought things might be alright.

For a long time, both sisters would remember 1978 as their last good year.

CHAPTER 17

Marietta State Penitentiary

July 22, 2020

She is a tiny woman with streaks of gray in her dark-blonde hair. Her red prison shirt and drawstring pants fit poorly, bagging at the waist and shoulders, cuffs rolled to accommodate her small stature. Her wrists are heavily cuffed and chained together. Even thicker steel cuffs ring her ankles. White socks and black rubber shower shoes. Her feet are small as a child's. Her eyes are down, and she does not resist as the two correctional officers seat her at the table across from Virgil. One of them pulls out a set of keys and secures her wrists to the iron ring, which is welded to the tabletop. They spend an inordinate amount of time crouched beneath the table, attaching her leg irons to a similar ring on the floor. The whole thing seems medieval.

When they are finished, both officers take turns yanking on the chains, presumably checking for a secure connection. Satisfied, they stand, give Virgil perfunctory nods, then step out of the room. The door swings shut with a heavy clank, and Virgil is alone with Janie Paradise.

Except for the scar, which runs like a fat white centipede up the left side of her face stretching from the edge of her top lip to her temple, this woman is everything Virgil expected her not to be. Petite, delicate featured, bright-eyed, deliberate in her movements, and, perhaps strangest of all, serene. Perhaps the icy wording of the Times article had conjured some monstrous creature to Virgil's mind. A hideously scarred female reincarnation of Charles Manson.. But Janie Paradise is not that. She is not tense or angry. She seems peaceful.

Her hair is smoothed into a low ponytail midway down her back, the ends neatly trimmed, her pale skin creases delicately around her wide eyes, and one side of her mouth is still smooth and perfectly formed-what Virgil's grandmother would have called a rosebud mouth. She smells of softly scented soap. Good soap would be an expensive indulgence in prison, Virgil knows.

There's a metallic click. Virgil glances up, catching the female C.O.'s face, locking the door, then peeking through the small she disappears. He turns back and finds the inmate smiling. Her teeth are small, both incisors slightly out of alignment, but a dimple has formed in her good cheek. She was lovely once.

"Hello, Miss Paradise. I'm Dr. Barrons. It's good to meet you."

"Yes," she says calmly. "I know who you are. You're down from the jail on Chartres, right?" Only she pronounces Chartres as Chawtiss. Her accent is pure southeast Louisiana.

"That's right," he says.

She nods. "Pleasure to meet you too, and you can call me Janie." Her hands, which lie flat, wrists cuffed snugly to the table surface, are too restrained for a handshake. Touching between prisoners and civilians is not allowed, anyway. She lifts her palm off the table and flips her hand at him in greeting. He's seen the gesture a thousand times. Ten thousand.

"And you understand why I'm here?"

"I do. My lawyer explained everything. I'm fully aware of the situation."

Virgil reconsiders. Her accent is there, but her words are pronounced fully. She's educated. Or well-read anyway.

"Ok, great. I'll need to do a brief review anyway, for the record. I'm sorry if you've heard it all before. That ok?" She nods and smiles. There is no sarcasm, no hostility in her expression. "I'm a psychiatrist in the state. Technically, I work for the governor, so this is not like a regular doctor-patient relationship. What you tell me can and probably will go into this record," He taps the chart lying on the table before him. "And later will be submitted to the court. It's not confidential. Do you understand that?"

"I do," she breathes. "That's all right."

"Ok, good. You also need to understand that I'm here for a specific purpose. I need to evaluate your competence."

"Yes, competence," she says—a slight smile.

Virgil clears his throat. He feels a twisting sickness in his gut. He's administered this procedure exactly once before. Somewhat ominously named a "last competency evaluation," he thinks it's bullshit. A matter of the state covering its ass. He wishes he were anywhere else, doing anything else right now.

"Specifically, your competence for execution." The law requires him to use those specific words. They feel like bullets from his mouth.

At this, her smile fades momentarily, but then she nods. "Yes, I know."

"To accomplish this, we will meet several times. I'll interview you as well as administer some paper and pencil tests. I will also interview other people who may have known you in the past or observed you here in prison. Finally, I'll look at all your records. Medical, psychiatric, legal, and anything else I think might be relevant. Then I'll prepare a report for the judge."

He explains the competency details, and she seems to listen, but he wonders. Does she really care? What difference does it make? Much of what Virgil says is scripted by law, and the outcome is already known. She asks no questions, nor does she interrupt Virgil as he talks. She seems mildly distracted. Her eyes dart around the room. She's looking for something. Finally, he finishes and asks, "Does all that make sense to you, Janie?"

She focuses her eyes on his. "So, after you do all that, you'll let them know they can kill me?" Inwardly, Virgil winces. There is no malice in her tone. She sounds almost sympathetic.

"Not exactly," he says. "I simply give the results to the court. The judge is the one who formally determines your competence to go forward." This legal technicality is a cop-out, Virgil thinks. The judge will make the final determination based solely on Virgil's evaluation. It's down to him—no escaping it.

"And then they'll kill me?"

He inhales deeply, and forces himself to look her directly in the eye. "If you are declared competent, then yes. They will carry the sentence out."

"The sentence which says they have to kill me?"

She's going to make him say it. Virgil curses himself for being such a fucking coward. "Yes," he says. "You will be executed."

She nods. Satisfied. "Can I refuse?"

"Refuse what?"

"To take part in the thing." She flicks her fingers. "The competence evaluation?"

Virgil sighs. There is a scripted answer for this as well. He's not allowed to deviate. "Yes, you can refuse to take part, but that does not mean I won't need to do my best to complete the evaluation. It will probably not stop things, only slow them down and possibly lead to an inaccurate result. Do you understand?"

"Not exactly," she says. "But it doesn't matter. I'll cooperate. I have no problem with it." There is a peculiar lightness in her tone, almost like cheerful anticipation. Her voice is clear with none of the posturing or resentment Virgil hears so often in the prisons. Her fingers, curled into fists, relax, and she rests her palms on the table. Smiles. "You should know something before we start. Is that ok?"

Virgil flips open a notebook blank for now and picks up his pen. "Yes, of course."

"I did what they say, Dr. Barrons. I won't deny it. I did it, and I was in my right mind. And I'm in my right mind now."

He sets the pen down and looks at her. "Ok," he says. "We'll start there then. But I have to ask. What about all the appeals and the insanity defense?"

"That was the lawyers. I never wanted to do any of that. Not really. I was young. I didn't know my rights back then. But now? Now I do."

Virgil knows well that an inmate may use the admission of guilt or the appearance of eagerness for trial or execution to mislead evaluators.

Underestimating the intelligence and manipulative capability of a convict is always a mistake.

"Miss Paradise," he says slowly. "Can you tell me exactly why you are here? In prison."

She sits back and looks at him. "I'm here because I killed a man. A police officer by the name of Jack Salvas. September 4, 2005. I had a trial, and they convicted me."

"And you understand the consequences?"

"Yes, of course. They aim to kill me, Dr. Barrons. I've made my peace with that."

"And how do they plan to execute you, Miss Paradise?"

"Janie. I think you ought to call me Janie. I've been told they'll inject me with somethin' to make me go to sleep and not wake up."

Inject me with somethin' to make me go to sleep. Virgil's mind flashes to the botched execution he witnessed as a newly minted prison psychiatrist so many years ago. The inmate had requested his presence, and Virgil agreed. The man had no one else. Eugene Carter killed three young women on the border between Mississippi and Louisiana. On some planet, Eugene Carter certainly deserved to die. But the image of his suddenly twitching fingers, his head twisting right, then left, then right again, the whole thing overwhelmed Virgil. That day, Virgil's opinion on the use of capital punishment changed forever. But here you are, he thought—judge, jury, and executioner all in one.

Suddenly Virgil's professional demeanor feels like a lie. He knows he should want nothing more than to get the hell out of this prison, away from this woman, and somehow, get on with his life. But there is a thing so mysteriously wretched about her, he feels drawn in. Beyond the scar. Beyond the imprisonment. Beyond even her impending execution. Looking at her, Virgil feels as if he can see the strength behind her sadness; he can sense all the heartbreak of her life.

"Ok," he says. "Ok, Janie. We'll start there then. In the beginning. Is that alright with you?"

"Sure," she says, smiling slightly. "I've got nothing but time."

CHAPTER 18

Devereaux, Louisiana

1980

Seventeen-year-old Tommy Lee Ashbury was leaning back against the corridor wall, one boot kicked up behind him. Rachel watched, partially hidden behind her locker door, as he leaned down to say something to Mindy Locklee, and she laughed. Mindy was everything Rachel wanted to be. A blonde-haired senior, Mindy had shiny, glass-smooth long hair, platform shoes with soles made of cork, and bellbottom corduroy pants with sparkly labels on the back pocket. She wore a gold necklace that hung halfway to her belly button, and, sometimes, while talking to boys, she'd pluck at it with her painted fingernails or push the charm in and out of her mouth between glossy lips. On top of all that, she was going out with Tommy Lee.

Tommy lifted a hand and grazed Mindy's chin with the tips of his long fingers. Rachel felt a shot go through her, electric and stomach sickening but weirdly pleasant simultaneously. She slammed her locker door. Both Mindy and Tommy Lee looked up, and she felt her face flush. Mindy rolled her eyes, but Tommy's smile moved his eyes and dimpled his cheeks.

God, she loved him. He had black hair and eyes so bright and pale blue they sometimes looked silver. Last school year, he'd been too skinny for his height-all elbows and ears that prompted girls to whisper he looked freakish-but over summer, he'd changed. Suntanned and twenty pounds heavier, girls whispered about him now, but nobody was calling him a freak.

Rachel wandered to her next class in a fog. Algebra. The chalkboard filling with symbols and numbers that she was not copying down. Her mind replaying Tommy's smile. He saw her, she thought. He saw her.

After school, Tommy was propped up against her locker, chewing on a ballpoint pen, waiting. He was bookless (apparently his perpetual state) and glanced up as she approached. Another electric pulse made her fingertips tingle. Her heart banged against her chest. Beyond him, someone had propped the doors to the high school open. It was one of those lightweight, lemony-scented days with brushy little breezes and nothing but sunlight and oak leaves as far as you can see. Rachel tried to focus on the stone steps and the light through the live oaks, dappling the walkway down to the street.

"Hey," he said as she neared him.

"Hey," Rachel replied, making a show of setting down her backpack and carefully twisting the knob of her locker. His nearness made concentrating hard, and she missed the combination twice. He smelled like cut grass, fresh tobacco, and something minty—breath spray.

"So, there's a party over at Mindy's. I'm gonna be there. You wanna come?"

"Uh," said Rachel stupidly.

"Tomorrow night. Her parents are gone."

"I'm, I'm," she was struggling. What to say? I'm too young for parties? I have to take care of my little sister. The idea of going to a party makes me want to throw up. She said, "Yeah. Ok."

"Yeah?" he said and stood straight away from the wall. "Great, you have a ride?"

"Yeah. Sure. But I don't know where Mindy lives."

He took her hand in his, pulled the chewy pen from where he'd stashed it behind his ear, and wrote the address in her palm. "There you go," he said. That smile again. Two boys were arguing, threatening to fight down the hall, and a teacher tried to break them up. Rachel ignored the cacophony.

"Ok. What time?"

He smiled. Shrugged. "Whenever you want. I'll probably show up at about ten."

She stood staring as he turned and left. Then she lay the marked palm against her cheek, then her mouth, imagining his lips burning there.

• • •

Rachel never made it to the party. She'd known she wouldn't. Ray and Pink went out. She had the kids. Instead, on her bed, her body was coated in sweat. The low ceilings and windows painted shut long ago made ventilation impossible. On sultry nights, she and Talia's little cubby bedroom sweltered.

Rachel leaned into the tiny plastic fan she'd stolen from the art room at school. Closed her eyes, tried, for the hundredth time, to think of a way to get to the party. But there was no way like so much of her life. One thing leads quickly to the next with no choices in between. Like a leaf caught in a river current, going nowhere. Going anywhere.

She lay back in her bed and slid her hands down the sides of her slim boyish body, wondering what a boy like Tommy Lee saw when he looked at her. She hoped he didn't know the truth.

Monday morning at school, he was waiting for her again. Dressed in the same faded jeans, he wore a new crisp blue T-shirt.

"Hey, you weren't there," he said, mock hurt on his face. He smelled pleasantly clean and spicy. Cologne or aftershave.

"I had to-" What? she thought. Babysit for my sister and this crazy little kid so my daddy and his trashy girlfriend could get drunk?

He leaned into her, one hand above her head on the lockers. The way he threw his arm up, lifted the hem of his T-shirt, and she could see the hard line of his stomach muscles and a narrow line of black hair just above his belt. They stood like that, saying nothing for a minute.

The bell rang a five-minute warning.

"Hey," he said coolly. "Don't worry about it. There'll be other parties, right?" He leaned closer, his face inches from hers, and whispered, "I'm gonna drive you home today." Then he straightened and smiled down at her. Just lips, no teeth showing. Turned, and he was gone.

He hadn't touched her. Not except the hand upon which he'd written the party address, which she'd been careful not to wash. And yet, she felt him. His body was against hers. His hands in her hair, his lips.

Tommy Lee drove a pickup truck. Not like the old shit-kicker, Ray tried to keep alive. Tommy's was smaller, midnight blue, with wheels raised crazy high, and a bumper sticker that said Fly Navy. Dried mud was spattered up the wheel wells and onto the rims. Now the Dairy Queen closes early. Had been ever since Chris Beaumont's first cousin from Jackson showed up and shot the place out looking for his girlfriend. Now, the boys from Charles Devereaux High School spent a lot of weekend nights drinking beer and turning three-sixties in the swampy expanses out east of town.

As Rachel approached the passenger side, he leaned across the cab of his truck, pushing empty drive-thru bags and cigarette packs off the front seat. He hopped out and came around to help her in. Even with the step, Rachel could barely reach. His hands were around her waist, lifting, white-hot.

"Alright," said Tommy, eyeing her from the driver's seat. "You wanna go for a drive?"

She nodded. She'd pay for this with Pink, coming home late, but she didn't care. He turned the ignition and switched on the radio. George Jones is crooning. *See that girl over there by the jukebox...*

"Oh man, I love this song," Tommy said, turning it up.

Well, you ask me if I know that she's lonesome...

"Me too," said Rachel, honestly. Mama loved the country songs about women who were wronged or women missed. It was strange to think about now, the way Mama loved to hear music about the bad things.

"Yeah?" Tommy looked at her. "What else do you love?"

And like that, she was telling him. About George Jones and Conway Twitty and Hank Williams. How, when she and Talia were small, they'd play Mama's Loretta Lynn records, dancing and singing like they were famous country singers.

Tommy's father managed the Circle K on Main Street. He gave them Cokes from the back without paying. He was a big, shuffling, balding man, and Rachel thought he always looked sad enough to cry. She wanted to get away as soon as they arrived.

They sat out back of the grocery, listening to the radio and watching the sky grow dusky purple over the telephone wires that crisscrossed the busted tar of the parking lot. They drank all six cokes and told each other different things. Stupid things. Secret things. She told him about Mama. He told her about his older brother, Cody, who died in Vietnam when Tommy was only nine-blown up by a landmine, so they had little of his body left to bury- and how his parents won't talk about it and how that's how come his Daddy looks sad all the time.

"There are pictures of him all over the house, like even in the bathroom, but nobody says nothing, ever. It's like livin' with a ghost."

She told him about Pink and the roller derby, and he laughed and said he'd never been to the derby, and they should go sometime. They talked about music, and he said they should make it to the city for a concert sometime. He told her how he'd planned to join the Navy, but his Mama cried when he told her. So, he started thinking about owning a store instead. A real store, not like where his daddy works. Selling auto parts maybe, with a place out back where guys could visit and talk about cars and whatnot. Maybe, he said, he'd sell drinks and food. She asked him if he wanted to own a store or a restaurant, and he laughed and said, or how about both?

After a long time, he slid closer to her. There was a split in the seat cushion's plastic material, a strip of silver duct tape holding together the edges. As he slid over, it unfurled, exposing yellow foam underneath. He stuck it back down with his thumb. He asked if he could kiss her, and she said ok. She'd known for a long time she wanted Tommy Lee to kiss her. She knew she wanted him in lots of ways, but, as he rested his palm warm and dry on the back of her neck, she stopped, knowing anything at all.

• • •

In the spring, they went up by the river, sat on the levee, watched the water, and talked. Sometimes they took Talia when Daddy Ray allowed them, and Rachel brought bologna sandwiches wrapped in brown paper, and Tommy got Cokes from his Daddy's store, and they had picnics.

Tommy Lee was great with Tee, and Tee adored him. He amazed her with his knowledge of the Waterbirds, fish and other creatures of the rivers and swamps. To Talia, Tommy was almost as impressive as Nona regarding the water.

"Daddy Ray calls me a little goldfish on account of how much I love the water," she told Tommy proudly.

"No, he calls you a goldfish on account of all the goldfish you have." Rachel smiled at her and rubbed the top of Tee's head.

Tee wriggled away. "Nope, it's cause I'm like a fish."

It was true. Talia was a water creature. She loved everything about the bayou. Rachel wasn't sure, but she thought there might be a dozen goldfish in fresh bowls in their room now. And Daddy Ray had given her that silly nickname. Tee loved it.

The three of them lay back on the bank of the levee and watched as the Snowy egrets and Louisiana pelicans sailed and spun overhead. Long beaks like silver arrows across the bright blue sky. They stayed quiet, waiting for the bird calls, especially the Osprey, which Rachel didn't have to explain to Tommy. Talia loved most of all.

When it rained, Rachel and Tommy went alone to the vast, empty lot behind the old Woolworths. Abandoned now for years, the building had been occupied at various times by retail outlets and crap furniture stores, none big enough to make a go of it. None of them were stuffed to the ceiling with the cheap junk that had made Woolworths famous. They would lie across the bench seat, Rachel nestled into Tommy's shoulder, and listen to the water on the truck's roof, watch it beat against the windshield. Tommy kissed her. His lips were warm and soft on her cheeks and eyelids and lips. Pulling her small body over onto his, pushing a hand under her T-shirt to touch her skin. They hadn't made love yet, although Rachel wanted to. Tommy said they had to wait. The minutes turned quickly to hours as they kissed, touched, and talked and nurtured their adolescent love while dreaming of a future that would never be.

CHAPTER 19

New Orleans, Uptown

July 22, 2020

The meeting with Cat Landry leaves Rachel feeling breathless and disoriented. Perhaps she's made a big deal out of nothing. Cat must be right. Camilla is crazy, or at the very least, lonely and exaggerating. Daniel is a good man. An honest man. *He's your husband; he loves you. He'd have told you if... if what? Goddamnit, if what?* Besides, Rachel should cut back on the pills, get more sleep, and see her therapist more often. According to her therapist, she avoids grief by "over-functioning" and "self-medicating" her anxiety.

It takes Rachel less than a minute at home to locate the extra study key. She keeps it along with the other duplicates in a velvet pouch at the bottom of her jewelry box. She's had it since Daniel installed all the interior locks years ago. He was forever losing keys, jackets, wallets, gloves and scarves. She's never needed to use the duplicates. He never barred the study door. She slides the ring back into the box and takes the key downstairs.

Rachel unlocks the study door, removes the key, slides it back into her pocket, and steps inside. Daniel's home office is a large room, book-lined and well-appointed in a modern, slightly stern style. His oversized desk, which is piled high with papers and files, centered the space. Daniel is not paper neat. Sitting down behind the desk, Rachel feels, for a moment, incredibly foolish. She takes a deep breath and exhales slowly, clearing her mind of the self-doubt, and then, she begins.

She's spends a long time pushing through the pile of papers, looking for nothing in particular, finding only bank statements, investment reports and a few pieces of banal business correspondence. Finally, she sits back, staring at the computer. She doesn't want to do this. It's a violation. They don't do this to each other. They never have. They are not *that kind of couple*. Spying. Reading one another's email. Going through each other's pockets. She doesn't check his receipts or follow up on his travel plans. She trusts him. She loves. Him, for fucks sake. Sitting here in his office, fingering his papers is terrible enough. She feels dirty, like a liar. She stands up. That's it, she thinks. This is over. She'll tell him. Tell him she was here. That she's worried. Tell him about Camilla and the bizarre meeting. They'll talk. Sort it out.

Rachel is halfway to the door, relief flooding her body. She can feel the half-smile on her face. She loves her husband. He loves her. Everything is ok. Her hand is in her pocket to get the key when it hits her. He bolted the door for the first time. He locked the door. And there's something else. Her key. When she went to find it, it was gone. She keeps her interior house keys on the iron hooks by the back door. Stupid for sure, but that's where she keeps them. They were all there, except for the office key. When was the last time she'd checked it? Never probably. Despite that, she's sure it was there. But not today. "Ah, shit," she says out loud.

She sits at his computer, hits the spacebar, and isn't shocked to find the desktop secured by password. She enters Alex's birthday, followed by an asterisk and her daughter's age. The password Daniel always uses. It opens. He must have assumed she wouldn't get beyond the locked study door. Daniel is an idea man. Fiercely intelligent and full of plans and dreams and inventions but lacking in certain practical skills. Relying on secretaries, assistants, his wife to keep things like passwords in order.

Rachel scans his web search history, opens a few desktop folders, and pokes around in his applications. Nothing remarkable. Not even porn. She sits back in his chair, feeling even more foolish but happily so. Thank God. She does not know what she's looking for. Evidence of his guilt? Over what? What is it exactly she thinks he might have done?

He could have secured the door for many reasons. Maybe Daniel bought her something, and he doesn't want Rachel to discover the gift. That would be unlike him, but it might happen. Or he's worried about the housekeeper or Alex's friends or...

She glances out the window beyond his desk. Two crape myrtles laced with delicate pink flowers frame the view across the smooth lawn and out toward the rectangular swimming pool Daniel had insisted he needed and now never has time to use. It's more often populated by ducks than people. The storm is clearing, and the pool is lovely, the expanse of water glistening in the newly hatched sunlight. Rachel feels a deep stab of guilt. Her life is good. Or at least as good as it can be given the accident. And it's all because of Daniel. He saved her. He gave her freedom, independence, money and so much love. He gave her their children. Alex. And Jeb, precious Jeb, for all the years they got to have him. But then, after Jeb died, hadn't it been Daniel who'd blamed her? Not in so many words. But it was there, in his eyes. At the hospital. All those days. At the funeral. And what had he said, her husband, her life partner? She'd coddled him. Been soft when the "problem" came up.

Rachel had not understood the accusation. Jeb was the easy one. He'd been the perfect child; he'd needed nothing. He'd been a brilliant student, a star athlete. Popular, everyone loved Jeb. Their daughter, Alex, took so much of Rachel's time and attention. Alex was the wild one, full of dreamy, clueless rebellion; she seemed perpetually at risk of dancing right off a cliff. Only she wasn't. Alex was kind, generous, deliberate, intelligent, and passionate as a young woman, focused now on her art, career, relationships and future. But Jeb, for him, it was over. So, Daniel's words that had made no sense at first, later, in the gray silence of Jeb's room, Rachel had understood. She hadn't seen it. She hadn't wanted to see.

Rachel's finger hovers above the keyboard and is about to log out when a notification appears in the screen's corner. New email. She hesitates, then hits the mail icon, her heart thudding as the page opens.

As she clicks the latest message, she feels the pulse in her neck. In her stomach.

In disbelief, she reads, then stares at the monitor as if the words might morph into something she can explain. She scans it again to make sure she's not misunderstood. No, she thinks, it's clear. She's frozen for a long time, uncertain what to do. Then, suddenly, she does.

CHAPTER 20

Devereaux, Louisiana

1981

By early spring, LooLoo had resurfaced. Sporting several new tattoos, one additional facial scar, and three fewer teeth, he claimed he was now disabled and permanently unemployed. He was back at the house and spending most of every day sprawled on the sofa. Rachel stayed away as much as possible and kept her sister away from him as well. But he'd started popping up when least expected. If Rachel passed too closely, he'd swat her on the behind, making comments like, "Sweet ass you got there kiddo," or "Breakin' any hearts yet? Yeah, you are."

By late summer, staying away from Loo was becoming more problematic. He'd taken to touching her when he thought no one was looking. A palm across her breast as they passed each other in the narrow hall, a grind from his hips behind her as she stood at the sink. Even when he wasn't touching or speaking, his presence was becoming unbearable. His breath and body were foul, emitting a smell far worse than the stale beer and cigarettes Rachel had become accustomed to. LooLoo's scent was unfamiliar. It was decay. At twenty-three, he smelled of death; he looked awful. Rachel sometimes wondered if he was really sick because he'd lost so much weight.

In retrospect, she would wonder if maybe that was why she told no one what LooLoo was doing to her. Perhaps she felt sorry for LooLoo, being sick and all. But she knew that wasn't it. Pink would never have allowed it. Pink, who hated just about everyone, probably even her own kids, loved her baby brother. She protected LooLoo, fought for him. No way would she believe anything, Rachel said. Worse, there was no way she'd allow Rachel to keep on saying it. Once she had an idea that Rachel might tell someone else, like Daddy Ray, Pink would be sure to send her away. Far from here. Far from Talia. So, no, Rachel couldn't say a word. Besides, Rachel reasoned, it wasn't that bad. LooLoo was like. Randy Galey is in fourth grade. Weak, stupid, slow. She could handle him.

Neither did Rachel tell Tommy Lee what was going on? He'd seek vengeance. He'd want to kill LooLoo. The thought of Tommy Lee coming after LooLoo made Rachel shudder. Pink had too many people in this town-cousins, uncles, friends-and they were all mean. All loyal to Pink's family. Rachel couldn't risk what they would do to Tommy Lee. So, she gritted her teeth and promised herself she'd hang on until LooLoo moved out. Finally, at the end of August, his disability checks came in, and LooLoo got his own place. For three glorious weeks, he didn't come around at all.

• • •

It was a scorching afternoon in September. Granny Nona had Talia overnight, and everyone else was out. Rachel was enjoying the alone time. She sat cross-legged on a rag rug in the front room, dressed in summer cutoffs and a bathing suit top. She held Pink's big sewing shears in her right hand and was using her left to flip pages of a Seventeen Magazine she'd lifted from the Walgreens. She was getting good at shoplifting. She could steal almost anything she wanted without getting caught. The priciest thing she'd ever taken was a gift for Tommy. A metal lighter with the American flag painted on the front. Tommy wouldn't use it. Only kept it in a wooden box in his room since it was so special. Rachel thought that was stupid, but she said nothing.

She snipped around the edges of a photo: a girl wearing a pale purple Gunne Sax prom dress with ivory lace trim. She was careful to remove the head in a quick slice. Rachel laid the clipping on the pile. She guessed there must be a hundred clippings so far. She'd have to cull the herd since her walls were already nearly covered with photos—

mostly headless models wearing gorgeous clothes. Talia hated the headlessness-said it made them look scary-but Rachel wanted the clothes to look like they were floating, without being possessed by anyone girl. It was all fantasy, of course. For one, Rachel wasn't going to a prom any time soon. For another, she wouldn't be buying any such dress. It didn't matter. She loved to dream.

The front door was ajar, and the cat squeezed through, padded over, and circled her a few times before finally settling into a sunny spot close to Rachel's elbow. Talia had named him Lucky, and really, he was her cat. He'd shown up on the back step around the time Rachel started seeing Tommy Lee. Lucky had been skinny as a jackrabbit. Fur so dirty, he looked gray rather than white and too timid to come near a human being. It was Talia who persisted in leaving milk and scraps on the step. Slowly, over a few weeks, he warmed to the girls, letting himself be petted, finally even kissed by Talia. He was still pretty skinny, but his fur was clean now, his eyes bright. He wasn't afraid.

Rachel reached out a hand to stroke Lucky's back. The feel of silky cat hair beneath her fingers and the warmth of the sun on her face felt good. She flopped to her back, rolled onto her side, and scratched him under the chin with one finger. Lucky purred contentedly and fell asleep.

A few minutes later, the back door creaked open. Lucky jerked awake, ears perked. Rachel sat up, a kernel of fear in her gut. She wasn't expecting anyone home this early. Pink and Ray were up in Slidell, collecting Matt and Nadine from their Dad's house. Weren't they? And Loo? Where was he?

She got up and stood still, her bare toes pushing into the bristly carpet. Listening. She heard nothing but a few kids next door playing in the sprinklers. A dog barking. She wondered if she could get their attention if she needed help.

"Hello?" she called. "Hello?" No answer. Her heart pulsed and quickened. She could smell her own sweat. Stepping out into the hallway, she stopped before moving toward the kitchen. A thickening in her throat made it difficult to breathe.

All at once, he was there. Looming ahead of her. The glare of sunlight coming from the back of the house cast him in a shadowy, swaying silhouette. LooLoo was Drunk. He looked massive, his skinny frame gone monstrous. Terror iced her insides. Her mouth was instantly dry as paper and her hands shook. Her brain screamed.

Run!

The word inside her head. Run. Run. Run! Her mind was screaming at her. But her legs were frozen. Her mouth. Her voice. Her entire body had become compacted, compressed. Turned to lead. Turned to stone. She was being sucked down into the crust of the earth by gravity. Down. Down. Down. Soon it would crush her. Burned by the core.

Then, he was on her.

His hand, stinking of grease and cigarettes and whiskey, across her mouth.

"Listen," he hissed. His soggy lips pressed against her ear. "You little prick tease. You keep fuggin quiet, or I'll hurt you. Hear me? You... keep... fuggin... quiet." He said the last part slowly as if he had to concentrate on getting the words out. His breath was hot and beery. She nodded. He loosened his grip on her mouth and, somehow, a sound, more like a bray than a scream, escaped the granite block that was her body. His fingers tightened, and then he slapped the back of her head with his free hand. Pain shot through her skull, making her eyes water.

"I fuckin told you. Shut up." This time his words were more precise. He did not loosen his grip. He shoved her against the wall and pushed his body weight against her back. She couldn't breathe. He yanked down her shorts, and she felt him drop his own pants. Suddenly he was hard and hot against her buttocks, and she was squirming to get away. He grabbed her hair and slammed her face into the wall. White pain shot up through her nose, into her head, and she wondered if he'd cracked her skull. Then blood, sticky, and warm, and coppery smelling, was coursing down her face, pooling on the floor.

He was leaning his full weight against her. Even at his diminished size, LooLoo was an adult man, and he outweighed Rachel by a considerable amount. Her left cheek was jammed up hard against the plaster surface of the wall, and her face pulsed wretchedly with the pain. Think, she told herself. Think.

LooLoo's drunkenness was slowing him down. He was having trouble with his balance. "Motherfugger," he whined and pulled her hair again with the free hand to steady himself. She winced but made no sound. She was running out of time.

Glancing down, she saw them. Pink's scissors still gripped in her right hand, the four-inch blades pointed directly behind her, now aimed at LooLoo's thigh. There was one shot. If she missed, he'd kill her. Rachel sucked in air through her broken mouth, gripped the implement harder, and jammed it backward with all her strength.

She felt it sink to its hilt into flesh and gristly tissue.

LooLoo made a sound, unlike anything Rachel had ever heard, then fell away from her. She turned to see him, pants around his ankles, sinking backward, descending. The shears were buried deep in his thigh, just inches to the right of his groin. Blood appeared to be coming from everywhere. Or rather, it was going everywhere. Down his leg, up over his abdomen, across the floor beneath him. Both his hands and arms were bright red as he grasped the wound. He continued to shriek and sob, clutching his leg, at the scissors, in the air. But then, he seemed to be rapidly losing touch with the world. Collapsing inward. Losing consciousness. It occurred to Rachel that he might die. He probably would die.

Suddenly, terrified all over again, Rachel carefully adjusted her filthy clothing, snatched up her sandals from the living room, pushed open the front door, and ran.

• • •

Six hours later, she and Tommy Lee rolled out of Devereaux, Rachel dressed in a T-shirt and sweats he'd taken from his mother's closet, their paltry possessions squeezed onto the seat between them. There'd been no choice; Tommy explained it to her. If LooLoo was dead, which he almost certainly was, given where she'd stabbed him-arteries, and all-they'd lock her up for murder, and it didn't matter if he'd attacked her. Not down here. Not with all the connections Pink's family had with the Sheriff. And if he wasn't dead, which for sure he was anyway, he'd kill her. And there wasn't time to explain it to Tee. Not now. She'd have to come back when it was safe. Tommy Lee promised they'd go back for Tee. They'd all be together. He promised, and Rachel knew it was true.

Rachel turned and watched through the rear window, whimpering as the two-lane blacktop unspooled into the darkness like ribbon.

CHAPTER 21

New Orleans, The Lower Ninth Ward

July 22, 2020

Rachel finds the house quickly. 1161 Charbonnet in the Lower Ninth. The address is written on the scrap of paper she'd received from Camilla. *Please, Rachel, please see for yourself. Go to the house.* That's what Camilla had said. The address isn't far from Good Hope.

Good Hope, she thinks. A hard pit in her stomach reminds her she should have done this yesterday. Instead, she'd run from the situation. Seen the horror at the nursing facility and run. It's no longer an option. Blind trust, denial, stupid laziness, or whatever she's been doing.

She turns down Josephine Street and is pleased to see a few brightly painted, newly constructed homes on a handful of treeless lots. They are small, boxy houses, put up quickly and cheaply, but a few are already inhabited by families—a hopeful sign. Two young children play with a makeshift wagon in one of the front yards: The little boy screaming happily, wiggling chubby arms in the air while the girl-his sister maybe-hauls the thing behind her over a patchy lawn. Their laughter was the only sound beyond the low rumble of Rachel's engine.

At the end of Josephine, she makes a right and then a left onto Charbonnet, cruising slowly, checking for the address. She pulls to a stop, shuts down the engine, and sits for a long time in the stillness.

Pushing open the car door, she steps out into the road. A mess of mud ditches and weeds and patches of old asphalt. She shields her eyes from the glare with her palm and studies the surroundings. Immediately to her right stands a mailbox, or the brick remains of one:

a tomb, waist-high, a black hole where the box itself washed away years ago. And behind the tomb, nothing. No house. No foundation. Only tall grass. A few scattered beer cans. Vines are grown so tall they engulf the trees—a littered jungle. There is a piece of thick, mud-covered black tarp unfurling into the street from beneath a thicket of bamboo, its purpose a mystery now. A torn blue work shirt. A plastic Winn Dixie bag. Cigarette butts. A doll's head.

Up and down Charbonnet Street, Rachel sees vacant lots with a handful of rusted large appliances-washing machines, refrigerators-turned sideways or upside down, a few small, dead trees, leaning at bizarre angles, branches twisted and snapped, a few concrete steps leading nowhere, and just two lots with structures left standing. Over everything, the sky arches a deep azure blue, so absolute, so clear Rachel can imagine seeing straight through it and beyond. The air is redolent with the sweet odor of growing things, of life. The grasses, clematis and honeysuckle run more thickly when not competing for space with urban construction. The earthy scent of wet grasses and swamp flowers. She knows the smell. This is life pushing its way back on its own.

The house on Charbonnet is a clapboard shack with windows either gaping and glassless or sloppily covered in plywood. The roof, missing most of its shingles, is patched with layers of black tarpaulin that look as if they've torn loose and been nailed down again many times. The paint, where it remains, is badly peeling and splotched with mold. High weeds encroach on all sides. Ivy has gotten ahold from the inside and emerges in long deep green tendrils from the plywood and window molding cracks. Someone has attached chicken wire to one side of the shack and spray painted the words DO NOT TEAR DOWN to one of plywood sheets. The front steps are all gone, but one bent and rusted railing remains. There is no door, only a broken door jamb, and rusted hinges. The house, Rachel thinks, is a long-dead thing. Like roadkill a hundred cars had run over. She suspects the words they wrote DO NOT TEAR DOWN years ago by someone still harboring a hope that no longer exists.

She spends only a few minutes inside the destroyed house. It is impossible to stay longer, given the air is so thick with mildew and the smell of mold and decay. But right away, Rachel knows.

This is a place Rachel has visited a thousand times, a million times before, in her heart. With its wrecked walls and rotting floors; its blown out attic steps and ruin of a kitchen; its books strewn across the rooms, bloated and waterlogged books about birds mostly, Rachel knows this place well. And everywhere, absolutely everywhere, delicately sketched but badly faded within the peeling and ruined paint on the walls, dozens upon dozens of tiny yellow goldfish.

This is Talia's house.

Stepping back outside, Rachel climbs cautiously down the splintered steps and returns to the street. She stands for a long time in the silence of the broken road. She is listening. Finally, she hears it. In the distance, the faint kee-uk-kee-uk-kee-uk whistling call of the powerful Osprey in flight.

CHAPTER 22

Devereaux, Louisiana

1981

Talia sat cross-legged in the weedy front yard of the little house on Blanchard Drive in Devereaux. Their fourth rental house since moving in with Daddy Ray and, so far, the worst. In the others, Rachel and Talia had their room or, like the first one, their own cubbyhole. But in the Blanchard house, they slept on the sofa, foot to foot, and Rachel was getting so big that Talia had to curl up tiny so both could fit. When Matt and Nadine visited, all four kids shared the living room, and Nadine always took the whole sofa, forcing the younger kids to sleep on the floor. But Matt and Nadine had visited little lately, and if they did, it was usually only Matt. He was quieter now, staying to himself, writing stuff in an army green spiral notebook he stole from the Shop-N-Save.

The size of the house wasn't the biggest problem. The Blanchard house also stank. Old, pet-stained, hi-low carpet covered most of the floors and the walls and windows were filthy. On days like today, the wet heat thick enough to cut with a knife, Talia thought the house smelled like moldy bread. She didn't mind as much waiting outside for Rachel to get home.

Pink had given only one house key to both of them and told Rachel to carry it. She didn't trust Talia, who was only nine. That meant on afternoons when the house was empty-most days-Talia had to wait outside for Rachel. The high school got out an hour later than Talia's elementary school and was an additional twenty-minute walk to the house. On icy days or when it rained, the wait could be excruciating.

Today, even with no watch, Talia was sure Rachel was late.

Talia shifted around on the patch of dirt she'd found. Her uniform skirt did little to protect her upper thighs and bottom, and her underpants were soaked through from where she'd inadvertently sat down in soggy grass. Talia had moved to drier ground, but now the prickly weeds hurt where they poked like little knives into her thighs. She wished she had a sweater to sit on. She stood up. Looked around the yard. Spotted a colossal palmetto plant and made her way towards it. With some effort, she pulled off one of the more massive fronds and dragged it out to the dry spot and sat down, legs splayed out before her. The soft, waxy surface of the palmetto leaf was soothing to the skin of her upper thighs, and she felt pleased with herself for solving the problem.

She picked up a dry stick and pulled it through the dirt, writing TALIA in giant blocky print. Then she rubbed it out and wrote D-A-M just to see. It looked stupid, and she banged at it with her fist. Until the letters disappeared. Matt wrote terrible words all the time. On his walls, his books. Once, he used a permanent marker to write F-U-C-K-Y-O-U across the outside of his door. Pink called him a "little shitty motherfucker" when he did that. Talia looked around. Making sure nobody was watching and then wrote F-U-C but stopped before finishing. Embarrassed. She stood up and stomped on the letters.

After a while, she wandered over to the spot under the eaves where Daddy Ray kept the hose looped around the faucet. She tried to turn the spigot, but it was stuck. Plopping herself down in the mud, Talia stuck her feet up against the house for leverage, and, using both hands and all her strength, she forced it free. Hot water shot out in all directions when it gave, and she was immediately soaked. She rolled away, screaming.

The water although sun-warmed, was not hot enough to do her significant damage. She let it run a while before taking a drink. It wasn't cold but even rubbery and lukewarm; it tasted delicious. She drank a long time, then squirted her arms and legs, paying particular attention to the many mosquito bites she'd acquired. The water washed away the itch and soreness, mud and sweat.

Then, she gathered more palmetto leaves and made them into a sort of pallet under the big live oak that straddled the property line between their house and the neighbor. Two of the tree's roots had broken through the earth and ran in parallel, each big around as Daddy Ray's whole body. She placed the fronds carefully cradled between them, then removed her school shoes, now wet from the hose, and put them under her head for a pillow. She laid down and tucked her small, damp body onto the pallet.

Her stomach rumbled, reminding her she hadn't eaten since lunch. She looked forward to the snacks Rachel always brought home. Desserts she'd saved for Talia from her high school lunches. Jell-O or packed cookies or pudding cups. Once, a whole Christmas cupcake with a red jellybean on top. It was too much for one girl to eat, Rachel always said. Talia could not wait to go to high school. She'd never seen too much food.

Another hour passed. She watched the sun through the trees to guess the time. And still, no Rachel. Maybe, thought Talia, she was busy kissing her boyfriend, Tommy Lee. Sometimes they kissed for a long time. Talia had seen them do that. Tongues in mouths. Eyes closed. Bodies smashed together. Gross.

Talia decided not to worry. Rachel would come soon and probably bring a pudding. Vanilla cream most likely and she'd tell Talia all about kissing Tommy and about high school, and then they'd do Talia's homework, and then... she yawned. She was really very tired.

She lifted her small hand to her face. Three of her fingernails were partially colored with pink ballpoint ink. She'd drawn a smiley face on the back of her arm, but it had become smeared by sweat and hose water and now looked all wiggly. It made her smile. Settling back, she let her arms go limp at her sides, and imagined she was a fairy princess, tucked secretly away deep inside the forest. She looked up through a billion leaves of the live oak and stared contentedly into the endless, brilliant whiteness of a Louisiana sky.

CHAPTER 23

New Orleans

1982

Tommy Lee hadn't lasted six months in the city. Sweet as he was, it turned out he didn't have the constitution for the life. Rachel had been lucky to land the waitressing job at Napoleon Grill. One of the other waitresses at the Grill, an older woman named Ruth let them rent the ancient trailer in her yard for cheap. They chopped back the purple top and cordgrass that had grown up around it blocking the entrance. They'd then worked together, scrubbing the surfaces and pulling out moldy linens and bits of trash. Rachel used bleach to kill the ants and wipe out the spots where roaches had nested. Ruth gave them a few dishes and a set of real sheets from the Goodwill; pale yellow with tiny blue irises.

The camper was small, barely big enough for a mattress, a fold-out table, and their meager belongings. The "kitchen" composed of a gas stove and rusty basin sink. Ruth gave them the use of her one bathroom and the extra fridge she kept under her carport. Twice weekly, they trudged inside to shower, carrying a white plastic basin, which held a sliver of soap, a miniature bottle of dime-store shampoo, and a change of clothes. It was ok for a while. At night they lay on the narrow mattress, staring up at the roof of the trailer and talking about their future. Tommy Lee often spoke about his auto parts store/diner, going into great detail late into the night.

For Rachel, it was all about Talia. She talked of little else. When they would have enough money, enough space for her sister, she missed Tee so much it caused her physical pain. In her gut and her chest.

Sometimes at night, she woke up from dreams about her sister having cried so hard, her head felt as if it was splitting in two. Sometimes, she wanted to give up. She wanted to go back to Devereaux turn herself in. Just so she could see Talia. Talk to her. And sometimes, Tommy Lee wanted to go back too. He was tired of life. It seemed only to get harder the longer they stayed. But Rachel couldn't go. What she'd done to LooLoo? It was a terrible crime. They could send her away. Put her in jail. Maybe forever. And then what? She'd never be able to take care of Talia. No, she told Tommy Lee, it was better to wait. Better to wait, plan, and then get Tee when things are ready. That's the way they had to do it.

They used the back porch when it was too hot to sleep inside. They'd strip off most of their clothes and lay together, skin touching moist skin, on quilts piled up to soften the hard floor. The only sounds were the chirping katydids, an occasional bullfrog and their hands slapping at the mosquitos tricky enough to find their way through the torn porch screen. Tommy Lee was gentle and patient; over time, Rachel's wounds- those inflicted by LooLoo and those accumulated years before- began to fade and scar.

They tried to make it work, and Rachel loved Tommy Lee for how hard he tried, but in the end, it was too hard for him. He hadn't been raised to tolerate so much discomfort. His parents had money. Or at least compared to Rachel, he wasn't poor. He'd never been hungry or cold, never worried about paying rent or buying shoes. Tommy Lee begged her to go back with him, promised he'd stand by her, no matter what. He cried. He clung to her, but she couldn't. There was no place for her in Devereaux, and for Talia, she had to make a new life. Finally, he left. She promised to write to call. There were a few awkward calls from a payphone, one or two desperate letters. He begged a few more times. Then Rachel heard he'd found a new girl, and that was it. Tommy Lee had broken her heart, but he'd kept his promise and told no one where she'd gone. All her life, Rachel would love him for that.

CHAPTER 24

New Orleans, Canal Street

July 23, 2020

It hadn't taken Rachel long to call the number. As soon as she'd left the house on Charbonnet, *Talia's house,* she'd called him. Dr. Virgil Barrons, the psychiatrist assigned to evaluate Janie Paradise. Rachel had been surprised when Barrons agreed to meet. He couldn't give any confidential information, he'd warned. He said he'd come, listen, and he would do what he could to help her.

The restaurant is busy in the late afternoon. Rachel's stomach is doing flips. She wants a cigarette, and she tries to remember why she quit. She cannot produce a single valid reason. Valid being a relative term. Lung cancer in twenty years versus losing her mind right now, for example. She thinks about the days when you could buy cigarettes from the bartender and get plastic go-cups of alcohol at the airport. For centuries, the city of New Orleans clung zealously to the antiquated idea that its citizens had an inalienable right to smoke and drink anywhere, anytime, all the time. *Those were the days*, she thinks. Jesus. When did she start having super old person thoughts? *What's wrong with kids these days?* And *It's too damn loud in here.* She'll have to do a better job at self-monitoring her brain and cut that stuff out. She read somewhere that thinking like an old person makes you into an old person.

Rachel pulls at her blouse, which suddenly feels snug, and glances around at the other diners. Nearly all of them members of the creamy-skinned under forty club. They're probably all grateful nonsmokers who eat quinoa and kale for breakfast and jog six miles a day. She blows out her breath and shifts uncomfortably in her chair, and fiddles with her sunglasses.

Her mind drifts. She's thinking about Talia. It's been so many years since she'd let her mind go there. Hadn't she tried? No, not hard enough. It was Rachel's responsibility. And what had she done? Made excuses. Repeatedly.

But it hadn't been as easy as Rachel had hoped. At first, it was Daddy Ray. He said she'd broken Tee's heart, and he wouldn't let Rachel do it again. Wouldn't even let her call. He probably threw away all the cards and letters too. So, Rachel had to sneak around. Asking favors, begging for rides, pleading with people to tell her where she could find her sister. Mostly though, Rachel stayed away. For Talia's good, she told herself. But the truth was something else.

Then there was the day at the middle school. Rachel hadn't planned to talk to Talia. Just get a glimpse. Thinking about it in the years after, Rachel knew the disaster had been inevitable.

It was a Tuesday in the fall. One of those spectacularly clear October days makes a body almost forget the fat rain and hot stink of August. Almost. The last bell had already rung, and, except for a handful of a few stragglers, the school was empty. Rachel caught sight of her sister, trudging rather than walking across the playground blacktop. It looked as if each step cost her some bit of blood or soul. Painful to watch. She wore a heavy sweatshirt despite the day, her beautiful hair yanked back and secured with a fat rubber band at the nape of her neck. A small book pack had straps digging into her narrow shoulders. Pale and thin, hands stuffed deep into the pockets of her ill-fitting blue jeans, she stared down toward muddy tennis shoes, which flopped with each step. Rachel found it hard to catch her breath. *How long had it been? Two months? Three at most. But Tee had changed. Maybe it was the weight loss.*

Rachel stepped out from her hiding place behind the administration building and followed Talia into the art room. As Talia entered the room, Rachel presented herself.

Talia dropped her paintbrush and ran for her big sister. She threw paint-smudged hands around Rachel's neck, making them both laugh. The class was empty except for Talia's art teacher, who happily excused herself and allowed them to sit and chat for a bit. Rachel asked about school (*fine, and I only like art and some of the books*) and about Daddy Ray (*he's ok, and he lost his job again*) and Pink (*she's the same and crazy*) and Nadine (*she never comes around no more*) and Matt (*he got himself sent to military school over the summer on account of vandalizing the Ford dealership and lighting Mrs. Tripstin's dog on fire*).

"What about friends? Are you making friends?"

Talia looked away. Her small face in profile, wide pale forehead and enormous eyes, and the dip of sculpted space between nose and upper lip. With her tiny body, she might well have been an exceptionally beautiful small boy.

"I'm ok. Mostly I don't like 'em. They're dumb. The girls, I mean. What they talk about." She looked back at Rachel. Smiled. But it was forced. Suddenly she tensed. "Daddy Ray picks me up in a few minutes. This is just my after school art time. The teacher lets me use the materials." She waves a hand at the easels and paints. "He'll be here..." her voice trailed off, and she glanced toward the door.

"I know," said Rachel. "I need to go as well."

Silence for a long time, then Talia said, "Take me with you. I'm big now. I can help. I can make money." Her eyes were wet and huge, her mouth open, and she was sitting on the very edge of the wooden chair, teetering as if she might topple to the floor at any moment. "Please," she added, her voice almost a whisper.

Oh, God. Rachel felt a knife slice right through the center of her chest. The pain was like fire, and she focused on it rather than look at her sister. Oh, God, no. "I'm so sorry, Tee," said Rachel. "I can't." How to explain. Again. No money. No place to put a child. No legal right to take Talia. They'd been over this. So many times.

Talia backed up in the chair. Her face changing. "Never mind. It's fine. I guess I knew that."

Life was stripping away Talia's carefully manufactured exterior. Hardening her. Rachel would have given up all the remaining days of her life to protect Talia from this pain. Without hesitation, she would give her sister everything. Briefly, Rachel's thoughts flashed to Nina. Those last moments in Devereaux were such a long time ago.

Pointlessly, Rachel tried to explain again. *What about school? Where would they live? No, it wasn't possible. Besides, Ray would never allow it. He'd hunt them down and drag Tee back. Give me time, she pleaded. A little more time.* But it was a speech. Meaningless.

"I know," Talia kept saying. "It's fine, I get it. You don't have to keep saying it, Rachel."

In the distance, a horn honked. Twice. The art teacher rounded the corner and came through the open doorway into the room. "Your Daddy's here, sweetheart," she said, smiling. "I think he's feeling a little impatient out there, so you best get your things together." The woman was young. She looked to Rachel like the sort of idealistic teacher who believed every kid had a real sweet Daddy with a job and a hug waiting out in the parking lot to pick them up.

"Yes, ma'am," said Talia.

Rachel stood and thanked the young woman and then forced a hug on Talia, wrapping her arms around the tiny child's stiff, unresponsive body. "Tee, I swear to God, I'll come back for you. Just a little longer. I love you so much. I love you."

Talia said nothing. Just grabbed her backpack, shoving her sweatshirt into the opening and zipping it tight. Then she stood looking straight through Rachel as if she couldn't see her at all.

CHAPTER 25

New Orleans, Canal Street

July 23, 2020

A sharp round of laughter startles Rachel from her reverie. She checks her watch. It's just past four. It feels as if she's been here for hours. Suddenly, she's exhausted, the sort of bone-melting tiredness that makes a person think about lying down in the middle of a restaurant, curling up right under a table, and having a short nap. God, she doesn't want to do this, she thinks. Whatever she was certain of yesterday feels like messages written in the steam on a mirror today; it's all gone now. That's it, she'll go home, take a Xanax, take a nap. Take a goddamn time out. She pulls her wallet from her purse, and removes a twenty, lays it on the table. It will more than cover the one café au lait she's ordered. She'll text the doctor, let him know... what? That she's had an emergency? Had a seizure? That she's out of her mind? She's pushing her chair back, getting up.

"Mrs. Thibodaux?" The deeply resonant voice comes from a tall, well-built middle-aged man who seems to have manifested himself from nothing and now stands beside her. "I'm Virgil Barrons. It's good to meet you."

Shit.

Dr. Virgil Barrons is a man with disturbingly blue eyes, and Rachel finds she is having trouble finding a spot upon which to rest her gaze. As he speaks, she lets her eyes bounce around from his shirt collar to his chin to his hairline and back to the shirt collar. She feels like an idiotic schoolgirl and is aware that, given her age, she probably gives the impression of being less a schoolgirl and more a victim of dementia, or she thinks, what's that thing Nona used to talk about? *One eye lookin' atcha and the other eye lookin' for ya.* She forces herself to steady her gaze and look into his eyes and feels immediately self-conscious and stuck. This is stupid, she tells herself. Cut it out. Mentally whacking herself in the face, she feels no better but is temporarily distracted.

Anxiety is a bitch.

"Yes, of course, Mrs. Thibodaux. I appreciate you calling me, and I'm happy to meet with you, but you should know I can't tell you anything. About a patient, I mean."

Oh, he's responding, thinks Rachel. That means she's said something appropriate. Probably she thanked him for coming as they sat down. It was automatic. She hadn't even noticed she'd done it. *Ok,* she thinks. *Carry on then. Good.*

"I know. I guess I just wanted to...to...I don't know. Talk to someone not involved. "Rachel breathes slowly. She's doing well. Less nervous now. She needs his help. He's easy to talk to. It'll be ok."

"Not involved?"

"Sorry, I mean, not personally involved. It's complicated. A friend of mine, a woman who was a nurse for AmHealth, suggested that I look into things. She's the one who gave me your name. Suggested I talk to you."

He glances at the ceiling, rolls his eyes. "Oh God, you're talking about Camilla," he says, blowing out a breath. "Camilla James, right?"

"Yeah, how did you know that?"

"We work together, downtown at the jail. Central lockup." He's shaking his head now. Frustrated.

"She didn't tell me that. I thought... wait, I thought you were at the prison. At Marietta,"

"No, no. I'm just consulting on this one case. That's all. Look, Mrs. Thibodaux,"

"Call me, Rachel, please."

"Rachel, then." He takes a breath. His expression is full of empathy but entirely professional. Rachel notices his teeth. He has beautiful teeth, not perfectly straight but nice and white and strong, well-positioned. She likes teeth. He's still talking. "I'm so sorry, but I'm not the one to help you. Honestly, I think Camilla has herself worked up over something that's, uh," he hesitates. "I'm not sure how to say this. I love Camilla. I've worked with her for years. She's a terrific nurse, very smart, and has always been totally reliable, but this whole thing makes little sense. I'm worried about her. I think all this stuff in the paper has triggered something for her. I can't share much with you, but Camilla is a friend of yours, so I will tell you I'm concerned she's not well. Not thinking clearly."

"I know," says Rachel. She picks up her coffee spoon, stirs her already stirred drink. "I thought that too at first, but now I'm not so sure. She was so insistent that there's some kind, I don't know, conspiracy, I guess going on. I know it sounds ridiculous. But Camilla believes this woman's execution should be stopped based on some theory concerning Good Hope and all that happened fifteen years ago."

Rachel feels a little ridiculous, listening to her own words. Out loud, they sound much crazier than she'd imagined. She forges ahead. Now looking directly at Dr. Barrons. Fuck it. She needs help.

"She gave me Janie's old address, and please understand, Camilla and I, we go way back. Way before the Water. She got me my first job nearly forty years ago when I wasn't even old enough to have a job. I mean, she saved me. Literally, I owed her. Still owe her. So, anyway, I did what she asked. I went to see the place, Janie Paradise's old place over in the Lower Nine." Rachel stops, surprised by the lump forming in her throat. She doesn't want to cry. Not here, anyway. She has to squeeze the rest of the words out. "Oh God, it was dreadful, Dr. Barrons. That's not even the word for it. Gruesome." I don't know if you've been over there?" He doesn't reply, only looks at her and nods for her to continue. "Look, Dr. Barrons, I just couldn't believe it. It was like it told the complete story."

"Virgil, please call me Virgil, and what does that mean? The whole story?"

The waiter arrives to take their order, and Rachel is relieved for the opportunity to collect her thoughts. She's so scattered. They order two regular coffees. This time, Rachel asks for decaf. She's too nervous to eat, but Virgil asks for the etouffee without looking at the menu. He's been here, she thinks and wonders why that matters. The waiter collects the menus and leaves.

Rachel sits up a little straighter, sets down the spoon she's been fiddling with, and looks at Virgil.

"That house is practically on the canal, just like Good Hope," she says. "You know what that means, right? That portion of the city took twenty feet of water. It's this tiny shotgun, you know, where you can see straight through to the back if you stand on the front porch, and that porch is raised up on concrete two or three feet at the most." In his face, Rachel sees that he's picturing the water breaching the Industrial Canal levees and coming over the riverbanks and rolling like a tidal wave down the road. "It had no windows or doors left. Like someone had just... blown them all out. The siding was all ripped off, and you could see the skeleton of the thing, you know the way the wood slats were all put together a hundred years ago or whatever. I mean, you could see the parts that were left, anyway. Like ribs. The roof, over the attic, was all caved in on one side." She grimaces. "But on the other side it was worse. I kept thinking that was where she stayed all those days, Janie. That tiny little space, with all that poison water around her." She stops, takes a breath. "They said it was days and days she was up there. I mean, my God, she had to be crazy by the time they got to her, right? I guess that's one of my questions for you.?"

"Six days, that's right," answers Virgil. "And I agree she couldn't have been entirely in her right mind. But that doesn't mean someone set her up or went there intending to harm her. It doesn't mean there's some sort of conspiracy." He's looking at her now sympathetically, and Rachel doesn't like it. She's seen the look before. It makes her feel like a patient.

"You're not hearing me. I need you to listen. Please."

"I am listening. I promise—more than listening. Because of my relationship with Camilla, I believe in her, I investigated it too. Looked at the history, the documents, the legal case. There's nothing. Eighty-seven people drowned at Good Hope; six were staff members. And yes, Janie Paradise survived along with a handful of others. Somehow made it back to her own house and holed up in that attic for nearly a week before being found. But, Rachel, it was investigated by at least three different agencies. The conclusion was obvious. It was an accident. That's it. If there's anyone at fault, it's the folks who built the MR-Gulf Outlet in the first place or those who put the damn building so close to the levees. Or even on the mayor for failing to order an evacuation until it was too late. I don't know but not on your husband's company and certainly not on the folks there on the front lines. It was a disaster waiting to happen. Guaranteed. From what I could find, it was inevitable."

Her husband's company. He knows about Daniel. Of course, he knows. Everyone in New Orleans, probably everyone in the state, knows she's married to Daniel. And everyone in the country knows about Daniel's position at AmHealth and, by definition, at Good Hope. The information is as close as the internet. Fuck.

"There's more, and it's personal." The words are out, and the tears come before she can stop them. She studies Virgil before continuing. His blue eyes are kind and honest. His expression is suddenly less clinical. "I have told no one this. I was hoping to..." she lets the sentence drift. He nods. Waits.

"It's ok. Go ahead."

"While I was in the Ninth Ward before I visited the house, I went by Good Hope. Or the remains of Good Hope." She pauses, looks down at the table, and runs a finger around the edge of the saucer that holds her cup. Looks up. "I found something. Or I think I found something." She inhales. "The doors. The doors separate the patient wings from the administration area. They were blocked. Rather, they had been locked. Dead bolted. You could see where the bolt had been sheared to get those doors open."

"Ok, so, I'm not sure what that means," he says.

"I'm not sure what it means, except that I've lived in Louisiana all my life. I've been through hundreds, thousands of storms, and plenty of floods. One thing you'd never do, I mean never, is deadbolt off part of a building. The risk is too high; someone might get trapped on the wrong side. You might barricade the doors against the water after everyone has moved to a safer location, but that's not what happened in this case. We know all those people died in the patient wings: in their rooms, cafeteria, and hallways. They hadn't been evacuated. They hadn't even been moved. Somebody, or several someone's, barred the only escape route. She looks up at him. "The water came in the building's front. You can see the high-water marks all over the patient's wings. They couldn't get out, Virgil. Even if they'd been able to get out of their beds and wheelchairs, they'd have been trapped."

Virgil freezes, a forkful of etouffee halfway between bowl and mouth. He looks up, studying her carefully. He says, "Wait, you're saying it was intentional?"

"I don't know. But I can't stop thinking about it. I can't stop wondering if Camilla is right? If someone locked those people in, even by accident, then it was possible there was some kind of coverup?"

"Ok," says Virgil, carefully setting his fork down tines against the edge of the China plate. He tents his fingers on the table surface, leans towards her giving her what she knows is his most empathic, professional doctor expression. "So, what if Camilla is right? What if something happened and there is some sort of conspiracy, and the worst is true? Why you, Mrs. Thibodaux? Why be involved? If Camilla is right, then this could be extraordinarily dangerous. For God's sake, this is your husband's company. It seems like you would be the last person interested in digging this up. Why put yourself in such a position?"

For a long time, Rachel says nothing. A twinge of pain behind her eye distracts her momentarily. Beneath the table, she crosses one ankle over the other to keep from fidgeting her feet. At the next table, a fat man wearing a black Saints T-shirt and Bermuda shorts laughs heartily at something his companion has just said. Rachel watches as he picks up a crawfish, cracks it, and presses the head against his oily lips, sucking the juices into his mouth.

"Rachel?"

"Sorry."

"Are you ok?"

She nods. "Why me?"

"I'm sorry?"

"You asked why me? Why put myself through this? Why put myself in such a position?"

"Yes."

"It's simple. I don't have a choice."

"I don't understand."

Rachel feels her throat tighten. "I've been fighting this ever since I first read about it in the newspaper. I think I knew even then. But things keep adding up, and now," she stops, takes a breath. "And now I'm certain. She's my sister Virgil. I don't have a choice because Janie Paradise is my sister."

CHAPTER 26

Devereaux, Louisiana

1986

Just after dawn, the storm that had been threatening all night finally made it to Devereaux. Icy rain needled then slammed into the windows in sheets, and black clouds turned morning back into night. Talia sat up in bed and watched beads of water leak through the cracked window frame and puddle on the sill.

Nona would have turned fifty-six yesterday if she'd lived. Her birthday passed without a whisper even as they made plans to drive down to Pichette for the funeral. She'd been dead less than a week, but the darkness inside Talia, which began with Mama's death and grew when Rachel left, now seemed to solidify. A thing tangible and weighty. It made her tired carrying it all the time. In dreams, she raced across flooded fields running from something sharp-edged, dangerous, and permanent.

She missed Nona already. When the weather was good, they'd go out to the bayou and sit on the bank and watch the dark water snake by. Nona smoking Paul Malls and pulling at the pendant she wore around her neck. Often, she was quiet. Other times she seemed to have more words than she had time. That there is Kentucky bluegrass, she'd say. And that one is yellow jessamine. Reaching a bony finger towards the water's edge, she'd pluck at the reddish leaves of pink sundew. She knew the birds too—the Louisiana herons, stripes running like neckties from chin to belly through their blue-gray plumage. The zebra-striped ducks Nona called goldeneye, their eyes like liquid gold.

Talia's favorite was the Osprey, with powerful wings spanning Talia's height. She loved the Osprey for its long life and its beautiful nest (she'd seen nests built of twigs and decorated with fishing net and rope and even bits of broken beach toys) and its loyalty to the water. It'll stay near the river all its life, Nona said. And near the swamp too, and it'll only eat fish. But most of all for its mastery over land and sea. When Talia spotted one, she and Nona watched until it disappeared across the river and into the distant trees, its striped tail feathers streaking the mist like jet fuel.

At the cemetery, a cool rain was steadily falling. The wind blew about pages of the preacher's bible. A handful of mourners stood over the grave, the men with their hats in their hands, the women pressing their skirts against the wind, palms flat against their thighs. Talia watched the low branches of the willows sway, the heels of her shoes sinking into the spongy grass, rainwater down her cheeks, mixed with tears. When it was her turn, Talia dropped a handful of dirt into the grave and watched it make muddy pools across the wet surface of the coffin. For the first time in her life, she was utterly alone.

•   •   •

Fall was an excellent time to die. Not too hot and unlikely to flood. But not so cold either, so folks were likely to show up. Rachel was thinking about that as she parked the Datsun at the edge of the cemetery and padded through the wet grass to the burial plot.

It was Pink that called. Your Granny is dead, she'd said, her voice hollow. Died in her sleep. Heart attack. Thought you'd want to know, is all. Then she'd hung up, leaving Rachel standing barefoot in her dark kitchenette holding the plastic telephone receiver against her ear, dial tone buzzing without empathy.

Mourners gathered around the gravesite. Rachel recognized no one. They'd been reduced to a clump of umbrellas gone bleary and colorless in the gray, wet day. She waited beside the broad trunk of an oak tree and strained to hear the unfamiliar preacher's words before they dissolved in the wind.

"Jesus gives us this faith when he says, 'Let not your heart be troubled. Ye believe in God, believe also in me. In my Father's house are many mansions. If it were not so, I would have told you. I go to prepare a place for you. And if I go and prepare a place for you, I will come again, and receive you unto myself; that where I am, there ye may be as well."

Rachel saw a young girl with her back turned to the left of the primary group, and her head ducked under one umbrella. Her hair, which made her stand out, was thickly braided down her back, and she was fidgeting foot to foot in the sludgy grass. Skinny legs clad in black tights, her sneakers badly splattered with mud. Talia.

She looked twelve, but she wasn't twelve. She was fifteen now. Fifteen thought Rachel. How did it happen? How did she miss all this? Rachel's eyes filled with unexpected tears. She squeezed them away and wiped at her face.

Rachel took a step forward, stumbled over a tree root, and had to step quickly backward to regain her balance, scraping her shoulder against the rough bark of the tree. Talia turned around, and Rachel-rubbing absently at her shoulder-caught her sister's eye.

Talia's face hardened, and she looked away.

Auntie Martha was not an aunt in the traditional sense. She was an aunt in the Louisiana-every older woman who is a close friend of my mother or aunt or grandmother or long-time neighbor- is my aunt sense. She'd been Nona's friend forever, and it was to her house the party retired after the funeral.

Auntie Martha lived in one of the tiny shotguns that had somehow survived a hundred years of hurricanes, near what Pichette locals euphemistically referred to as downtown. The house was barely twice bigger than the minivan camper Rachel had lived in with Tommy Lee was neat and perfectly maintained. A wooden sign planted in the yard said: God Bless this House, which was funny because right next to it was another one that said: BLESS YOUR HEART BUT GIT YOUR RAGGEDY ASS OUTTA MY GARDEN. Auntie Martha was like that. But then, so was Nona.

People were milling about up and down the steps, the front porch, pouring out the doors, around the side yard. They leaned against the house, smoking cigarettes or sucking on cans of PBR. A few spit streams of tobacco juice into the dirt. Rusted-out pickup trucks lined the narrow street, and Rachel had to park nearly two blocks down and walk up. Who knew Nona had so many friends? Or maybe people came for the free food and beer.

Rachel's heart pounded as she made her way through the front gate, up the brick path to the house. No one she knew. A big man in black jeans and a plaid work shirt stood leaning against the doorjamb at the entrance. He stepped back and held the screen door open, nodding at Rachel in acknowledgment.

The house was stuffy despite the cool fall weather. The smell of boiling crawfish floated into the front room from the kitchen, and people crowded into the tiny space.

"Rachel!" She turned and squinted her eyes in the voice's direction. "It's me...you know me, c'mon."

LooLoo was smaller than she remembered. Painfully skinny except for that same potbelly (bigger now) he'd been unable to hide inside his too-tight button-down shirt. It hung over his grease-stained jeans like he had a half watermelon stuffed in there. Bloodshot eyes. She stared at him, uncertain of what to do. Why hadn't she prepared for this? She knew she'd see him, of course. She hadn't wanted to think about it. Before she could move, he was approaching.

"Well, hey Rachel, long time girl! How ya been?"

She took a step back, her mouth thick and dry, her palms sweaty. Nausea rising. She would not vomit. She peered at him, into his face, as if she might find something there. Something to explain what he'd done. But he only grinned. Stupidly. Tobacco-stained teeth. Gum stuffed with chew, it pushed his lower lip forward, twisting his mouth into a repulsive smirk. There was a dining chair beside her, and she stepped quickly behind it, grasping the back of it like armor.

"LooLoo," she said. It was a reflex she could hardly help, but his name tasted foul in her mouth. She wanted to spit. Her knuckles grew white, where she clutched at the chair. He stank—alcohol and chewing tobacco and vaguely, fish.

"You grow'd up even prettier, even goddamn prettier Rachel," he said, letting his eyes drop to her breasts where they remained. She let go of the chair, and folded her arms across her chest, looked around for anyone. Anything. "Too bad for us, huh?" he added and took a lurching step closer.

"I gotta go find Ray and them," she blurted.

"Ah, sure," he said. "Out back." He jerked his head toward the kitchen, but before she could move, he leaned in closer, lowered his voice. "You got me good, didn't ya? But I forgave you, right? I figure we's even ok?" He narrowed his eyes. "Right?" She said nothing. "Ok then, ok."

She could feel him still staring as she turned and walked away.

Rachel pushed open the swinging door to the kitchen. Women were buzzing around inside the tiny room, fussing at plastic-wrapped Tupperware containers, stirring big pots on the stove. A few were handing various items to children with instructions. "Take these over to your Uncle Ben," or "Go give this to your Maw Maw and tell her the gumbo ain't gonna get no hotter."

Someone had propped open the backdoor with a cinderblock, and Rachel could see directly through to the outside. Talia sat on the concrete steps, her back to Rachel. She still wore the tennis shoes and black tights, and now Rachel could see she also wore a long-sleeved black sweatshirt, with the hood pulled up over her head. She sat alone, elbows on her knees, chin propped on her hands, a plate of food untouched on the step beside her. Rachel took a breath and nudged her way through the kitchen toward her sister.

"Tee," said Rachel crouching down on the step. Talia turned, looking startled.

"What the fuck?"

"Sorry, I didn't mean to scare you."

Talia pressed her lips together and shook her head. She was silent for several seconds, then she said. "What are you doin' here? What do you want?"

"Want? Why would I want something?" Rachel studied Talia's face. She wore heavy black eyeliner, much of which had been smeared and reapplied. She'd been crying, her eyes swollen and red. The makeup made her look older in some ways, but younger too. So angry. The way she held her chin as if she expected to be punched.

"Why else would you be here? You don't give two shits about us. About Granny Nona." Her tone was sarcastic, but her voice broke on that last word. She was trying not to cry.

"Oh God, Tee, I'm so sorry. I'm so sorry about Granny Nona."

"You ain't! You never liked her. You weren't even nice to her. You don't care nothin' bout us."

Rachel bit back the pain from Talia's words. She deserved it. Her voice was gentle when she spoke, but the words came out all wrong. "Of course, I do. You know that, Tee. Jesus Christ. I've been trying to reach you for a year. A goddamn year. You're the one who won't take my calls. Won't answer my letters. What was I supposed to do?"

Rachel wanted to suck the words back into her mouth as soon as she said them. She knew what she should have done. Nothing should have stopped her from reaching Talia. She should have come back down here and made Tee listen. Instead, she'd lived day to day, justifying her absence from Tee's life by telling herself the work she was doing would make their lives, both their lives, better in the future. What future? She wondered now. How much damage had been done to Talia while she'd waited?

"You think that's what I wanted? Oh my God, you're so pathetic." Talia stood up. "Just leave me alone, ok? You left me here twice already, just... just leave. We don't want you. I never needed you here. None of us did."

Rachel stood up as well. "Tee, please. I know you're angry. I know you don't understand. But I couldn't take you with me. Not last year. I...," She stopped. It sounded pathetic. It didn't matter that it was true.

Talia stood on the step, half-poised to leave. She pulled a thick splinter of wood off the edge of the step and began picking at it with her fingernail. There of silence between them, but Talia didn't turn to go. Rachel didn't speak, afraid to lose the moment. Finally, Talia looked up, and Rachel knew in that instant what was coming.

"So, take me now." Talia's eyes did not shift from Rachel's. She held the sharp piece of wood away from her body. Like a weapon. Rachel opened her mouth to respond, but before she could answer, Talia said, "Forget it, just forget it." She tossed the scrap into the dirt at the bottom of the steps where it lay, useless. Quietly, without looking again at her sister, Talia added, "You could if you wanted. But forget it. I'm fine, anyway." The harsh tone was unmissable.

You're not fine. Look at you. You're so thin you practically disappear inside those clothes; you look tired and sick and scared. Nothing is fine.

"I'm sorry," was all Rachel could think of to say. She felt dizzy, tunnel vision threatened. What was she doing? Was it possible? Could she just take a fourteen-year-old girl away? It wasn't even legal. No she couldn't do that. But how to make Tee understand.

"It don't matter. I'm ok here with Pink. With Daddy Ray."

And LooLoo thought Rachel. Oh, my God. What about LooLoo? "Talia," she said as gently as she could. "Does anyone ever... hurt you? Does LooLoo ever hurt you?"

Talia shrugged and shook her head, rolled her eyes as if the question were ridiculous. "Hell no," she said. "I'm fine. I'm not a baby. I'm almost fifteen, Rachel. I can take care of myself now."

Rachel reached out to touch Talia, but she jerked her arm away. "Besides, Loo told me what happened."

Rachel froze. "I don't understand."

"He told me what you two did, Rachel. He told me, he said that's how come you left."

"What?"

"Loo said you took off on account of his not wanting to, you know, be with you no more."

Rachel was stunned. No wonder Talia hadn't responded to her letters and calls. "When?" She asked. "When did he say that?"

Talia shrugged. "Last year. He said it after you came to the school. He said a lot of other things too. Told many people around here about you." Then, she dropped her voice, almost whispering the words. "I didn't want to believe him." Her face changed. Softened just a little. "It's not true." It wasn't a question exactly.

"It isn't true, Tee. None of it. Look, stay away from him. Ok? Just promise me. You'll stay away from him. He's dangerous." Rachel reached out and touched Talia's arm. Under the pads of her fingers, she could feel the thin edge of Talia's bone straight through the thick fabric of her sweatshirt. Talia wrenched her arm away again and narrowed her wet eyes at Rachel.

"Just go. Look, Rachel, I'm grown up now. I ain't no baby. So, you can stop worryin'. Ok?"

"Tee," Rachel tried again.

"Just go. I'm fine," Talia spit the words like tiny stones. Before Rachel could say another word, Talia disappeared up the steps and inside the house.

CHAPTER 27

Marietta State Penitentiary

July 24, 2020

Virgil is standing at the prison gate, watching a car approach in the distance. The sun in the cloudless sky is a cruel and brutish thing, and the air is so still he can hear the inmates slinging insults at one another back in the yard. He wishes that he'd worn sunglasses. He glances at Beaumont, who stands beside him with his hands on his hips, staring straight ahead. Beaumont doesn't squint but purses and un-purses his thick lips. A man like that thinks Virgil. A man like that is well suited for waiting.

Beaumont, who notices the glance and takes it as an invitation to chat, says slowly, "Now why would a woman like Rachel Thibodaux come all the way up here anyway, doc? She's on my roster. That's who y'all waitin' on, right doc?"

Virgil considers this. He could tell Beaumont to fuck off; it's not his business, which of course, it is not. He could lie, but there would be no point since the truth would be out in about one minute. And alienating Beaumont makes no sense. It won't help things. So, Virgil says, "Yeah, that's right." He says nothing more, hoping silence will follow.

Beaumont only takes a step toward him. "Oh, c'mon, doc. How come a rich lady, a rich white lady, is coming down to the asshole of nowhere?"

"Ok, Beaumont, ok," says Virgil shaking his head. "You know I can't discuss that with you." He'd tried to keep Rachel's name off the visitors' list. Janie refused to see her, anyway. He'd explained that to

Rachel over the phone, but she'd insisted on coming. Maybe she thinks this will change things. It won't.

"That her doc?" Virgil jerks his chin toward the Range Rover, rolling toward them.

"I'm sure," says Virgil. "Who else, right?"

"Okey dokey." Beaumont turns. "I'll get her documents started." Virgil nods, his eyes on the dark vehicle as the woman's face comes into view.

Fifteen minutes later, Virgil has guided Rachel through security and into the tiny windowless box he's been given to use as an office while he works on the Paradise case.

"Nice," says Rachel as Virgil closes the door and offers her a seat. She smiles slightly. "Sorry," she adds.

"Yeah, well, it's not much different from any other government issue office I've ever had, if you want to know the truth." He looks around. "In fact, I think it might be nicer than my permanent office at Central Lockup." He laughs. "If I wanted a nice office, I guess I would have gotten a different job." He sits behind his small desk and watches as she sits down across from him. There are no other chairs in the room, so no options for less formal seating. He mentally kicks himself for not moving his chair around front of the desk before her arrival. Now it feels a bit like she's a student he's asked to visit the principal's office.

He shouldn't have done this. Virgil knew this was a bad idea. How many years of therapy has he had? Four? No, five. It's been five. And he's a psychiatrist, for fucks sake. What will it take for him to stop trying to save every hopeless situation he comes across? And yes, if he's honest with himself, the codependency is exponentially worse with women. But then there's what happened with his brother. Fixing people who don't want your help is about control; that's what this is about. It's not about helping, right? That's what Lucinda loved to tell him. In fact, that's the last thing she said before slamming the door of their apartment over twenty years ago. *You are such a controlling asshole; I can't breathe with you anymore.*

Their marriage lasted two years. Now, he's well past a half-century old, and he's managed exactly four years in a stable relationship (Virgil likes to include the two years he and Lucinda lived together before getting married, although the word "stable" is a stretch in describing that period.) Ultimately, he told everyone (friends, colleagues) they broke up because she wanted children, and he wasn't "ready." Only a part-lie. She wanted kids, and he wasn't ready. But he wouldn't ever be ready. The thought of kids scared the crap out of him. He loved children. Other people's children. But his genes, his family, his inability to keep a houseplant alive. The whole thing made him want to run. That's what he thought then. Now, he regretted the decision. It seemed stupidly short-sighted. The selfish cowardice of youth. And he'd lost the love of his life over it.

He focuses on his guest, putting aside his worries for now. He'll do what he can, try not to make any promises. That's all. Yes, he tells himself. That is all.

"It's cozy," says Rachel, a wider smile- a gorgeous smile- and light flashing behind her dark eyes. She's tucking away her sunglasses, and he sees her hair is pulled back softly, and she wears simple pearl drop earrings accentuating the strength and elegance of her long neck and jawline. She's stunning. It's impossible not to notice. She's wearing a pale cream-colored skirt and blouse and crosses her legs carefully as she sits down. Her calves are toned and shapely, her ankles delicate. She might be the most beautiful woman he's ever seen. Even more striking than her photographs. Her face is well-loved, well-documented by society photographers, but she's different in person. Somehow, he'd missed it yesterday. Then he remembers. The sunglasses are the sort actors wear to avoid being recognized. At the restaurant, she'd never removed them. He wonders if she does that in public all the time. Now, her face is bare. And undistracted, he sees her. He really sees her.

"Thank you for having me here, Virgil," she says. He feels a sharp but not unpleasant twinge in his stomach as she says his name. Her mouth is small but perfectly shaped, and with a start, he realizes he's seen her mouth before. Not only in photographs. Cupid's bow, he thinks.

"Absolutely," he replies, plucking a pen from the pencil cup on his desk for no particular reason. He puts it back. Smiles. Folds his arms. Unfolds them.

"I just feel safer somehow, being a long way from the city, and, of course, you know I want to see Talia." She laughs weakly. "Janie. Miss Paradise. Oh, God. I don't even know what I'm doing."

"It's ok," he says. Immediately calmer, more comfortable sliding into this role. *Doctor.* He knows how to do *doctor.* "It's difficult. There are no rules, no protocols for a situation like this, right?"

She nods. "Thank you. Really thank you. Not just for having me here but for understanding."

"I'm sorry, I can't do more, Rachel. I just have no control over who she agrees to see. I mean other than-"

She holds a hand up in a stop gesture. When she speaks, her voice is full of humility that sounds authentic. "You don't have to explain it again. I'll wait. Until she's ready." She pauses, dips her head then looks up. "I'm just hoping if she hears about what's going on, she'll become ready."

"Fair enough," says Virgil, feeling a little like he's lying. The office is stuffy, and he can feel his shirt sticking to his back. He'd love to remove his jacket but fears that it would appear too casual. Personal even. Rachel, in contrast, seems clean and unrumpled in her linen suit. Money, he thinks. Money has a way of insulating people. He supposes she's been rich a lot longer than she was poor. Only that's not fair. This woman has had more than her share of pain. He sees it. In her eyes, in the way she holds her back so straight, tilted forward a bit in the chair. Defensive. That's wrong. More apprehensive. As if she might need to fend off an adversary or leave quickly. Her hands are folded in her lap, her fingers entwined to keep them still.

"Look, there's another reason I've come."

"Ok."

"I need to tell you about her."

"About Janie?"

Rachel smiles. "Talia, Janie, yes."

"I apologize. Talia, yes."

"There are some things you need to understand. Things I know she won't tell you herself."

"Yes, of course. Great." He opens his desk and removes a notebook and pen, opens it. "Ok, if I take notes?"

"Yeah. Please." She pauses. "So, the thing is Talia's been alone most of her life. She's had to fight on her own, and it's my fault. I was supposed to take care of her. That was my job, and I failed."

Virgil waits. Resisting the urge to comfort. He says nothing.

Rachel continues. She tells him about losing Nina and Granny Nona and Daddy Ray and Pink and then, "When I was sixteen, something bad happened. I had to leave Devereaux-that's where we lived then. With our father. I ran away. Just left her there. Didn't even say goodbye." She stops for a moment, steadies herself, and then adds. "Talia was only nine."

 "But she wasn't alone; she was with your father, right?"

"He had this girlfriend, Pink and our father, Ray, spent a lot of time trying to make Pink happy, and she was never happy, just always sort of angry or righteous. Maybe he tried to keep her more mollified than happy. Anyway, I know it was hard for Talia. Ray wasn't an evil man, he loved her in his way, but he was not a good father. I kept telling myself I'd be back for her once I'd got my life together. The thing I didn't realize was that during that time, she was growing up. Changing, and not in a good way. That world she was in was wrecking her. It grates on you over time, you know. The poverty, the hopelessness, just the sheer emptiness of it all. I don't know what life was like for you as a child, but for us, it was like standing in the middle of a dead marsh that stretches out into infinity and," she wipes at her eyes, but there are no tears, "just waiting for someone to come by and rescue you only nobody ever does and it never, ever gets any different. And I left her in the middle of that, just left her."

Rachel stops talking. Pulls a tissue from the box on Virgil's desk and crumples in her palm. She looks around the small space, her gaze lighting on a photograph on the bookshelf behind Virgil. It's the only personal item Virgil keeps with him. He carries it as a reminder.

"Can I ask who is in that picture?"

Virgil turns and picks up the small frame. "Sure. It's my brother and me. He's about five in that picture."

"How old were you?"

"Eight. I was Eight. We were on a camping trip that weekend."

"Where is he now?"

Virgil sets the photo down on his desk. Looks up at Rachel. "He passed away a few years ago."

"Oh, I'm sorry. I..."

He shakes his head. "It's ok."

She nods as if she knows something about his grief. She shakes her head and plucks another tissue from the box on the desk. She dabs at her nose and mouth, then balls it into the palm of her hand and looks up at Virgil. She's left a tiny smudge of tinted lip gloss along the curve of her upper lip. He thinks about offering her the wastebasket and decides against it.

CHAPTER 28

Devereaux, Louisiana

1987

Talia ate dry cereal, then carried the bowl to the sink and rinsed it out. The window over the counter had been cut out and replaced with a glass enclosure that included shelves for growing herbs. Pink called it a garden window, although nobody gardened. It sat empty, the outside of the glass mud-streaked and bug-splatted, the inside filthy with dust and kitchen grease. Talia ran a finger along one of the glass shelves, leaving a clear streak in the grime. Outside, the sky was marbled gray and heavy, and a drizzle had begun. It was rapidly escalating, and water tunneled off the corrugated roof of the empty chicken coop. It made wide muddy pools across the dirt expanse that was the backyard and soaked up through the porch's slats and under the floor, giving everything a slightly rotten, mildew smell.

By the time she arrived at school, Talia's shoes were soaked through, and a half-inch of water was sloshing around under the soles of her feet. She wore no socks, and her thin sweater had done little to keep her warm, let alone dry. Her first-period teacher took immediate notice of her wet clothes, blue fingers and chattering teeth, shook her head pitifully, handed Talia a hall pass, and shoved her out the door to see the nurse. Everyone's head turned; a few of the girls laughed behind cupped palms, and one kid flicked something at her as she passed his desk. She gave him the finger, not caring if Mrs. Stevens saw it or not. Her face flushed hot as she exited the room.

It irritated Talia that the teachers treated her like she needed caretaking. Sometimes she wondered if it was her abject poverty, so obvious by the chronic state of her clothes, that made people treat her this way. Or, and she thought this more likely, was it her diminutive size? At sixteen, she was still barely over five feet. Worse, she was nearly boobless and looked like a child. Talia blamed it on Nina, who, according to Nona, had been "petite" as well. Talia had no solid memory of her mother. She had snapshots in her brain, scattered in no particular order. They felt terribly unreliable, as if she'd picked them up from other people's garage sales and then put them all together in a book labeled "My Life." Nona wasn't a tall woman either, but she believed she was Amazonian, so it mattered little. That meant there was no height on that side of the family. Rachel had gotten all of Daddy Ray's size, which seemed to Talia tremendously unfair.

Arriving at the door to the nurse's office, Talia hesitated. The nurse, a middle-aged woman, built like an icebox and so stubbornly mute some long-ago student had started a rumor she'd lost her tongue in childhood. The nurse had thick fingers that poked and prodded at you in painful, private places, small piercing blue eyes that made her look as if she were reading your mind. Talia sucked in her breath, shoved the pass into her pocket, spun around, and hurried away. She didn't stop until she was down the hall, out the front doors, down the steps, across the walk, and halfway down the street.

After that, she mostly skipped school, attending class just enough to keep Daddy Ray off her back but not enough to pass any subjects other than art, which she enjoyed, or at least did not despise.

Talia had one friend, Mandy O'Leary, who also did not go to school. Mandy never went. As in zero. She believed mandated schooling violated her "right to live free and unencumbered by the man" and pointed out the letters M-A-N in the word mandate. Talia thought she had a point.

Mandy's family lived three doors down, and she claimed she hadn't been to school since sixth grade when the whole family left New Orleans and moved down to Devereaux. She also claimed her mama wasn't around because she'd gone off to join up with the Peace Corps and was, at this very moment, in Africa saving lions, or in Alaska saving whales. She wasn't sure which. Anyway, Mandy never got registered for school, she said. She might've been lying-Mandy lied about almost everything. Whether it mattered-but Talia didn't care.

At sixteen, Mandy was a head taller than Talia and built like a full-grown, very well-endowed woman. She was showy and loud and full of bosomy, blonde-haired, spice-scented hugs and the sort of whispered wisdom and promises only a girl like that could give. Mandy was a beautiful, unapologetic predator. A motherless osprey in a world full of pigeons, Talia supposed she was a little in love with Mandy.

And the other thing about Mandy was that she always had a plan.

Mandy knew a boy, she said. Up in the city. A friend of another boy she knew. Mandy knew lots of boys. He'd let the girls stay with him, Mandy said. They could both stay a while until they got jobs and could afford a place on their own. All they had to do was get there, Mandy said. And how hard could that be? And besides, who wanted to stick around Devereaux and get old and fat and die like everybody else?

Then July came, and Mandy met Quinten. And Quinten had a guitar and a better plan, and in August, the two of them took off for Seattle.

Just before they left, Mandy stopped by to say how sorry she was. She was so awful sorry, she practically wailed. *'But it'll be ok, Tee, because you can go anyway.'* Mandy, who smelled like weed and cheap perfume she'd been stealing from the Shop-n-Save. Mandy fluttered around Talia's room, wearing the brand-new fake silver promise ring Quinten had given her. Mandy said, *'it'll be great, you'll love it, Tee, and I'll write you for sure, and later we'll visit and everything.'*

Talia sat on her bed, listening for a few minutes. When she could no longer stand it, she told Mandy to shut up and get out of her room. That made Mandy cry for real.

• • •

By the end of August, Talia had saved enough to make it down to New Orleans on her own. It was late afternoon on a Friday, and she stood on the riverbank. Talia stood on the riverbank. The air at the wharf felt dense and hot with the coming storm, as it might compress the surroundings-the structures, the vegetation, even the people- with its weight. She had to be careful to keep her feet well above the steep slope of river rock and yellow grass, which sloped down to the water. She'd read about how, without warning, the current could suck your feet out from under you and deposit you like trash into the Mississippi. She stared out over the river. To date, she'd only seen it in books, on television. In real life, it was a hundred times more magnificent. A thousand times. Not at all the muddy stream she'd imagined. Today it churned dangerously, picking up energy from the wind and drawing on the enormous power of the storm high above. In the distance, through the thickening mist, she could just make out the twin cantilevered bridge, which, according to her map, was the Crescent City Connection. It was stunning, the entire scene. The behemoth of a waterway, the bridge, the city. She tried to focus on the beauty rather than its enormity, which made her feel diminished and lost and some other thing she couldn't identify. Talia hadn't expected the limitless loneliness. She'd left Devereaux so filled with anticipation and emotions, mostly anger, there'd been no room for anything else. But slowly, as the bus approached New Orleans, it had encroached. A peculiar sort of emptiness she'd not experienced before. Deeper and seemingly inexhaustible, it had only grown with each passing minute. Now, standing here, at the wharf waiting for a boy she'd never met, her body felt too light, unmoored, as if she might blow away with the winds picking up off the water.

It would be long before Talia could identify this feeling as fear.

She pulled the small duffel from her shoulder, balanced it against her knees, and tugged back the zipper. A sharp gust smacked at her face, whipping hair into her eyes. She dropped the duffel and cursed out loud, feeling immediately ridiculous. Crouching, she rummaged inside for something to cover her shoulders. It wasn't cold. The temperature was probably still above eighty, but she didn't want to get soaked if it could be helped. She found a thin jacket and put it on, yanking the too-small hood over her head, then zipped the duffel and stood up.

"Talia?" She turned to see a man coming towards her. "Sorry I'm late," he said as he approached. "Ah, you're wet. Oh, man, I'm sorry."

Her first thought was that he was old, really old. In his twenties, at least. Mandy had said nothing about him being old. Only that she knew a boy. A boy! Not a man. Talia forced herself to focus. Breathe. He wasn't big, five foot seven or eight, strong, well-muscled, nice-looking, pretty eyes. Not that bad, she thought. He had dark hair cut short on the sides and shaggy on the top, almost like he'd forgotten to trim that part, and he wore a white tank top and slouchy jeans with holes in the knees. The jeans were tucked inside heavy black boots that looked made for soldiering rather than walking around a city like New Orleans. And he was smiling. As he got closer, she could see his eyes sparked hard, like flint.

"Hi," she said. It sounded dumb. She tried again. "Hi, yeah, Antoine?"

He nodded. Smiled again. "Yeah, right? Here let me take that." She handed him the duffle. "That's my truck." He gestured at the pickup she'd noticed earlier.

Antoine's place turned out to be a rented room above a tiny liquor store called Mid-City Grocery (although they didn't appear to sell groceries, only shelf after shelf of bottled booze and about a hundred brands of cigarettes), on the corner of Palmyra and Pierce. They had to pass through the alley to get to the entrance, and the darkness behind the old buildings was solid, moving, like something alive. Talia held her breath against the stink. Her stomach ached a little. He jingled a key ring with what looked like a dozen keys hanging from it and pushed one into the narrow steel security door. Inside, she followed him up a narrow staircase, the soles of his boots making shushing sounds on the concrete steps, two bare lightbulbs flickering from the ceiling overhead.

The apartment, a converted attic spanning the building's width, was bigger than she'd expected. It was all exposed brick, sharply sloped ceilings, and ancient honeyed oak floor, well-worn, heavily scratched, but still beautiful. Furniture was scattered about, somewhat haphazardly, but roughly it appeared Antoine had divided the space into living and sleeping areas. An old sofa upholstered in brown plaid-it looked solid if not soft-was flanked by two milk crates turned on their sides and fronted by a walnut veneer coffee table that had seen better days. Ashtrays overflowing with cigarette butts and roach clips littered the table; beer cans, some squashed accordion-style; sticky-looking plastic cups, and other paraphernalia Talia wasn't sure she recognized. The place smelled like weed and stale beer and sweat.

A half dozen aluminum beach chairs were scattered around, the green nylon seats and backs badly tattered. Antoine was using some of them as catch-alls for blue jeans, old tools, a couple of guitars, and lots of pages of sheet music, spiral-bound notebooks, magazines and unopened mail. "I'm a musician, well, a songwriter, really," he offered apparently as an explanation for the clutter.

A cubby cut out of one wall served as the kitchen: mini fridge and a two-burner electric stove. A small folding card table-the kind Daddy Ray used to pull out of the garage and set up for poker nights-and two folding chairs (one with the back bent as if somebody angry had tipped it over and possibly stomped on it a few times).

Talia thought, it wasn't terrible.

The rain was coming now in pea-sized drops, beating against the windows at a severe angle. Wind howled through cracks in the ancient moldings, and outside, the storm rumbled on.

"You like it?" Antoine asked.

"Yeah, it's ok," she said. "Kinda messy." She smiled, then stepped toward the back of the apartment, beyond the white sheets and past the mattress that sat flat on the wood floor without the benefit of a box spring. "I like these," she said, examining a series of magazine photos and album liner notes with which he'd covered the back wall like wallpaper. They were all photographs of people like Antoine. Like Antoine, only more so. Girls with hair bleached so blonde it was colorless; eye makeup so black it turned their eyes into unreadable pits; skinny boys with shaggy hair; boys bald except for a stripe of hair that grew like dry marsh grass straight up the middle of their skull; kids in plaid pants and leather jackets; kids scowling into microphones; kids sweating and growling across a tiny, dimly lit stage.

"Who is that?" She asked, pointing at a black-and-white photo- a girl in ripped jeans scream-singing into a microphone. One arm in the air, fist clenched, her back arched, knees bent, and heels kicked up off the floor. Her hair flew off her shoulders in thick ropes of black and blonde. Her head was turned slightly, and her huge eyes-exaggerated by liner and shadow, had caught the camera lens just at the moment the shutter clicked. "I think she's beautiful," Talia said without turning to look at Antoine.

"Yeah," he agreed. "That's Exene. She's a singer, a poet, really. You heard of X?" Talia shook her head. She'd never heard of X. Nor had she heard of all the other bands he pointed out pictured on the wall: The Clash, Black Flag, The Sex Pistols, Fear, The Dead Kennedys and a dozen others. He played some of the music for her, and the plaintive, screeching sounds, the dark lyrics immediately struck her. The youth and anger of it. She loved it all.

Antoine knew about a lot of things Talia had never heard of. The music, the art, the people. And, yes, the drugs. Antoine knew a fair amount about drugs. She stayed with Antoine and his roommate for several months. The roommate's name was Oscar, a slightly chubby, genial man even older than Antoine (possibly even thirty). Oscar was a cook at a French Quarter restaurant, a small but reasonably excellent Creole Italian place with the unlikely name of Marsha's. Talia liked him, not least because he brought bits of amazing food home at regular intervals (shrimp cakes, turtle soup au sherry, sesame biscotti) but also because he was kind to her, right from the start. It took Talia about five minutes to sort out they were more than roommates, which made the situation that much easier for her. They enjoyed having her around, and she felt safe with the two of them. Antoine and Oscar's friends were interesting. They talked to her like equals. Taught her things but not like teachers. Like friends. They went places: clubs, bars, the ragtag bunch of places the friends—mostly musicians and artists- inhabited. They drank, and smoked a lot of pot, but Talia stayed away from the other stuff. At least, at first.

Talia met a boy. He was a year older and still lived with his parents in some Uptown mansion, but he spent a lot of time sneaking out, going to clubs, smoking weed, and rebelling. Oscar said he was "bad news," just wanting to be part of "the scene" to give his bougie parents a hard time. But Talia loved the boy's hair and his smile and the way he tore pages out of poetry books and gave them to her. The first time he kissed her, he'd pushed at her lips with his tongue until she'd opened them. It hadn't been unpleasant, their tongues touching, but it hadn't been exciting either. Her heart was pounding, but she didn't feel afraid exactly. Nervous that it might hurt. Anxious that he'd know she was a novice

He lay her down, kissing her face, her neck, her shoulders. She arched her back to meet his body-it felt reflexive. He held one arm under her waist and pulled at his jeans, and she shimmied out of her shorts. The kisses had become faster, and it was ok. The pot helped. She loved him, she thought. This boy, this beautiful boy. From a world so different from her own. His body was taut. He smelled of weed and toothpaste and sweat.

He made love to her slowly at first, the pain was sharp and then very dull, and then it subsided entirely. The humid air between them was like a blanket. They moved from the couch to the floor, and he held her in his arms and nuzzled his face into her neck, her hair. They lay sweating, side by side, staring up at the ceiling. The day had gone brilliant. Sunshine poured in through the dormer windows and fell in great shafts across the oak floor. He reached for Talia's hand and laced her small fingers between his strong ones, and she closed her eyes and let the sun warm her cheeks and still her mind. But she wasn't thinking about the boy. It had surprised her that the experience had amounted to as little as it did.

CHAPTER 29

New Orleans, Uptown

1988

The wedding, just two months past and still perfectly fresh in Rachel's mind, had been an affair of monstrous proportion; an avalanche of white silk and white roses and white people the likes of which the old Rachel could never even have fathomed. She'd asked for a small reception, and Daniel had agreed, but the thing mushroomed, and a four-course, sit-down dinner for three hundred guests, had become, according to Daniel's mother, the absolute minimum. Rachel felt sure it had something to do with overcoming the social disaster that had been Daniel's first marriage. Despite Daniel's claims to the contrary, that marriage had not exactly been "over" when he'd started up with Rachel, although it had been troubled, or so he said. His wife, he told Rachel, was five years his senior (thirty-one to his twenty-six) and sole heiress to an impressive fortune. The prenuptial agreement said he'd lose everything should he divorce her before ten years of marriage. Daniel's parents were not supportive of his decision to leave the marriage regardless of how strong his insistence that he no longer loved her, nor she him and the separation inevitable.

So, mostly to appease Daniel's mother, they'd carried on in secret for several months. At various times when the office was sparsely populated, they made love on the desk, or the floor or the small sofa he kept in there; shushing each other and laughing together like children. They met in hotels, friends' apartments (his), and out-of-town restaurants, anywhere they wouldn't be seen. In retrospect, the affair was a blur. Months filled with more hours of longing and heartache than love and sexual satisfaction. Assurances came in every flavor. Gifts, flowers, short notes, long love letters. So many promises.

Rachel might have gone on like that forever. But the first Mrs. Daniel T. would not. She discovered the affair quickly and, even more quickly, filed for divorce.

Sometimes Rachel isn't sure if she fell in love with the idea of Daniel or Daniel, the man. A bit of both if she's honest with herself. Rich, good-looking but not beautiful, soft-spoken, intelligent, flawed, and enough of a cynic to not be an intolerable bore. She loves him, but she might love the idea of him a little more.

They were married in as public a way possible. Rachel wore the creamy silk ball gown of a duchess and was assigned a personal photographer. The one guest she cared most about did not receive an invitation since nobody knew how to find her.

Talia was constantly on Rachel's mind. She'd driven back down to Devereaux twice before the wedding, the last time to find that Talia was gone. No explanation. Daddy Ray refusing to talk about it. He only said she'd taken off. Nobody knew where. He didn't invite Rachel inside, only stood behind the screen door, his face gray and unshaven. He'd lost weight. He held a bent beer can in one hand, his eyes were flat and Rachel could see he wanted her to go.

"I don't know. I don't know where she's gone. Off in the night. Kept saying she'd go, and she went. Couldn't have stopped her, anyway." He kept repeating the same thing. Convincing himself. *"Nothin' they could do. Sheriff said. Nothin' nobody could do."* He shrugged, squeezed his face with his thumb and fingers. Sniffed. *"She called a few times for money. Then nothin'. She's getting on ok, I guess."* Ray did not know.

Rachel noticed Pink was gone too. She'd taken her furniture, and over Ray's shoulder, she could see the place looked dark and empty. Rachel didn't ask about Pink. Didn't want to know. She felt sorry for Ray, for his aloneness, for his pain. He wasn't a wicked man. Only a broken one.

It was about three weeks after the wedding that it happened. Rachel was in the foyer, staring into an enormous hole in her ceiling. Rachel, who had never been particularly interested in the art of home decoration, had, since moving into the spacious Uptown house Daniel's parents had helped them buy, discovered she was not only disinterested but remarkably untalented. The floor of the entryway had been reduced to rubble as workers had jack hammered the old marble, but she had not yet chosen the replacement, and so she stood amidst ruin looking up at the enormous space in the ceiling where the beautiful antique chandelier once hung. Daniel had found "the old crystal fancy thing utterly depressing" and asked her to find something more contemporary.

"And what is that?" she'd asked him. "What does that mean exactly?"

"Oh, you know, updated, sort of edgy?" He'd answered distractedly, putting on his tie.

"Uh,-huh."

"Don't worry. I trust you." He gave her a smile. Then he checked his tie in the mirror and took it off, and tied it all over again.

She'd liked the old crystal fixture. Mammoth and very ostentatious, but it worked with the house, or she thought it did. Rachel had liked the ridiculous bling of it. The way it threw disco lights all over the entryway in the evening. It felt very roller derby, and she was familiar with roller derby. She sighed and looked up again, mouthing the word edgy to herself. Shit.

It was amid this dilemma that the doorbell rang. Didn't ring exactly; sort of screamed and squawked. It was another mini-project Daniel had requested. "Can't we do something about that bell? It sounds like the greeting at a haunted house." So, he'd had it disconnected, and the new one had more watts or jewels or thingamabobs than the house could handle and therefore sounded not like the beautiful song of the wood thrush Daniel wanted but like hundreds of birds being killed on the front porch.

Rachel pulled open the front door. The winter day was clear and freezing, and the mid-morning sun shone so brightly that, at first, she could see nothing but the dark silhouette of a slight figure holding what looked like a bag or small suitcase. The figure stepped forward.

"Rachel?" The voice was exceptionally soft, but she knew it right away. "It's me."

Talia sat on the big sofa in the family room while Rachel filled a carafe for coffee and pulled random food from the fridge: cheese, pickles, and yogurt. Her sister was so thin. Terribly thin. Rachel guessed she must be under ninety pounds. As she plated the food, she watched her Tee pulling off the jacket she wore. Black combat boots, a pair of torn jeans with black tights showing through the holes. A thin t-shirt and a ski cap as her only other defense against the cold. Her face was drawn, her eyes huge. She pushed her pack up underneath her legs as if someone might take it from her.

Rachel set the food down on the coffee table then sat beside her sister, careful not to come too close. She felt Talia stiffen just a little.

"I can't stay long," said Talia.

"Ok." Rachel bit back all the words, all the questions threatening to pour from her mouth.

"I have to... meet someone. I just need to ask a favor."

"Tee,"

"Don't call me that, ok? It was my baby name."

"Sorry."

"It's ok."

"Talia? Please, tell me what's happened. Where have you been? Who have you been with?" Rachel wished she could suck the words back into her mouth.

"It doesn't matter, ok. None of that matters. I'm fine. I just need to borrow some money."

"Yeah, yeah, ok. But it's been so long." How to ask. "Why now? What's happened now?"

"I don't know what that means, Rachel? Nothing. Nothing happened now. I just know where you are now. You married a rich guy. It was in all the papers. So, it was, uh, pretty easy to find you, right?" Her voice sounds strange. All the words flattened like they were coming out of a machine. Identical. Rachel wants to hug her, shake her.

"Ok, whatever you need. But please talk to me."

"No, I can't right now. I just need to borrow some money. Ok?"

Rachel pushed away the sick feeling of disappointment. Could this be true? That's all this was. Money. She'd seen the wedding announcements and found Daniel and then found her way to Rachel. For money? Rachel stopped the thought. It was selfish. So what? What difference did it make why Talia was back? Anything that brought her back was good.

"I love you, Talia. I love you so much. I'm so sorry." She paused. Where to start? "About everything. About leaving. Everything."

Talia's face softened, but it made the darkness under her eyes even more prominent. "Look, Rachel. I'm grown now. I don't need you to take care of me anymore, ok. You don't have to worry. Really." She looked right at Rachel. "I have a job, ok. Or I had one, but I need to get another one, and that's why I need to borrow some money just to get by for a little while, ok?"

"Yeah, yes, of course, how much? What do you need?"

"Really?" A lift in her tone. A break in the steel façade. Thank God.

"Yeah."

"Maybe two hundred?"

"Fine, that's fine."

Talia smiled. "Look, Rach, I'm not mad anymore, ok? I mean, I know why you had to do what you did, ok?"

Rachel nodded, wishing it were true. "Ok. Will you eat something at least, stay for a little while? Rest?" She studied the lavender circles under Talia's eyes. Her beautiful sister looked a hundred years old. Her teeth were stained, her hair greasy, unwashed for a long time, and she smelled like she hadn't bathed in days or weeks. "Do you have a place to live, Tee? A safe place?"

Talia bristled. Rachel saw her retreat inside herself. "Of course. I'm not stupid."

"Sorry. But you're still...." She stopped. It wouldn't help. "Anyway, if you want to sleep, shower, just have something to eat. I'll stop asking questions. Ok?"

Talia studied her. Finally, she said. "Ok. Yeah, ok. I'll rest for a while, but I can't stay overnight, ok?" She pulled in her knees, tucking her calves a bit more firmly against the bag.

"Great. Let me show you the guest room. There's a bathtub and everything you need. Just take whatever time you need, ok? Please. I'll bring you some lunch soon."

"Yeah, ok," said Talia, and she grasped her backpack with both hands. As she stood, she transferred the pack to her left hand, letting it dangle palm out, giving Rachel a clear view of the skin on the inner side of her arm. Rachel averted her eyes quickly, and they both stood, crossed through the kitchen, and headed up the back stairs toward the guest room.

An hour later, when Rachel took lunch up the stairs, she found Talia was already gone. She'd used the shower, but the bed remained made.

She'd taken the money Rachel had left for her along with two decorative silver teacups and a Waterford crystal clock from the mantlepiece.

CHAPTER 30

Marietta State Penitentiary

July 24, 2020

"And that was the last time you saw her?"

Rachel shakes her head. "No, it was more complicated than that." She looks up at him. "She came back several times that year and the next. She kept coming all the way through '88, always for money, but I'd lost her by then. You know, emotionally. We had no genuine connection. She was on more drugs than we could identify. So malnourished. Each time in even worse shape." Rachel shifts in her chair. "Then, this one time, she shows up in terrible shape. These awful bruises around her face and neck and so strung out she could barely stand up. She had all this makeup smeared around her eyes, and I remember, I couldn't tell how much was that and how much was bruising. Her eyes like gigantic craters." Rachel stops suddenly, a palm to her mouth, and Virgil thinks she won't speak again. But then, after a few moments, she goes on. "Seventeen." Rachel swallows a sob. "A kid. Anyway, it was Daniel who took action. Not me."

"Daniel?"

"Yeah, he sort of took over. She refused to go to the emergency room, so he had a friend, a doctor, come and see her, and then, after that, he made all the arrangements."

"What sort of arrangements?" asked Daniel.

"Daniel had been saying for some time that we needed to have professional help. Talia would die, and it would be our fault. She would die from drugs or malnutrition or being beaten to death, but regardless it would be our fault." Rachel hesitates. "He was right, of course. I just didn't want to see it." She squeezes tears from her eyes and lets her hands drop. "So, he called some people-Daniel knows many people-and two days they came, they took Talia, and I did nothing. I just folded myself up and didn't move and watched as they took her, one on each side; this man and woman, they walked her out. I remember they had these gigantic hands, even the woman, especially the woman, huge thick gripped around Talia's arm, digging into her flesh.

"They were probably transport staff. It's not uncommon for staff to take children and move them to rehab or psychiatric facilities to diminish the flight risk. Where did Talia go?" Virgil immediately wondered why he'd said that. Trying to soothe an old injury. Not his place.

"Tee didn't fight. She just walked downstairs in the pajamas I'd loaned her, which were far too big, and walked out. She never even looked at me."

"That must have been very painful."

"Combat boots."

"Excuse me?"

"They let her take the time to lace up her combat boots. That's how she left, her boots, my pajamas and her jacket."

"Where did she go, Rachel?" he repeats the question.

"Somewhere in Utah. A facility for kids."

"And how long was she there?"

"I don't know exactly. Maybe a few months. At least that's how long Daniel was paying the bills. At some point, she got Ray to go out there and get her discharged. And, after that, I never saw her again."

"I'm so sorry."

"You want to know the truth? I thought she was dead. I'm not sure when I started believing that, but it was long ago. You know that thing people say about *knowing* their loved one is alive out there somewhere? How they'll never give up looking because they can *feel* the aliveness." She waves her hand around in the air. "I think I believed that. I wanted that to be true. It made it easier for me to live. See, I felt nothing. We were so close, and yet I had no sense of her. Nothing. So, if someone had asked me, I'd have said she must be dead. Surely if she were alive, I'd feel it, right? That sense of nothingness gave me permission to go on with my life, so I grabbed it. I took it and ran with it instead of looking for her. Instead of spending my life searching for her."

"I understand," said Virgil

"I don't think you do. See, I was wrong. Completely wrong. And I've known that I was wrong ever since Jeb died. When my son died, there was no middle-of-the-night brain zap. No sudden feeling of slipping away. Nothing. Just a god damn phone call. That's how much awareness I had that he'd died. Zero. When the call came, it might have been a wrong number for all I knew, until the voice on the other end told me what had happened." She looks at Virgil. He's stopped writing now, holds the pen loose in his right hand. He's studying her. Trying to understand. She isn't sure why, but suddenly it matters that he understands. It matters a great deal. "To me, Jeb is still here. I can feel him. All the time, everywhere. But I know he's dead. I saw his body. I buried it. So, it makes no difference. They can be alive. They can die. They can hover in some goddamn cosmic limbo, and we don't know. We can't know. Our feelings, our sense of them, is about us. It's not about their position in the cosmos. All that is a bunch of crap we tell ourselves so we can feel better. Feel more in control of the unfathomable. But really, if they aren't with us, there is no magic, no safety net. We won't know unless we are told. All we can do is wonder all the time, every minute, every second. It's the wondering Virgil. That's what is so goddamn difficult. It takes a stronger person than me to live with the hard truth for all those years. My sister? She's strong that way. That's Talia, not me."

"So, what about now?" says Virgil. "What do you think now?"

"You know something? Maybe I've always known." She rubs her eyes. "Even before Jeb. Since the arrest anyway. How could I not? That name she chose, Paradise. If I didn't, I should have. I'd know her with a fucking bag on her head. It was like the longer she was gone, the easier it got for me to harden my heart against her, to blame her somehow, to make her invisible. I needed her to be invisible." Rachel looks at Virgil, shaking her head. "I was just too scared."

"Too scared for what?"

"To look, Virgil. To look."

CHAPTER 31

Marietta State Penitentiary
July 24, 2020

A strong hot wind pushes itself through the oaks and magnolias that line the road leading to Beaumont's office. That's how he likes to think of it. His office. That's what Beaumont tells his Mama. She doesn't know it's just a kiosk outside the prison. He keeps pictures of her and PawPaw in there alongside his radio. Makes the place so it feels personal. He also keeps other stuff in there too, but most of that is hidden away. Wouldn't want any of the C.O.'s coming across it.

He's standing outside leaning against the door frame, smoking; he's getting great at blowing smoke. Today he's working on circles inside circles. He was up to four until the goddamn wind picked up. Overhead the sky is thickening. By late afternoon, he'll be closeted inside for hours if he wants to stay dry. It's the one part of the job he hates. He doesn't mind the heat if he can be outside.

The phone in his pocket buzzes, an illegal phone he isn't supposed to have while working out here. He looks around, then steps over the threshold and picks up the call. "Beaumont," he says in his official voice.

"Yeah, you called?" says the voice. Beaumont's stomach does a little whirly gig. He's been waiting all morning for this call. The extra thousand a month he gets for keeping watch on things means a lot to him, but the respect of powerful people like this means even more. He doesn't want to sound stupid.

"Uh, yeah, I got somethin for ya."

"Yeah?"

"Uh, so she was here." Silence on the other end. He continues. "She was here with that doctor. Come to see him bout somethin, I guess. I dunno what, but she was here a couple hours." He checks the log and gives the precise times. Then adds. "And after she left, I saw on the roster that doctor, he put in a request for her to get in to see that inmate. Janie Paradise."

"When?"

"It ain't been approved. Don't know if it will be."

"You let me know."

"I will."

"Good work."

Beaumont starts to answer, but the line is already dead.

CHAPTER 32

Highway 10

July 24, 2020

The rain begins before Rachel is five minutes outside Marietta. The water comes down in strings of plump drops, fat, soft, unapologetic. Mama used to tell Talia you could hear music inside the storm if you listened hard enough. So they did, all three of them, even though Rachel was too old for such nonsense. They'd sit on the old broken porch at Nona's, getting soaked and watching water sluice around their feet and all agreeing they could hear trumpets or saxophones or French accordions playing. Talia always insisted she heard steel guitar, which made Mama laugh because nobody knew where she got such an idea.

Rachel taps out a melody on the steering wheel, squinting to see past the smear of water on the windshield.

She's glad she made the trip. It's the furthest she's driven in years. Even before Jeb died, she rarely traveled alone over thirty minutes outside the city. But she'd done it today without chemical aid. And, Rachel thinks, she'd trusted someone. The burden is not lighter because of it, but it feels less malignant.

Fifteen minutes later, the rain is letting up. A ribbon of sunshine breaks through the cloud cover and pours down over the road. Storms are that way down here. Erratic. Dramatic. Here and then gone.

She's back in the city and headed up St. Charles when Daniel calls. He's leaving the office but has a dinner meeting. Won't be home until late. Over the years, Rachel has become accustomed to these calls. Two or three times a week, Daniel is late. He always lets her know. Until yesterday she'd considered it thoughtful.

"Thanks for letting me know," she says, unable to keep the low hum of anger from her voice.

He didn't notice, or at least he didn't say he noticed. "Sure. See you later. Love you."

"Bye," she says and hangs up the call.

Rachel makes a U-turn at Jefferson and heads back toward downtown and the offices of AmHealth Corporation.

She pulls into the Claymore building's parking lot (an enormous glass and steel structure erected in the nineties with AmHealth Corporation boom money and then completely rebuilt after the storm), shuts down the ignition, and sits, staring through the windshield for several minutes. The heat inside the car is expanding, pushing at the doors and windows like an over-inflated balloon. When you don't know what you're doing, it's better to be doing nothing at all. Who'd said that? Daniel maybe. She smiles. There's an irony there. Rachel considers continuing to sit until clarity descends on her like a prophecy from God but then remembers she doesn't believe in God.

She takes a deep breath, unhitches her seatbelt, and gets out of the car.

In the lobby, the security guard smiles and nods as she enters. He lets her know the office alarm is off and tells her it's real nice to see her again.

"Just getting my wallet, Charles. Seems I left it in my husband's office," she says. He waves and goes back to whatever he was doing, which she suspects might have been sleeping.

AmHealth occupies the entirety of floors ten through twelve. They've come a long way from her first introduction to the company in the 1980s, and she'd been awed back then. The offices are closed now, and the soft whoosh of the elevator doors sliding open to the cavernous vestibule sounds clangorous in the dense quiet. Rachel steps out and pulls a card key from her purse, which she passes over the electronic lock mechanism attached to the entrance doors-a pair of walnut monstrosities spanning the height of the space to the ceiling. She's never had to use this key before Daniel gave it to her for emergencies only. She experiences two seconds of panic, wondering if it will work. A click, a slide, and she pushes the steel handle down. The door opens, mutely brushing over the thick carpeting beneath.

"Hello," she calls, just in case. The lights are dim but not completely off. "Hello, anyone here? It's Mrs. Thibodaux. Just picking something up." She waits for a few seconds. Nothing. Then continues. As she walks, her heels sink deep into the Persian rug. She looks down. Intricately patterned silk threads, turquoise, blues, cranberries. It's new, or it's a new, incredibly old piece. Expensive. Original artwork on the walls. Some she recognizes. The whole place smells like money.

Cameras, of course. Up to the right and left of the doors and over the reception desk. Tiny red lights blinking. She wipes sweat from her forehead and pushes her hair back behind her ear as she opens the double doors to Daniel's office. No cameras here. Daniel has always been adamant about his own privacy.

It takes some time, but Rachel finds what she's looking for. Daniel is remarkably inconsistent with security. His office files are not locked, although his desk and all its drawers are secured by a passcode. Like the one at home, his computer is also password-protected, but the password is identical to the one with which she is already familiar.

An hour later, everything she needs tucked neatly into her bag, Rachel stands at the frameless windows stretching floor to ceiling across two walls of Daniel's corner office. The view stretches over downtown all the way to the river and across the Crescent City Connection. From here, the battered city appears flawless in the night, a glittering, perfectly cut diamond.

• • •

The road uptown from the central business district looks different in the dark. At I-90 interchange, murals of graffiti layer the overpass's cracked concrete, and homeless encampments populate the weedy, overgrown expanse beneath. Big Charity, abandoned but still standing, is a gray ghost ship now. Shattered windows. Black mold staining the towering stone walls. A fence has been built, topped by rolls of barbed wire, like a prison.

Rachel pulls to the stoplight at the end of Tulane Avenue, cranks up the air conditioner and waits for the light. Continues to wait. There are no other cars on the street, and the light, she thinks, is doing this on purpose to frustrate her. Rachel taps her right foot against the floorboard and bangs her hands against the steering wheel. There's a man huddled back against the barricade beneath a streetlight. He's wrapped in layers of blankets, and thick strands of his long, unwashed hair are visible against the light gray concrete. There's a sign balanced against his knees, requesting a specific amount of money. She wonders what he can buy with fifty cents.

When she's safely back on St. Charles, she dials the number, breaking the rule against cellphones and driving because she cannot find her earphones and is lousy at using the speaker function. He answers after two rings. She speaks at once.

"Virgil, I have to see her. You've got to make it happen."

"Rachel, what's happened? Are you alright?" His voice was rough from sleep.

"Yes, yes, I'm fine. I've been to Daniel's office. I've found some things. I'll explain later, but you must promise me, Virgil. I have to. We have proof. Or at least a start on proof. What she's doing, it makes little sense."

"Where are you? Are you somewhere safe?"

She peers into the darkness; the live oaks on St. Charles are so tall the streetlights illuminate them from beneath, and the blackened branches twist across the entire avenue, embracing one another in a macabre dance.

"Yes," she answers.

"What is it, Rachel? What did you find?"

"That cop she shot, or supposedly shot."

"What is it?"

"Daniel knew him. Daniel and that cop knew each other way before the flood, and Daniel collects people like that. People he can use later. People who owe him. And there's more. I found a file. Several files. I think I might know what happened." For a moment, there is silence on the other end. "Virgil?"

"Rachel, I'm so sorry. I thought about calling you earlier but," he hesitates.

"But what? What is it?"

"She won't do it. I got a call a few hours ago. It was so late I thought you'd be asleep. Janie, I mean Talia, she's put in an official complaint. The warden called me. No more requests from you. No visit. That's final."

"I don't understand. What does that mean?"

"It means we can't even ask. That's her right. Rachel, let this go. She doesn't want to change this. I'm so sorry."

Rachel lays the phone in her lap, too stunned even to switch it off. The street is deserted now. A single streetcar sits stilled and empty on the tracks of the neutral ground. Its olive-green paint has gone a dim, dead gray in the darkness.

• • •

Rachel feigns sleep as Daniel comes in. She hears him pad softly to his closet and drop his clothes to the floor. He runs the shower and stays in it for a long time. She waits. Finally, he emerges from the bathroom, and she opens her eyes to narrow slits; he stands in the light from the bathroom, his white robe open at the waist. He's a handsome man. Tall, toned, flat stomach under his T-shirt, square chin and good gray hair. He shuts the light, approaches the bed. He smells sharply of woodsy soap and toothpaste and, despite the shower, sweat. He tiptoes around to her side of the bed. She steadies her breathing. Remaining still as he presses closed lips to her cheek and kisses her. "Goodnight, Rach," he whispers. His breath is sweet and warm.

Then he goes to the door, opens it, and steps out of the room.

She opens her eyes as the door clicks softly shut. For a long time, she stares out into the darkness.

Rachel doesn't know how much time has gone by, but he doesn't return. He's probably gone to sleep in the guest room. He does this sometimes when he works late and doesn't want to disturb her. That's what he says, anyway.

Sleep is a distant thing. Growing not closer but less attainable with every passing minute. Guilt plays on her consciousness. Guilt and doubt and fear. Fear like ice in her gut. To lose Talia again, after all this time. After coming so close. Is it possible she's misconstrued everything? Clouded her own judgment with pills and unresolved grief. How many people have brought it up to her recently.? Five? Six? Her daughter, her doctor, her best friend. Her husband. Could they be right? Is it possible Talia wants this? Wants exactly this. For a second, a brief flash of a moment, Rachel allows herself to feel the relief in that. What if she let it happen? What if there was no choice but to let Talia have her way? Would that mean she could go back to her husband? Her family? Her life? Forget all about Good Hope, Camilla and her girl Francine.? Why not? What good does this do? Bringing it all up now? She thinks about Daniel at the door. His eyes were warm, and his kiss soft on her cheek. He loves her; she knows that. No matter what he's done. He loves her.

She sits up and switches on the bedside lamp. Leans back against the padded headboard and wraps her arms around her knees. She's trying to think, but her brain is muddled with fatigue, fear, and the Ambien she swallowed an hour ago. After a while, she gives up. Reaches over to switch off the light.

That's when she sees it.

It's such a small thing. Nestled within the pattern of an indigo flower in the woven rug beneath their bed. The carpet she and Daniel picked out together on a trip to Thailand. In a lovely gold baroque setting, a pearl the size of a good pecan, a statement piece without being garish. A classic. As she plucks the piece out of the carpet, Rachel thinks she knows this earring. She's seen it many times. She borrowed it once, along with its mate, and wore the pair to a performance of Tosca at the Met on one of her and Daniel's trips to New York. She knows the earring, and it does not belong to her.

Pieces are tumbling into place. All the relief of seconds ago is torn away, replaced suddenly with fury and terror and grief. For a long time, Rachel tries to sort out what to do, but there is nothing to be done in the middle of the night, and after a while, there's no more thinking to be done, and her head hurts from thinking, and finally, she swallows four Xanax and buries herself under the duvet expecting to lie awake for a long time. Instead, exhaustion and medication overtake her, and within minutes, she is asleep.

They sit on a blanket beneath a two-thousand-year-old live oak. Prehistoric ferns, so green they look as if they might glow in the dark, cloaking the charcoal branches, which stretch and up and over the marsh. Mama tucks her blue sundress under and kneels on the blanket. A paper sack with Winn Dixie-The Beef People written on the front is set out between them, and Mama unloads its contents. Fried shrimp sandwiches, collards, coke bottles, and thick pecan pie wrapped up in brown paper.

It's a warm blue day, a few dandelions sparkle in the soft grass, and the water bubbling around them smells sweet and ripe. After they finish eating, they stretch their bare legs and feet out before them, giggling at the sight of all thirty toes wiggling in the sunlight.

Rachel closes her eyes for only a few seconds, but when she opens them, her sister and mother are gone. For a long time, she sits and waits for them to return. Watching the light through the branches of the oak tree as it dances across the flowered pattern of the tablecloth, turning the skin of her legs and arms a pale dappled silver.

• • •

When she wakes up, he is gone. The bedroom is awash in mid-morning sunlight. Standing, she feels momentarily dizzy, her limbs awkward and uncoordinated. When her vision suddenly tunnels and bright white stars appear before her, she leans her forearm against the wall to steady herself before continuing to the bathroom. She turns the tap and fills a small glass with water, drinks it down, fills it again, and drinks. Her reflection over the sink appears pale, her eyes slits, the surrounding skin puffy and red. Her mouth and throat are painfully dry. She opens her mouth and leans forward, trying to peer inside. Her tongue feels thick, as though if she were to speak, the words would be slurry.

She feels... drunk.

A note on the kitchen counter says he wants her to rest for the morning, and they'll talk later. She pulls her robe tight and climbs the stairs to the guest room. Still feeling unsteady, she leans against the doorjamb, arms folded across her chest, an elbow cupped in each palm, and studies the unmade bed. Daniel left the ceiling fan switched on, and the wide wooden blades make a rhythmic thwop thwop thwop as they turn. Her gaze falls on the bed, where'd he'd been sleeping. There's a dent in the pillow where his head lay during the night. She approaches and runs her finger along with it suddenly no longer able to stand, she folds her body into the bed, aligning herself with the impression his body has left in the sheets and soft duvet. Lays her cheek on his pillow—still warm. Closes her eyes, listening. The fan turning slowly. A loon just outside the window. The distant warning bell as a streetcar clangs to a stop on St Charles Avenue. Sun streams in through the south-facing windows flooding the pine floors with golden light.

Is it possible? She thinks. That this man she has loved so much. This man with whom she has made a life, created children. Lost a boy. This man about whom she thought she knew everything. Is it possible she never knew him at all? As she buries her face deeper into the sweet-smelling pillow, the world recedes. In the distance, she hears a phone ring, but before she can get up to answer it, she's fallen back asleep.

•   •   •

Someone is banging on the roof. Construction workers. Rachel will have to tell them not to start so early. Her head pounds, and she tries calling out. "Stop, shut up." But no words come. The banging continues. Wait, not on the roof. On the door. Someone is at the door.

Rachel sits up. The world spins, and she squints to clear her vision. Only it won't clear. Now someone is shouting, but she can't make out the words. Down the stairs, forcing her eyes open so she won't fall. It's Virgil. Why is Virgil here?

"Jesus, I've been trying to reach you all morning."

"Sorry, I must've passed out. Come in."

"Rachel, are you alright?" He steps inside and reaches out to steady her. "What did you take?"

"I'm fine," she says, struggling to make the words come out clearly. She can tell he doesn't believe her. "I took my anxiety medicine. Probably too many."

"Is that all? Are you sure?"

She nods. "Yeah, I'll be ok." She is feeling better. Her head is clearing. How many did she take? She'll stop. That's it. No more of that. She needs a clear head. How to explain everything to Virgil. The files. The earring. "Wait, why are you here? What's going on?"

"Well, first, I woke up to four incomprehensible voicemails from you." He holds up his phone to show her, but she can't read the display. "Don't know what that was about." He shoves the phone into his pocket. "And Janie Paradise changed her mind. I don't know why, but I got a call, and as of this morning, she's changed her mind. She'll see you."

"What? Why?"

"Like I said, I do not know. But she agreed. I spoke to her this morning, and she agreed. She'll see you today."

CHAPTER 33

New Orleans, French Quarter

1990

It was late, way past midnight. Canal Street, right next to the Quarter, was nearly empty. That meant the time was somewhere in those weird hours when even the worst drunks had gone home, passed out, or been arrested, but before the early risers were back at it again. *Shit*, she thought. Talia did not know how long she'd been walking the streets. No idea how she got here. She must have been running at some point because her legs ached, and she felt that sort of panting physical exhaustion. She wore just a thin tank top and a pair of sweatpants. She was barefoot; the soles of her feet were shredded, and bleeding, and a gash had appeared along the outer edge of her right foot, the pain suddenly excruciating.

There was a small overhang protecting a dark doorway, and she curled her body within it and lifted the lacerated foot to her face. The wound was deep, blood-soaked, although no longer actively bleeding. *Shit, shit, shit.*

Eighteen months. That's all it took for Talia's life to unravel completely. She tried Antoine again after the bullshit with rehab but left when he started acting like a daddy, or at least he'd acted like she imagined a regular father might act. Giving her rules and caring about who she hung around with. He hadn't cared until Rachel and Daniel sent her to rehab, and then there had been the whole thing with THE BOY. Talia refused to think of that stupid kid in any other than THE BOY or THE RED-HAIRED BOY. Antoine had been right in the end. Talia thought she loved him. Now she wondered if love was even real.

The kid had been an asshole. Not a monster (Talia knew what a monster was, there were plenty of those in Devereaux). He was lousy in the usual lousy boy way. He wanted sex. He was nice to her, gave her a lot of drugs, and when he'd had enough, he took off. But Antoine went a little crazy. Started "supervising." Talia couldn't handle that, so she split.

At first, it was great. Lots of kids were on their own. Doing what they wanted, living downtown in vacant buildings, mostly around the Central Business District. It was essential to stay out of the nicer parts of the Quarter. Cops picked you up fast there, and you'd wind up with social services. Or, if you were over eighteen, like Talia, they'd take you to jail. But nobody cared what you did if nobody could see it. She graduated from weed and speed and Quaaludes to doing crack and even a little PCP while living with those kids. It was the crack that pulled her down and the PCP that really fucked her up.

God, her foot hurt. She shuddered, thinking how much filth she'd packed in walking around the New Orleans streets with an open wound. She'd probably die of blood infection before anyone finds her here. Twenty years old and dead in a fucking doorway. God, what a loser.

She knows what happened. Sort of. Flashes of someone telling her not to do it. And her screaming back and a booze bottle cracking-that must be the glass she stepped on-and the pills. All the pills. And then smoking the joint, which wasn't just a joint. And it wasn't the first of the night. What was she thinking? She should be dead. That's what the doctor told her on her last trip through Charity ER. 'You should be dead, miss, with all the drugs we found in your system, you should be dead.' And what had she said to him, to that nice old doctor who was trying to help? Oh yeah. 'Fuck you.'

Luckily, her entire body now hurt as much as her foot, the pain a distraction from her thoughts. The inside of her head felt like someone trying to burrow their way out; her mouth was twelve times too big for her face. She realized she wasn't running; the muscle aches were everywhere. Every single muscle in her body had been strained to the limit. On top of all of it, she's going to throw up. A few seconds later, she vomited, but nothing came up. Only a bit of greenish bile. She was dizzy and so tired she lay down on the concrete. Within a few seconds, she was out.

• • •

A cabbie found Talia and transported her to Big Charity's ER, where they cleaned and dressed her feet, gave her fluids, and a kind social worker came and asked a lot of questions: ***Were you assaulted? Who gave you the bruises? Do you have a place to live? Is there someone we can call for you? Were you trying to harm yourself? Do you intend to harm yourself?*** And possibly most bizarre of all, ***do you own a gun?*** To most of the inquiries, Talia gave vague answers. To some, she outright lied. The woman gave her phone numbers: AA, NA, Alanon, a women's crisis line, The Suicide Hotline.

"Because you have a place to live, and you are not suicidal, the doctors can't hold you against your will. They will discharge you, but," the social worker made a serious expression as she said this part, dipping her chin and knitting her brow, "we are genuinely concerned about your well-being Miss Fontenot." Talia was fairly sure that this woman might be concerned, but the over-worked medical staff mostly didn't give a shit.

"Ok," said Talia noncommittally.

"I'd like to give you this number just in case you ever need help. Other help." She handed Talia a card with a number on it, and Talia crumpled it in her palm, fully intending never to call.

CHAPTER 34

Marietta State Penitentiary

July 25, 2020

The hard thing about knowing when you'll die isn't knowing *when* at all. It's knowing *how* that's the real bitch of the thing. At least that's true after you've had a bit of time to get used to the when. Talia lies on her bunk, watching narrow bands of light move slowly across the floor of her cell. She is counting the time it takes for the band closest to her to stretch long enough to touch the inside of the steel door, where, she supposes, it will stop and curve upward again toward the concrete ceiling. Or it will disappear altogether. She's not studied it carefully enough in the past. This is unfortunate. She has only twenty-two more chances. Today included.

Dying does not frighten her. She has often wished for death. Or rather, the absence of life. To be snuffed out in an instant, the way we can snatch a candle flame from existence between two fingers. But the process of separating her consciousness from the body she's known fifty years, specifically the idea of being strapped to a table and injected with drugs, forced to sleep, and then given a lethal concoction, is vile.

It is impossible not to think about how it will be. Whether death is the pouring out of the thing that is her memories, images, and loves, in a slow liquid release like water from a jug. Or more of a sudden dismantling of consciousness, bits flying around discombobulated like Dorothy's flight through the tornado to Oz. Or would there be nothing? Just a switch pulled from ON to OFF. She thinks that's best.

She goes back to following the band of light. She's lost count, but it's within a fraction of an inch of the bottom of the door. She sits up, slides to the floor, and moves over into the light. She watches it closely for a long time. Pushing her face nearer the spot where the door makes a right angle to the floor. She cannot miss it like a rare and precious eclipse.

She has twenty-one more chances.

• • •

It's well past lunch when they come to tell her the visitors have arrived. Talia isn't customarily allowed unscheduled visitors, but the rules seemed to have been loosened this month. It was Cindy Pitre who convinced her to see Rachel. *You gotta see her, at least one time*, said Cindy. She's one of the older guards, even older than Talia. She's a tall, skinny woman with graying dark hair pulled back into a severe low ponytail. Cindy is from rural Mississippi, long-faced and narrow-lipped. She looks every bit like the cruel spinster schoolteacher. But she is fair-minded, warm, and even reasonably kind. She brings the books Talia requests, supplies extra blankets when the cellblock is frozen winter, and always ensures medical concerns are quickly addressed. But that's not why Talia likes her. At least not the main reason. Cindy is a bible thumper. She's passed along to Talia more than one bible and dozens of HAVE YOU BEEN SAVED? pamphlets, and the thing is, she won't give up. Even though Talia is a hopeless case-her belief in nothingness in place of God firmly entrenched- Cindy will not give up. The woman has an honest passion and an authentic desire to help other people, and Talia finds that remarkable. More than remarkable: saintly. She's not sure she's ever met anybody like that. So, when Cindy pursed her thin lips, pointed one long, bony finger skyward, and told her, "You ain't doin' yourself any favors refusing visits from your friends and family. Dr. Barrons says this one's real important, and besides, you know you gotta git things right." Then she added, staring at Talia with both eyebrows arched, "You gotta see her, at least one time."

So, Talia agreed. She'd meet with Rachel once. What she couldn't tell Cindy or anyone else about was the message she'd received a few hours after Dr. Barrons' visit the night before. It had come like all the others, inked on a bit of rolled paper, stuffed inside a paper straw: SAY NOTHING.

Talia is waiting for her visitors behind a pane of thick plexiglass. Her heart pounds painfully against her ribs, her mouth is dry, and she's thinking about a boy she knew in fourth grade.

There'd been a fire. Something to do with the kid's mama falling asleep with a lit cigarette. One of the kid's legs was so severely burned it wound up shorter than the other, which made him walk strangely despite the special shoe they made him wear. His leg wasn't even the worst of it. He was missing part of his right hand-three of his fingers melted down into a hard-apricot shape, the skin stretched taut and stringy, the color of wax. Then, there'd been his face. That's what Talia is thinking about now. That kid's face. The way the fire had scarred that little kid's face.

Through the plexiglass, Talia sees the door open and one of the C.O.'s steps inside. She keeps her eyes trained on him, reminding herself to breathe. He steps back to allow the visitor to enter. Dr. Barrons looks terribly thin. Wrinkled dockers and a button-down that has seen better days. Talia wonders if he's slept since the last time she saw him. He sits down and picks up the telephone, and looks at Talia for a long time before speaking.

"Hi," he says. The skin around his eyes is puffy. He's not slept, she can tell. "Thank you for seeing me. I want to make sure you are ok with this."

It's strange viewing him through the window. Every other time they've met, it's been in an interview room, without a physical barrier between them. She'd come to think of him as part of her world. This place, the concrete walls. The locks. But he's not. He's part of something she hasn't known in over a decade. To come and go. To make choices. When to eat. When to sleep. When to get in your car and go to a goddamn movie. Virgil Barrons is something that is entirely not her. He's free.

Talia shakes her head. Smiles. "Hell no. I'm not ok with it, but she's not going to give up, is she?"

He smiles back. "Yeah, I don't think so."

"It's dangerous. For her, I mean. For her family. I don't even know. I only agreed this morning because now that she's this far in, I don't know if it's worse for her to see me or for her not to see me."

"I told her that."

"And she's still here?" Of course, she is. "You know something, Doc?"

"What's that?"

She changes her mind. "Nothing. Sorry. Never mind."

He waits, studying her. Then says, "Ok. So, you ready for me to get her?"

"Yeah, sure," Talia says, feeling not at all ready. She's pressing the telephone so close against her ear it still aches after she hangs it up.

•   •   •

Talia rubs her palms together and tries taking deep breaths. She's suddenly panicking. She isn't ready. They aren't ready. This shouldn't be happening. Not now. Absently she runs a finger down the scarred side of her face. It's been a part of her so long she rarely thinks about it anymore. Only when she's about to face someone who's never seen it. Which, on death row, is not very often. But it's not just the scar, is it?

On the other side, the door opens slowly. She turns her face away. From the corner of her eye, Talia sees Rachel sit down and pick up the telephone receiver. She turns even farther away. Rachel can't see her.

The C. O snaps at her. "Paradise, what the hell are you doin'? Either pick up that phone, or I'm takin you back to your cell right now. I ain't got time to babysit you."

The air grows heavy. Fraught. It takes all her will to move. She is visibly shaking as she turns slowly toward the glass and looks up, allowing Rachel to see her face. Rachel blinks, her face reflecting confusion, then shock, then suddenly understanding. Her mouth drops open, and her eyes widen and fill with tears. Talia still hasn't picked up the phone. She can't hear Rachel, but the words are clear from the way her lips move. *Oh my God*, she is saying. *Oh, my God.*

Rachel has her palm up against the window, fingers splayed as if she is trying to force them through. Tears are streaming down her face. Please, she says. Please.

Finally, Talia picks up the receiver. Her throat is tight, and her mouth so dry she can't speak. At first, Rachel is silent as well. Only her soft breath. Then, in a voice so small it's a whisper, she says the words Talia has dreaded hearing for a long time.

"It's you, Tee. Oh my God, it's you."

PART THREE: WATER

The Louisiana wetlands. Seven thousand years to build. Soft spring river water rising and over-topping the Mississippi's natural levees, carrying with it the makings of a new world: sand, silt and clay. Sediment deposited in thick layers more quickly than the river could wash it back out to the gulf: lush rainfall and fertile ground, a climate advantageous to things that grow. From the new deltaic plain came tall reeds and grasses along the river's edge, thick forests of live oak and vine just beyond. Reaching further inland, a complex network of life-giving cypress swamp and brackish estuaries. Saltwater marshes nearer the sea. Graceful seabirds, snowy white and pale silver. Catfish, crawdads, shrimp. Snapping turtles, snakes, frogs and alligators, and white-tailed deer, fat raccoons. Blue dragonflies, katydids and butterflies of every variety, some big as small birds. At the dawn of the twenty-first century, it is disappearing faster than the river can bring it back. Some say before the twenty-second century, it will be gone, and the Lower Ninth Ward, a glorious tapestry of landscape and living creatures, will be among the first to go.

CHAPTER 35

New Orleans

1991

The women housed by Catholic Charities were a uniformly depressing lot. Their lives, a series of bad men, bad choices and bad luck. Talia told herself she was nothing like them repeatedly when sleep failed to come. This shelter was housed in a beautiful, if dilapidated old house on Esplanade Ave, halfway between the Garden District and the French Quarter. Run by nuns, who wore jeans and T-shirts that said things like In Jesus We are Loved, and buzzing with the elderly volunteers who smiled constantly and called all the girls sweet girl and darling, the place itself was not depressing, only the women. Talia, the youngest by far, avoided most of them; it wasn't difficult given that they avoided her as well. The one friend she made, a skinny twenty-one-year-old junkie from Bogalusa named Marcy, got herself kicked out when she disappeared for three days and showed up high in the middle of the night. Talia thought it was fucking unreasonable to expect a drug addict to never show up wasted. They should at least have some sort of three strikes deal. And the nuns ought to give partial credit for showing up at all.

Nevertheless, Talia spent four months at the shelter, which provided her food and medical care and, in return, asked only that the women try to find outside work, help with household chores, and, of course, follow the RULES, read-NO DRUGS OR ALCOHOL. She stayed because she sort of liked her social worker, because the food wasn't bad, because they had bookshelves full of paperback novels, only half of which were vacuous bits of fluff. Mostly, however she stayed because she had nowhere else to go.

She found a job, not a great one, but it paid exceptionally well. A lot of the women were doing it. They lied to the nuns and said they were waiting tables. Not a total lie. They did wait tables, just without clothes.

At six months clean, the caseworker found Talia space at a sober living house downtown. She'd be living with six other women, all clean from drugs and alcohol. There'd be more freedom but more responsibility as well. Did she want to move on? Was she ready? Talia rubbed her thumb and forefinger over the six-month sobriety chip in her pocket.

Yeah, she was ready. Yeah, she wanted to move on. Absolutely.

CHAPTER 36

Marietta State Penitentiary

July 25, 2020

The scar cleaves Talia's face chin to temple on the one side. In newspaper photos, Talia had turned her head away, and the malformation was indistinct, but up close her entire face was unrecognizable. This ruined middle-aged woman, thin and weathered, bears almost no resemblance to the sister Rachel remembers, and at first, she feels nothing. Not nothing. More like the numbness induced by Novocain. A lumpy, painless presence and nothing more.

She sits stiffly, perched the way a person might if they were waiting for a bus to arrive shortly. This wasn't a good idea, she thinks. But then, she is taking up the telephone and drawing it up to her ear. Rachel lets her eyes pass over the woman's gray hair, dull skin. No, Rachel thinks, she doesn't know this woman at all.

Then the woman turns slightly; there is a strip of smooth skin across her neck, and Rachel recognizes the narrow protrusion of her scapula, delicate as a bird's wing. In the movement, Rachel sees her.

There's a thud, a cry, something guttural and Rachel turns to find she is alone on this side of the small vestibule. She presses her hands, both palms, to the glass, and she is crying. A great gush of tears, brand new ones mixed with those bottled for years, sluicing together now, boundless. It's you, Tee. Oh my God, it's you.

Talia tucks her hair behind her ear and opens her mouth to speak, the phone receiver pressed hard to her intact cheek. "I'm so sorry," she says. Her eyes are wet. But her expression is not of sorrow. She holds her mouth tight, her back straight. Resolute. "I'm sorry, and you have to believe me, ok?"

The voice is the same, a little older, more sophisticated pronunciation, but the lullaby sweetness, the pitch. All the same. How could Rachel not have seen? The way she leans forward and juts her chin as she talks. And her face. Everywhere the scar isn't, she looks so much the same. Older, of course, and so tired. But her features haven't changed. Mama's eyes. And her pretty mouth.

At first, Rachel can't respond. The lump in her throat is so big it threatens to choke her. Finally, she says, "No, Tee. No, don't say that. You've nothing to be sorry for." Rachel presses her palm against the glass, wanting so badly to touch her baby sister. "This is my fault. I should never have left you. I'm the one. I tried to find you. Oh, God, Tee. I tried, but it was too late."

Talia grimaces and shakes her head. "I didn't want to be found."

"I should have kept looking, never stopped."

"Look," says Talia. "Rachel, we don't have a lot of time." Her voice is stern. Her eyes dry now.

Rachel stifles a sob at Talia's mention of time. "I know that. That's why I've been trying to see you. I know what happened, Tee. Or I know some of it. I have evidence. Daniel, he knew that cop. And Camilla, she came to me. You were, I don't know, set up or something or-" She's babbling. She needs to calm down.

A tiny shake of Talia's head. "No. Stop."

"What?"

"It's not up to you, Rachel. Not this time. You need to let this go. Do you hear me? You need to get up and walk out of here. Don't come back."

"What are you talking about? I thought when you said you'd see me that-"

"I know, and I'm sorry about that. It was the only way I'd get you to stop. I knew I'd have to tell you myself."

"No." Rachel is shaking her head. "I won't accept this. I just told you, I have-" She can hear the edge of hysteria in her voice. Inside her chest, she feels something cracking open. A brittle thing she'd barely held together all these days, these years.

Again, Talia stops her. This time more vehemently. Her lips pressed tight. She mouths the word "Stop." A siren explodes in the distance, and reflexively both sisters glance up for a few seconds before looking back at one another.

Rachel is starting to hyperventilate. Panic. "I don't believe you did what they say. I know you. It isn't possible. You didn't kill anyone." The words are tumbling out of her mouth. She feels a roaring in her ears above the sound of the siren.

"It's ok, Rachel. I'm ok with it. I did what I did. I have to pay for it, right? I've been settled with it for a long time."

"No! I'm not ok with it, Talia. I'm not!"

She watches as Talia glances at the guard standing off to Rachel's right. Then back at Rachel. "You're not hearing me. You have to leave it alone. It's dangerous. Go. Just go."

"No. I won't leave it." She struggles with what to say next. There are so many questions. So much she doesn't know. Where has Talia been? Why change her name? What happened to all those years? But there isn't time. Not right now. "You have to explain, Tee; I can't leave like this." She is unable to stop the tears now. "Please."

The screaming siren stops as suddenly as it started. Talia shakes her head. Quietly she says, "They hear everything you say." Her eyes barely flick toward the door to her left. "Do you understand? So, stop. Right now. You have no idea."

Rachel looks around. She was expecting to see what? Cameras? Of course, there are cameras. It's a prison. She rubs her temple. She's trying to think. But nothings making sense. "If you hurt someone, you had a reason."

"You're wrong," says Talia. "It happened. Just like they said. I was half out of my mind, stuck in that attic for days. But I knew what I was doing when I did it. I killed that man. Unprovoked, I killed him." She glances over her shoulder at the guard stationed behind her. Then she looks into Rachel's eyes. Her stare is hard. "Please," she says. "Leave it alone, Rachel. The only reason I agreed to see you today is so I could tell you to keep the fuck away from me. Jesus. I knew you wouldn't stop."

"It's my job to take care of you, Tee. I've always-"

"It's not your job, Rach. That's the problem. It's always been the problem. You won't listen to anyone. You just barrel ahead without asking. Whatever you think is right must be right. And that's just not true."

Rachel is stunned. She says nothing.

"Do you hear me? Not everyone needs or wants your help. Sometimes people just want to be left the fuck alone. I do not want your help. Ok? I don't need it. I don't want it. I want you to go."

"You're not making sense. Why wouldn't you defend yourself? What good can it possibly do to sacrifice yourself? It's insane.

"Fine, whatever. But it's my life. Just leave me alone, Rachel."

There is a pain flaring in Rachel's chest, rage from the place Talia's words have torn open. She shouldn't speak, but she does. "You stayed away all these years out of some childish resentment over my sending you to the hospital or rehab or whatever. Just because I tried to help you. And now you still resent me trying to help you? What the hell, Talia?"

"Is that what you think? That I disappeared because I resented you? That I'm practically volunteering for execution because of some adolescent chip on my shoulder? Really? Jesus. Rachel, in your mind, I never grew up. I'll never grow up. I don't think you let people grow up."

Talia motions for the guard and says she's ready to go. "Remember what I said. Leave this alone."

The rage evaporates, replaced by something much worse. "Please, Talia," says Rachel. "Don't go."

Standing, Talia turns back toward her sister. Her expression is softer. "I love you, Rachel. Go home. Please just go home."

As Talia turns away, Rachel is a small child, standing alone beside an abyss; as she watches the steel door shut behind her sister, she feels herself lean foolishly out over the edge, trying to catch a glimpse down into its depths.

CHAPTER 37

New Orleans

1992

Way down Tulane Avenue to the river, but not as far as South Rampart Street loomed Big Charity. A multi-winged, twenty-story, million square foot, art deco building made of clean white limestone. A sheet of decorative metal, two stories tall, fronted the building. It contained an elaborate carving by Enrique Alferez, a flying duck, a nod to the DEE DUCT box of Huey Long's days. This particular night, Talia stood in the frozen air at Tulane and Bienville's corner, waiting for the light to turn, staring up above "de Duck in de Aluminum Grill," as it was affectionately known. She'd waited through several cycles already. She did the same most nights. Standing on the corner, staring up at the windows of Big Charity's fourth floor. It gave a sharp comfort like pinching oneself awake from a nightmare.

The walk to work would have been shorter had she skipped this part. The back way, across Canal, cutting behind the row of big hotels and then over to Bourbon, was possibly five minutes faster, but she didn't care. Rachel was in there. Not all the time, but often. Rachel volunteered as a baby holder, one of the women who came to the newborn ICU to hold the infants who had no one else. Talia saw Rachel's name on the list once when she'd been passing by the hospital's registration desk. One day, she'd have courage enough to approach her. Talia hoped so. First, things needed to be right. She needed to get cleaned up. She wanted to show Rachel she could do it. Do life on her own.

The light changed again, and this time, she stepped off the curb, careful not to wade through the water that pooled slick across the gutter. She wore a pair of Vans, picked up at Goodwill for a dollar. A nasty hole in the canvas at the toe meant a wet foot for sure, so puddles were to be avoided. At work, she'd switch them for the five-inch plastic stilettos she carried in her purse.

Inside the Quarter, wet patches of indeterminate depth pockmarked the narrow streets, and Talia was forced to tiptoe carefully to avoid them. She thought about the paper boats she and Rachel made from torn magazines back in Pichette. Setting them down at the swamp's edge, they would watch with renewed disappointment, as each time, the paper would become immediately waterlogged, sending the edges curling up and the little ships down beneath the surface; not so much sunk as swallowed. That's how Talia pictured New Orleans; just a cruddy paper boat sitting on a swamp, waiting around for the day it would be unceremoniously swallowed whole.

The Quarter was crowded despite the cold. Bourbon Street especially. Music pouring from every open window and door, the taxis screaming, and she had to push her way past a clump of blingy middle-aged tourist women standing outside the bar, sucking orange liquid from enormous plastic tumblers through ten-inch straws.

Big D's was already jammed. Purple and pink neon lights flashed up at the stage where a skinny new girl in half a red bikini hugged a worn brass pole. Talia watched her a moment. She wrapped one leg around the pole, pressed her crotch to the metal, and arched backward, allowing her white-blonde ponytail, which was so obviously fake Talia felt embarrassed for her, to brush along the ground. Her breasts were enormous, the size of cantaloupes, and barely shifted as she swung her body against gravity. She wore black stockings and stilettos. Her feet were ridiculously small, and she kept forgetting to smile. Later, she'd catch hell for that.

The crowd was mixed tonight. Business travelers with loosened neckties, middle-age bellies, sweaty underarms, cigars. A few tan lines where the wedding ring usually sat. Young guys too with wonderful hair, T-shirts emblazoned with the name of their college or favorite beer or, worse, their fraternity. Throwing back shots, professing their brotherly adoration of one another (Love ya bro), and occasionally lurching forward to stick a buck in a dancer's G-string. For a buck, they figured they owned you.

Two bouncers by the front door, May May, an enormous Samoan who spoke three languages, never smiled, and, as far as Talia could tell, never ate, drank, or took a pee either, and Rupert, a square-jawed, nice-looking thirty-something, who, despite a build, approximately the size and strength of a college football player, looked positively puny next to May May. Both were friends to Talia. Telling her often she needed to get out of this job (What's a nice girl like you doing in a place like this?), to which she'd smile politely and tell them to fuck off.

Big D's was always redolent with the stink of cigar smoke, stale cigarettes, spilled beer, sweat and sex, and, by the time Talia left, she'd smell of it too.

Jimmy was waiting as she emerged from the dressing room, leaning back up against the wall next to the cigarette machine. He held a brand-new pack of Marlboros, cellophane partially peeled but dangling off where he'd pulled the thin gold strip. He was already smoking the first one. Talia hated the way Jimmy smoked. Like a girl. First, two fingers flared up and back, lips pursed. Made him look freaky scary on account of him being such a mean sonofabitch.

He grabbed her elbow, leaned into her ear, and hissed, "What the fuck?"

"Huh?" She tried to yank her arm away, but he dug his fingers deeper into the soft flesh of her upper arm. He kept the nail on his left ring finger long for scooping coke and heroin, and Talia felt it break into her skin.

"I told you bitch, five hundred, and what did you give Aaron last night? Two?" Jimmy released her, shaking his head. He inhaled deeply on the cigarette, looked up at the ceiling, and tapped the toe of his boot against the side of the cigarette machine. Lizard skin, or alligator, it could be fake, thought Talia. Probably fucking not. Jimmy liked expensive things. Alligator boots, shiny suits. He probably had his stupid car (some ground-hugging space-age thing that Talia thought looked like it'd be the first to take on the water should New Orleans be suddenly overwhelmed by a flood) parked illegally nearby. One of his people was ready to bribe or break the face of any NOPD who tried to ticket him.

"Sorry, Jimmy, it's everything. I know. It's slow for me, is all. Slow night. You know how it is." She didn't look at him. He'd know the truth if she did.

"Don't be givin' me that. Don't even. Rochelle gave me six hundred, and I got twice that from Ruby. They ain't near what you are, and you know it, baby." He ran his thumb under her chin and up the side of her face. He made his voice softer. Talia felt sick at the thought that she used to fall for this. He'd speak to her in a voice so sugary gentle, and she'd swallow it like chunks of candied apple.

Exhaustion rippled through her body, beginning with the place where his finger was in contact with her skin. It felt suddenly like his nearness was sucking the energy from her. She ducked away from him. "I got to go. You want me to work? I got to go."

Later, in the VIP room- just a glorified walk-in closet with black lights, red velvet sofa, pounding music, ceiling mirrors, and cloyingly sweet air freshener called Tropical Paradise- Talia pushed her G-string back into place, slid her feet into the stilettos, and stood up. A glance back at the unconscious man lying against the sofa cushions, dockers around his ankles, mouth agape. He wore a white T-shirt under his cheap blue button-down, and somehow, he'd managed a lipstick stain (not Talia's) across the T-shirts neckline. She noticed his hairline was receding, quite a bit for a guy in his late twenties. He'll be bald by thirty. The thought gave her a weak satisfaction.

Talia tapped his bare shin with the toe of her plastic shoe. Rule was no customers left alone in the VIP room. The manager of Big D's was a small, squinty-eyed unforgiving woman named Cheryl, and if she found this guy back here, she'd have Talia's ass. Talia banged harder at his leg. Nothing. She kicked him. Then bent over his face and shouted above the pounding base music, "Hey! Wake up!"

His eyes popped open. They were shot through with red vessels.

"Ah, shit," he said, only it came out long and exaggerated like "sheeeee-it." He dug the heel of one hand into his eye socket, rubbed it a few times, and then reached down to pull up his pants.

"Come on," Talia said. "You gotta go. Now."

He raised an eyebrow at her, smiled slyly as if they had some sort of understanding. He reached for her like he planned to pull her down on top of him. Like she was his girlfriend, and they'd just snuck out of a party for a quickie.

"Fuck no," she said firmly. "Deals done. Go." She moved to the door and put a hand on the tarnished brass knob, liking the metal's solid feel in her palm. He stood, tucking in his shirt but kept his eyes on her. Then, he moved towards her.

"Why you gotta be so mean," he said in a voice meant for a girl he was courting, not one he'd just paid three hundred bucks to fuck in a closet at the back of a strip club. He was confused, Talia decided. Or retarded.

She opened the door. "Out," she said. He gave her sad puppy dog eyes like she might change her mind. "Now," she said, and he left.

Talia bent and checked her makeup in the rusty mirror attached to the wall next to the door. A basket sat on the edge of a wooden crate by the door; it held old lipsticks and a few cheap face powders. Things the girls left for touchups. She re-applied a semi-dried red lipstick and used her finger to rub it into her lips. She smacked her mouth a few times and studied her reflection. The false eyelashes Trina had convinced her to start wearing on work nights had been a good idea. They stayed put better than globs of mascara and made her gray eyes look big as moon pies. Yeah, she thought, good enough. Jimmy wanted more money. The fucker would get more money.

She stepped out and let the door close softly behind her. She ran one hand over the back of her hair and tugged at her costume a bit, then started back to the floor. This job no longer bothered her. She didn't feel the men's eyes or hands on her or their pricks inside her. She didn't feel anything. Not even fear. Jimmy used to frighten her. What he'd do to her if she didn't bring him the money he wanted. Now she felt nothing. Except for exhaustion. All the time.

CHAPTER 38

New Orleans

July 26, 2020

Rachel is up early and on the road by nine. The light is dim. Fat raindrops splash against the windshield, leaving little blurry starbursts in Rachel's field of vision. First one, then several. Soon it will be a downpour. She steels herself. You can do this. You have to do this.

She'd wanted Virgil to go with her. Would probably have asked him to drive. But Virgil, it hadn't worked out that way. Their conversation had been brief.

"I can't let you continue to do this, Rachel. Technically, she's my patient. She's asked you to keep out of it. And, even more importantly, I really think there could be a danger here for you?"

They'd argued. No, that wasn't fair. Virgil had been reasonable. Rachel had argued. She'd gotten nowhere, finally promising Virgil she'd at least think things over and talk with him before doing anything else. She'd lied.

It was true what Talia said, stopping to ask if people wanted her help never even occurred to Rachel. Was that bullying? Controlling? Probably. She'd spent her life deciding things for other people, making decisions for them. For Talia, for her children. Why didn't Talia understand that Rachel had no choice? Why couldn't Talia see how Rachel had failed to help Nina, which had been the whole problem? Nina got into trouble, got them all into trouble because Rachel didn't help her figure things out. Rachel was the one who was supposed to fix things, and she'd failed. Rachel let Errol hurt Nina. Rachel let Nina leave them at Bubba's that day. If Rachel had done something, anything screamed, run after Errol's truck, told the man in the restaurant Nina's name-if she'd dared to do anything at all, it would have all turned out different.

Then, as always, there was Jeb. If Rachel had made different choices for him. Sent him to a different school, maybe. Urged him to take another job, something less high pressure, away from the world of finance. Everyone knew what those people did to themselves to keep up. Suddenly a million variables threaten to crowd her mind and drive her crazy. Rachel squeezes the thoughts away. There's no time for that now. Talia's life is on the line, and Rachel will help her this one last time, even if it means Talia hates her for it.

As she passes through Bayou Manchec, the downpour thickens, and the route narrows. Both hands wrapped tightly around the steering wheel; she focuses unwaveringly on the road ahead.

CHAPTER 39

New Orleans, Mid-City

1993

Talia sat on a bright chrome chair, the frame digging into her buttocks through the thinly padded seat cushion. A big yellow sign over the door read: WELCOME TO OPDCS in a cheerful script as if this were some sort of clubhouse instead of what it was. The Orleans Parish Department of Children's Services. Probably the least popular place in the city, second only to Central Lockup.

The room was large, windowless, and lit by overhead fluorescent panels that hum-buzzed occasionally in that annoying fly zapper way. It smelled like vanilla air freshener and Clorox and faintly of urine. Beige indoor/outdoor material that looked tough enough to survive Armageddon stretched wall to wall covering the floor. There were three more chairs identical to Talia's, a large, deeply scarred laminate table, and a child-sized bookcase that held a sad collection of toys. A one-eyed baby doll, a handful of soft blocks, a few tattered copies of The Hungry Caterpillar. Someone had tacked posters to all four walls, mostly flowery landscapes, and sunset beaches captioned by phrases like DON'T GIVE UP FIVE MINUTES BEFORE THE MIRACLE and YOU MATTER, YOUR BABY MATTERS. A large glass panel, mirrored on Talia's side, centered one wall.

This meeting was important. With luck, it would be the last one. After this, the nightmare would be over. With luck. But luck, Talia thought, wasn't easy to come by. More than once, the caseworkers and social workers had reminded Talia she had no reason to be nervous, but sitting there alone in that antiseptic space, anxious and terrified, were the only emotions she could muster.

As it turned out, the exhaustion Talia had been experiencing in early 1992 was more than stress and overwork and "living the life." She'd been pregnant and completely unaware.

Her baby was born at Big Charity two weeks shy of her due date, in the summer of that year. An easy delivery-if such a thing existed-and a healthy baby. Talia named her Delilah Magdalena (a nod to Nona). And she gave her child the last name she could no longer carry herself. Delilah Magdalena Fontenot. Talia called her daughter DeeDee and fell in love with her immediately.

The baby had to be Jimmy's-he was the only one who didn't use protection with her. He'd been the club boss. He hadn't given any of the girls a choice. If you wanted to dance in the quarter (at least if you wanted to work anywhere decent, you had to do what Jimmy said.) Fucker. Sex with Jimmy was obligatory, a sort of graft he extracted in addition to the portion of their earnings he demanded. The timing was right, but that didn't mean much. Plus, and Talia hated to admit this, Dee looked like him. She was a beautiful girl, like that asshole in no other way, but the physical similarity was undeniable. Jimmy could never know. Talia refused to name a father for the birth certificate, claiming unknown.

When DeeDee was two days old, a caseworker Talia had never met came to ask questions. Talia, who didn't lie, failed to give the right answers, and the next day when it was time for discharge, the woman came back with a stack of papers, and they took her baby away.

Talia howled and refused to leave the hospital. She threw the papers into the air, and they scattered around the room like so much confetti. You need to provide us proof you have a place to live and means of support to take your baby from the hospital. Talia only grew more hysterical. Alternatively, you could provide the name of the baby's father. Talia screamed and lunged for the nurse. They were sure she was on drugs. She wasn't. They were convinced she was withdrawing from drugs. She was not. Certainly, she was psychotic. The doctor became concerned. Talia became more violent, and finally, she was sedated and transferred to the psych ward, where she spent a week in a medication-induced fog before being released. DeeDee was sent home to a foster family.

So, before she'd gotten Dee back, Talia ran. It was because of DeeDee she'd had to run. But it took a year for her to make the Department of Children's Services understand. Her social worker had helped. She'd explained that Talia had no choice if she wanted to be safe. Wanted her baby safe.

Talia changed her name and found a place across the canal. She quit stripping. She left behind a lot of debt and a lot of bad people. It never occurred to Talia to run further than the Lower Ninth. Crossing the canal seemed like a million miles away. Besides, where else would she go?

Letting go of Rachel had been the hardest part; letting go of the *possibility* of Rachel. Jimmy would look for Talia. He'd want her back. She earned a lot for him, and he wouldn't give that up easily. Plus, she owed him. Talia wasn't even sure the amount. Thousands, at least. His exorbitant interest rates piled on what she'd borrowed to deal with her medical expenses and living expenses while she was pregnant. She'd promised to come back. Now, she had no way of paying any of it. Even if Talia could convince Jimmy to let her stop dancing, he wouldn't forget about the money. He'd go after Rachel if he thought they'd had contact. Let it go, Talia told herself. So many times, let it go.

It had taken Talia over a year to set her life straight. To find her waitressing job, which social services deemed acceptable, accumulate enough money for a solid place to live, and, she hoped, establish her doctors and caseworkers' trust. Talia suspected it was her stint in the psychiatric ward following Dee's birth, making it difficult for her to regain full custody of her baby. She'd been coming to these visitations twice weekly, peeing in a cup, attending parenting classes, providing proof of employment (not stripping or hooking). She'd done everything they'd asked. Still, they'd kept Dee.

Talia glanced at the one-way glass. Placed a hand on her bare knee, holding it down to keep it from jiggling. Looking down at the dress she wore (it was her best), she felt stupid with its white eyelet hem and girlish cap sleeves. She pulled from her bag the sweater she'd brought along and slipped it on. What had she been thinking? Dressing like a child. The social workers, doctors and therapists already thought she was too young, too irresponsible to take care of a baby. Wasn't that why they took Dee? At the hospital. No, she thought. They took Dee because your job was dancing naked and turning tricks at a strip club and you lived with a bunch of other hookers in a place barely fit for a dog. Get a grip. Things are different now.

The heavy door creaked, and a young caseworker appeared smiling. Talia jumped to her feet. Suddenly unsure what to do. Her heart raced, her mouth cotton-stuffed, and the room, arctic minutes earlier, suddenly felt like an August afternoon in Pichette. The sweater felt heavy and sweat pooled in the small divot at the bottom of her spine.

"Hi, I'm Melissa; I'm one of the caseworkers. Are you ready?" the woman's tone was too light as if she were about to bring in a birthday cake rather than Talia's daughter. "Why don't you have a seat in the play area?" She pointed at the bookcase.

Talia croaked, "Yeah. Yes ma'am. Thank you." She practically curtsied. Cut it out, she told herself. Act like a grown-up. She sat down cross-legged on the small rag rug beside the toys.

Melissa nodded, stepped out of the room. Returning almost immediately. All at once, there was Dee in this stranger's arms. It made no matter how many times it happened. Talia's breath stopped every time she saw her baby. Every time, like that first time. Melissa knelt and placed DeeDee on the floor in front of Talia.

Talia resisted the urge to collect Dee up into her arms, into her body, squeezing until the two of them were one thing again. Instead, she held out her arms and said, "Do you want to play with me today, Dee?"

DeeDee sat, staring at Talia for a moment. She cocked her head, placing one chubby finger in her mouth, blinked her green eyes as if trying to make up her mind, and finally broke into giggles. Dee was a cautious baby. After all these visits, she knew Talia, but she had another family. She'd lived with that family nearly her whole short life.

It doesn't matter. It can take forever. I can do this.

The visit was difficult. Talia's panic and desperation rising and falling at regular intervals, the pain so enormous inside her, pulled her attention away from Dee and whatever they were doing. Playing blocks or 'feed the baby' or 'bedtime story.' She was too aware of the one-way glass behind which sat any number of supervisors and social workers in whose hands her fate and DeeDee's fate rested. It was all Talia could do not to throw her body down before them and plead with them, the ghosts behind the mirror. Please give me my baby, please let me have her, or I'll die. I'll just die. It took everything she had to turn pages slowly in The Hungry Caterpillar and smile when all she wanted to do was snatch up her daughter and race for the door and never stop running until they were far, far away.

• • •

A week later, Talia was at work, sliding an order of shrimp 'n' grits off the counter and ignoring the catcalls coming from a couple of regulars.

"For you," Walter, the cook and owner, looking impatient, was holding the phone out, away from his greasy apron, a dishtowel over his shoulder.

When she got the news, Talia's knees buckled. If not for one busboy standing close by, she might have hit her head on the chrome countertop or pulled the phone clean out of the wall.

Instead, the young man guided her to one booth in the back and sat her down. Talia buried her face in her hands, still smelling of shrimp and the coffee she'd poured all morning. For the first time since DeeDee was born, she felt herself smiling through her tears.

CHAPTER 40

Devereaux, Louisiana

July 26, 2020

Rachel is in Devereaux before noon. The cloudburst is long gone, but the sky remains gloomily overcast; the air is hot and dank. Standing on the dilapidated porch, she hesitates before stepping forward. A board creaks suspiciously under the heel of her boot. She pauses and glances down, testing it a little, before pressing on it with her full body weight, then moves on. The screen door has several nasty rents, and the whole thing is pulling away from the frame across the lower edge. A horse fly buzzes lazily inside the webbing in no hurry to find a way out. There's a sharp smell as if something died under the house. Or inside.

He hadn't been difficult to find. It seems Ray Larson moved around a lot in the last few decades but never more than a mile from where Rachel left him back in 1981. He was listed, although the listing was wrong. Outdated by a half year. The woman who answered the phone-her cigarette-scarred voice dropping into something steeped with barely suppressed anger at the mention of Ray's name-knew exactly where Rachel could find him. "And you give the sonofabitch a message for me, will ya?" Rachel had agreed to carry the message, although she'd forgotten it as soon as she'd thanked the woman and hung up the phone.

Carefully pulling open the broken screen, she raps at the door, waits, knocks again, harder this time. Nothing. Checking for a doorbell, she finds only the remnants of one; the aluminum chipped and peeled, ringer button missing. Finally, she hears something. A voice from inside the house, although it sounds muffled. Strained.

"Hello!" She calls through the door. "Anyone home?"

A minute later, an incredibly old man stands at the door. He wears wrinkled pajama bottoms and a white t-shirt, yellow stains under the arms. There are deep crevices around his eyes and across his forehead. He is missing several teeth, and his lips curve inward across his gum line. Unshaven, bristles of gray beard sprout in patches over his sallow, sickly skin. His eyeglasses are broken, secured across the bridge of his nose with black electrical tape and when he speaks, his breath is fetid. Rachel takes a step back, careful to avoid the loose board.

"Who are you?" He spits the words more than says them. It's the voice Rachel recognizes.

"Ray, Ray Larson." She says. It's not a question, but he takes it as one.

"Pends on whose askin'." He glares at her.

He is barefoot, and Rachel sees his toenails are thick and yellowed, and, for a split second, she considers turning. Running. In her mind, Ray hadn't aged. Not like this. He was still the handsome, slightly wrecked, forever hard lucked Daddy-Ray she'd known. Moody, selfish, and drunk as a wayward teenager, but not this horrible, mean-looking, catastrophe of a confused old man. She's enraged at herself for caring.

The words come, but they are forced. "I'm Rachel. It's me, Ray. Nina's daughter." She couldn't say "your daughter." That had never been true. Silence. Then he takes a half step backward and squints at her.

"Well, I'll be goddamned."

He looks amused, and for some reason, this inflames Rachel's anger further. "Look, I need to speak with you," she says to fill space and keep herself from turning and walking away. "It's... important."

"Is it now? How many years has it been? Now you need somethin?" She sees him glance at her diamond wedding ring and over her shoulder at the Range Rover, then back at her. "What the hell," he says. "Come in. Come on in." He steps back from the door, and Rachel takes a step inside.

The dark hallway is rank with the smell of body odor, stale alcohol, cigarettes and cat pee. Ray leads her into a claustrophobic living room. The drapes are drawn, and a single reclining chair-the seat cushion badly worn, and sagging-is positioned three feet in front of an enormous television. Beside the chair sits a hospital rolling table, crowded with items: a television remote control, a plate full of crumbs, a China dish he's using as an ashtray, an open can of PBR, a lighter, and a crumpled pack of Marlboros. A trashcan beside the table is full of empties. Rachel wonders if they are from last night or this morning.

On the television, there is a talk show. Two men who might be skinheads or might just be assholes with attitudes are screaming at each other. Ray picks up the remote and mutes them.

He lowers himself into the recliner. Points at a lumpy sofa. "Sit, you wanna beer?"

She shakes her head. "No, no thanks. I just need some information."

"He picks up his beer, takes a long sip, and sets it down again. Peers at Rachel. A gummy grin. "So, ya gonna tell me where ya been? What's it been, Rachel, thirty years? Jesus fuckin' Christ. How'd that happen, right?"

More like forty years, but she's not in the mood for small talk. Not with him.

"Listen, I need your help."

"Yeah?"

"I found Talia." Ray shakes his head, stares at the muted television. Says nothing. "Did you hear me?"

"Yeah, I heard you. You found Talia. What do you want? A prize?"

She sighs. "Jesus Christ, Ray. She's your daughter. Don't you even care where she is?"

He looks at her, his eyes narrowed. "You think I don't fuckin know where she is?"

For a moment, Rachel is unable to speak. Questions fly at her from all directions. How long had he known? Why had he lied to her? Would he lie now? Sonofabitch. She had to be careful here. She did not know who this man was, not really. She'd known him all of a handful of years. She'd invented him in her mind. Talia knew him. Rachel did not.

"You knew? About prison?"

He takes another sip from his beer. "Yeah, I knew. She killed a fuckin cop. They put her in prison. That's what happens when you kill a fuckin cop." He picks up the remote and unmutes the sound, and sets the remote back down, but this time on the table between them. It's a challenge.

Rachel stands, takes the remote, mutes the TV. "But her name. Her... her scars. How'd you know, Ray?"

Ray sets down the beer. "How'd I know what? That she changed her name?" He smirks. "You know where she got that name, don't you?"

"Yeah," she says. "I don't know."

He pauses for a while, staring ahead at the television, but Rachel can tell he's not really watching it. He's considering something. "It was a cartoon show she used to watch. When she was a kid, she spent a lot of time on her own after you left Rach." Rachel grimaces at his jab and his use of her childhood nickname. "She watched a lot of television, I think." Is there sadness in his voice? "Anyway, there was this show. I don't recall the name. Buncha little fairies, I think. Different colors, ya know? All had the same last name. Paradise. One of em I remember was like the magic one. Had powers. Talia talked about it a lot. Went on and on for a while. Anyway, this one fairy could do all kind of shit. Go invisible. Fly around. Grant wishes." He laughs. "Save the fuckin world, you know. I think maybe that was the main thing. The saving. Anyway. She loved that show. She had a stuffed doll looked like that one fairy. Ya know, I never knew where she got that thing. Probably stole it. Little thief, she was." He looks at Rachel, and this time she sees the sorrow in his eyes for sure. "You know what that one fairy was called?"

Rachel nods. "Yeah," says Rachel. "Yeah, I do."

"That's right," he says. "Janie fuckin Lucile Paradise. So, soon as I saw that news after the storm, I knew. I knew it was her. Goddamn knew it."

How had she missed it back then? The name. It had all been right there. Talia must have wanted her to know, on some level, and Rachel never saw it. She remembers the story, the Katrina survivor who committed capital murder. It was big news for a while. All the surrounding chaos. But she'd been busy trying to protect the children from the rest of Katrina's aftermath. They'd stayed up in Baton Rouge that whole year until the city cleared and the Good Hope fiasco was settled. Had she paid so little attention? Even Ray caught on. Rachel takes a deep breath. "She didn't murder anyone Ray. You know that."

He shrugs, but there's something in that shrug. "Course she didn't murder nobody. Not Tee. But what's done is done. They ain't gonna change their mind."

"I need you to help me."

He shakes his head, sticks out his lower lip, and looks away. "Nah, can't be helped. What's done is done," he repeats.

"Jesus, Ray, they're going to execute her. We can't let that happen."

"Yeah," he says flatly. "They're gonna execute her." He thinks for a few seconds, then adds, "She's got a daughter, you know? Or she had one."

"Oh, my God."

"Yeah, names DeeDee. She'd be bout." He rubs his chin. His nails are filthy. "Bout thirty now. If she's alive, I mean. Seemed like after the storm, maybe Talia went crazy. You know? That's how I figured it. I know she'd been livin' over there in the Lower Nine. She was lucky to survive. I figured her girl didn't make it. Maybe that's why... "Another long sip of beer. He's empty. "I gotta go get another beer. You sure you don't want nothin'?" He hauls himself heavily out of the chair.

"What's her last name? The daughter? DeeDee?" Rachel stands to follow him as he heads for the kitchen.

"Uh," he pauses. Then pulls open the fridge. It's nearly empty save eight or ten cans of beer, a hunk of cheese wrapped in plastic, and something unidentifiable on a plate. He takes two beers and slams the fridge door. "Her last name? Lemme think." He shuffles back into the living room, sets the cans on the table, and plants himself in the chair. Looks at Rachel. "You got any money? I'm a little short. Been on disability for a while now. My back. But the checks don't stretch if ya know what I mean."

A shakedown, Rachel thinks. Isn't that what they call this? Still standing, she takes her purse off her shoulder, opens it, and pulls out her wallet. Feeling his eyes heavy on her, she removes five twenty-dollar bills and places them on the table. "What's her last name, Ray?"

He grins. "Fontenot. The name is F-O-N-T-E-N-O-T. Same as you. Same as Nina. Same as old Magda. Same as ever crazy bitch I ever knew. But like I said," he pulls the top on his beer and shrugs. "She's probably dead."

She looks at him. "Ray, are you doing ok? I mean," she says, looking around the ruined house. "Oh, I don't know what I mean."

He picks up the remote and unmutes the sound. The screaming men are no longer on stage. Now the host is speaking to a guy in a jumbo wheelchair who looks like he weighs four hundred pounds.

"Yeah," another toothless grin. "I guess I am Rachel. I guess I am."

She can't help herself. "What about me, Ray? Did you know where I was the whole time too?" She regrets the words immediately.

He nods and smacks his lips together. Then, without pulling his eyes from the television. "Yup. I did. The whole goddamn time."

Of course, he'd known, Rachel tells herself as she gets back into the car, swallowing hard to clear the bitter taste from her mouth. Her name has been all over the society pages for years. Decades. Ever since she married Daniel. It would have been hard to avoid knowing all about her life. Why it hadn't occurred to her earlier, she couldn't say.

That means Talia knew too. All these years, Talia knew. But she'd stayed away. That's what she'd meant. I did it to protect you from me. Talia didn't want her life, history and problems to damage what Rachel and Daniel had built. Suddenly it hits her. It's been this way their whole life. Talia is the strong one. She's protected both of them. She's allowed Rachel to think she was the one taking care of Talia when it's been Talia sacrificing herself for Rachel all along.

CHAPTER 41

The Lower Ninth Ward

1999

Clear gold spun light filled the front room as Talia pushed open the door to the house on Charbonnet Street. The blue jay song above in the oaks intermingled with children's voices outside in the street. Always so many children outside. She smiled broadly, gave herself another minute, and then hurried to the bathroom to shower and get ready for work. She and Dee had been renting this tiny shotgun house for almost five years, even so, she never stopped noticing the little things about it. Like the way the sun filtered in through the time-worn kitchen curtains she'd decided to leave hanging because she liked the patina the years had given them. Or how the thousands of hand-hammered nails in the hundred-year-old oak floors had been worn entirely flush and soft as the wood.

Talia loved the neighborhood. The houses were cheap, and public transportation made it an obvious choice for someone like her (meaning poor), but she lived there for more than convenience. It was the only proper home Talia had ever had. She knew her neighbors. Trusted them. Trusted her daughter with them, trading babysitting time for yellow squash and collard greens grown in backyard vegetable patches. She'd sat on their porches drinking sweet tea from a mason jar, gossiping as the day fell softly into night. These people had been her only family for a long time.

Life wasn't perfect. There were nightmares. Talia woke up sweating, crying, and screaming sometimes. Not always able to remember. But often, there were people in her dreams. Men mostly. Faces of men she didn't know. Not always cruel. Sometimes just indifferent. She dreamt of Mama and Rachel occasionally. Never Mama's face. She couldn't remember her face, and there were other things, but she tried not to think of those. Instead, she concentrated on Dee. Her daughter was all that mattered now.

The Charbonnet house was just a handful of rooms piled together inside a brick box. A rickety porch with a busted front step. Not a lot more than a raised shack, but Talia and DeeDee loved it. There was a small front yard with a low fence, two magnolia trees, and a swinging wooden gate. A kitchen bright with a window box for growing things and two tiny sunlit bedrooms, one for each of them. It was possible to see the moon, high over the fence posts and washing lines, and telephone wires from the kitchen steps—pale gold and hopeful.

Overwhelmingly, the population of the neighborhood was black. But there were also French-speaking Catholic creoles and Italians and Greeks and Cubans. No one asked questions. They just took Talia and her daughter in and kept them both safe. Those who lived in the Lower Ninth saw it as home, a refuge, a special place to be treasured and protected. Not so with the rest of the city.

Forever cut off from the city by the Industrial Canal in the early twentieth century, the downriver portion of the Ninth Ward became utterly isolated except for a single streetcar line connecting it to the city center. The repository of virtually all municipal dis-amenities (railroad yards, petrochemical plants, slaughterhouses and the city's sewage treatment plants) and populated by the city's poorer and less educated residents, the area was consequently neglected by the city government and virtually ignored by the rest of the city's inhabitants. The final blows came with the Intracoastal Waterway excavation directly behind the Lower Ninth and, later, the Mississippi River-Gulf Outlet Canal, profoundly exaggerating the flooding risk. The residents of the Lower Ninth were now surrounded on three sides by water.

All of this created a virtually guaranteed disaster.

In 1965, it arrived as Hurricane Betsy. Most of Talia's neighbors remembered Betsy, even the young ones. They'd been told the stories by their parents and grandparents so often that the catastrophic hurricane had become part of the neuronal connections that made up their memory center. It was practically part of the collective DNA. Some of the oldest residents could not speak about Betsy without breaking down in tears.

Talia was pulling her door closed and locking it when she noticed her elderly neighbor wrapped in an afghan sitting outside on her porch. She glanced at her watch, plenty of time before the start of her three pm shift. She felt hollow and happy inside, so much space for others today.

"Hey, Miss Gloria!" Talia called across the narrow swath of dirt that separated her house from the next.

"Well, now, hey, your own self. How is y'all doing today?" Miss Gloria was waving one long thin brown arm in the air. Gloria Wright was one of the neighborhood's oldest residents. She claimed to be ninety-two, but without birth records, it was hard to know. Most mornings, she could be found on the porch of her pale blue shotgun house, sitting upright in her wheelchair, brightly colored blanket stretched across her lap and lace shawl around her shoulders. She drank sweet tea only, although Talia thought she smelled a brief spike of something more potent on the old woman's breath once or twice. "Come on over here," she said, smiling wide at Talia. "I want to see ya. Seems like I ain't had a good look at my girl in a long time." They'd spoken the morning before, but, over the past year, Gloria forgot a great deal. She could recite from memory the names of every Louisiana governor since William Wright Heard in 1904 but ask what she ate for breakfast or anything about a conversation that happened hours earlier, and she'd draw a blank. Talia had learned to agree was easier and gentler for her.

"Oh, I wish I could, Miss. Gloria, but I'm late for work. I'll come by after, ok?" A pang of guilt at the lie.

"Sure, sure." Miss Gloria kept waving and smiling as her eyelids fluttered down, distracted by the feeling of warm sun on her face.

"Miss Gloria?" Talia called over the porch railing. The woman didn't respond. She only sat with her face turned up to the sunlight, ashy dark skin a myriad of lines and wrinkles, so fragile it looked as if tissue paper had been balled up and flattened out again, stretched delicately over her bones. Talia stepped off her porch and started across the shaggy patch of lawn. Likely Miss Gloria had just fallen asleep. Still, Talia would check that Gloria's grandniece, Charmaine, was awake and watching her before leaving. The girl, nineteen, had lived with the old woman since birth. She was well-intentioned, but sometimes Talia found her a bit lacking in common sense. Mama would have said she was a few tools shy of a shed. Talia thought she was just immature and not especially bright.

On the porch, Talia gently touched Gloria's shoulder and called her name softly. Gloria's eyes popped open. "Yeah, well, hello. How are y'all this morning?"

Great, they could start all over again.

Just then, Charmaine emerged from the house, rubbing her eyes. A tall girl with ebony skin and wide, black eyes, she had a cigarette, unlit, between her lips and wore rubber flip-flops and cut-off shorts, and she'd painted her long fingernails a deep sparkling purple.

"Well, hey, Charmaine," said Talia. "Miss Gloria seemed like she fell asleep, so I just popped over to check."

"Hey there, thanks for that. I got her now." Charmaine smiled and patted Miss Gloria's shoulder, then took a seat beside her aunt and stretched out her long, bare legs in the sun.

Talia peered at the young woman's face. She looked tired. "How are you doing, Charmaine? I haven't talked with you lately."

"I'm doin' fine. I got no complaints." She smiled and picked up a lighter that lay on the small table and lit the cigarette. She sat back. "Hey, how's Dee doin', anyway? She's a busy little girl running in and out." The smell of cool menthol drifted, mixing with the magnolia.

"Yeah," said Talia, "She's starting over at St. Chris, you know. I think she's more excited about the uniform than anything else. She's already talking about college." Suddenly Talia realizes how these words might impact Charmaine, not that many years older than Dee but with far fewer prospects.

Charmaine smiles and shakes her head. Draws on the cigarette. "Yeah, that's a lotta money, right? But she's a smart girl. Real smart. She'll do it, I bet." The words were warm and full. The generosity of people always struck Talia. Charmaine meant it. She would be genuinely happy for DeeDee to make it to college.

"Thank you, Charmaine. What about you? What do you want to do?"

"Ah, I don't know. Right now, I kinda got my hands full, ya know?" She dips her head toward Miss Gloria. "But could be later, I'm thinkin' bout beauty school. I'm good at that stuff. Hair and such."

"Wow, that would be great," said Talia. "Yeah, I could see you'd be good at that." She smiled, and Charmaine smiled back, nodding thoughtfully.

Talia stepped off their porch and headed toward the bus stop. She glanced back once to see Charmaine had put out the cigarette and was leaning forward, one hand on her aunt's arm. She was whispering something, and Miss Gloria laughed, her dentures flashing brilliant white in the sun.

CHAPTER 42

Kenner, Louisiana

July 26, 2020

DeeDee Fontenot is not dead. Rachel finds her on Google in less than ten minutes; she is in Kenner, across the river, nine miles and a million lifetimes away. The two-story complex is on a busy, treeless thoroughfare. Mid-century. The apartments face the road, two rows of dulled black doors, the paint peeling, some with strips of laminate coming away dry and bleached from sun exposure. A wrought-iron railing runs the length of the upper story; it is ornate, like a French Quarter balcony rail, but very flimsy, giving the whole place a sad, fake feel. A single brass colored plastic number has been stuck to each door. A few have lost their numbers and have only the glue residue remaining.

DeeDee's is number nine. Her number is polished and someone had attempted to re-glue the peeling laminate to the door. The weather, however, is winning that battle. Outside her door are several potted plants. A fern, lush and healthy, and two potted geraniums still blooming bright red. In pink letters, a straw mat reads: WELCOME.

The girl who answers the door is not DeeDee; she's too young, mid-teens. She wears low-slung jeans and a tie-dyed T-shirt. She's mixed race, skin the color of milky coffee, and dark hair pulled back from her face. High cheekbones, small perfect mouth. Her eyes are pale gray. There's a young baby in her arms, swaddled in a blue baby blanket, his pink face pinched and wrinkly still bears the bruises of birth.

"Hi," says Rachel as gently as possible. "I'm Rachel; I'm looking for DeeDee Fontenot."

The girl looks skeptical like she does not believe Rachel is looking for DeeDee or does not believe Rachel is named Rachel. "Who are you?" she says, her voice sounds intentionally thuggish.

Rachel sucks at the air and runs a hand over her damp forehead. It's hot standing outside the apartment. "Uh, I'm Rachel," she repeats. "My name is Rachel Thibodaux. I'd like to talk to DeeDee. It's about her mother."

The girl's face tightens, and she says sharply, "She don't want nothin' to do with her mama. Besides, she ain't here right now." Still sounding thuggish, although a bit more forced. Rachel wonders if this is her natural voice. The girl steps back and starts to close the door.

"Um, please. Can you tell me when she might be back? It's important that I speak with her."

The girl stops, one hand still on the door. She peers at Rachel. She's trying to decide. "She's at work. But like I said, she don't want nothin' to do with her mama. She ain't gonna talk to you about her."

"But why? Why is that?" asks Rachel. The girl is silent, staring at her. If she doesn't do something quickly, Rachel will lose this opportunity. "Look, my name is Rachel, like I said. And my married name is Thibodaux. But my name used to be Fontenot. I'm DeeDee's aunt, and I need to speak with her."

The child loses herself for a moment. Her face softens, becomes curious. This girl is not the street-tough she was trying to project when she answered the door. She is, thankfully, just a child. A little girl. She twists her mouth, squints her eyes while she thinks. Finally, she says, "OK, you wait, lemme call her first." And she shuts the door and is gone inside.

Rachel waits less than two minutes, and the girl is back, still holding the quietly gurgling baby.

"Ok then, she says you can come in. She made me tell her what you looked like."

"Oh," says Rachel. "Well, thank you. Thank you very much."

"Come on then," the girl backs away from the door and motions for Rachel to step inside.

They sit across from one another in the sunny living room. Someone freshly painted the walls a cheerful yellow. Inexpensive prints hang on the walls. The furniture is worn but clean, and a lovely hand-knitted Afghan is folded over the back of the sofa. The girl pours sweet tea into tall glasses with ice and watches Rachel. Her expression is the sweetly curious, mildly suspicious one of a child who has snuck out of bed and sits hidden on the stairs to spy on her parents' unfamiliar visitors. There is no hostility, only childish curiosity mixed with a dash of adolescent self-righteousness.

After a bit, she says, "I'm Colette." She's still holding the baby against her. "And this here, this is Liam." The baby has fallen asleep. It's hot in the apartment. Colette has removed the swaddling, and he lies one cheek pressed up against her skin. One tiny, perfect hand curled into a fist against his face. Rachel says nothing for a moment. Studying the girl. Her eyes are Talia's, as is her narrow chin.

"You're DeeDee's girl, aren't you?" she asks.

The girl nods slightly. Rachel resists telling Colette how much she looks like her grandmother. She makes Rachel think of what Talia might have been had she been redrawn somewhat larger than life. Colette is much taller, her skin darker, and her features bolder, but all the outlines are the same. The gestures are so similar.

 She studies the infant again-only a few weeks old. Was it possible?

"And Liam?"

Colette glances down at the infant curled snaillike against her. She looks up, smiling—Talia's smile. "I'm just sittin' with him. His Mama lives next door. She pays me to stay with him when I'm home. Money's good, and he's a good baby." She smiles down at Liam again.

Rachel feels an unexpected sense of relief over this. Colette is tall, but her body and face are childlike. She's much younger than Rachel first thought. She can't be fourteen years old. "Can I ask you how old you are, Colette?"

"I made thirteen in April." Wide smile.

Rachel takes a moment to process this. At forty-nine, Talia, her baby sister, is not only a mother but a grandmother.

"Wow," says Rachel à propos of nothing. She picks up her glass and takes a sip. The bite of lemon mixed with the sugary tea and ice is delicious. She can feel the coolness down her throat after she swallows.

"You like that?" asks Colette grinning.

Rachel laughs. "Yeah, I guess so. I don't have sweet tea often enough anymore. This is excellent, thank you."

"Mama made it. She leaves it every day. It's sugar. And she puts cranberry in it."

"Huh," says Rachel holding her glass to the sunlight. Indeed a few tiny bits of bright red cranberry are floating in the pale-yellow liquid.

"So, how come I never met you?" Colette screws up her mouth, suspicious again.

"It's my fault," says Rachel. "I... I lost track of..." she starts to say Talia and changes her mind. "Your grandmother. A long time ago. And I didn't know."

"You didn't know what?"

"About you. About your Mama. I'm sorry for that."

"When you see Mama, don't talk about her family, especially her mama. I've never even met her. I told you. I used to ask, but she made me quit. Said it wouldn't do me any good, and there wasn't nothin' I needed to know, anyway. Said she didn't even know where her mama was." Colette shrugs. "You know what I think?"

"No, what do you think?"

"I think that isn't true. I think she knows, and she won't tell me."

Rachel has no answer to that. What can she say? Colette is staring right at her, so Rachel shifts her gaze, takes another sip from her drink. She feels like a coward. She sets down the glass and asks, "And your father?" Rachel is immediately angry at herself for asking.

Colette's face drops. She glances toward the window and looks out for a moment. Pushes a strand of hair out of her face. "He died." The words are flat, airless.

"Oh, I'm so sorry."

"I didn't know him. He died before I was born." Rachel says nothing. She doesn't have words. "He was visiting his family over there on Jackson Street. Got shot. "Rachel thinks about the empty lots she'd seen. Mailboxes still standing, servicing nobody.

"I'm sorry you didn't get to know him." There's a hollowness to her words. She searches but has nothing else.

"It's ok."

Rachel waits, thinking Colette will say more, but she doesn't continue.

Colette, who has her head bent toward Liam, cooing at him, looks up suddenly. "Do you want to hold him?"

"Oh," Rachel is surprised. "No, that's ok. I think it's better if I don't. But thank you." She watches as Colette rocks Liam back and forth gently in her arms. The baby is making small burbly noises and blowing tiny spit bubbles between chubby lips. Colette giggles.

"He's real cute; I don't even mind watching him. I'd do it even if Aliana didn't pay me anything. But she always makes me take something. Liam's such a wonderful baby."

"He seems like it."

"I don't think I want kids, though."

"You don't?"

She shakes her head, "No, I'm going to be a surgeon, and surgeons don't have kids."

"Really? And why is that?"

"No time. Too busy saving people's lives and all that." She looks at Rachel seriously, then nuzzles Liam for a few seconds and says, "Or I will.. I could get one of those Or Pairs, right? Who lives with you and helps all the time, like that? That would work, right?"

Rachel corrects Colette's mispronunciation of the word "au pair" and then stops herself. Instead, she says, "Sure, lots of busy people do that."

"Yeah, I don't know. I'll decide later. I have some time."

They sit in silence for a while, watching Liam do extraordinarily little.

"You have kids?" asks Colette.

"Yeah."

"Boys or girls?"

"I have a daughter," says Rachel. "And I had a son." She says this for the first time. I had a son.

Colette looks at her. Very plain. "What happened?"

"He died." For the first time, Rachel does not add a qualifier. She does not say that Jeb died in a car accident. She does not mention that it was not his fault or that the police found no evidence of speeding. She says nothing. She knows that if Colette asks, she will tell the truth.

Colette is quiet for a while. Contemplating. Then she says, "In sixth grade, I fell off the monkey bar and broke my arm so bad you could see the bone sticking out."

"Oh my."

"I screamed and screamed, and they had to hold me down in the emergency room. I thought it was the worst thing that could ever happen to a person."

"I bet."

She nods slowly, her eyes suddenly dark and serious. "But it wasn't. I learned that. It was just the worst thing that happened to me. But about your boy? I bet that's the worst thing ever, and I'm just sorry that happened to you."

Rachel felt the tears immediately and swallowed a few times, blinked them away.

"Thank you, Colette, and you know what I think?"

"What?"

"I think breaking your arm, so the bones stick out, is pretty darn gross and terrible, and I also think you'll make a terrific doctor."

Colette smiles wide, and then they both laugh, and then Colette pours them another glass of sweet tea.

CHAPTER 43

The Lower Ninth Ward

2004

Talia pulled a finger down the classified ads one more time than dropped her pencil to the table. She pushed the paper away, picked up her coffee mug, and let her gaze drift to the window. Sipping at the coffee, she grimaced at the bitter liquid. She'd been sitting staring at the paper longer than she realized—a million jobs but, so far, not one better than what she had already.

Outside, DeeDee watched two little girls, granddaughters to Earle Clarkson, a widowed schoolteacher who lived across the street, as they played on the weedy lawn. The girls had uncoiled the garden hose and connected it up to a rusty-looking lawn sprinkler. Broken, it shot a steady stream of water up and out at a forty-five-degree angle from the dirt. The children ran back and forth through the spray screaming. The smaller one, Talia couldn't remember her name, was five or six years old. She kept losing her nerve. Jumping up and down and then skittering away giggling instead of running through the water. Her small brown belly protruded adorably over the top of her fuchsia bikini bottoms. The bathing suit top was both superfluous and oversized. It kept riding up around her neck.

Talia thought about Earle living alone with those two little girls. He and his wife had raised them from babies; his daughter, shot to death in a drive-by years ago. Earle's wife died suddenly, leaving him to take care of them on his own. He was sixty-seven now and retired from school, but he continued to work part-time as a handyman for extra money. Dee took the girls whenever she could help. But Dee was only thirteen and a young thirteen, so what she could do was limited.

Earle and Miss Gloria and Charmaine, and so many others were the reason Talia had stayed here in the Lower Ninth long after she could have afforded to move elsewhere.

Dee sat in an aluminum lawn chair as the children played, painting her fingernails periwinkle. Occasionally, she looked up and hollered jovially at them to quit getting her wet. There was an old tire beside the chair and, she rested her long legs on it, occasionally glancing down to admire her recently pedicured feet. Talia loved how DeeDee's body differed from her own; Dee was an athlete, a soccer player, built strong and lean, and so tall. At twelve, Dee was already three inches taller than Talia.

"Dee!" Talia called, poking her head through the half-open window.

"Hey, Mama," DeeDee looked up. Smiled.

"Hey, baby. Listen, you watch those two, alright?" Talia motioned toward the children. They'd stopped running in the water and were watching Talia. Eyes wide.

"Yeah, Mama," Dee answered with only a hint of pre-teenage 'whatever you say' disdain in her voice.

"I'm serious," said Talia, more firmly. "No more nails, girl. You pay attention!"

Dee made a face, twisting her mouth slightly and rolling her eyes.

"Hey!"

"Sorry, Mama." Dee smiled.

You are my life, sweet girl, Talia thought.

The sun shone bright and hot, and the table fan which Talia had pulled up-close did little more than blow hairs around her perspiring face. Days like this, when the air was stone-still, it could be hard to breathe. Hard to think, and she needed to think. She pulled the paper toward her and opened to the jobs section again.

Money, she needed to think about money. They were doing ok, for now. Finishing her high school diploma had helped her find jobs, but it hadn't earned her anything extra. It seemed like high school graduates were everywhere. College was the thing. And there was no way for Talia to get to college.

But Dee, she thought. Dee was going. No matter what. For that, they needed money.

She flipped to the next page of the newspaper. Her eye fell on a half-page advertisement. A photograph of a long, low building, so white it nearly glowed. Lush green lawn. Perfectly shaped boxwoods and one enormous live oak shading a circular drive. She read the caption: GOOD HOPE—NOW HIRING. ASSISTED LIVING FACILITY/LONG-TERM CARE AIDES NO EXPERIENCE NECESSARY. WE WILL TRAIN! The starting wage was more than she made now, even with tips. Too good to be true for sure, but Talia picked up the pencil and circled the ad, paused and circled it again.

. . .

Bernard and Ellie Coen were two of the first residents to be moved into the new facility in the Ninth Ward across from the Industrial Canal. Both in their nineties, married over seventy years, they lived together in room 294, side by side in hospital beds, close enough to reach out and touch one another, any time they liked. They'd chosen Good Hope specifically because it offered them the opportunity to stay together no matter what the future might bring. It was a promise few other facilities would make. Good Hope made it without hesitation.

They'd been scientists, both of them, ecologists working with the National Wetlands Research Center up in Slidell since the 1970s. Ellie retired years ago, but Bernie stayed on until the Center became the Wetland and Aquatic Research Center, a USGS division, and moved to Lafayette in the '90s. He was nearly seventy-five. After that, Bernie continued to write and lecture at LSU as often as he could.

They called her kiddo, Bernard and Ellie, which Talia, at thirty-four, found sweet. They had a combination of ailments between them: diabetes, hypertension, degenerative joint disease, neuropathy and Mrs. Coen- a small woman with large curious brown eyes, smooth silver hair and a quick smile had recently exhibited confusion in the evenings. It frightened Bernard to watch his wife slip away for a few hours every day. Murmuring to dead relatives, unaware of her surroundings. She returned after a dose or two of medication and was always clearer when the sun came up, but Bernard had trouble just the same.

Bernie was a big man. In his prime, Talia guessed he'd been well over six feet and had probably weighed over two hundred pounds. Now, his frame was still broad and strong but hollowed out, like a sailboat without sails. His eyes were cloudy blue but wide as a child's. Full of curiosity and goodwill, Bernie trusted everyone. Talia held his hand while the nurses administered injectable medications to his wife. Sometimes Ellie was combative, and it became necessary for an orderly to restrain her during treatments. Moving Bernie from the room was not always practical, and it pained him terribly to hear Ellie's screams. Talia held his hand and encouraged him to look out the window as the evening light paled to lavender and the tree branches moved gently in the breeze. She whispered words she hoped might soothe him.

"It'll be alright," she'd say. "Ellie will rest soon. Not to worry."

Most evenings, Talia returned to see them after she'd finished her rounds. She'd sit, smoothing the hair away from Ellie's forehead as the old woman babbled to her son, dead now nearly ten years, or her mother or older brother. Sometimes Ellie thought she was at home in Chalmette. In the comfortable brick house, the couple had shared for over forty years. Sometimes she was in another place. A place Bernie didn't know.

The job at Good Hope had turned out to be both more and less than Talia had expected. More work, more hours, more back pain, and significantly more fulfilling. But less organized and far less clearly defined than she'd hoped. Good Hope was perpetually short-staffed, the training scant to non-existent, the infrastructure complex and the bureaucracy thick with unnecessary paperwork. She loved it.

Most of the patients, like the Coens, were elderly, some with dementia, severely disoriented, and often frightened. She bathed, dressed, and fed them. Changed sheets and bedpans and chatted with them. Almost only about their pasts, although a few expressed an ongoing interest in Talia's life. They mostly wanted to know about her daughter. Youth, it seemed, was an elixir to their suffering.

It was late October, and Talia had been working at Good Hope for nearly four months. Bernie sat up in his bed, a mass of pillows propped behind him. He wore eyeglasses and held a book with enormous print but did not appear to be reading. Instead, he was watching his sleeping wife. She'd been worse lately, the confusion coming on earlier in the day and lasting most of the night. There were times now when she had difficulty recognizing her husband. Bernie looked up as Talia entered, his face brightening.

"Hello, kiddo," he said. "Good to see you."

Talia pulled up the steel nursing stool and sat down beside his bed. "I'm so sorry, Bernie," she said, looking at Ellie.

He didn't answer for a long time. Then he said, "It's no use, you know?"

"What? What's no use?"

"It's not the rain," he said. "It's the levees that'll get us in the end. The water will overtop those levees, and that'll be that."

It took Talia a moment to understand. They'd had a terrible storm three days earlier, the severe thunder and torrential rains frightening many residents. The risk of flooding had been high, and it became apparent that Good Hope's emergency plan was lacking. In the end, the damage at the nursing home was minimal. A few trees went down, two windows cracked, and a flooded parking lot. But no injuries other than psychological. Bernie had been intermittently obsessing about it ever since.

"You mean flooding? Is that what you're talking about, Bernie?"

He nodded, glancing back at his wife. Then, he set down the book and laid his glasses on the hospital table. His hand trembled. He'd lost weight. "You want to know what's going to happen to this city, kiddo?" She wasn't sure she did but said yes, anyway. He needed to talk.

Talia sat for a long time, listening to Bernie Coen explain the profound dilemma that was New Orleans. She'd had a vague understanding of the danger all along. Most city residents, especially those in the Ninth Ward, knew that living in a place many feet below sea level and surrounded on three sides by water was inherently untenable. Still, she guessed she hadn't understood the extent of the problem.

"Subsidence," said Bernie. "We've been sinking for three hundred years. And right here." he poked his index finger down towards his mattress. Talia was confused. "Here, we are twelve feet below sea level. Twelve feet! And water everywhere." With incredible energy, he swooped his arm in a circle to show the scale of the problem. "Lake Pontchartrain and the Waterway to the north, the river to the south, the Industrial Canal to the west. We live on a soda cracker, and we float in a bowl of water!" He waited for her to react. When she said nothing, he continued. "And that is not the biggest problem! It's worse than that."

"I don't understand," said Talia. How could it be worse than living on a soda cracker floating inside a bowl of water?

Bernie placed his hands together, palm to palm as if he were going to clap. Instead of applause, he suddenly shot them forward like a rocket taking off, and he made an enormously loud whooshing sound with his tongue and breath. The total effect sent Talia reeling backward with surprise. Bernie didn't seem to notice; he was so absorbed in his lecture. It occurred to her that Dr. Coen must have been quite the teacher in his day. The thought made her smile.

He glanced at her, arms still straight out ahead of him. "Confluence," Bernie said. "That'll be the final straw." He explained how the human-made waterways had torn through the wetlands creating a direct route for the turbulent waters of the Gulf to shoot missile-like up the canals and over the levees into New Orleans. When those waterways met, a funnel would pour directly into the city. A great rush sending enormous waves west down the canal and then south into the Ninth Ward via the Industrial Canal, which linked the river and the lake. And then, according to Bernie, flooding of the Ninth Ward and much of Saint Bernard Parish would be inevitable and catastrophic.

"But it's not happened yet," protested Talia. "I mean, like you said, New Orleans has been here for centuries, Bernie."

To this, he only shook his head sadly. "For a time, we've gotten away with it, but not much longer." He sat still, hands folded across his chest, and watched his wife for a long time. Then he said, "And when it happens, they'll say it was an unfortunate tragedy. Something like that." He looked up at her, and his eyes were shining. "I'm ninety-two," said Bernie. "I've been down here, looking at this problem, seventy years, and I've seen the worst humans can do. Ignorance, laziness, Misplaced priorities. I don't know." He waved an arm around vaguely. "I'm an optimist. No other way to be." He smiled and looked at Ellie. "But all this will not get better." Talia didn't know if Bernie was referring to the environment or his wife. She didn't ask, only sat with him for a while in silence, and together they watched Ellie sleep.

•   •   •

Ellie opened her eyes around nine. She'd been sleeping for hours, the result of the injection she'd received. Her eyes were clear, her smile bright. "Is he talking your ear off, dear? He'll do that, you know, if you let him."

"I am not," said Bernie. "I'm just passing along a little critical information. That's all."

Ellie smiled. "I know, dear. I know." She winked at Talia and then closed her eyes. Quickly drifting back to sleep.

Bernie made a face. "She thinks I blabber on. She's always telling me to stop. You'd think by now she'd have given up." He smiled, but there was a touch of melancholy on his face. "You know, kiddo, you need to find someone. Someone for you. Children are terrific, but they leave. They grow up and move on like they're supposed to." He looked again at his wife. "Get yourself someone and then hang on. Real tight."

CHAPTER 44

Kenner, Louisiana

July 26, 2020

DeeDee arrives home as the afternoon sun is paling and the sky is going silver, blue. Rachel stands as the younger woman pushes open the door. She's dressed in a navy-blue skirt, stockings and business heels, and she's carrying two bags of groceries, a heavy briefcase slung over one shoulder. Talia's daughter is not what Rachel expected. She's tall, her features are bold, her skin darker than Colette's, and her eyes a startling green. She looks a little older than her years; Rachel guesses she can't be more than her late twenties, possibly thirty. Life has been hard for her, Rachel thinks, with a sharp stab of guilt.

"Hey girl," DeeDee calls as she's pulling her key from the door balancing the groceries on her hip. "Come on and help me. I got dinner."

"Mama," says Colette. She's put the baby down in his bassinet. "Mama?" DeeDee turns around and suddenly stops when she sees Rachel for the first time. "This here is Rachel." Colette seems unable to continue; she steps forward, takes the grocery bags, carries them over to the counter that separates the living area from the kitchen, and sets them down.

Rachel moves toward DeeDee, extending her hand. "Hi, I'm Rachel Thibodaux. I'm so sorry to barge in and surprise you like this."

"I know who you are," says DeeDee icily. Then she adds, "I've seen your picture in the paper." She's looking at Rachel hard. She knows more than what she's seen in the paper.

"Oh," says Rachel, dropping her hand. She waits for a beat before adding, "Ok. Well, I wanted to talk with you. About your mother."

DeeDee shakes her head, drops her keys and purse on a small table by the door, and kicks off her shoes. "No, I don't talk about her." She glances at Colette then back at Rachel. "We don't talk about her. Colette, take Liam and give him his bath, get him nice and cleaned up. Aliana will appreciate it. She'll be by at six to get him."

The girl obeys, although she monitors DeeDee as she carries the baby from the room. DeeDee watches her go. When they are alone, she turns to Rachel. "Look, I can't help you. I can't talk about anything. I told Colette to let you wait for me because I didn't want to make her do this, but the truth is we have nothing to say to you. You can't be here."

"Can you at least tell me why? I don't understand. Do you know what's going to happen? I mean, of course, you do. But I can help. I just need more information. Please." She waits, watching the younger woman, who only looks back at Rachel. There comes from the bathroom the sound of running water and the indistinct murmur of Colette, making soothing baby sounds. For a few seconds, Rachel thinks DeeDee will not respond. Then, suddenly, her face crumples. She sinks onto the sofa and buries her face in her hands. Rachel sits beside her, waiting.

DeeDee rubs her forehead with her hand, closes her eyes. "I'm tired; you know that. Just so tired of all this." She glances up at Rachel. "It's been a long time."

Rachel nods. "Let me help."

"You don't understand. You don't know."

"That's right; I don't. Nobody will tell me."

"Look," she says. "I want to help. But I can't. I made a promise."

"To your mother?" DeeDee only nods. "I get that," says Rachel. "I also understand your mother is trying to protect someone. But she doesn't need to. Just tell me the truth DeeDee."

DeeDee says nothing, just sits staring down at her lap, fiddling with a thread from her blouse. Rachel feels the familiar tightness in her chest. Her tea, now half-full, still sits on the coffee table. The ice is melted, the outside of the glass slick with condensation. Rachel notices the coaster for the first time. She leans forward and runs her finger over its etched surface.

"Did your mother make this?"

DeeDee looks up, glances at the coaster. "Yeah." She smiles. "Yeah, she did. They do stuff like that. In prison, you know. Make stuff, I guess. To sell."

"She loves those birds, doesn't she?"

DeeDee's face relaxes, and Rachel can see her fighting tears. "She used to say I was like an Osprey. Loyal, powerful, beautiful, all that. She was full of words. I guess that's why she gave me those. I've got four of them, all painted with the same damn bird."

"So, you've seen her?"

DeeDee stiffened. "No, not in a long time." She pauses, then adds, "Even if I help you, even if I tell you what I know, she'll still refuse to go along."

"Why?"

"Cause she's decided. She wants to die. She's been waiting for this for a long time. She thinks it's the only way."

Rachel shakes her head and closes her eyes as if this will make everything make sense. When she opens them, the world has only gone more sideways. She opens her mouth but can't say anything more than, "She thinks it's the only way for what?"

"To protect you, to save me. Me and Colette."

"She's wrong, DeeDee. Whatever she thinks, it's wrong."

DeeDee wipes her eyes with the heels of her hands and pushes the hair out of her face. She takes a long shuddering breath. Rachel can see the fear and indecision in her eyes. Her voice is small and so quiet Rachel must lean forward to hear her.

"It wasn't her fault," she says. "She didn't murder anyone."

CHAPTER 45

The Lower Ninth Ward

August 24, 2005,

Five Days Before

Night falls over the southeastern Bahamas, hundreds of miles from Florida and nearly a thousand miles from New Orleans. Out where the Caribbean seawater is deep and warm, heated tropical water spirals upward, and the wind whips and folds and spins, licking across the ocean's surface at an alarming rate.

Two hundred miles southeast of Nassau, a pair of Lockheed-Martin WS-130J aircraft out of the 53rd Weather Reconnaissance Squadron cruise the airspace over the open ocean. Both crews check and re-check their onboard instruments, the pilots communicate one last time with their respective control towers. They circle once, receive their last instructions, and then fly directly into the center of the developing storm.

•   •   •

On breakfast rounds, Wednesday morning, Talia found Bernard asleep, his long, bony frame wrapped in the Hello Kitty quilt he'd received from his granddaughter. Ellie was wide awake. She was sitting up in bed wearing her glasses and squinting at the television. She glanced briefly at Talia as she came in. Her eyes were bright with excitement behind the wire-rimmed spectacles-more alert than Talia had seen her in months.

"Well, hello, kiddo," she said, grinning, and Talia could see she'd applied pink lip gloss missing her lips and hitting her teeth in a few spots. Ellie smelled like bubble gum and artificial strawberry this morning, the lipstick likely another gift from the five-year-old granddaughter.

"Wow, Ellie, you're up and about early," said Talia moving across the room.

"Have you seen this, dear?" She pointed at the muted television screen.

"You're watching the weather channel?"

"Oh yes, dear, of course," Ellie replied without looking at Talia, her tone suggesting she did this all the time. "We should all be watching today. This could be it, the big one."

"The big one?" Talia knew the term "The Big One," especially when used by longtime residents of Orleans Parish, but she wasn't sure that was Ellie's meaning. Frequently Ellie had conversations that involved people or events that existed only in her mind, and she had a habit of neglecting to fill the listener in on all the details. Talia suspected this habit might even predate Elie's dementia. She set the breakfast trays, stacked one on the other atop the long, laminate dresser the two shared, and turned toward Ellie's bed.

"THE-BIG-ONE," Ellie repeated, emphasizing each syllable as if Talia was a slow student. "Surely you know about it?" Talia took a step toward the small wall-mounted television, trying to read the words running below the image. She squinted: THE STORM IS EXPECTED TO PRODUCE A SIGNIFICANT HEAVY RAINFALL EVENT OVER THE CENTRAL AND NORTHWEST BAHAMAS... AND SOUTH FLORIDA... WITH TOTAL RAINFALL ACCUMULATIONS... MAXIMUM AMOUNTS OF 15 TO 20 INCHES POSSIBLE.

"Ellie," said Talia. "That's the Bahamas. Maybe Florida. That's way out in the ocean, a long way from us. And it's only a tropical storm. You don't need to worry."

"You don't see," said Ellie, removing her glasses. She set them carefully on the hospital table that sat neatly across her small belly and rubbed at the bridge of her nose. Her face looked craggier this morning, if that was possible. The vertical lines between her eyes and the furrows in her brow appeared to have deepened and darkened overnight. "Everybody thinks it's so far away, but." She shook her head. "You young people don't remember Camille." She glanced back at the television. "That one started in the Bahamas. They ALL start in the Bahamas or some such. But it traveled. That's what they do. Travel."

Talia went to work, setting out Ellie's lunch tray, peeling back apple sauce containers, opening cartons. When alert, Ellie liked to feed herself, but the mess she created took so long to clean up, Talia tried to minimize it by maximizing the preparation.

"Oh, I think we'll be fine. Look outside." Talia gestured toward the window. "It's a beautiful day." Outside, a pale blue sky dotted with meringue clouds looked so calm. It might have been a still life if not for the soft breeze brushing the tops of the trees lining the parking lot.

"No, nope. I don't believe it," said Ellie, even as she glanced toward the window.

Talia stopped arguing. Ellie got like this sometimes: rigid, even paranoid. There was no debating her out of it. A week earlier, she'd become convinced someone was sneaking into her room, absconding with her undergarments. She'd insisted on going through each pair of stockings she owned, none of which she'd worn in probably two decades, counting, reorganizing, taking inventory.

Talia noticed a tiny pink plastic barrette clinging to a few strands of Ellie's hair. Sort of dangling haphazardly near her right ear. She reached out, "Ellie, what's that? Would you like me to fix it?"

Ellie raised her hand, touching her sparse hair. "Oh, oh, dear. I forgot about that. I wonder how long? Bernie. Bernie!" She looked at her husband, who gave a small snort and curled tighter into sleep. Ellie shook her head in mock disgust. "He'll remember. I'm not sure when they were here last."

"Who? Who was here?"

"Oh, oh. You know who gave me that?"

"Your granddaughter,? Did she give you that?" Conversations like this could go on for quite a long time. Talia picked up a spoon and scooped a little scrambled egg.

"No, no, that was my little niece."

It was always tricky, deciding whether it was best to correct Ellie or let her slip into the wrong decade, the wrong family, the wrong set of circumstances. Today, Talia didn't have the heart.

"Oh, how nice? I didn't know you had a niece Ellie." She held the spoon handle toward Ellie, hoping she'd take it and start eating.

"Chantal. That's Chantal. She's almost six."

Talia set the utensil down. "Chantal?"

"I have a picture of her. She gave me that too." Suddenly, she was looking around, struggling to push herself up. "She's not our real niece but, I like to say that you know. Help me find that picture, will you?" Then, "Oh, there it is, I knew it was here." She was pointing at the small cork bulletin board she and Bernie hung on the wall between their beds. There were dozens of cards and photos pinned to it, but the one Ellie was pointing at was a little girl.

"I see," said Talia, genuinely surprised. She needed to stop underestimating Ellie. She was often wholly lucid.

"Yes, she and her mama visit us sometimes. They live just a few blocks from here, you know."

In the photo, a tiny girl was sitting cross-legged on an old oak floor somewhere, holding a baby doll, pretending to feed it, and looking up directly into the camera. Big dark eyes, shining smile, hair filled with pink and purple barrettes, and smooth, gorgeous deep brown skin. Talia studied the picture for several seconds, trying to fit the pieces together. Finally, she gave up. It was good enough that Ellie was happy.

"She's adorable."

"I worry about her," said Ellie tipping her head toward the television screen.

"Worry?"

"The water, you know, the water." Then Ellie reached for the spoon, hitting it with her wrist. The utensil somersaulted into the air, spun several times on its way down, and landed in the carpet, leaving runny, scrambled egg splatted against the wall like abstract art. For a few seconds, Ellie and Talia stared wide-eyed at one another, and then both burst out laughing.

Bernard woke up as Talia finished feeding Ellie. He seemed confused at first. Eyes closed. Calling out for someone named Shirley- his dead mother, Ellie explained.

Talia pressed the control button on the side of his bed, raising the head to a steeper angle. "Hello, Bernard," she said. "You've been sleepy today."

He opened his eyes a narrow slit and looked at Talia. More curiosity than recognition. "Who are you?" He raised his left hand a few inches as if he wanted to touch her face.

"It's me," she said, suddenly apprehensive. Acute disorientation could mean anything to someone like Bernard. Simple morning grogginess through to sepsis, which could be fatal. She touched his arm with two fingers and leaned closer to his face. "You know me," she said gently and told him her name. The familiar pang of guilt she always experienced using her new name with people she'd grown to love. It felt duplicitous. Bernie looked dubious. His deeply wrinkled face twisting as he tried to sort out who she was. She added, "Kiddo."

"Kiddo!" He said, his face breaking into a toothless grin.

Thank God, thought Talia. She hadn't realized how close she'd grown to these two nonagenarians. There were others at Good Hope she felt affection for, but Bernard and Ellie were unique. They reminded her of something she couldn't quite put her finger on.

"Hey," she whispered. "There you are. Good morning." She smiled at him. "How about some lunch? Are you hungry?" He shook his head. Not a good sign. Lack of appetite could be a harbinger. "You should eat something, Bernard. The night nurse told me you missed breakfast too."

"Ah," he said with a wave of his hand. "Breakfast is the pits here. You know where those eggs come from?" He raised his bushy eyebrows. "Cartons! Who heard of chickens shaped like milk cartons? No sir, not for me."

"Oh hell, Bernie, eat your lunch, will you?" This was from Ellie, who had replaced her glasses and was back staring at the television.

He looked at her and then back at Talia. "Well, she's the boss," he said and winked.

"Good," said Talia. "Let's get your teeth in first, ok?"

"Yep. I'm a lot better lookin' with teeth," he said.

She retrieved the cup next to the bed that held Bernard's soaking dentures. Helped him insert them. He clacked a few times and then smiled broadly at Talia.

"Bernie, you need to see this," blurted Ellie. Talia turned. Ellie was sitting straighter in the bed. Unnerved. "Bernie," she repeated.

He was still fiddling with his teeth. A thumb and forefinger pushing at them inside his upper lip. "Hmm?" He murmured around his fingers.

"For god's sake, stop with the teeth and pay attention!" Talia had never seen Ellie frustrated with her husband. Her tone was always light and teasing with him. Flirtatious even.

Bernie looked at the television, but Talia knew he couldn't see much. His eyesight was significantly poorer than his wife's, even with glasses. He pulled his fingers from his mouth. "What is it, El?"

"It's a storm Bernie, a big storm."

Talia unfolded Bernie's napkin, handed it to him, and pulled the plastic cover off his lunch tray; some kind of noodle casserole and a small heap of dried-looking peas. She turned back to the television. On the screen, a pale eye was barely discernible at the center of a swirling cloud mass. It appeared to be moving counterclockwise, its tails waving like white streamers, all the way across the Gulf of Mexico. She read the caption rolling across the bottom of the screen:

DEPRESSION STRENGTHENS INTO TROPICAL STORM... HURRICANE WATCH AND TROPICAL STORM WARNING ISSUED FOR FLORIDA... HURRICANE CONDITIONS ARE POSSIBLE... WITHIN 36 HOURS.

Oh, God, thought Talia. Now it had a name: Katrina.

CHAPTER 46

Marietta State Penitentiary

July 27, 2020

Talia twists the chrome knob and watches as the thin stream of lukewarm water turns to a dribble, then a drip, then nothing. Still wearing her orange shower shoes, she crosses the aqua tiled floor of the shower room, moving toward Officer Dupart, who holds out a thin grayish towel. In the past month, Talia has been on twenty-four-hour observation, including showers. Nobody wants her to commit suicide. It's a fact Talia finds ridiculously funny, but the irony is lost on Dupart, which makes joking about it irresistible.

"I might hang myself with this, you know," Talia says, taking the towel from the guard.

"Shut it, Paradise; you have two minutes left."

Dupart is a veteran corrections officer. She takes the job seriously and, mostly, abides by the rules, which is better than most. Talia likes her ok except for the fact that she's zero fun. She's heard Dupart has a bunch of grown kids somewhere. No husband. She works a lot of overtime. There's a real sad story inside the woman, making it impossible for Talia to dislike her.

Talia swipes at her hair, then dries off quickly and trades the towel for clean prison garb. Once she's dressed, Dupart cuffs her and leads her back to D block through Ad-Seg and back into her cell.

Rachel will be back today. Soon. There are so many things to say, so much to make her understand. Talia isn't angry; she never was, only terrified. For fifteen years, Talia has been thinking about a way out, and there isn't one. At least, there isn't one that won't harm other people, and she's not willing to do that. Making Rachel understand without putting her in danger is a trick for sure. Rachel doesn't give up easily. She never did.

• • •

An hour later, Talia and Rachel sit looking at one another through the plexiglass window. The cubicle is overly air-conditioned, and Talia shivers as she picks up the phone. Rachel has not slept; Talia can tell. She's tied her hair into a messy bun, gray streaks at her temples, and she's not wearing makeup except whatever mascara might be left over from yesterday, which remains smeared under her lower lids. She wears a man's athletic club sweatshirt, and she is beautiful.

They exchange awkward 'hellos' and sit in silence. Rachel opens her mouth to speak again but says nothing. The C. O posted behind Talia is Officer Gergen. He's new, young, dumb as a stump, and completely inflexible. Talia knows he will remain standing at his post throughout her conversation with Rachel, and he will religiously report any deviation from the rules to his superior. She needs to be extraordinarily careful.

"You found Dee," says Talia, careful to keep her tone neutral.

"I'm sorry."

"She called me."

"Of course."

"She told you everything didn't she?"

"Yeah," says Rachel.

"It's ok," says Talia. "I should have known, right? I mean, it's how you are."

"I'm so sorry, Talia. You're right. I do barrel forward. I don't ask. All those things you said, every single thing is true. I never once asked if you wanted my help. I just assumed I was right when I sent you away." She pauses. "When I let Daniel send you away. When I tried to make decisions for you. And now."

Talia nods. "You know who you're just like?"

Rachel does, but she's hoping Talia won't say it.

"Yeah. That's right. You're just like her, Rachel. Nona asked no one for an opinion. She knew what was right for everyone every time, and if she didn't know, she knew anyway." They both laugh. "And I loved her. I loved her so much."

"Yeah, but sometimes she wasn't right, was she?" asks Rachel. "She wasn't right at all."

"No, sometimes she wasn't," Talia puts a hand to the glass. "but she was doing the best she could, Rachel. All that time. After Mama died, dealing with Ray and everything was hard for her, and she was trying. Everything she did was out of love for us."

Again, they are silent for a while, but the quiet is no longer awkward.

"You have a granddaughter," says Rachel. "She's amazing."

Talia's smile grows wide, her scar nearly disappearing into her dimples. "I do," she says. "And she is that. I'm glad you got to meet her, Rachel. I really am."

"She told me she wants to be a doctor. A surgeon."

Talia rolls her eyes, "This week. Last week I think it was a geologist. She's a smart girl. A good girl."

Outside, down some distant hallway, an inmate screams a stream of obscenities—an alarm sounds.

Talia is careful to keep her voice low, but her words deliberate. "Rach, listen to me. I need to tell you some things, and I need you to really listen, ok?" Rachel nods. "I want you to know first that I have a long messy history. I stayed away from you, from your family, for lots of reasons. But not because of you. I couldn't drag my past into your life. Do you understand? There had to be a distance."

"I know. I understand that."

"I don't think you do." Talia looks hard at Rachel, trying to transmit her thoughts without speaking them aloud. The prison monitors all conversations, and she has no idea who is listening. "I knew about Jeb. I mean, of course, I knew." Rachel looks away, and Talia continues. "But what I mean is, I really knew."

"How? How is that possible?"

"Information is easy in here, that's all. Especially anything you know, criminal. But the thing is, I knew you were suffering. I thought reaching out to you would only make it worse."

Rachel covers her mouth with her palm. Her eyes are filling with tears. "Tee, Oh God, what did I do?"

"You protected him, Rachel. That's all. In the end, you protected your boy. But it wasn't your fault. His death was not your fault. And I should have been there to tell you that back then. I should have been there to tell you that years ago, Rachel. All this shit," Talia looks right and left, "It's not your fault, stop blaming yourself." Talia sucks in her breath, willing herself not to cry. "It's like they say, Rach, shit happens, right?" She forces a smile.

Rachel smiles weakly. "I love you, Tee."

Talia leans into the glass. "Then stop. Stop trying to make everything ok for everyone all the time. You can't do it."

Rachel is silent for a long time, then she says, "You're right. I'll let this go if it's what you want. It's your life. So, I'll do whatever you ask of me but only what you ask, ok?" She pauses, leans in, a palm on the glass. "I know things, Tee. I'll take-"

Talia shakes her head, but she keeps the movement small hoping Gergen doesn't see. She silently mouths, "stop," and Rachel is quiet.

"Five minutes," says Gergen. The angry obscenity spewing inmate is apparently undergoing an extraction from her cell. Her screams have escalated, and Talia hears several pairs of boots hurrying down the hall that runs along behind the visiting cells. She's grateful Rachel can't hear the howling inmate, the rush of boots. Any average person would find violent commotion disturbing.

An idea is forming, and Talia studies Rachel carefully, considering. The long stretch of light in her cell comes to mind. There are now nineteen more opportunities to count the time it takes for the light to reach the inside of her steel door before curving upward again toward the concrete ceiling. Nineteen more and then, nothing. Both Talia and the light will be over. Talia because of some arbitrary date written on a piece of paper, and the light, because no matter its magnificence, it only exists as a neurochemical process in a brain that will no longer be. Suddenly Talia is gripped by the desire to share the light with DeeDee. With Rachel. With Colette. Nineteen chances seem suddenly absurd. Obscene. She's not ready.

"Tee?" says Rachel. "Tee? Are you ok?"

"Yeah, sorry. Yes."

"You seemed absent for a second."

One shot, they may have one dangerous longshot. "Ok, listen," says Talia. "I don't remember things so well these days, you understand?"

"Ok," Rachel says, looking confused.

"What I mean is, memory is a funny thing. But other people might remember better. Other people who would recall things or events I wouldn't know."

"I don't..." Rachel begins. Then she raises her hand to her mouth as a look of comprehension washes over her face, "Oh God, I'm so sorry, Talia." She lets her gaze flick to the officer. He appears to be staring idly into space. Looking back at her sister, Rachel whispers. "Alright."

Talia touches one finger to her lips, then relaxes, folds her hands together on the counter, and sits very still. Then, silently, she mouths the word, careful to form each syllable clearly: "LAN-DRY."

•   •   •

As Rachel drives the bayou highway back down toward the city, rain begins. Water hitting the asphalt in thick slabs, blinding her through the windshield. She's not thinking about Talia. Instead, she remembers.

It was the paraphernalia that did it, of course. They'd found it in his car when they'd gone to pick it up from impound. The police had agreed to drop the investigation after Daniel had done whatever Daniel did to make things happen. The coroner's report was ambiguous, leaving room for a conclusion of accidental death because of injuries sustained in a motor vehicle accident, but the coroner had required some financial encouragement to leave the toxicology findings off the final record. If he'd not been willing to do that, enormous amounts of opioids in Jeb's system — (enough to kill a fucking elephant, Rachel overheard the ER doctor tell another staff member)—would have been difficult to ignore. Still, in the days following Jeb's death, Daniel and Rachel had been willing to believe the accident was just an accident. It was dark; Jeb had been tired, working sixty hours a week in his first year at the city's most prominent financial firm. He'd come around a curve and lost control of the car. The robust construction of his luxury SUV could explain the minimal damage to.

But then they'd had to pick up the car. Daniel had walked into the kitchen carrying the contents of the glove box. The pristinely intact contents of the fucking glove box.

There'd been signs. More than signs. Rachel had seen Jeb high multiple times on visits home. She knew what it looked like. But he was doing so well. It didn't seem possible. Once or twice, she'd asked him about it. He'd laughed. The very idea was ridiculous. Jeb? On drugs? Mom, what are you thinking? She'd been relieved. Let it drop. It was ridiculous. He was Jeb, for fucks sake. He was good, always, Jeb was great.

So, yeah, Jeb was on drugs. Hard drugs. But it also turned out he'd lost his job. Lost his girlfriend. Lost his apartment. And he owed many people money. The truth — (the whole truth) — was that Jeb died following a minor accident in which he sustained an injury that would have been non-life-threatening had he not first been rendered unconscious by the heroin in his system, which resulted in his bleeding to death over the next fourteen hours.

Rachel has to lean forward and peer between the wiper blades. She ought to pull over. Wait it out. It would be safer. She presses her foot to the accelerator, and the car speeds ahead.

• • •

Cindy Pitre was on duty when Talia got back to Ad-Seg. Fresh from two days off, she looked less pinched than usual, and she'd even dabbed on a bit of lipstick, which made her face more cheerful.

"Afternoon, Officer Pitre," says Talia.

"Afternoon Inmate," says Pitre, using formalities for the benefit of the escorting guard.

"Hey, you got any more of those Bibles by any chance?"

"What happened to the last three?" Pitre is smiling. She knows what happened to them.

"Dunno. Can I have another one?"

"Sure, I'll bring it by."

Ten minutes after Talia is settled in her cell, Pitre pushes the door open and stands there, holding out a bible with a soft white cover.

"Here you go. I gotta ask. Why now?"

"You look real nice today, Officer Pitre."

"Nice try."

"I don't know. I have a lot on my mind. I just think it can't hurt right."

"Sure, holding a bible can't hurt. You think a little prayer can't hurt too?" Pitre asks, handing Talia the bible.

"Yeah, ok, that too. A little prayer."

CHAPTER 47

The Lower Ninth Ward

August 24, 2005,

Four Days Before

Tropical storm Katrina moves toward Florida, picking up speed and power over the water; it becomes a Category 1 hurricane two hours before making landfall at Keating Beach, two miles south of the Fort Lauderdale International Airport. There are four fatalities. With winds at 85 mph (137 km/h), the eye of the hurricane moves directly over the office of the National Hurricane Center.

Katrina lasts six hours on land over the Everglades, losing some of its power, before finally reaching the Gulf of Mexico. Upon hearing of Katrina's downgrade from the hurricane to a tropical storm, a collective sigh of relief can be heard in New Orleans. Perhaps, once again, a storm had graciously side-stepped the Big Easy.

Less than four hours later, Katrina regained all its force and more. It is again a hurricane, and within twenty-four hours, national news outlets call New Orleans an area of "particular concern." In addition, the same news media are reporting on the FEMA 2001 study identifying the three most likely disasters facing the U.S.: an earthquake in California, a terrorist attack in New York City, and a devastating hurricane in New Orleans.

CHAPTER 48

New Orleans, Bayou St. John

July 27, 2020

Virgil hands Rachel a mug of hot tea and sits across from her at his kitchen table. Briefly, he wishes he'd had time to put away his pile of folded laundry or the lunch dishes he's left washed and stacked by the sink. He shoves a stack of medical journals to the side with his elbow and kicks at an unopened Amazon delivery he's left on the floor beside his chair. It slides noisily and clatters into the cupboards. Virgil isn't dirty exactly. He cleans up after himself or has a weekly housekeeper who does, but he's messy. At home, anyway. He blames it on being busy, too busy to organize and put things in their proper place. Maybe that's true, or he likes the clutter. Or perhaps it's something else.

"Rachel, take it slow, ok? You're giving me a lot here." She's flushed, sweating, but it's not just the heat. When he'd opened the door, she'd practically lunged past him to get inside, as if someone was chasing her. She'd nearly stumbled over Louis, who had strolled over to check out the commotion. She'd seemed, not quite frantic, but undoubtedly agitated.

She's calmer now but still anxious. The old lab now is curled at Rachel's feet, and now and then, she reaches down to give his neck a good scratch. The gesture is sweet, if surprising. Virgil hadn't imagined Rachel Thibodaux a dog lover.

"I know, I'm sorry. But Talia's agreed. I went and saw her again this morning, and she's at least allowing me to look into things a bit."

Virgil listens as Rachel reviews the conversation she had with her sister earlier in the morning. He feels significantly less optimistic than

Rachel sounds, but he says nothing. Under the table, Louis opens his mouth and makes a loud yawn-whine sound that means he'd like someone to continue scratching him, please. Virgil pokes gently at the dog with his toe.

"You know what that means?" she continues. "We have what? Twenty days? Less than that. Nineteen days to stop this from happening."

By this, Rachel means the execution. And she doesn't have nineteen days, thinks Virgil. Nowhere near that. She does not know. He's seen this before—a family's desperate attempts to stop the process at the eleventh hour. It is agony to watch even when one is not invested, and this situation is intolerable. It's his goddamn fault for getting mixed up in it. It's more than his fault. His responsibility. He's created this mess.

He studies Rachel. Has he ever known anyone with this intensity, faith, love-whatever it is-for another person? She believes in her sister's innocence. With evidence. Without it. Rachel knows her sister did not do this. God, he thinks, what if she's right?

"Ok, so tell me about the daughter again. DeeDee?" Virgil says. "What did she tell you, exactly?"

"She told me it was an accident, Virgil. That's it. Just a stupid accident."

"And DeeDee knows this how?"

She hesitates. "I can't tell you that. Not yet. I promised I wouldn't."

Virgil blows out his breath and sits back in his chair. Maybe this is better, he thinks. Rachel, a woman he doesn't really know, asks him to believe a crazy story based on what? Nothing. Nothing he can verify anyway. It should be easy for him to let go. Why is it not? Why the hell is it not?

"I know this is ridiculous. For me to ask for your help but, she's telling the truth, I swear. DeeDee knows my sister didn't do this. Look, Virgil, Dee told me. That cop, he'd come to hurt Talia. Not save her. Somebody sent him. But she didn't kill him. He died, yes, but it was all a freak accident."

"But she confessed, Rachel. Why would she have done that? This makes little sense."

Rachel rubs her forehead with the heel of her hand. "I know," she says. "Shit, shit. Ok, listen." She looks at Virgil. "They're scared. That's why they're hiding."

"Hiding?"

"Dee. They're hiding Dee. That's why Talia confessed to Virgil. Protection. She was protecting her child."

"I don't understand, Rachel."

"She was there," says Rachel. "The day it happened, after the water. Dee was there."

• • •

Virgil had tried insisting she needed his protection. He'd wanted to drive her, but Rachel had refused. She'd wanted his help in a particular way. Finally, he'd agreed, and then she'd left. And he'd let her go. Now he sits at the kitchen table with the pile of original documents she left behind, feeling a combination of worry, guilt, relief, and misplaced pride in this woman who seems not to need his rescue after all.

He removes the envelope's contents. There are several sheets of paper stapled together. He thumbs through the sheets, recalling his and Rachel's conversation.

"Looks like bank transfers. I don't get it. Who are these people?"

"Those are former employees from Good Hope,"

"Ok," said Virgil, still confused.

She'd pointed at the folder still in Virgil's hands. "I got that from Daniel's Claymore office downtown. He's been making bank transfers to those people for years. The first one is dated two weeks after the storm. The last one, less than two weeks ago."

Virgil nodded, studying both lists again, his eyes flicking back and forth. "And these people..." he let his voice trail off.

"Those people are the survivors. There were eighty-seven deaths and eight survivors. Of the survivors, one was Rick Landry, my sister, and those," Rachel pointed to the list, "are the other six. All six of them are staff. Not a single patient survived."

"Payoffs? You think Daniel was paying these six for their silence?"

"I don't know," said Rachel. "Paid, bribed, maybe gifts out of guilt. Who knows? But that account number, the one from which Daniel made the transfers? That's my account. One of them anyway. I never even look at it. Daniel handles all our financials. He sets up accounts for tax purposes. That's what he says, anyway. I've been stupid. Just signing documents, he puts them in front of me, I sign. That's my name on that account."

"Jesus," said Virgil. He ran a finger down the list of transfers next to each name. The sums, taken one at a time, were small, in the hundreds of dollars. But it had been nearly fifteen years, and there were six people involved. He did the rough math in his head. It came to seven figures for sure. How could anyone not notice seven figures missing from their accounts, even spread over fifteen years?

Virgil had experienced a wave of something ugly, as he'd thought: rich people. Then he looked at Rachel. She was not that. He believed her; she hadn't known about the money; she was no criminal.

"And if those are payoffs, or hush money or blackmail or whatever, then it's not a matter of the past; this is still going on," Rachel added.

He'd looked again at the dates. She was right. The last transfers were two weeks ago.

"He set you up."

She nodded, looking relieved at his understanding. "Yeah." Rachel paused, swallowed, and took a breath. Virgil could see how difficult this was for her.

"So, all this," she gestured at the documents., "means that Daniel knew my sister knew something." The implication was clear. If Daniel knew, Daniel or someone under Daniel's control must have given the order to have Jack Salvas go after Talia. At the very least, Daniel would have known about the miscarriage of justice all these years.

"I'm so sorry, Rachel," Virgil had said, and he'd wanted to cringe at the hollow sound of his words.

Rachel ignored the comment. "Look, there's something else."

"Ok."

"What is it?"

"I think Talia gave me more. She won't let DeeDee come forward. That makes sense, of course. It's too dangerous. At least until there's more to support her case. But I think Tee tried to help me when I saw her today."

"How?"

She gave me a name. It was confusing at first. She said, "Landry. I mean, Rick's gone. No one can find him. How can I get anything more from him, right?

"Right. So?"

"I don't think she meant Rick Landry." Rachel exhaled and looked at Virgil. "She didn't mean Rick at all."

•   •   •

And so, Virgil pushes the papers back into the manilla envelope and stands up, looking around the cluttered kitchen for his keys. Louis raises his colossal head from his dozing position under the table, mildly curious. "Sorry, dude," says Virgil. "You can't go this time."

A few minutes later, Virgil is driving to Marietta for an unscheduled visit with Janie Paradise.

CHAPTER 49

The Lower Ninth Ward

August 26, 2005

Three Days Before

A raw wind snakes out of the east, low and wet, through the trees of the city. The Mississippi tosses river rocks onto the shore, and out near Salvador, small trees come up by the roots and lay stranded in the mud like beached whales. The levee at Bayou Mercier stands impassive as water laps up hard against its inside edge. Way out in the parishes, down Bayou Dupre, beyond New Orleans, where a half-century ago, the wetlands were slashed open making way for ships, the water moves through the channel then flows out toward Bayou Terrebonne. Under the Interstate-10 Bridge, just outside of New Orleans, another concrete waterway dissects the wetlands like an open wound, deep and wide across the Louisiana coastline all the way to the Gulf. Where the two meet, a dangerous confluence is formed.

On Friday, the Governor declares a state of emergency for Louisiana, including activation of the state's emergency response and recovery program under the office of Homeland Security and Emergency Preparedness to supply emergency support services. Federal troops, including 922 Army National Guard at 8 Air National Guard, are deployed to Louisiana to coordinate operations with the Federal Emergency Management Agency. By 4:00 pm, the hurricane is located 66 miles southeast of New Orleans.

•   •   •

DeeDee, who had been busy reading the back of a Frosted Flakes box as her mother left for work and therefore never heard the gentle warning to "keep an eye on the storm," forgot all about the weather until late afternoon. She'd been delighted to have the day to herself. An entire Friday alone, without homework hanging over her head. A gift. She'd shoved an enormous load of laundry into the washer and then stretched out on the sofa with a battered Nicholas Sparks novel. She'd fallen asleep, finally waking when the mid-morning sun shone so brightly through the un-curtained window that her face stung from sunburn.

An hour later, DeeDee was outside clipping sheets to the washing line; a light breeze that had been pushing itself around the humid air in the yard all afternoon suddenly expanded, twisting into something peculiar. She stopped and looked up at the sky—a brilliant blue, nearly cloudless, and completely benign. But the sheets she'd already hung were folding back upon themselves. The motion was chaotic, indecisive. Despite the sky, the wind had taken on a curling, insidious feel.

A dog barked in the distance. A high-pitched yip. Once, then again. Then, after a few moments of silence, the barking started up, this time without ceasing. That's when she remembered. "Dee, keep an eye on the storm today, and you call me if you need anything, ok?"

She dropped the clothespin she was holding, missing the laundry basket entirely; it landed in the dirt. She left it there and went up the steps and into the kitchen. Switching on the television, Dee found the local news and turned up the volume.

There'd been a time when DeeDee hated storms. As a small child, she remembered falling asleep in a closet in which she'd taken refuge when a storm's thunder became unremitting. She awoke hours later, buried among winter coats and junk-filled cardboard boxes, her mother standing over her, smiling. But she was grown now. She wasn't afraid of the weather. Not usually. But as she watched the news report, something of the old dread resurfaced. Heading for the Mississippi Coast, this storm, with winds over a hundred miles an hour and the possibility of a twenty-foot storm surge and massive flooding, was something way beyond simple weather.

She sat at the table, folded into a narrow chair, knees up to her chin, watching as the governor told the people of Louisiana that they needed to be prepared for the worst.

Five minutes later she picked up the phone to call her mother.

CHAPTER 50

New Orleans, Uptown

July 27, 2020

Cat Landry stands at the sink holding an empty coffee carafe, and Rachel has a terrible vision of her cracking it across the stone counter and lunging at Rachel, a shard of glass drawn out like a dagger. She forces herself to look away, out the window at a collection of brilliant purple bromeliads and fuscias—an expanse of lush lawn bordered by a sea of blue hyacinth beneath the shade of the magnolias. The entire kitchen smells of the cut flowers — (gardenia and English Rose) --Cat has delivered weekly. Rachel looks back at Cat, who is now filling the carafe. A special filtered tap, a thin silvery stream of water.

Cat steps toward the table and pulls out one of the heavy deco chairs. Its legs scrape along the stamped concrete floor, making an ugly screeching sound Cat seems not to notice. She sits down kitty-corner from Rachel, and her knee grazes Rachel's before she pulls away. She's pulled her hair into a tight ponytail, and gray half-moons have surfaced beneath her eyes. She's tried to cover them with makeup, but the result is concealer drying in the tiny lines Botox couldn't relax. Cat clears her throat, shifts in her chair. The soft linen of her blouse bows away from her neck, exposing the sharp, emaciated detail of her collarbone.

Rachel stares at her, saying nothing. It's hard to breathe.

"All of this," Cat waves a hand in the air. Rachel does not know what she means to indicate. The fat diamond of her wedding ring slides loosely around her finger. Cat shrugs and begins again. "If I'd known..." she doesn't finish the thought. She looks at Rachel, studying her, searching for something. "What? What is it you want me to say, Rachel?"

Rachel says nothing for a moment. She wants to choose her words carefully. Finally, she says, "I want you to tell me the truth, Cat. I want you to explain how this happened." She pushes the bank transfer documents across the table, fanning them out across the glossy surface. Suddenly she's glad she brought only copies. Virgil had insisted she leave the originals with him for safekeeping. She'd thought he was dramatic, but now, looking at Cat, she's changed her mind. "Explain."

Cat licks her lips, moves a strand of hair away from her face, and straightens.

"Please, Rachel, you can't be that naïve."

"You know what I'm going to do with that," says Rachel pointing at the file. "They'll investigate it. I have emails, everything. I know you're involved." She swallows painfully. "You and Daniel." There's a stab of pain thinking about the message she found on Daniel's computer. It's unexpected, and she feels herself flinch. The email, the earring. Goddammit. Why does she care?

Cat kicks her head back, looks at the ceiling, and laughs, the sound high-pitched and brittle. When she looks back at Rachel, there is a tight smile on her face. "Me and Daniel? Is that what you're thinking about? Jesus, Rachel. Right now? Whatever happened between us is the least of your problems."

Rachel forces herself to maintain Cat's gaze. "That's not what this is about."

"Oh yeah? Then why are you here? Why not go straight to the police?"

"Tell me the truth Cat. What did you do? What exactly did you do?"

Cat shrugs. "You can't go to the police."

"Of course, I can," Rachel says with authority, but something inside her feels like it's cracking.

"Right, so you'll go to the police and say what? That your husband and me and Rick and I don't know who else, we all tried to cover up something that happened at Good Hope during Katrina. Something that makes us culpable for all those deaths, that tragedy. And here's the kicker, you don't even know what happened. You have to tell the police you're accusing one of the biggest health care companies in the country of covering up a crime, and you cannot even say what that crime is." She shakes her head. "It's ridiculous. How far do you think that will go?"

She's right thinks Rachel. Or she would be right, except that she doesn't know about DeeDee. "So, tell me then, what about all this?"

"What do you have?" Cat pokes at the papers on the table, one glossy fingernail shoving them askew. Rachel notices two of the nails on that hand are imperfectly polished, the white tip chipped, in need of repair. "Some money transferred. So what? Maybe Daniel felt sorry for those people and made donations? Who knows? What's your theory? That Daniel is bribing survivors to keep quiet? Please. And your sister, what happened to her? Do you think she was a loose cannon, so we sent someone after her? To what? Kill her? Think about how crazy that sounds, Rachel? You plan to take that insanity to who? The governor? Good luck. You have no proof. No witnesses. I won't say anything. Rick is gone with the wind. And Daniel? No way, he's in too deep. And the truth you say you want so badly will ruin you. You and your husband and everything you know. Besides, your sister confessed. You can take this whole conspiracy to the police, and somehow, they'll put a bunch of little pieces together, and it'll add up to her being released?" She shakes her head, almost laughing. "You'll accomplish nothing. And just going to the police with insane allegations, regardless of the outcome, will ruin your life and everyone else's. They'll take your house, your money, your company, your reputation." She inhales sharply. "You will lose everything, Rachel. Everything. So, I don't think so," she says again. "I don't think you'll do it."

Gray, fog-like dizziness threatens to overwhelm Rachel. She shakes her head to clear it.

"Rachel, what you want is someone to blame, and there isn't anyone. Not really. What happened that day was an accident. Or a series of accidents or poor decisions. But nobody intended all those people to die. There was no evil plan—just a tragedy. And as for your sister? Who knows? She was stuck up there in that attic for days. I'd have gone crazy. I'd have probably killed someone too."

"I saw the deadbolt Cat. I went to Good Hope. Those doors were locked."

Cat smiles with the corners of her mouth. "That? You saw that, and it made you think what?"

"It made me think that someone at Good Hope barred those doors deliberately."

Cat was suddenly silent, the smile gone from her face. She contemplates Rachel for a moment before saying, "Ok, fine. Listen to me; I'll tell you what you want to hear. But you still won't go to the police. You can't. You're as deep into this as the rest of us. You profited as much as anyone else. Just look at your life Rachel, look around, and you'll see." Cat pointed at Rachel's expensive bag and shoes. "Look at the fucking car you drive and that house you live in. But you want to know? Fine. I'll tell you. But there's one other thing you should know first." She pauses, her eyes narrow, and Rachel feels sick anticipating what Cat is about to say. "Jeb, your precious, perfect Jeb. You should know that I know everything. It's so predictable what a man will tell you when he's vulnerable, Rachel. You should know that. And Jeb? He's part of your truth, isn't he?"

Rachel stands too suddenly—stomach-churning-the walls are closing in; she reaches out to steady herself on the edge of the table.

"Sit down, Rachel. I changed my mind; it would be best if you heard this. It'll make more sense coming from me."

CHAPTER 51

The Lower Ninth Ward

August 27, 2005

Two Days Before

In the early morning hours, Saturday, August 27, Air Force reconnaissance aircraft out of Keesler Air Force Base flies 435 miles southeast of the mouth of the Mississippi and straight into the eye of an enormous hurricane. The storm's wind speeds are measured over 115 miles per hour, and by 5:00 a.m., Katrina has become a Category 3 hurricane. Its tendrils stretch hundreds of miles across the Gulf of Mexico, and it moves at a remarkable pace towards the Mississippi Gulf Coast. Neighboring parishes begin evacuations early in the day, and, at 5:00 p.m., local officials will call for voluntary evacuation from the city of New Orleans.

• • •

Talia awoke Saturday morning to find Dee sitting beside her on the bed, her face ashen, her brow furrowed.

"What?" said Talia pulling herself to a sitting position. "What's wrong?"

"I think we need to go, Mama," said DeeDee.

"Go?"

"Yes. Leave the city. It's getting worse."

"What's getting worse?" Talia rubbed her eyes.

"The storm, Mama, the storm is worse."

Talia swung her legs out of bed, slid her feet into a pair of well-worn slippers, and stood up. "Sweetie, I can't go anywhere. I'm working a double today. And tomorrow." She put both hands at the small of her back and stretched, wincing as her lower back cracked painfully. At thirty-five, she felt relatively young and strong most days, but mornings like this, facing back-to-back double shifts, it could be a struggle to get going. She stood; DeeDee stood up and stepped in front of her.

"I don't care about any of that. We need to evacuate. And I think we should take Miss Gloria and her niece with us."

"Evacuate?" Talia blinked. This was an overreaction even for Dee. "What are you talking about, honey? We aren't evacuating. Besides, where do you think we would go? And how would we get there?" She smiled gently and put a palm to her daughter's smooth cheek. She looked as if she might cry. Talia softened her voice. "Hey, hey, now. Come on, think about it." She raised her eyebrows. "No car, and I don't know about you, but I don't have the money for a hotel. So no, we are not leaving."

Talia reached for the robe she'd slung over the bedside chair the night before and slipped it on. The silky material felt good against her skin.

Dee let out an angry sigh. "Jefferson and St. Bernard are already going, Mama."

"What? Going where?" Talia felt a twinge of worry. The Big One. What had Ellie said? That's what they do. They travel.

"They're evacuating, Mama. Voluntary evacuation. You need to come see." DeeDee headed for the bedroom door. "Come see the TV," she said over her shoulder as she left the room.

There'd been only one other voluntary evacuation Talia could remember, and the results of that were devastating. She hurried through her morning routine in the bathroom and was still cinching her scrubs as she entered the kitchen. The room smelled of chicory coffee and warm biscuits. Dee was seated at the tiny table they used for everything from meals to homework to paying bills. She had an untouched biscuit before her and was staring at the television.

"Thank you for making breakfast, sweet girl," said Talia. At thirteen, DeeDee was amazing for the level of responsibility she assumed. In so many ways, she was older than her years.

Dee grunted but did not look up. The news anchor was speaking.

"Katrina has now reached Category 3 intensity. It is currently moving westward in the southeastern Gulf of Mexico and is expected to strengthen and turn west-northwest. A hurricane watch is now in effect for southeastern Louisiana, including the metropolitan New Orleans and Lake Pontchartrain areas."

Shit. Talia took a deep breath and moved to the cupboard, where they kept coffee mugs. Taking one down, she poured coffee into it slowly, stalling for time to arrange her face before turning around to look at Dee. They sat silently and watched the news together for a while. Outside the kitchen window, the sky was clear and still. Sun poured in through the old panes of glass, sending wavy yellow ribbons across the table's surface and onto the floor. The light softly illuminating one side of DeeDee's worried face.

Talia checked the clock and stood slowly. "Dee, look, I am going to have to go into Good Hope, probably earlier than I thought today. Those people will need to be moved, and I have to go in and help."

"What?" said Dee, the shock clear in her voice. "No. No Mama, you need to."

"I need to do my job, Dee. But you're right about leaving. I'll sort something to get you out of here today."

DeeDee looked more confused than angry. "No. I'm not going anywhere without you, Mama, Mama. And what about Miss Gloria and Charmaine? And everyone else? No way. I'll wait. Mr. Earle and the girls are here, anyway. He'll come by. I'll just wait for you to come back."

Mention of their other neighbors sent a chill of worry through Talia; she told herself they'd be alright. At least until she could get back to check on everyone. Maybe she could arrange some sort of transportation for a few of them. Although she knew this was unlikely.

Few had cars. And nobody had money. She needed to focus on getting DeeDee out of the city. That might be the best she could do.

Talia sat back down, placed a hand on Dee's arm, and looked at the television. On the screen, a satellite picture showed the storm over the water. A tremendous white swath that virtually obliterated the Gulf of Mexico.

•   •   •

The Good Hope staff spent Saturday afternoon preparing for evacuation and reassuring family members who were reluctant to leave their loved ones with the threat of the oncoming storm.

Don't worry, we'll take good care of your mother, or You need to and take care of the rest of your family, get out of the city now, or Our staff has everything under control, we'll keep you well informed.

By evening, most family members had cleared out. A few stragglers remained one or two requiring physical encouragement to leave.

Joey Guardino Jr., the fifty-year-old son of eighty-four-year-old Joseph Guardino Sr., was one of those more resistant to leaving. Joey Sr. suffered from emphysema and semi-paralysis wrought after two strokes. He was bed-bound and oxygen-dependent and moving him in a personal vehicle would have been both foolish and cruel. Joey Jr. insisted he be allowed to take his father out. You ain't gonna tell me what I can do, and get the hell outta my way, and I pay you to do what I say... that sort of thing.

"Please, Mr. Guardino, he could die if you do that. You're not equipped to handle his medical needs, and the drive out of town is going to be very long." Talia tried explaining to him multiple times with no response beyond a solid shake of a stubby fist and Get the hell out of my way.

Finally, a nurse administrator intervened. "I just can't let you take him," she said. "It would be negligent of us to let him go." Two of the bigger-boned male nursing assistants escorting Joey Jr. from the premises followed this.

Talia, who was helping another nurse change Joey Sr.'s sheets, waited until the nurse exited the room to fetch fresh supplies, then she jogged to catch up with the younger man. "It's ok," she said, her voice soft and sympathetic. "I know everybody is scared. But we'll take good care of your father."

She held the younger Guardino's stare until his eyes softened and filled with tears. He nodded at her. "Ok," he said. "Ok. But please, please promise me you'll make sure he gets out if... well, you know if it comes to that.

"Of course," said Talia. Then she added something she'd come to regret. "I promise," she said. "I promise."

CHAPTER 52

New Orleans, Uptown

July 27, 2020

It's been nearly an hour by the time Rachel emerges from Cat's. Her hands are trembling as she pulls her seatbelt on, and it's difficult to fasten the buckle. Once she's back on St. Charles, she waits until she's a safe distance away and pulls over beneath the shade of a magnolia and dials his number.

"Is she ok?"

"Talia's fine, I've just finished checking in on her, and I plan to stay here until we've got things finished, ok? How about you?" answers Virgil. His gentle voice is soothing to her.

"Thank you, Virgil. I don't know what to say about—"

"Stop, it's ok. Just tell me what's happening. Tell me if you are all right."

"I'm good. You know, I don't think Cat was ever a danger to me. Not really. She thinks she's got me pinned down; she thinks we care about the same things, that I won't want to lose everything, you know? And what she told me means blowing up her life, my life, the whole thing."

She can hear him as he blows out his breath. He's worried. "Really, I'm ok. I'm on my way—" She stops herself. "I'm fine. I'll check in soon, ok?"

"Be careful; it's just really dangerous. The whole situation."

"I know," she whispers.

"Of course," says Virgil.

A minute later, Rachel is back on the Avenue. As she rolls the car to a stop at Nashville and St. Charles, a streetcar clangs by, and she waits for it to pass. She thinks about that day long ago, riding uptown in the pouring rain. For a moment, part of her leaves her body and floats around outside the car. Once again, she's riding that streetcar, contemplating the magnificent Victorian mansions that line the avenue. Formal porticos, urns overflowing with maidenhair, curving brick walkways flanked by dogwoods and marigolds. She floats through the windows into the high-ceilinged drawing rooms to find Talia. They throw open the front doors, step outside barefoot, and from their magnificent porch, they'll watch the streetcars trundling by.

When Rachel came back to herself, her mind no longer split into pieces. She tries to remember the precise threat Cat Landry made. What was it, she said? You will lose everything, Rachel. Everything. The thought makes Rachel smile. Cat is right. If she does this, Rachel will lose everything she once believed she wanted. Everything she once felt certain would keep both her and Talia safe.

CHAPTER 53

August 28, 2005

One Day Before

Two hundred and fifty miles south-southeast of the mouth of the Mississippi River, Katrina continues to rage. With sustained winds over 160 mph, it is now a Category 5 hurricane, the most dangerous storm known to exist. A hurricane warning is issued for the north-central Gulf Coast, including New Orleans, and, by the end of the day, the projected storm surge will be 18 to 28 feet high enough to overtop the levees multiple times. That is if they hold. By 10:00 a.m. city officials issue a mandatory evacuation order. The city positioned its buses around New Orleans in locations that have never been flooded. At around the same time, the National Weather Service issues the direst weather warning in its history:

"DEVASTATING DAMAGE EXPECTED... A MOST POWERFUL HURRICANE WITH UNPRECEDENTED STRENGTH... MOST OF THE AREA WILL BE UNINHABITABLE FOR WEEKS... PERHAPS LONGER... AT LEAST ONE-HALF OF WELL-CONSTRUCTED HOMES WILL HAVE ROOF AND WALL FAILURE... TO THE POINT OF COLLAPSE... THE MAJORITY OF INDUSTRIAL BUILDINGS WILL BECOME NON-FUNCTIONAL... AIRBORNE DEBRIS WILL BE WIDESPREAD AND MAY INCLUDE HEAVY ITEMS SUCH AS HOUSEHOLD APPLIANCES AND EVEN LIGHT VEHICLES... PERSONS, PETS AND LIVESTOCK EXPOSED TO THE WINDS WILL FACE CERTAIN DEATH IF STRUCK. POWER OUTAGES WILL LAST FOR WEEKS... WATER SHORTAGES WILL

MAKE HUMAN SUFFERING INCREDIBLE BY MODERN STANDARDS. DO NOT VENTURE OUTSIDE!

The Times-Picayune reports that an estimated 112,000 people do not own cars. At the Superdome, the Louisiana National Guard stocks enough MREs to feed 15,000 people for three days. By the end of the day, there are 30,000 people at the Superdome, most dropped off by buses provided by the Rapid Transit Authority. The Coast Guard mobilizes to respond after the storm hits. Several parishes and the City of New Orleans announce that emergency responders will stop venturing once the wind exceeds 45 mph.

•   •   •

By Sunday morning, everyone was exhausted. Talia spent Saturday night at Good Hope along with the remaining staff and the director, Rick Landry. There was too much to do for her to make it home, and she'd called DeeDee to let her know. The mayor's mandatory evacuation order came just after 10 a.m. Talia arranged for Dee to get out of the city with one of the geriatric internists, heading north to Baton Rouge with his family.

"Come with us," the doctor had urged, but Talia shook her head. They were short-staffed, to begin with, and since the storm's escalation, many more had called in sick or no-showed. People like Ellie and Bernie depended on Good Hope to keep them safe and move them to higher ground. Her mind was also on her neighbors, Miss Gloria and Earle Clarkson, and their families. Without cars or means of any kind, they wouldn't be leaving. She'd have to make it home, at least briefly, to check on them. Even as the doctor reminded her, "You've heard what they're saying now? If you must stay? Buy an ax, right? You'll have to hack your way to your roof." It couldn't possibly get that bad, she thought. But it had happened before. Hurricane Betsy trapped many people in their attics. Those who couldn't get out, those without an ax or a pick or hammer, died. And many died anyway. Some local authorities advised citizens to fill upstairs bathtubs with water as there would be no other drinking water source after the storm.

By midday, Good Hope was down to a handful of aids, two nurses, a few admin assistants, and Rick Landry. Thirteen staff in all. And eighty-two patients.

Evacuees jammed the roads and highways leading out of New Orleans to the point of near impassability. The Superdome, meant to be a shelter of last resort, was quickly becoming overwhelmed. Busses continued to drop off trapped residents, while canceled flights and closed hotels made it the only refuge for stranded tourists. People lined up by the thousands. The numbers were proliferating as it became apparent that evacuation plans all over the city were limited or non-existent.

It was Rick Landry who came to them with the news just after eleven in the morning. The staff sat silently in the windowless conference room, watching as he leaned against the wall nearest the door. He looked like a trapped animal, Talia thought. He was a pale, diminutive man who seemed mildly sickly in the best of times. Landry raked a hand across his scalp, and he looked them over. His eyes were small and hard inside the round face, like peach pits. Beard stubble and fatigue shadowed his face.

"We're not leaving," he said. "Orders came down to suspend evacuation efforts." He paused, casting his gaze to the floor. "We are supposed to shelter in place."

"What the? Shelter in place, Ricky? And how do we do that?" blurted Toni Guidry almost before he'd finished his sentence. Toni was the assistant director of nursing, a no-bullshit veteran of clinical nursing and southeast Louisiana weather. She'd been a child for both Betsy and Camille, and, contrary to some, she didn't believe the city could manage another similar hurricane. "People will die if we stay here, and you know it." She stood up and was leaning forward, balancing herself with fingers tented on the table.

"Yeah, I know that Toni, but it's not my decision. This is coming from corporate. No choice. Besides, there are no ambulances to get us, anyway. Most are busy, and the ones available have no drivers."

"Jesus," said Toni. "What's the hell does that mean?" She narrowed her eyes at him. Accusing. Toni didn't like Landry and had never made any attempt to hide it. But she wasn't stupid and never directly countered him either. This was the most aggressive Talia had seen her behavior toward him. "What is the point of an ambulance contract if they don't come when we need them?"

Landry's face flushed. He shook his head. Beads of sweat collected on his forehead and upper lip. "I don't have another answer for you, and I'm sorry. But we have to do the best we can." He pulled out a chair and took a seat. There were murmurs across the room.

Talia said nothing. There was nothing more to be said. But Toni was not letting up. She straightened and stared down at Landry, hands on her ample hips. "Do the best we can? Are you kidding? There is no making the best in a situation like this. We are overcrowded, understaffed, and have no alternative plan. No escape Rick. If those roads flood," she pointed vaguely toward the front of the building. "You know as well as I do what will happen."

They all knew; they'd been watching the news all day. The reports coming in were dire. If it hit New Orleans, the storm, now a Category five hurricane, would slam the city with the force of a hundred atomic bombs. They would lose power for sure. Emergency services discontinued—the destruction of buildings and infrastructure astronomical. And, of course, they all knew what was going on at the Superdome.

"We are twelve feet below sea level, Rick, and that," she pointed in the canal's direction, "will send water over those levees and into our goddamn lobby as soon as that storm surge arrives."

Landry took a deep breath, pursed his lips. "Come on, Toni, that's the worst-case scenario. We don't even know if the hurricane is coming our way."

"Yeah, of course. It's the worst case, but that's the reason we evacuate. Because of the worst case, right?"

A few others spoke up, but Landry retreated into what sounded like corporate public relations copy. "The hospitals and nursing homes have been exempted from the mandatory evacuation order... some patients are too fragile to be moved... the reality is the risk to their lives by evacuation outweighs the risk of staying for the storm... blah... blah."

His arguments sounded weak. Landry was no longer listening to anyone; he was barely even pretending to listen. Finally, he closed discussions with, "there's nothing I can do."

Staff spent the rest of the afternoon and early evening returning patients to their rooms and beds, which they rolled as far as possible from the windows. Sometimes, they moved people out of their rooms and into the hallways. Those who weren't engaged in moving patients were busy explaining the situation to terrified family members via computer email since the phones were already overwhelmed.

"You need to go home," Toni said without looking up at Talia. They were re-wrapping a ninety-two-year-old Alzheimer's patient into her blankets. The woman lay on her back, bony knees sticking out under her short nightgown; her arms, rife with purple bruises, were jerking randomly in the air. Her pressure socks had unrolled down to mid-shins, and she made low moaning sounds, twisting her head about, eyes wide, like a frightened animal. Toni gently straightened the socks, and Talia rolled a towel into a sausage shape and pushed it behind the woman's back to keep her positioned onto one side. She patted the woman's gnarled hand, settling it down on the blanket, and then glanced at Toni.

"Go," Toni said. "See about your house, then find a way out. Just get out of the city."

"I can't," said Talia. "I can't leave everyone." She picked a warm washcloth from a basin next to the bed and ran it carefully up and down her patient's arm, gently soothing the spot where a new skin tear had erupted. "Besides, if we have an ambulance contract, won't they come, eventually? I mean when there are drivers available. If we need them?" Talia could hear the desperation in her own voice.

Toni sighed and lowered her voice. "There's no contract."

"What?"

"Camilla called."

"Camilla?"

Yeah, she was trying to get down here, but the city is impassable. She's stuck in Hammond. Can't even get past her street. Anyway, she told me to pull the paperwork in the business office. To see what the ambulance contract looks like." Toni shook her head. "I should have known."

"Known what?" Talia had stopped moving the washcloth and now held it in the air a few inches above Cory's left hand.

Toni glanced down at the old woman, who'd closed her eyes. It looked as if she'd gone to sleep. Then, glancing back at Talia, she said, "It's meaningless. Just a piece of paper on Southeastern Transportation Company letterhead."

"I don't get it."

"There's no such company," said Toni lifting the lid on the laundry bin and tossing in the ball of dirty linen. "They just drew it up, created a company, and filed the paper. To show the parish they had completed the evacuation plan. You know, ticked the boxes. There's nothing behind it. Southeastern Transportation isn't a real ambulance company unless you count the two eight-person passenger vans we have parked out back. I should have known. Camilla should have known. Another Am Health executive signed the contract."

Talia's stomach clenched. "Who? Toni, who signed it?"

"The CEO. Daniel Thibodaux."

Talia felt an icy sting in her chest, around her heart. Toni looked at her curiously. "You don't know him, do you?"

Talia shook her head. "No, no. It's just..." she hesitated, unsure how to finish the sentence. She took a breath. "So, no one is coming? I mean, even if we need to evacuate, there's no one?"

"Right. So, I want you to go. I've got four other nurses' aides here, and none of them with kids or a house in the Lower Nine. They've all opted to stay. That's enough."

"Thank you, Toni," said Talia smiling. She glanced down at Cory, clean white sheets pulled up to her chest, breathing softly. Definitely sleeping. "I'm ok. I want to be here. Really." She looked at Toni. "What about you? Your people?"

"Ah, thanks. My kids are grown all out of state. My Dad, a stubborn old guy, he's retired down in Mississippi."

"Mississippi?" said Talia, alarmed.

"Yeah, Gulfport, actually. Smack in the storm's path, but I can't get him out with a crowbar. He built the house with my mom, and now he won't leave." She shrugged. "I talked to him a few hours ago. Made him promise me he'd go if it got real bad. Thing is, I'm not sure how he'll define real bad. Anyway, nobody ever forced my dad to do anything so, nothing for me to do but pray." She smiled, but Talia knew how scared she must be.

"I'm so sorry."

Toni was already moving toward the sink to wash her hands. She pulled a paper towel from the dispenser and turned back to Talia. "Ok, so let's get to work."

• • •

Dee lied to the doctor, and she guessed she'd lied to Mama as well. She'd promised to go, but when the time came, and the doctor showed up Sunday morning, she couldn't do it. She was sitting on the porch beside Miss Gloria, who was blessedly unaware of the impending disaster. They weren't talking, just sitting quietly, Miss Gloria running her gnarled hands over the afghan covering her lap as they watched a bluebird twitter between the branches of a magnolia tree. The air was redolent with the magnolia's smell and the day so crisply beautiful, anything so malignant as a hurricane seemed impossible

So, DeeDee lied. She told the doctor she had another ride. A friend's family would pick both her and her mama up later in the day. The doctor made DeeDee promise to have Mama call him. Then he let her stay with Miss Gloria. Dee guessed he would have tried to call Mama himself, but nobody was getting through on any of the phone lines by then.

After he'd gone, Charmaine brought a radio out onto the porch, and the three of them, DeeDee, Charmaine and Miss Gloria, sat listening to the news and following along as the storm tracked closer and closer to New Orleans.

It was mid-morning when the mayor issued a mandatory evacuation for the entire City of New Orleans. But, by then, it was too late.

CHAPTER 54

August 29, 2005

In the starless night, over the Gulf of Mexico, hot air rose in maniacal swirls off the blackened ocean. Waves peaked and crested, rolling higher and higher hundreds of miles from the coast. Over four hundred miles across, a monster hurricane pressed its belly down onto the ocean's surface, pushing water out and up and over the shores like a stone dropped in a teacup.

At 2:00 A.M. on Monday, August 29, the storm made landfall in Mississippi. Bands of rain and hurricane-force winds extended twelve miles inland, creating a storm surge twenty-eight feet high, and spawning eleven tornados. Within hours, all coastal Mississippi towns were ninety percent flooded; Buildings were gutted to the third story. The damage was catastrophic.

Simultaneously the Mississippi-River Gulf Outlet was filling with dangerously warmed water. By morning it would overrun the flood wall and shoot, missile-like, up the outlet, between the stone walls of the canal towards New Orleans. Waves would smash furiously at the sides of the Intracoastal and Industrial Canals walls, which split the ninth ward in two. Water would hammer the shores of Lake Pontchartrain, and the levees would struggle to hold back the rising tide of water.

Within a few hours, all around the city, the levees would give way. Enormous chunks of concrete blown away like so much paper wreckage, and the Gulf of Mexico would come like a tsunami into the city.

* * *

In the night, the storm became a living thing. Bright and fierce. In the distance, they heard it whooping, riding at them headlong like a warrior. The brick and mortar of Good Hope swayed and bent beneath it. Bowing like some supplicant to the black and lightning ripped sky.

They lost power just after midnight, the engineer returning from the generator room, khakis dark with water to the knees, sleeves rolled back into dripping cuffs, he cursed. "Goddamn below sea level. Who in the hell puts a backup generator below goddamn sea level?" No one answered, and he dropped into one of the metal folding chairs and went to work on his boots, picking at the laces now agglutinated into impenetrable globs by the water.

They huddled together in the conference room lit hauntingly by two lanterns gleaned from the supply closet. The windowless room was so stifling, they could smell one another's sweat and taste the fear. Thirteen of them now. Five aides, three nurses, and five administrative staff. They took turns, all of them rounding on the patients. When it was Talia's turn, she took up the silver flashlight and stepped cautiously into the pitch-black hallway. She went first to see Bernie and Ellie, their room at the far end of North Wing, nearest the cafeteria. They'd been medicated, like many of the others, before the storm, and they both slept peacefully, mouths agape, their drawn faces slack in the circular light. Talia touched the sheet that lightly draped Ellie's childlike figure. Folded the edge back and smoothed it down across the old woman's chest. Then she checked Bernie's breath. Steady and strong despite the snore. Despite the rains lashing their window and the wind that screamed and howled overhead.

Up and down the hall, she checked each room. One palm sliding coolly along the chrome handrail that ran the length of the corridors, the other clutched around the butt of the flashlight—the light jerking side to side in a frenetic dance.

Back in the conference room, she handed the flashlight to Francine James, next up to make rounds, and took a seat, wiping sweat from her face with a paper towel pulled from the dispenser over the sink. Near 2:00 A.M., Rick Landry stood, his figure up-lit by the yellow light of his lantern. Half cantaloupe-sized sweat stains at the underarms of his dress shirt, and he'd removed his tie. He wiped the sweat from his brow and began.

"Ok, folks!" he shouted over the din of the storm. "We'll need a plan to handle the power outage the rest of the night." His voice sounded grave and tremulous despite its volume. He was still speaking loudly when the wind died suddenly, and his shouts seemed suddenly farcical. Talia giggled, then covered her mouth, embarrassed.

One nurse stood up suddenly, pushing back her chair so aggressively, it made a horrible scrape across the linoleum tile. The darkness wholly shrouded her figure, but her posture made it clear she was upset. She threw her arms up in a *what the hell gesture.*

"Rick, the med cabinet is electronically locked. No way to open it without power. And the crash cart..." She didn't finish; Landry cut her off.

"Yep, I realize that. We'll have to make do." A dissatisfied murmur moved across the room in a wave.

"And when they start waking up?" the nurse continued. "Some of them are going to panic. Maybe more than a few. How are we supposed to handle that?"

He had no answer, only shifted back and forth on his feet uncomfortably.

They made lists. Supplies. Medicines. Patients. Staff. They made schedules. They made plans.

Near 4:00 A.M. came a crack of thunder so loud it was as if the entire planet had split in two. A few seconds later, the room flashed with electric white light. One of the aides screamed, and two others began to sob. The rain turned to a deluge. The water is thrown down in thick angled sheets. After that, the air felt pulled tight, bow strung by the unspoken danger. The canal is just fifty feet away.

• • •

At Miss Gloria's, they'd collected candles, filled the bathtub with water, boarded up a few windows, and brought in the cats. The phones were out, but they still had electricity. The three of them, DeeDee, Charmaine and Miss Gloria, sat in the stuffy living room, listening to howls and scrapes against the shake roof; it sounded like a freight train passing directly over their heads. The worst thing, besides the wind, was the heat. They sweated through their clothes, changed clothes, and sweated through them again.

DeeDee sat in a small, cushioned chair clutching an embroidered pillow to her stomach and trying hard to appear less than terrified. Of the three of them, Miss Gloria was the calmest. She sat cupped by her wheelchair, which seemed suddenly enormous around her. Afghan over her thin thighs, ash-colored ankles protruding from below. Feet stuffed into a pair of fuzzy yellow socks, which were pushed like beanbags into her black sandals. Mr. Booties, her Cat, lay across her lap, and she stroked him with gnarled fingers and cooed down as if he were a human infant. Mr. Booties was blind and likely deaf, which, Dee imagined, accounted for his lack of alarm at the storm.

"Just need to set awhile," Miss Gloria kept repeating. "Set awhile, Mr. Booties." When she grinned, her big dentures glowed in the dim light. She cocked her head, listening as the wind screamed.

Outside one streetlight remained illuminated, and DeeDee could see trashcans blowing across the pavement, whipped like paper hats. As the storm neared, the winds picked up. Trees bent nearly to the ground across the street. One neighbor had a blue plastic pool in their yard, and it blew suddenly up and then out over the fence, bouncing its way across rooftops and street signs. When the rain started, it came down in sideways sheets, nearly parallel to the ground. Pelting the roof and then banging the windows like bullets, hard enough to send cracks spidering across the glass.

After a while, she stood and moved toward the couch where Charmaine lay curled into a ball. Dee leaned down and put her mouth to the girl's ear, and said, "We need to move to my house. It's higher. And we have the attic. We can't stay here."

Charmaine looked at her, then glanced at Miss Gloria, and then looked at DeeDee again, her lips pressed together, eyebrows raised.

"I know," said Dee. "It won't be easy to move her, but we gotta try."

"I ain't goin' nowhere," said Miss Gloria, obviously overhearing their exchange.

DeeDee studied Miss Gloria, who hadn't stopped stroking the cat. Charmaine was right. Moving Miss Gloria and her chair and her oxygen tanks and her cat would be a challenge in fit weather. For the two of them to do it in the middle of a hurricane would be impossible. And the attic stairs? There was no way.

"Ok, but we gotta get away from these windows, get as high as we can."

DeeDee thought her voice sounded reasonable, almost calm, despite her unstoppable internal monologue focused almost only on all the ways a storm like this could kill a person: drowning, crushing, or whisking away by winds strong enough to destroy houses. And then, there was her mother. She couldn't even allow her brain to go there.

An hour later, they had Miss Gloria in Charmaine's tiny back bedroom. The room had been a late and somewhat poorly constructed addition to the house. Access required that Charmaine and DeeDee drag both Miss Gloria and her wheelchair up two rickety steps and down a narrow and roughly carpeted passageway. The bedroom was at least a few feet elevated compared to the rest of the house and slightly insulated from the storm's raging winds. A neighbor boy had boarded those few windows on Saturday, but he'd run out of lumber before getting to the front of the house.

The move caused Miss Gloria severe pain in her back and lower legs, and she needed to lie down. They got her into Charmaine's bed and pulled chairs from the kitchen for themselves.

They turned off the lights, plunging the room, with its boarded windows, into absolute blackness. They lit candles, but the wind through the cracks in the siding blew them out. For hours, they sat together in hot, wet darkness. Buried alive, listening to the pounding of rain on the roof and the scream of the wind in the night.

CHAPTER 55

New Orleans, Uptown

July 27, 2020

"She knows," Cat says as soon as he answers the phone. Her voice is controlled, but he can hear the rage. He has been expecting the call.

"I know."

"You know? What is that supposed to mean?"

"She's been to the office, up to the prison, into the computers. My wife is a smart woman Cat. How long did you think it would take? Hm? Once Camilla got involved?" He places emphasis on the word *'wife,'* and he's not sure why.

"You need to do something?

"What would you have me do?"

"I don't know, Daniel, but I would say this is your mess to clean up. Explain it to her, threaten her, take the kid. Whatever. Fix it! How do you think it's going to look?"

He laughs. "Look? You're worried about appearances. You're kidding, right?"

"You're drunk."

"Yes, and getting drunker," he says and sips loudly from his glass.

"What in the hell are you thinking?"

"I'm trying not to think.

"Jesus. Fucking fix this." Cat is losing her cool, Daniel thinks. This is kind of fun.

"Catherine, I do not think this is fixable. Not even for you. Not now."

"You're wrong, Daniel.

"Maybe," he says casually. He closes his eyes and lies back on the sofa. "I am often wrong."

"So, do something."

"Nope."

"Fine, I'll do it. I'll do what has to be done. She is on her way over there. Just don't fuck this up. Ok, Daniel? Just do nothing to make it worse."

"Um," he says, debating whether it's worth messing with Cat Landry on this point. He could say something that would really get under her skin. God knows she deserves it, but suddenly he's overwhelmed with exhaustion. He wants to sleep. Just sleep and sleep and sleep. So, he says, "Ok, Cat, no problem." A small drunk laugh escapes with that last word, '*problem*.' He can't help it.

"Daniel," her voice is sharp. She doesn't believe him. He gave in too quickly. "Rachel can't do anything as it stands. She won't accomplish anything for her sister, and she'll only wreck her own life. I don't think she'll take what she has and do anything with it. But like I said, don't be stupid. Don't fuck things up. Make sure she understands."

He laughs again; this time, it comes out harsh and ugly. He doesn't care. "Fuck this up? Fuck, up what exactly? Never mind. Don't answer that. I have to go."

CHAPTER 56

August 29, 2005

THE WATER

At dawn, the bravest of them ventured to the front of the building. They stood watching the storm from the relative safety inside. The blue gum trees across the parking lot swayed and bent to the ground; some cracked and fell, and their tangled roots yanked out, exposing the earth's underbelly. Obscene. Chunks of debris blew like paper across the blacktop: car fenders, traffic lights, a trash receptacle from behind the building.

Bernie was awake the next time Talia visited; he sat up in bed, his face gray and toothless, his smile weak. He said something, but the wind drowned out his voice. She approached his bed, but there was nowhere to sit. The metal stool had been removed from the room. She lay a hand on top of Bernie's and tried to reassure him with her eyes. The sound of cracking came through the scream of the unspooling storm, as if an enormous lake had finally lost its freeze, the surface shattering all at once. The windows, those not boarded, were finally giving way.

The crash woke Ellie, her eyes wide with confusion and terror. Her mouth opened. She was making sounds that Talia could not hear. Talia went to her and whispered words she hoped were soothing. Ellie settled. Before exiting the room, Talia looked back at them once more. Both had their eyes closed now. Their faces glowed in the silvery dawn light as the wind screamed, the rain battered, and the storm went on and on..

• • •

It was just light when DeeDee ventured outside to peer into the dawning day and check for signs of damage. The wind had died down to an intense bluster, and the streets held no more than an inch or two of water. In some spots, the blacktop was dry.

Stepping off Miss Gloria's porch, DeeDee could see around to her own house. They'd lost the picket fence that had stretched around the postage stamp of a lawn. At least they'd lost most of it. A few mud speckled pickets still stood, disconnected and forlorn. Windows up and down the street were blown, bits of glass decorating the landscape like jewels. A few houses were missing doors or gates or, like DeeDee's, fences. An aluminum lawn chair sat upended in their front yard. Mailboxes faced into the ground; their posts bent like broken spines. And so many trees snapped like twigs or ripped by their roots from the earth. Mr. Clarkson across the street was on his front porch inspecting. Noticing DeeDee, he waved and shook his head.

"Y'all ok over there?" he called out.

Dee nodded. "We're good. Thanks. No electricity or phone. How about you?"

He gave her a thumbs-up and a weak smile. "Lost the windows a course, and this." He held up a piece of his porch railing, a thin spindle that had been snapped in two. All the other spindles were missing altogether.

Dee made a sympathetic face. "Yeah, us too." She pointed at the fence and decimated the porch. Let us know if we can help with anything."

He smiled. "Y'all take care." He shuffled back inside his house, still holding the now useless piece of wood.

DeeDee stood watching the paling sky. The sun peered around the edge of the thick cloud cover, and the wind ceased, and the air became curiously still.

With the phones, electricity and internet all down, DeeDee and her neighbors had no way of knowing that the storm had already destroyed vast swaths of Mississippi. Nor could they know that at 6:10 am, Katrina had made landfall just east of New Orleans, crushing St. Bernard parish, wiping out the entire emergency communication infrastructure, and killing scores of people.

At 6:30 A.M. that Monday, even if they had known, nothing could have prepared them for what was to happen next.

• • •

Good Hope was built like a squat letter T, the top of the T running north-south along the street facing the canal. In the center, the entrance lobby, visitor check-in, and the central nurse's station. To the right and left were locked doors behind which were residents' rooms on one side to the north and record storage and administrative offices on the other to the south. The third set of locked doors directly behind the nurse's station led to the east-west wing; it had supply storage, facility management, the kitchen and conference rooms. The main conference room was at the far end of that hallway, most distant from the canal and, by design, most distant from the north wing residents. At midmorning, eight of the thirteen remaining staff members, jubilant over having missed the worst of the storm, were busy prepping food trays for residents. Mostly, bread, boxed juice, and fruit cocktail cups. Without electricity, there would be no cooking. The collective mood was near ecstatic as they threw open all the doors and sunshine peeked in through the broken windows.

Francine James (Camilla's daughter), Toni Guidry (still unaware of her father's fate in Gulfport), Talia, and five others, cleaned up the broken glass and made rounds on patients. Talia was peeling back the plastic seal on a cup of fruit when she heard it. A scream. She froze, one hand still holding the circle of plastic. A few seconds later, one of the young aids, Ivan Lemont, came stumbling, arms waving, down the hallway, his face pale. Terrified.

Talia could see the wetness across his chest and the front of his pants. He looked as if he'd been sprayed by a hose.

"Go tell him to cut it out. He's gonna scare everyone," said Toni in a hushed voice, "Go!"

Talia jogged out into the hall, approaching Ivan, but he wouldn't stop. She had to run to keep up with him as he headed toward East Wing. "Ivan, Ivan! Stop it." He ignored her.

He was frantic. Screaming, "Water! It's the fucking water."

Several other staff members had heard him and collected behind Ivan near the conference room in the East wing. Landry emerged and tried to place a hand on his shoulder, but Ivan shrugged it off. Breathless now, "It's water coming." He was pointing. West. Toward the canal.

Then the sound, a tremendous gushing, like standing in a culvert as thousands of gallons of water came down the pipe.

Rick Landry was yanking something from his pocket. Keys. He was out of the room and down the hallway before anyone could ask what he was doing. The rest followed. The sounds of rushing water growing in intensity. Screams and car alarms and the whoosh of the wind.

They stood peering out the windows along the west hallway, waiting. Then they saw it. A wall of water had come straight over the levee. Black and tumbling with street signs and tree roots and slabs of concrete and entire automobiles. Talia knew it would slam into the front of the building first. Come through the air vents into the patient's rooms, drown them in their beds. *And Toni was in there. And Francine and, Oh God, Ellie and Bernie and so many others.* She was the first to rush the steel double doors that separated the back of the building from the north and south wings. Without thinking, she banged her palm into the automatic open button on the wall. Nothing. No electricity. She pushed on the chrome crossbar. Locked. Jerked it hard. Tried slamming her body into it. The heavy doors didn't budge.

"They're locked!" She was screaming, hands still on the door handle. "Someone fucking locked them. Keys! I need keys!"

"Try these." Suddenly Ivan was behind her, a ring of keys in his hand. They tried one over another. Then another. They could hear people shrieking, banging, crying out for help on the other side of the door.

"Landry," said Talia. "He did this. He locked these doors. I saw him. Fucking coward. He thinks it'll give us time, get us out the back, up the roof. Fuck. I thought he was... Oh, my God. They'll drown. They'll all drown." She stared at Ivan, momentarily unable to think.

Talia was shouting for Landry, begging him to stop. "I know you did this, Landry. Come back. Goddammit, we need those keys. Help us." But he was disappearing around the corner into the stairwell. He heard her. She knew he heard her. She was down the hall and halfway up the stairs, yelling for him to throw the keys back, but he was out of earshot, gone, and there was no time, and she was running, pounding heel over heel down the hall back to Ivan.

"We can't do anything. These are steel doors. Bolted fucking steel. Landry, fuck, fuck. I'm gonna kill him." Ivan was wailing and pounding on the doors, but Talia stopped him, with a hand gripped tightly on his shoulder.

"We can't get them open," she said, leaning as close to Ivan as possible. "Ivan, we can't. The weight of the water, it's the weight of all that water on the other side. There's no way." Suddenly she was aware of the tears streaming down her face. She was moaning and shaking her head. "Oh, God, oh God, Ivan, listen."

Suddenly, Francine's voice broke through and, for a few seconds, Talia heard nothing else. *The water. The water. Please. The water.* Talia looked down. Water was coming in under the crack beneath the doors. Pooling black and stinking around their feet. The smell of oil and sewage and dead fish.

"They have nowhere to go but out the front," she said to Ivan. "Nowhere but out the front straight into the water." Then Talia began again. Banging over and over, hard, and hopeless on the door. She leaned against it and then threw her body sideways into it as hard as she could. All her weight against all that water. "Fuck! Fuck!" she wailed and threw herself again and would have kept going except that Ivan wrapped his arm around her waist.

"Stop, stop it. We have to go," said Ivan.

"No," she jerked away from him. Pressed her ear again the door. Called out for Francine. For the others. But the screams were diminishing. Francine did not answer.

"Look, we have to go. Now!" said Ivan pointing down.

The water was up to their calves. The supply room was flooding. Medical supplies bounced on the current like small boats. Pill bottles, packets of sterile bandage, stainless steel bedpans, many wound care implements-scissors and scalpels, and debridement packs. It was too late. There'd be no way to open the doors against the weight of the water on the other side even if they'd had the key.

Ivan pulled Talia back down the hallway. Someone was yelling about the roof, a boat. As Ivan pushed open the door to the roof stairs, Talia looked back to see the water now seeping in between the two hallway doors, to the top.

"Go," he said. "Go right now. You tell them. Tell them that Landry did this. He trapped all those people."

"No." She dug her fingers into his forearm.

"I'm going to open the doors. You go up to the roof."

Talia thought about her neighbors. Miss Gloria. Mr. Clarkson. Charmaine. The little girls. So many people. They'd never get out on their own. "I can't go up there. I gotta get home," she said.

"You'll drown. There's no way."

"I have to. I have people at home."

He nodded. "Try Remington street. I heard someone say it was still dry. Or at least passable. Please be careful."

"You?"

"I'm ok, just go." And before she could argue, Ivan had turned and headed back through the water, wading to his chest now, west toward the screams coming from the front of the building.

Remington street was indeed passable. Flooded only a couple of feet, although laden with debris: sandbags floated past. Lawn chairs. Appliances. A dead dog. She saw a brightly colored beach ball bouncing carelessly across the surface.

Crossing Remington, Talia waded between the houses of Carter Street, through the backyards, and two more streets over to Charbonnet. Racing down the middle of still dry Charbonnet Street, toward Miss Gloria's, as she approached her own house, she saw with horror her daughter climb the broken porch of their own home. Talia screamed, but apparently too far to hear, DeeDee disappeared inside.

*   *   *

It was mid-morning when DeeDee left Miss Gloria and Charmaine sleeping together in the back bedroom and walked down the steps at Miss Gloria's, placing her feet gingerly in case the steps had lost their support beams and planned to drop her through to the underside. The grayed and splintery steps held firm, and she made it to the sidewalk and over to her own house.

Their own stairs had not fared as well as Miss Gloria's. There'd been three of them, and now all were severely cracked and precarious locking. She hoisted a leg onto the decking without attempting the steps. Reaching out, she grabbed a remaining porch post and pulled herself up and over the edge of the wooden deck. A splinter dug itself into her right middle finger, and she squealed, nearly losing her balance. Upright again, she stood, waving her right hand in the air to relieve the sting. She studied the finger. An enormous black sliver lay beneath layers of skin on the underside of her third finger. She picked at it for a moment but got nowhere. She'd have to deal with it later. Find some tweezers.

The front door was still attached but only by one hinge, and it hung open, giving the house a terrible gap-mouthed appearance.

Inside was dark, even darker than Miss Gloria's. She'd left the blinds pulled. She'd read somewhere that windows with the blinds down would be less likely to break in the wind. It hadn't worked. Nearly every single pane was shattered. Glass coated the living room floor, some of the furniture. Pictures had come off the walls, and books toppled from bookcases, and some smaller items rocketed to new locations by the wind. Other than that, most of the damage wasn't too bad. Kitchen items knocked out of open cupboards, off shelves, a box of cereal, a set of plastic bowls, the toaster. Dee thought her mother would be pleased it wasn't worse. Much worse.

Mama, she thought suddenly. She had to find a working phone and call. Let her know she was ok and that she'd weathered the storm here rather than leaving for Baton Rouge with the doctor. One neighbor could have a better landline or a cellphone on a different service.

The sound of Talia's voice behind her interrupted her thoughts. "Come on, Dee, we have to go. We have to go."

"Mama?" She turned to see her mother's tiny figure; water was dripping from her scrub top, her pants dark-stained wet to the thighs. She stood, panting, at the half-hinged front door.

"The waters coming, Dee. The floodwaters breached the levees. It's coming."

"The levees?" Terrified, DeeDee still hadn't moved.

"We don't have time; come on." Talia was pulling Dee by the hand, leading her back toward the kitchen. The attic stairs. "We have to get up. Up high. Right now."

In the distance, car alarms began screaming, one after another in succession. Dee glanced out the window onto Charbonnet street. A wall of inky water, twenty feet high, was coming straight at them. A tidal wave crossing Jackson just a few blocks away.

"Oh my God, oh my God, Oh my-"

"Stop it. Come on. There is no time," Talia interrupted her, now dragging DeeDee across the front room towards the kitchen. They snatched up plastic bottles of water from the kitchen's storage pantry, and Talia yanked the cord that pulled down the attic stairs. She shuffled Dee to the first step. "Up now. Go unless you wanna drown in all that water."

Dee scrambled up the attic ladder, landing with a thump on her buttocks. Steadying herself, she reached down for the water bottles as her mother pushed them up. Then she helped pull her mother along behind her. Talia turned and pulled up the attic hatch, and slammed it shut.

They sat frozen together, DeeDee curled, her head against her mother's chest. Talia's arms wrapped tight around her. Eyes wide, in the dark. In the heat. Waiting.

A sound, an inevitable low gush coming towards them—a moaning giant. Dee's mouth went dry, and something vile expanded in her gut. The furious thrumming of her heart in her chest. Short, panting breaths. Second, over second, the sound outside grew more intense. It came closer. Closer still. Then, suddenly an ear-splitting crack like a thunderbolt had struck the house, followed by the deep whoosh of the water rushing in.

CHAPTER 57

New Orleans, Uptown

July 27, 2020

Rachel finds him in the living room when she gets home. He's lying back on one of the paired sofas with his shoes on, but he's thrown his jacket on the floor. There's a bottle of Chivas and an empty glass beside him on the coffee table. The room is dim and smells dank. He sits up as she enters, and she can see how his confident, handsome face has gone colorless; he looks ancient.

"Hello Rachel," he says, his voice has a fractured quality.

"Daniel," she says and stops several feet from where he sits.

"Sit, please, we need to talk."

She perches carefully on the edge of a chair across from him, possibly needing a quick escape. She already knows most of what she needs to know. But there are questions she has for Daniel only he can answer.

"How long?" she says.

"How long what?"

"Did you know? How long did you know about Talia?"

He shakes his head. "I didn't. I mean, not until the end. When you knew. We just sorted it out. How could I have known? Talia did a good job burying herself, Rachel."

"She was an AmHealth employee, for fucks sake. Don't you do background checks or something?"

"Oh, come on. We have a thousand employees. First, I wasn't involved on that level, and second, she'd been Janie for a decade by then. More than a decade." He drops his head into his hands. "Fuck."

Looks up. "You have to believe me. I didn't know she was your sister. You know I loved Talia; think of what I went through for her? I couldn't have allowed all that to happen to Tee."

Rachel cringes at Daniel's use of her sister's baby name. She sits back in the chair, watching him. "So, I'm supposed to believe you sent a cop to kill a woman you'd never met because why? To cover up some stupid decision Rick Landry made. A stupid, cowardly decision that accidentally killed a hundred people? Why would you do that?"

"God, no. I didn't do that." He seems energized suddenly. Vehement in his denial and even surprised by Rachel's accusation. "Is that what you thought? That I sent some kind assassin after Janie Paradise? Jesus Christ, Rachel."

"So, who? Rick planned all that? I can't believe that. Rick isn't an idea, man. He's a follower."

"No, Rick was a coward, but not a killer. That was Cat. She planned it and had it done before I knew anything about it. She knew Jack Salvas; she arranged for him to go along with Rick to do the job. I didn't know about that until it was too late."

"But you knew him. Salvas."

"So? Many people knew him. He was a corrupt cop. He was useful."

"And you knew what really happened out there that day? You knew it was an accident. You knew Talia, or Janie, or whatever you thought her name was. You knew she wasn't guilty of murder. You let an innocent woman sit on death row for fifteen years when you fucking knew."

"I had no choice, Rachel. What would you have had me do? Run and tell the cops that my partners arranged the whole thing to cover up their own stupidity?"

They sit in silence for a while. Daniel refills his glass from the bottle of scotch. Offers to get one for Rachel, which she declines. He finishes his drink in two gulps, sets the glass on the table, then sits with elbows on his knees, waiting. Rachel watches the dipping sunlight glint off the crystal of the glass.

Finally, she says, "I don't understand why you couldn't let Rick Landry take the fall for his own choices Daniel. I saw the deadbolt. I think I figured it out right then. I can only imagine that he thought it would slow down the surge, that he'd have more time to save himself. Jesus." Rachel closes her eyes and takes a deep breath. "I just didn't want to think you could be involved in something so awful. But, if this was Landry's disastrous mistake, why cover for him? Was it Cat? Were you... are you with her?"

He shakes his head and looks straight at her. "No, Rachel. You know that. I love you. I've always loved you."

Maybe she believes him, but probably, she thinks, she only wants to believe him. Even after everything. Maybe for Alex. For Jeb.

"So why?"

"Look, Rachel, Rick's an idiot. He made a stupid panicked decision in the end, but it wasn't all on Rick. It was a whole series of shit decisions. A lot, my fault. I never should have sent him to Good Hope that weekend. To the fucking Ninth. I mean, I should have sent someone halfway competent, at least. But way before that, years before, we'd been writing up our own evacuation plans, skirting certification, falsifying those stupid ambulance contracts for years. Not just at Good Hope. It saved a lot of money. But mostly, it saved a lot of bureaucratic headaches. It mushroomed, we did it more, and I allowed it. Never in a million years did I think it would matter. Then it mattered, and it was too late. If I'd thought there'd be a surge and a fucking levee breach, I'd have driven there myself, evacuating every single person one at a time myself, but nobody thought that. Nobody ever thinks that. Not really." He picks up the near-empty glass and throws back the last dregs, sets it down. "And then, Rick panicked and did the worst possible thing." Daniel picks up the bottle. "Jesus Christ," he says, refilling the glass. "We were looking at a minimum of negligent homicide. Dozens of counts of negligent homicide. It would have ruined us."

"It would have ruined you," says Rachel.

"No! Us, Rachel. Everything." He waves his hand around, and Rachel is reminded of the gesture Cat made in her kitchen earlier in the afternoon. "This, all this shit," Daniel continues, some of the gold liquid sloshing over the edge of his glass and landing on the ten-thousand-dollar sofa. "And yes, prison for me, for sure. So, anyway, we bribed witnesses to tell the story we needed them to tell. And it might have worked except Cat found out about Janie and decided not to leave loose ends."

Rachel feels a painful ratcheting down in her brain as the ugly pieces fit themselves into place. Daniel keeps talking, explaining, but Rachel stops listening. There are no lamps in the room, and with the sun fading, the space is growing peacefully shadowed. When Daniel finishes, he drops back heavily against the cushions, apparently exhausted.

She's leaning forward now, tracing circles on the table with one finger.

"Was," she says quietly.

"What?"

"You said Rick Landry *was* a coward. Not is."

Her bag is on her lap, and she reaches inside, pulling the small object from an inner pocket. She leans forward, placing it carefully on the table before Daniel. The gold in the elaborate setting glints in the soft light, and the pearl's sheen is exquisite against the marble tabletop. Daniel barely looks at it before turning away. In that one movement, he tells her everything she needs to know.

Rachel studies her husband in the fading light, the way a clump of his hair, uncombed at the back, stands up straight in the manner of a young boy, the slump of his big shoulders. She waits, but he says nothing. Instead, he sits staring down into his lap, the fingers of his right hand twisting his wedding band around and around.

CHAPTER 58

Lower Ninth Ward, September 3, 2005

Five Days After the Water

Five days later, hunger big and hollow ripped through DeeDee's body. They'd run out of food almost immediately, quickly consuming the box of energy bars Talia grabbed when the water came. They'd rationed the bottled water, making it last as long as possible. Still, they had little left. The water continued to rise. There was a small space, only an inch wide, between two pitched roof beams. DeeDee sat on a full paint bucket someone had stored in the attic decades ago. Through the narrow opening, she watched the streets fill. By Friday, the water was over many of the roofs. Nothing but a few shingles and a chimney poking through the inky surface. Some houses had been torn from their foundations, moved with the violent current onto another property altogether.

In the daytime, DeeDee and Talia lay on their backs, sweltering in the stench and the heat. At first, optimistic, they spoke of rescue. Later, as their energy drained and their brains slowed from hunger and dehydration, they lay in silence. The nighttime was worse. The temperature barely dropped, and the dark was so thick it had a taste. A touch. It was like being sucked down into a quicksand; DeeDee felt like gagging as it swallowed her feet, her hands, her face. Down and down until blindness and stink were all that was and all that would ever be.

Nutria and rats scrambled across the roof; some sounded big as dogs. Other times snakes surrounded the little house, swimming in the waters around the attic. As the hours and days passed, they could hear their neighbors trapped and calling for help. Eventually, the sounds waned as people became sick and eventually died.

No rescue came. Nobody came.

DeeDee kept track of time by the cycles of light and dark. It was Saturday when they saw Miss Gloria.

Dee was peering out through the roof beams. The water level, she thought, might stabilize, although it remained an un-swimmable, toxic soup, full of rotting food and oil and sewage and dead things. Bodies. So many bodies. Bloated, blue, and unrecognizable. Maybe that was a good thing. Not knowing who or what you were looking at.

Then she saw it,

"Mama," she said.

"What is it, Dee?" answered Talia, without opening her eyes or moving from her position flat out on the floor.

"Come look."

Outside caught up against an electric pole and bobbing on its side in the water was Miss Gloria's wheelchair. Amazingly her afghan remained tangled in the spokes of one wheel.

"Oh Jesus," said Talia.

"Maybe she's ok? And Charmaine?"

"Maybe. But I don't know."

"I hope so."

"I hope so too, sweetie. I hope so too."

DeeDee kept watching. Miss Gloria's house was submerged completely; not even the chimney poked through. Survival, Dee knew, was unlikely. But maybe, she told herself. Maybe they got out.

• • •

Hours later, the sandals would tell the entire story. The thick orthopedic sandals Miss Gloria had insisted on wearing over her fuzzy socks. They were absolutely identifiable; they were tiny but heavy like miniature military shoes. Dee spotted one of them as the chair finally came loose. The little black sandal floated like a small boat, perfectly upright, undisturbed by the water.

Then, rising to the surface, another sandal. This one, still attached to a foot. Dee screamed. If she'd had food in her stomach, she'd have vomited. Instead, she gagged, dry heaved. Screamed again.

As Dee wept, Talia held her, and they rocked together, their tears mingling with sweat. Thinking about Miss Gloria and Charmaine and Mr. Clarkson and his little granddaughters and Bernie and Ellie and Chantal and her mama and so many others. Talia's thoughts frequently drifted back to Landry. Repeatedly to Rick Landry and what he'd done. What they'd all done.

After that, Talia tore a strip from her white undershirt and tied it to a piece of molding, and shoved it through the hole. Blocking the view.

"It's an SOS flag," she told Dee. "Don't be looking out there anymore."

CHAPTER 59

New Orleans, Uptown

September 3, 2020

In September, DeeDee showed up six weeks after Daniel's confession and two days before Talia's prison release. Talia's full pardon had come quickly following Daniel and Cat's arrest and arraignment on multiple charges. It turned out Cat had been terribly wrong not only about Rachel but also about Daniel. He was a terrible liar. A cheat as well. But he wasn't a murderer, not directly at least, and, strangely, he loved his family. In the end, he chose prison over forcing his wife and remaining child through the ordeal of a lengthy trial.

It must have rained on her way over. Dee stood in the doorway, wearing a purple LSU sweatshirt so wet it looked as if it weighed as much as she did.

"I have something to tell you," she'd said. "It's about what happened that day, in the attic. You should know the entire story. I mean before my mom gets out. You need to know."

Seated under the garden's portico, glasses of sweet tea on the table between them, they watched as water dripped off the roof onto the grass. Rachel waited silently until DeeDee spoke.

CHAPTER 60

New Orleans, Lower Ninth Ward,

September 4, 2005

Six Days After the Water

In the late afternoon, the silence began to thicken with the stench and the heat. The food was gone. Water is extremely low. The minutes ticked by like hours. Everything is slow, sticky, and endless. And then from nothing, voices. Downstairs. A man. More than one. Impossible to know exactly what they were saying, but they were coming closer into the kitchen and under the attic stairs.

DeeDee started to call out, but Talia shushed her. One finger to her mouth. They were here to help, or they could be here to make things worse. Talia shook her head at Dee. They waited. The intruders pulled the attic stairs down with a loud creak.

Toe of a boot-tapping each step as the man climbed. One... two... three... four.

"What you got?" said a man. Talia recognized the voice.

Suddenly, an artificial light pierced the room. Dancing across the shadow of Talia's face. Along the dusty beams and cobwebbed corners of the attic.

The cock of a gun. Its black barrel coming up over the edge of the attic hatch.

"Hey, Chief!" A man's voice from below.

Then like the lifting of a curtain to reveal some dreaded scene, DeeDee knew. The men weren't here to help.

Suddenly Dee was up, on her feet, her long, sturdy legs ready. She turned and looked at her mother's face only once, then turned back. Seeing everything as it was happening but in slow-motion and from a sort of distance, like a video. In the days and years after, she would replay that video thousands of times, back and forth, looking for the breakpoint, a pause in the action, and never finding it.

DeeDee stepped back, her filthy sneaker landing inches from Talia's hand; her mother could have snatched it then, grabbed her daughter's foot, and pulled her down, but she didn't. Then DeeDee backed up another step and kept her gaze laser-focused on the barrel of the gun, then her foot, the one in the tattered sneaker, almost of its own accord, shot forward, connecting with the side of the paint can. It spun so fast, it blurred as it disappeared through the attic hatch, and all at once, Dee heard the gruesome organic crunch as the can collided with the man's head, his face. Simultaneously, the man screamed, the gun went off, and the bullet tore an enormous hole in the roof, flooding the space with bright white sunlight.

Then, Talia was thrown backward by the gunshot. She lay in a heap against the far wall of the attic. Legs bent crookedly beneath her. DeeDee had no time to think. Blood was running down her mother's neck, her chest. Setting coppery smelling pools across the surrounding floor. When Talia touched her face, both hands came away covered in blood. A coppery stench immediately filled the room. The bullet that had torn through Talia's cheek and then shattered a portion of the roof had blasted a hole big enough to climb through. The light fell wide across the attic floor. Talia was looking for Dee.

Talia screamed, "Go! Go now, baby!" Dee was confused. Disoriented. "Go, Dee. Get out of here."

Dee scrambled towards her mother. "Mama," she said. "Oh my God, Mama." She knelt, hands and knees in the rapidly pooling blood. Panic in her eyes. Then, her blood-soaked hands fluttering around Talia's face. "You're hurt, you're-"

"Go. Go." Talia grimaced, and through clenched teeth, she said, "I don't know who all is down there... but..."

"I'm not leaving you, Mama."

"I'll be ok. You leave. Now!" She spoke the last word as harshly as she could, given the pain and blood loss. "Dee, there's more than one of them down there. We heard them. And they came for me. Ok? They don't even know you're here. Now you do as I say, you go, and you say nothing, ok? No matter what."

"But" Dee looked towards the attic hatch. Soundless now.

"Nothing. It's done. Go. I love you."

Dee hesitated, fat tears in her eyes. Then her hands trembling violently, she grabbed at the edges of the ragged hole in the attic ceiling. She looked back. Sobbing.

"I love you, Mama." Then she climbed out onto the roof without a glance back; she was gone.

CHAPTER 61

Marietta State Penitentiary

September 8, 2020

Rachel stands just outside the prison gates. Shifting back and forth from foot to foot, the crunch of gravel under her boot heel. No breeze breaks the air, and a muggy stillness settles around her. She reminds herself to breathe. And then to breathe again. She feels almost as if she needs to remind her heart to beat, her blood to flow; all of this is so unreal.

It's mid-morning when the electric gate finally rolls open, so slowly it appears to be stopping rather than starting up. The smell of tar, the sound of greased gears. The low creaking as the wheels track. In the distance, a bell, more of a siren, really.

Then, from nowhere, a pale figure barely discernible against the gray fence, Talia steps outside, into the open, and the gate wheels close behind her. She is dressed in the street clothes of a younger woman. Low-slung blue jeans, a fitted T-shirt. A hoodie draped over one arm. And in her hand, a large transparent plastic bag, half full. Her belongings. The sun peaks out momentarily as Talia walks toward the last exit, and Rachel sees her scar is a sparkling white. A radium river down her face. Strangely beautiful. Rachel moves cautiously then stops, reluctant to approach too quickly. Talia moves toward her without hesitation.

They hold each other for a long time. Rachel buries her face in Talia's hair, shorter now but still the same sweet smell. Finally, Talia pushes back and catches Rachel's gaze. "Thank you." She smiles, but the smile fades quickly. "I'm different, you know?"

"I know."

Talia shakes her head. "I mean inside. I'm not the same." Her brow furrows. "This place... everything. I don't know if I can do this." Talia gestures over Rachel's shoulder, down the path, and past the outer gates, where the rest of the family waits.

Rachel looks back. Through the wire fence, she can see Dee fidgeting with the strap of her purse, her expression anxious and elated, hopeful, and tired. Colette, tall and gorgeous, her smile bright, her face awash in all that nervous, forgiving optimism of youth. Virgil is here too. He'd been delighted with the invitation, although to Rachel, it had seemed obvious that he would come. Virgil, she is learning, is that way. He takes nothing for granted. And he listens. Really listens, and somehow that's enough, at least for the time being. Rachel likes him quite a bit, but they need time, and she intends to take the time. They'd discussed it, and he'd agreed. After everything they'd both been through, *slow sounded good*, Virgil said. He stands silent, a few feet apart from the others. His hands clasped before him, like a preacher. It's right that he's here. It's right that they're all here.

"You can. You will," says Rachel, her hands set gently on Talia's shoulders. "We will."

"You think so?"

"I do."

"We don't really know each other anymore, do we?" asks Talia, and Rachel thinks she's asking something else altogether.

"I guess we don't," says Rachel. "But we'll learn, won't we?" Talia nods. Whatever answer she needs, that seems enough for now.

"What's going to happen, Rach? How's it going to be?"

"I don't know, Tee."

Talia looks at Rachel, then up at the sky as if the answers might lie there. "Jesus, God, I don't even know where to start."

"Neither do I," says Rachel. She smiles, and Talia smiles back, and something tangible and familiar drops between them.

"Ok, then," says Talia with a laugh Rachel has not heard in many years.

The sun has fully emerged now, turning the sky a vast, brilliant blue. Talia puts her hand in her sister's, and together they start down the long gravel path.

EPILOGUE

Three Months Later

Present Day

It's winter—icy cold but clear. A soft wind rustles the evergreens and pushes the soft silk of Rachel's scarf up against her cheek. She pulls at it several times, finally tucking the ends into the back of her raincoat. It won't rain today. The air is dry. Lightweight and spicy smelling. She pulls off her sunglasses and looks up through the oaks into the vivid sky beyond. She smiles and replaces the glasses.

The beautiful Uptown cemetery is small and incredibly old. Across the street Lunaro's Family Grocery. In the store window, there are handwritten signs—crawdads for a dollar and homemade marmalade.

Small brass bells hang from a silk cord inside the door, jingling sweetly as she pushes it open. She drops her sunglasses into her purse. The store smells of olive oil, flowers and mint tea. On the counter over the deli is an enormous mason jar. Amorphous beige objects float inside, taped to the surface an ivory index card. Sharpie marker lettering: Pickled pigs' feet three for $2. Behind the glass case stands the manager. His name is not Lunaro but Jamal, and he knows why she's here.

"Mrs. Thibodaux," he calls out in heavily accented English. He comes around the corner, already holding out his hands. "It's so nice to see you again." She gives him her hand, and he takes it in both of his thick palms. She can feel the callouses under his fingers. "I have irises today," he says. "Beautiful." Only he pronounces it bee-A-oo-teeful.

Jamal is a short, dark man, round in the belly and balding. He was an accountant in his country once, but that was before. Now, he manages a grocery. "Also, daffodils, if you like." He walks her to the corner of the store, where blue water buckets, about a half dozen, are stuffed full of cellophane-wrapped flowers and greenery: yellow and white daffodils, purple hyacinth and iris, ivory mums.

It's in his eyes what he's lost. She'd have known even if he'd not told her three years ago. Jamal knows grief. The bottomless pain of losing a child. Both of his sons were murdered years ago before he fled his home country. Therefore, Rachel comes here each time. Not for the flowers. She comes to see Jamal. He doesn't expect her to get past it. He knows the pain does not ease. It only moves aside so you can breathe one day to the next. He is always happy to see her, and he never asks her how she is. He already knows.

"Thank you, Jamal, they're lovely. I'll take these." She hands him the daffodils, and he bows slightly before returning behind the counter to wrap them in paper.

In the cemetery, she spreads the blanket she's brought with her and lays the flowers before the marble headstone. She reads the inscription for the thousandth or millionth time. Then she sits down, crossing her legs beneath her, folds her hands in her lap, and lowers her head.

She talks to Jeb for a long time. She tells him all about Talia and DeeDee and Good Hope. About Rick and Cat Landry. She cries some. She tells him about Miss Gloria and Francine, and Charmaine. And she talks about Daniel. His tragically confused love for his family. And in the end, his sacrifice. She talks to Jeb about the truth. Finally, she tells Jeb the story she heard from DeeDee. The one she promised to keep to herself—the one about the attic.

It's late when Rachel finally gets to her feet, brushing dirt from her slacks. She carefully folds up the blanket, tucking it under her arm. She kisses her fingers and then lays them across the headstone, cool against her skin.

Leaning against the hood of the car, she finds Talia. Her shadow a delicate silver splash on the pavement. She's wearing a new red wool coat and tall boots with zips from ankle to knee. Her hair, darkened and fresh-cut at her shoulders, is smoothed down around her face, pink on her nose and chin with the cold. The scar, treated by a surgeon now and covered with a bit of makeup, is a thin line of white inside, and when she smiles, it disappears.

"They said you'd be here," she says. "Thought I could help."

Talia opens her arms, and Rachel lays her left cheek against her sister's and closes her eyes, allowing her breath to ease and her thoughts to drift. A light rain begins, and in the distance, Rachel can hear the low rhythm of someone playing a steel guitar.

ABOUT THE AUTHOR

W. A. Schwartz writes short stories and novels of literary fiction focused on psychological suspense and interpersonal relationships. Her work has been given special mention by the itinerary journal Glimmer Train (2018) and has been long-listed for the Alexander Chee Short Fiction Prize (2020). Born in Berkeley and raised in both the US and the UK, Ms. Schwartz was educated at the University of California and LSU in New Orleans. She and her husband, a native of Baton Rouge, spent many years living and working in Louisiana. She holds a BS in biochemistry and an MD from the University of California. She studied literature at UC Davis and novel writing at Stanford. These days, she lives in Northern California with her husband and children. *The Weight of Water* is her second novel.

"One of the strongest authorial voices I've heard in a very
long time. A formidable story that broke my heart,
and ultimately gave me hope."
—Anna Quinn, author of The Night Child and Angeline

AS FAR
AS YOU
CAN GO
BEFORE YOU
HAVE TO
COME BACK
A NOVEL

ALLE C. HALL

NOTE FROM W. A. SCHWARTZ

Word-of-mouth is crucial for any author to succeed. If you enjoyed *The Weight of Water*, please leave a review online—anywhere you are able. Even if it's just a sentence or two. It would make all the difference and would be very much appreciated.

Thanks!
W. A. Schwartz

We hope you enjoyed reading this title from:

www.blackrosewriting.com

Subscribe to our mailing list – *The Rosevine* – and receive **FREE** books, daily deals, and stay current with news about upcoming releases and our hottest authors.
Scan the QR code below to sign up.

Already a subscriber? Please accept a sincere thank you for being a fan of Black Rose Writing authors.

View other Black Rose Writing titles at www.blackrosewriting.com/books and use promo code **PRINT** to receive a **20% discount** when purchasing.